RLY

ROADKILL

NEARLY

AN INFOBÄHN EROTIC ADVENTURE
BY CAITLIN SULLIVAN & KATE BORNSTEIN

ROADKILL

HIGH RISK BOOKS

NEW YORK / LONDON

First published 1996 by
High Risk Books/Serpent's Tail
4 Blackstock Mews, London N4 2BT
and 180 Varick Street, 10th floor, New York, NY   10014

Library of Congress Catalog Card Number: 95–72971

A full catalogue record for this book can be obtained from the British Library on request

Cover design by Rex Ray
Text design by Philip Kovacevich
Printed in Finland by Werner Söderström Oy

Dedicated lovingly and thoroughly by us both

to Ava Apple

and in loving memory of Mildred Vandam Bornstein

THANKS TO EVERYBODY
FOR THEIR HELP

Online: Becky, Gleth, GA Smith, CJasmine, Drumcircle, Soluna, Quirk, Cayenne, Midishamen, TroiSura, jplummer, Collette, Notnilla, NukeNewt, Leogrrl, Ingenue VT, Grrl Bear, LAntoniou, and the officers and crew of the *USS Republic*.

Thanks for initial reads by Bryher Herak, Iris Landsberg, Bob Redmond, Nadja Schefzig, Dragon XCalibur; to Carol Tiebout for thorough reading, insight, and wisdom; to Amy Scholder for extraordinary editing; Malaga Baldi for support, savvy and patience; to Phil Kovacevich who so deftly and with good such humor translated our page layouts into such a pretty book; to Paula Bell, Teresa (goddess) Dietze, falcon and the amazing Jordan Buck for healing; to Ava Apple for reading, ideas, insight, humor; and to Philip E. Sullivan for words.

For support and/or love: Harriet Baskas, Dana Blumrosen, Justin Bond, Alan Bornstein, Marsha Botzer, Bonnie Brown, Frank Byrum, Sue Ellen Case, Shannon Coulter, Marna Deitch, Diane DiMassa, John Emigh, Frank & Linda of the East Beach Lodge, Val Fields, Val's desk, Elizabeth Freeman, Pat Friedman, Diana Gard, Bill Germano, Elsie Godden, Alison Greene, Gwydyn, David Harrison, Sophie B. Hawkins, Jenny Hubbard, Holly Hughes, Robyn Hunt, Jackal, Jamie Kae, Julia Kaplan, all the KBCS folks, Gail Leondar-Wright, Susan Martin, Dona Ann McAdams, Shea McGuier, Melissa Murphy, Rose Pascarell, Cid Pearlman, the gang at Post Option, Isabella Radsna, Raven~Light, Kim Robinson, Martine Rothblatt, Liz Rudd, Sylvia Salget, Isabel Samaras, Eleanor Savage, Carla Stevens, Sandy Stone, Strawhat, Dana, Lesa and Marianna Sullivan, Tristan Taormino, Kate Thompson, Roz Warren, Lois Weaver, Gretchen Wenner, Susan West, Riki Anne Wilchins, Ingrid Wilhite, Lauren Wilson.

CHAPTER ONE

Journal Entry by Toobe, if anyone cares

You can pretend it's the future if you want to. I don't give a rat's furry behind what you tell yourself, what you need to believe. You can say this kind of stuff doesn't exist yet, or that it's really close, like tomorrow, but not today. There's no such thing as the kind of shit I'm writing, you can say, if that makes you feel better. Heh heh heh. G'head.

Two people got it started; I want it all to be recorded. Two little idiots who don't know anything. One's confused and one's a ditz. Real revolutionary material. Maybe they sound all full of the passionate fires of political idealism, but believe me, they kinda stumbled into this one. First of all, they're too damn happy if you ask me. Happy like oblivious you know? There's all this insidious shit with the govt and electronic invasion and they act like damn porpoises on some kind of perpetual cyberwave.

But they've always been funny about one thing in particular: gender. Both of them, so it's ironic that they met, I guess. They refuse to submit to pronouns. It's some kind of thing with them. So what they run into with people is amazing. People get really pissed. And they have all this sex! Online I mean. Talk about doubling your chances if you swing both ways—they swing both sexes. They both tell me all about it, which is cool. Except knowing who does who and what sex they are kinda seems important to me—at least as a *perspective*. Then Scratch goes into hir "what's gender?" rap. ("Hir" is what they use to avoid gender pronouns.) And I start sputtering cuz "what's gender?" is a stupid question but it's not easy like I think. What kind of fool would ask you what gender is? It's the only thing we know, goddammit.

It's the only thing we're told from birth on out, says Winc, we don't really *know* it, no one questions it. Ze says (that's another one—pronounced zee, if that helps), ze says gender gets assigned at birth but we never choose, not like we choose our clothes, jobs, cars, or lovers. Especially in this country, where you think you can choose anything, where we have so much control over everything. Except the one thing that determines how we'll be treated the rest of our lives we don't choose. Can't argue with that one.

I'm doing double backups of everything I write about them; things are coming down and I have a feeling the media is gonna have their usual field day with those two, and I don't want to lose any of it. Truth is, I save everything I can get my hands on.

Me? I'm not really important, but Winc would kill me if ze heard me saying that. I live with my dad in a little apartment in a big city and I'm not a nerd but I'm not the school president either. I'm at an age (that's what Scratch always sez) where I feel this whole life is a huge mass of water pulling down into a drain and I'm trying like hell not to go with it. It's pulling me to be a boy, it's pulling me to be a grown-up, it's pulling me to be socially adjusted, all these *things* I don't have a clue about. I was just a person and then I turned into a teenager and now everything's different. Why would that happen, everything different all of a sudden? I don't want to be those things, but I don't have an alternative, so I feel kind of formless and weak. Scratch sez I will be something, that I'll have to choose. Winc sez I won't have to choose, but that I don't have to make up my mind ever. Sometimes that's a comfort, sometimes it just makes me more confused.

I like to think that somebody will find this journal and it'll be poignant like the *Diary of Anne Frank*. (That's another thing about this water whooshing down the drain thing. I'm not supposed to be interested in books like that now. Who made that rule?)

Anyway, the first time S and W met, they were hot for each other. Still are! They wouldn't tell each other what they were, I mean what sex they are, or anything else for that matter, like how old or what color. By now it's become a game with them. I'm not sure anything could make them reveal themselves. It drives me crazy, but they seem to like it. They used to trip out on whether they might be falling for someone of the "wrong" gender, but then they got a little compulsive if you ask me, about making sure they *didn't* find out. Like taping a football game and not wanting any contact with the outside world cuz someone might tell you the final score and ruin the whole thing for you.

But I know what they both are, or at least what they were when they met me. I keep the secret for them, I still keep it from everyone else. But I start to burst sometimes, you know, cuz of that sex stuff. They made up this pronoun game, this "ze" and "hir" thing, well they ripped it off like they rip off so much other stuff, so I use it to write about them, so nobody will know. Funny thing is, I can't remember as quickly as I used to, what they really are, I mean. Christ, I sound like them.

///The Eyes are here to help you.///

Oh, that reminds me. Can you believe that screen message popped up just as I was writing in my own journal? Okay, I was online, but still, this computer communication service promises complete privacy but as you see … Well, this is why Scratch and Winc sometimes write things to me, and not to each other. They have to talk to me cuz of the Eyes. That's a new thing, well, a new term for an old concept.

See, we're all connected via computers. There are services that make all those connections for you, but basically we're all connected one way or another. You can be "live" with somebody, communicating with them right now, or you can send electronic mail (email for short). You type onscreen and the message gets sent to another computer, is the simple version. So for a long time it was all chaos and everyone was connected, but then the govt got wind of it and the ad agencies too and they said, Unregulated? No way! So they started doing little things to make sure everything was monitored. (Censored. Protected.)

The Eyes are online, electronic beat cops. Real friendly. If you see a message like the one above that means the Eye's with us now. You can say anything as long as it's not subversive. Sometimes if two people have a communiqué more than once, then the Eye will note that, for everyone's own good.

///Perhaps some assistance here?///

No thanks, Eye, signing off soon.

///Eye now in nearby sector. Please call if you need——///

Fuck that noise. You can block them when they go to the next sector. So if two of you are in one place online, but another friend is in another, and you're conversing back and forth among the three of you, it confuses them. That's why Scratch and Winc sometimes communicate through me.

Scratch, Winc, they have an advantage on this pronoun thing. They met on one of those big, commercial computer online services, cuz they were weenies then and didn't even know how to hook up with people on the Net. So they have all their hot scenes with each other there. Oh, you pay for the private thing, but let's just say I'm paranoid. The walls have eyes, knowhatimean? Still, they think it's private. It doesn't matter to them what they are. They say they'll meet one day, and that it won't matter then, but I say it will.

Even though these are some early letters from Winc, I think it shows what ze's like. I keep it around, cuz it cracks me up but also makes me wanna hug hir. Just to make it all clear, I'm using excerpting marks to show you where hir letter begins and ends, which look like this: >>excerpt<<.

>>To: TOOBE
From: WINC
Subj: IS THIS WORKING?

HEY DUDE, GOT MY MODEM HOOKED UP AND I MADE IT ONLINE. WOW OH WOW OH WOW THIS IS A WAY COOL WORLD. HOPE I'M SENDING THIS RIGHT AND THAT YOU GET IT.

HUGS TO YOU,

—WINC<<

So I wrote back:

>>To: Winc
From: Toobe
Subj: Read you LOUD and Clear

Got your message. Welcome to the Net! One little note: don't write in ALL CAPS okay? That means you're shouting when you're online. And since you mentioned it: if you want to send hugs, you can do it in a couple of ways . . .

{{{{Winc}}}} means I'm hugging you. The more {{{{{{()}}}}}}, the bigger the hugs. A lot of people use them. I don't because they're kinda cutesy, but I might give you a few sometimes. Or, you can put stuff in double colons, like this: ::hugging you:: Anything in a double colon means an action, not what you're actually saying. And if you want to emphasize something, just put an asterisk around the word; you may have noticed you can't use your *italics* command.

Have fun. I'm glad you're here.

Your Pal,

—Toobe<<

>>To: Toobe
From: Winc
Subj: Ohmigoshl

::shaking my head in amazement:: I am having so much *fun* here, Toober! Sorry for the all caps, I'd never shout at you!

My mind is boggling at the possiblities of stretching who/what I am in this space. The bottom line here seems to be sex (as in making love and all its permutations: seedy to glorious). So that's where I started. Listen, listen . . .

I went online last night, and I used a couple of different names, right? (Thanks for teaching me *that* one.) I went into one of these online rooms called the Flirt's Nook, and this guy said, Wanna go private? and I said, Sure, and I didn't know what it meant, but he gives me the name of this room, right? So I go there and he starts *taking off his clothes*! I mean, online he does. He used that double colon thing, ::I'm stripping off my shirt:: etc. I don't know what he's doing at the keyboard, but I can just imagine. It's amazing! So ::blush:: we have sex right there! He asks me what I look like,

4

what I'm wearing, and Toobe, it's kind of like the phone sex
work I do only better, because there's even *more* to the
imagination! So he has his way with me ::grin:: and then he
signs off! ::wryly:: Guess he came, huh? That's what guys
do on the phone line, they come, then they hang up.

At that point, I figured in for a penny, in for a pound. So I
signed off, then signed back on as, get this, a major macho
dude! HAHAHAHAHAHA! And I had *more* sex with some
women this time! *Then* I signed off and signed back on as a
DRAG QUEEN! And I had all this sex with straight boyz and gay
boyz AND straight girlz! (Drag Queen's a mighty popular
thing, I discovered. Did you know this already?) Thank you
thank you for introducing me to all this! And you've been
traveling in this world all this time? You are one wise cookie,
don't you ever forget that, you hear me?

{{{{{{{{{Toobe}}}}}}}}}
—Winc<<

Winc always makes me feel good. Just when I think ze's a major flake, ze comes through.
Ze's a friend, a real one. Doesn't treat me like a kid. I'm glad ze has the phone sex work cuz it
pays the bills but ze doesn't have to go to an office, which would kill hir like it kills most people. Even though there *is* sex online, lots of people use it for research and other serious things.

A couple of weeks later, ze sends me this:

>>To: Toobe
From: Winc
Subj: Thoughts
Toobe . . .

This online stuff: I can explore different ways of relating
with people. I can be brave one night, timid the next. I can
saunter or mince, attract or pursue. It's like when I'm working the phone sex line, being someone else for some guy.
Only, online it's really *me*, a different aspect of me. *For*
me, Toobe. Not for some guy who's payin' me to be his fantasy.

Like when I ride my bike, depends on what neighborhood
I'm in, I'm seen totally different in each one.

I want to learn to do *that* in the real world. Know what I
mean, bean?
—W.<<

I totally get what ze means, but my outside self sez what a ramble, why does ze think I would get that? But even if I act like a shit ze still keeps talking to me like I understand, and so . . . I do.

End Toobe Entry

Narrative Entry by Jabbathehut

Green walls. Darker green trim. Wherever one might glance from the vantage point of Wally Budge's well-worn government issue swivel chair, there's some shade of green. The brightest green is the monitor into which Wally Budge is now peering: it's positively *glowing* green. The lone window in his office at the Federal Bureau of Census and Statistics is a pale brown-yellow: Layers of nicotine obscure nature's one shot at adding some real green to Wally Budge's life. Wally Budge couldn't describe the color of his office walls if you paid him. He's 46 years old, and the best he can come up with is: "The same color I went to school with."

Cigarette wedged between his fingers, he reads the daily reports offered by the Federal Bureau of Census and Statistics' twin Cray supercomputers; he's sucking at a hole in his teeth, an annoying habit, but Budge has no one left in his life to annoy. Three failed marriages and two lost custody battles left no one in Wally Budge's life to care about his three-pack-a-day cigarette habit, no one to wince at the soft sucking sounds his tongue makes as it pokes the well-traveled cracks and crevasses of his teeth. His nicotine-stained fingers are, ironically, well-manicured; they now dance clumsily across the worn and battered keyboard of one of the Bureau's oldest desktop computers as he adds information to his database. He peers up at the screen from time to time in search of a clue, a pattern. And for someone *outside* a pattern.

Wally Budge knows that once you have a pattern down, criminals show up outside it; criminals will inevitably break the patterns laid down by the law. He begins humming a mangled version of "London Bridge is Falling Down." Good sign for him, bad sign for some poor sap trying to escape the length of this particular lawman's long arm.

His monitor beeps, and on his screen flashes:

To: Invest@FBCS.gov
From: DevilsOwn
Date: (transmission garbled)
Subj: Think about this, my fine-fettered friends . . .
"Of course, the entire effort is to put oneself
Outside the ordinary range
Of what are called statistics."   Stephen Spender
—Devil

Budge snorts once and hits Save. The hackers are getting downright poetic. At first he'd been alarmed by the ease with which some of these people could read his files; but he learned there is nothing you could do about them except collect what they send you, save their electronic "signatures," and build a profile. His files on them are getting fat. Who knows, it might come in handy some day. He has, however, the persistent suspicion that they are only letting him collect what they *want* him to collect.

Patterns. It was easy enough to spot patterns in the old days: The object of everyone's desire had been money, and money had very few possible pathways—into and out of banks, or into and out of the black market. Follow the money there, and eventually you'd find your criminal. But money is on the way out, and the world is trading in information. Information, Budge has discovered, can come from anywhere and can go anywhere else. There is no clearly-defined black market for information. Well, none that the Registration Enforcement Task Force is aware of. That's why Budge is humming happily: He's discovered a pattern, and it's finally starting to pay off.

Not that any of his supervisors had wanted to hear about it. A month ago, he'd tried to explain it to them: "Most people sign onto the Net with whatever name they're given by the system or whatever name pops into their head at the time," he'd said to the roomful of FBC&S brass. "They tend to go to more or less the same areas of the Net time after time."

His audience had looked at him blankly. He was used to it.

"Okay," he'd begun. "Let's say some Joe out there is going online using the name JoeBlow, and let's say you're going to find him night after night in a corner of the Net called, say, Flirt's Corner. One guy, one name, one place to hang out and shoot the electronic breeze. With me?"

Heads nodding tentatively.

"Right," he'd continued, buoyed slightly.

"Then there's this other type: the guy who changes his name night to night from JoeBlow to JoeCool to CoolBlue to Blue Velvet to whatever, but he's *still* there in Flirt's Corner, no matter what his name is. He always wants the same company, the same thing every time. He's got a lot of names, but only one personality, like a *core identity*. He's no different, really, from the first guy."

The half-dozen faces had said nothing aloud, and the looks bore the unmistakable "Yeah, so?" But Budge was on a roll.

"Finally, there's the guy who keeps changing not only his name but his entire identity."

His audience had looked decidedly uncomfortable with *that* one. Budge forged ahead. "These folks might hang out in Flirt's Corner one night, Bible Talk the next night, and Love My

Puppy the next. If they're doing that *online*," he'd concluded triumphantly, "they'll do that *offline*, too. *Those* are the folks who aren't going to register their identities, I'll lay you odds."

It was the undersecretary of Census and Statistics who'd broken the uneasy silence. "Even if that is true," she'd said quietly, "how do you propose to find them? Follow every person on the Net?"

Budge's tongue had found a particularly rich vein to mine in his teeth, so his grin came out somewhat lopsided. "No, no, we don't have to follow them. That's the beauty of it all! We just have to study the PR printouts," he'd said happily. "We just have to study who's getting which ads."

Blank stares—all those words and they still hadn't got it.

Budge himself is staring off now into the smoke hanging lazily near the ceiling of his office. His reverie is suddenly interrupted by the memo flashing on his screen:

To: Invest@FBCS.gov
From: Inspections&Reports
(time/date stamp)
Subj: quotas

It has been noted that several departments have not submitted a projection on the status of Registration evaders. To complete the Divisional report, we need:

1. a projection (in percentile figures) of Registration evaders in your online sectors;

2. a summary of the tactics you plan to employ to identify the evaders.

Kindly respond by day end.

—RR

He shakes his head. Right. Good plan.

"Look," he'd tried to explain to the undersecretary back then, "Ol' Joe, he keeps going into Flirt's Corner, pretty soon he's going to be targeted for breath fresheners, time-share condos in the islands, and adult videos. Fits a pattern. But someone who's changing his or her identity all the time, they're going to be getting ads for everything from——" and here Budge had paused, glanced down at a printout, smiled, and said, "mutual funds to skateboard insurance. The Triumverate Association of Businesses, representing virtually every company that spends more than a nickel a year in advertising, is keeping records of who it's targeting these days, and *how* it's targeting them. All *we* have to do," he'd pointed out, "is find someone who shows up in one too many marketing windows."

More blank stares, but Budge ignored them. He had a pattern, and he'd found some folks he suspected were breaking it.

"Those are the folks who aren't going to register an identity, the ones who don't have an identity to begin with—those are the folks we want. Those are the folks who are telling us about themselves right now, three months before the Registration deadline." They'd looked at him with polite smiles, dismissing him without really saying a word. He'd seen that look before: they were giving him just enough rope to hang himself. Perhaps he would.

But that was four weeks ago, before two names fell practically onto his screen, right out of one too many marketing windows. And now he stares at the printout again:

Scratch/WINC
a.k.a.: (no alternates located)

"What's W-I-N-C stand for?" he says out loud to his empty office with the green-green walls. "It's an acronym for something, right?"

source: persLOG/budge/harddrive

End Jabba Entry

Toobe Entry

You can give yourself any name you want online. Then you can set up "rooms" online: little virtual places where people chat about whatever. Or rather, it's pretty specific, like if you go into some room called Love of Christ with a name like SatanDear, you might have a little trouble. That's why it's fun to come back five minutes later as Christonacrutch or something . . .

Anyway, one time Scratch chose the name of hir father's ancient Hibernian clan to go cybersurfing cuz ze thought it looked kinda neutral, but in fact it had "bear" in it. Each room would have a different perception of what that meant. In the pagan room they thought it meant that Scratch's totem was a bear. In the Love My Beastie room, they thought that Scratch did it with bears. In the gay room the men there thought it meant ze was a gay, hairy guy. That was hir first cybersex scene, as O'Bere. Ze was kinda delighted and terrified to be simulating sex online, it was too good to stop. Scratch sent me the whole transcript the next day.

That's the weird thing, they both think I want to hear all about it. Winc sez I have no blinders on, like they left them off at the baby factory. Scratch sez I have no idea what's taboo or not, and I'm mostly just curious, curious, curious. See, I'm supposed to be gathering all this info about what's taboo or not, or I'm not supposed to be interested in what boys are like, or girls are like, but only in what *I'm* like, but I think I'm boring and I want to know what everyone *else* is like.

So S and W laugh at me cuz I'm always getting technical, asking how women's bodies work, or what it feels like for a guy to come. I know how it feels to me but if one will tell you why not ask him? Both of them know what both kinds of bodies are like, by the way, or at least they describe it real well.

I don't know what Scratch looks like in the real world, I met hir online. But I do know what sex ze is. It used to influence me. But now I talk to hir like a normal person. I mean, without thinking about what ze is.

Scratch can get into these loops where it's hard to get hir out. Ze starts spiraling down some helix that I can't follow all the time. Ze says that's what everyone says about hir and not to worry about it. But one loop was pretty cool, where ze explained why this whole online world thing is so addictive.

>>To: Toobe
From: Scratch
Subj: Online

I just got off the phone with my brother and started thinking. He doesn't get communicating online at all. He gets the technology, but he doesn't get why people spend so much money to talk to strangers or have more email than they can handle. Stumped me for a minute, but then I got a theory (ready for another one, ol' pal?):

It used to be you could talk to people on the street. You could chat about the weather or the news and it would be nice and then you'd go your separate ways. But now you have to worry that they're psycho or they're gonna ask you for something, or worse, that they'll think *you're* weird. So we've shut ourselves down. We size somebody up in a second and we cross the street, either literally or figuratively. We judge people by how they look, of course, but it's a complex assessment—in a flash!—based on so many little things that it takes up too large a portion of your brain.

The thing is, people still want to connect. Behind all that cynicism is this desperate need to connect. You know when people do good deeds accidentally, like keeping a whale alive when it's washed onshore or helping somebody out during a fire or something? They all feel so fucking good, and they can't quite explain it.

So in cyberspace, they're talking to people again! They don't have to worry that somebody's gonna pull a gun if they say the wrong thing. Or even if someone *is* psycho, they can go ahead and talk to them, they never have to "see" them again. They can even enjoy talking to a psycho. They're safe enough to connect. And for women! Whoa! Suddenly they can tell assholes to fuck off without getting killed, or be really sexy in a way they would never be normally, and just enjoy it. Even though the majority of onliners are men, I think it's gonna change, if for that reason alone.

Which leads me to why so many men pose as women online. It's like cyber-crossdressing. They give up the male role for awhile. Or pretend they're lesbians. What cracks me up is that they're probably doing it with other guys who are acting like women that night too. Oooh, baby! I got off the track. But do you know what I mean?

—S.<<

Toobe Entry con't

Here's more about the word *hir.* I was reading some old English novel in class and found out that the English language used to have gender assigned, just like German and most other romance languages have. We still have some of that left over, like ships are shes, and Mother Nature is she, and of course, everything else is he. There's a line from Chaucer, "Whan that April with his shures sote," a stanza every kid in my high school had to memorize. See how the April is a he? I grabbed that April/his thing, and found this other word, which is like "its." Which was the word "hir." That's how they used to say the possessive when they didn't know the gender of the noun, or it was a neutral noun. Way back then! So it would be "The person sat down at hir computer and began to type." (It was pronounced "here" sort of, with an English accent so who really knows. It's as dead as ancient Greek.)

So Scratch and Winc keep meeting in different rooms online, like sci-fi rooms or I'm-cheating-on-my-husband rooms, and it's like they toss a coin to see what sex they'll be.

The weird thing is, I don't know if Scratch and Winc really know this yet, but they keep running into each other online, no matter who they're being at the time. They'll be in a room called Fooling Around and maybe Scratch has chosen for hir persona that night a big strapping, hunk of a sexist pig, and sure enough Winc will have chosen tiny damsel in distress, and they'll play it out, and then one of them will recognize the other's "fucking style" or something and they'll crack up. Then one of them will say, I *know* you're a woman now, and the other one will ask how do you know, and they'll be off on that noise.

Or they'll both send me a log of the whole thing, separately, mind you, like "Look at the cool scene I had," only I get the logs at the same time, and it's clear they had this cool scene with *each other.* I don't always tell them, it's too weird (and also don't forget those Eyes). I think they'd be blown away if they knew most of these scenes happen with each other.

I'm a chronicler, I guess. And I'm a guy. I call myself Toobe (pronounced tube) cuz I think it sounds cool. Fuck what age I am.

Here's an example of Scratch torturing some poor dude who just wants hir to be a girl. But ze won't cooperate. The other one's not Winc, though. Just some guy who found Scratch online.

>>FORWARDED CHAT LOG: Scratch--->TOOBE

AWESOME: You a guy or a girl?

Scratch: Does it matter?

AWESOME: I'm pretty loose about most things, but I don't fuck no dudes.

Scratch: Ah, that's a shame, hon. You'd probably enjoy it if you loosened up. That's OK, I'm not anything tonight.

AWESOME: I take it you enjoy watching guys together. No, I don't think I would enjoy it, and yes, I am pretty loose.

Scratch: I enjoy lots of things, like guys who can be receptive, as it were. :)

<<

That little :) symbol is a smile (turn it on its side and you'll see). I don't use them, way too cute for me. Scratch doesn't usually either, but I guess ze was "in character."

>>AWESOME: I can be very receptive to certain things. But I enjoy it more when I do the giving.

Scratch: Ain't that sweet. And rare . . .

AWESOME: So do you just naturally have a fucked-up attitude, or is this your way of weeding out certain people?

Scratch: What the fuck do you know about my attitude, dude. ::firing up weedwhacker::

AWESOME: Somehow I get the impression you're a guy. If that is the case, bring the weedwhacker over here and I will demonstrate on you how it is used properly . . . ha ha. Your attitude is all fucked up. But I think that is just great. LOL.<<

LOL means laugh out loud, so you can show somebody you thought something was funny, without writing "That was funny." People also use ROTFL, which means Rolling on the Floor Laughing.

>>Scratch: Don't give a fucking shit in hell what gender I am . . . try to leave it in the car with the windows rolled up as much as possible.<<

I like when Scratch and Winc send me stuff. It makes me more brave.

End Toobe Entry

Narrative Entry, Jabbathehut
(Note: sample log, socialization, the Net.)

There's a "pub" in the virtual world, which, despite the unlimited possibilities of description, the "patrons" have chosen to create as a slightly tacky lounge for more than tacky people to frequent. It's all there——the polyester, the smoky haze, the blender drinks and the elevator music. At any given time, day or night, this bar can be full of people, with a wide range of handles reflecting their status——usually heterosexual, married, and restless. They come because there are others like them; this is their first tentative step onto the worldwide connection to the Net.

It is here that Scratch has found hirself, bored out of hir mind but unable to sleep. Ze has signed on as Scratch, without a gender, waiting to see if someone else will fill in that blank for hir. As ze fends off the third of a series of polyester advances, ze realizes wryly that ze must be giving off the scent of someone female, and ze muses on the invisible cues cyberspace somehow allows. Pissed off but curious, ze decides to give them what they want, but takes time crafting hir profile. Ze can see out hir window: riotgrrls with backward baseball caps, combat boots, and skirts. They're scary, angry, frenetic, and beautiful. Funny how even in this androgynous new generation, there is still a gender uniform for girls and boys.

"Okay," ze says. "You want a girl, I'll be a girl."

Into this bar skateboards Winc, oblivious of the hour, the patrons, the atmosphere. He (for that's the pronoun chosen at this point) shakes the rain out of his long dark hair like a puppy, again clueless of the startled stares his presence provokes. He turns on his "All Messages" option, allowing him to receive not only Private Messages from the other patrons, but also the news, public service announcements, and advertisements. In this virtual world he sits down at the bar, orders a beer, and surveys the place.

"Cool," he says. Onscreen is a lottery game, inset with a football broadcast, which he idly watches. He has a small waterfall tattooed under his right eye. His body is lithe, boyish, and he's added a bit of mascara tonight.

Meanwhile, Scratch puts the final touches on "her" transformation. She has created an online profile, a summary self-description that may be called up by the curious, the bored, or the painfully longing. If some unsuspecting soul were to type in "Scratch," then select "Get Profile," they would see:

Member Profile

Name: Scratch

Occupation: Fully

Quote: Fuck your gender

◎ click here to read more

"More" is what Scratch is working on. Immediately after creating her profile, Scratch starts receiving advertisements. Since she selected more info about fragrances, she has been pelted with pleas from the fashion industry for her attention, her time, her body fat, her virtual crow's-feet. It's helping. Her profile is getting more solidly centered in "pissy." By the time a pastel-colored layout urges her to buy the latest PMS medication, she's in full swing: young, female, angry. She hits the "refuse" button hard, almost breaking her mouse. She recovers by surfing the other patrons' profiles, whose scintillating conversation is revealed:

×××Online Host: You are in "The Tavern."×××

Fredman: Hey, honey, come sit closer to me.

Scratch: No thanks, I'm fine right here.

Tomgun: Don't mind Fred, he's harmless. But I'm not. ::grin::

Fredman: Not that harmless.

Scratch: Winc, how long is your skateboard?

Winc: Oh, it's not a long one, it's about average.

Aza: LOL, Winc, tell her it's huge!

Winc: ::startled:: huh? What do you mean?

Scratch: I'm sure it's long enough, babe.

Hanzoo: Scratch wants your body, man.

Scratch: Thanks, Han, but you can go do yourself now.

Winc: ::to Scratch:: So I missed that one, eh? You want my body?

Scratch: Why don't you come with me and see?

Winc: ::gazing at Scratch from beneath hooded eyes:: What's in it for me?

Hanzoo: Go, Winc!

Scratch: ::shrugging:: Suit yourself, cautious one.

A soft chime sounds in the background. Everyone in the bar instantly becomes "quiet" and listens—no one is typing over the soothing "voice" of the message, written so you can almost hear it purring:

The silence continues until the last of the announcement fades from the screens of the Tavern attendees. Then gradually, the room's ambience, such as it is, begins to return.

> **Fredman**: I know someone who won last week's lottery.
> **Hanzoo**: Wow, what I could do with $6 million!
> **BarBun**: You do, Fred, really? ::pouting:: I suppose I should Register.
> **Fredman**: It wasn't six million, Han, that's only the grand prize. You haven't Registered, Bun?
> **Hanzoo**: You haven't Registered, BarBun? Get with it, woman!
> **BarBun**: I know, I know, it's just all those questions they ask you!
> **Winc**: I'm with you, BarBun. Major ick!
> **Hanzoo**: No bad questions, BarBun . . . just the standard age, sex, race, income, stuff like that . . .
> **Winc**: ::whispering the name of a private room to Scratch::

Azazello: Yeah, and what else . . . simple stuff like
sexprefs, brandprefs, zip, zip-plus, famzips . . . it's
not hard.
Scratch: Got it, Winc . . .
BarBun: All right, all right, you guys, I'll fill out the
forms now. Geez!
Winc: ::waving::
Fredman: If you win, BarBun, take me to the islands! I
have a timeshare condo, but no way to get there!

End Jabba Entry

Toobe Entry

Did I mention I save everything? I still have Scratch's note to me about the first time ze met Winc. They met in a kind of "virtual pub." It's an excerpt from Scratch's journal. I can't wait to show it to them in ten years.

>>Scratch Entry

The first time I met Winc was unbelievable. Perfect that ze was there. If I'd heard another stupid line I would've thrown up right into my keyboard.

Member Profile
Name: Winc
Age: 28
Occupation: hahahahahahahaha!
Hobbies: Skateboarding, it's my life.
Quote: jus' wanna be yer cherrybomb!

But just as I was to join the Winc dude in a private room, I get one of those Private Messages . . .

Private Message from Thesman:

Thesman: Um, Scratch, just being friendly here, but if any member of this service catches your profile (you wrote: "the F-word your gender") it will mean a quick end to your online days. You might want to take that offending word off and replace it with something more mainstream.
Scratch: Thanks, oh my goodness, that word! I'm taking out my frustrations with Winc. Catch you next time.

<<

Toobe Entry con't

The worst thing is that this guy Thesman isn't even an Eye. After awhile we won't need an Eye, we'll just do it ourselves. Here's the rest of it.

>>Scratch Entry con't

I didn't even care what this guy was or if he was a guy. I was trapped in "girl," with all these lounge lizards around me. Thought some cybersex would be nice. I gave him a whole lot of attitude, but he stuck around anyway.

You have entered Private Room "Apt. 3G."

Scratch: Warning: I'm pissy and I'm horny and I want...
Winc: Yeah? ::grinning:: What is it you want?
Scratch: I don't care how old you are or even what sex you are, I just wanna fuck. If that's too rough for you piss off.
Winc: ::leaning forward, putting my hands on your shoulders:: Do your stuff, Scratch.
Scratch: ::crotch zing:: I like that in a partner. Gotta know about your hair. Long or short?
Winc: ::laughing, turning away, tossing long hair out of my eyes::
Scratch: <--- likes long hair.
Winc: You?
Scratch: Short, bristle, you have to ask to touch it.
Winc: What if I don't wanna ask first? ::turning and walking back closer to you::
Scratch: Then you get a kick in the balls.
Winc: ::stopping short:: Ah . . . well . . . With what kind of shoe?
Scratch: They're boots, dude. Bet you're pretty in that long hair.
Winc: ::dropping to my knees, pressing my cheek against your boot:: ::purring:: I'm as pretty as they come.
Scratch: ::grabbing hair:: ::pulling face up to look at me:: Stay with me, though . . .
Winc: ::jerking to my feet::

Scratch: ::kissing your neck, pulling hair::
Winc: mmmmmmmmmm . . . nice, very nice . . .

I'll summarize a bit; it was so real I can tell it like a story: It's a bare room, there's a mattress on the floor, but we're nowhere near it. I can practically hear our voices echoing, it's so real. I'm horny as hell, urgent, with a kind of intensity I've never felt with men. Like I don't care what he wants. I'll use him anyway, I'm not obligated to his rhythm.

I push him against the wall, and he gasps.

"You like it rough, huh girl?" he asks.

My hands are hungry, rough on him, rougher than I wanna be, but now I understand "I can't help it." He shudders, I bring my hands to his chest, squeezing his nipples. I squeeze them hard, and his eyes go wide. It makes me laugh softly. I've pegged him, his hardness turns me on, but it's the way he yields that takes me over the top. I've never been here before, it's not some bitch in high heels with a whip I'm doing, but I'm definitely running this thing. I can feel my own desire take over, spill out, let it guide my hands. I lift his shirt, suddenly impatient: "I want it off!"

He tosses his head, making his hair whip my face a bit. "Make me," he says. He still doesn't get it. He's describing himself, and I begin seeing him. Lithe boy body, soft hair on his belly, sinewy. I ease up to his chest, kittenish, unassuming, kissing his chest, but then bite his nipples hard. He gasps.

"Shirt off," I repeat. He's breathing hard, but pauses, maybe in confusion, maybe still impudent. "Off!"

He pulls his torn T-shirt over his head, and I tease him, telling him I can see why it's torn now. He's slightly offended, folds his arms across his chest: I knead his chest with my hands, pulling his arms down. He gasps, and I press myself fully against him, kissing him deeply.

He lifts his arms up and around my shoulders. I lean into him, suddenly grateful for his strong body, his boy strength. "Yes," I say, "hold me strong." He opens his mouth wide for me, pulling my tongue deep inside. I press against his pelvis, and he moans into my mouth. My hands are around his back, digging in.

Winc: ::pushing hard against you, kneading your shoulders with long strong fingers . . . my cock harder now::
Scratch: ::Hand drifting absently down to the top of
your jeans::
Winc: ::whimpering::

I feel his jeans pull away from his body; he shivers. I rub his
bulge through the jeans.

Winc: Oh
  my
  gosh
Scratch: ::backing up, pulling off my shirt::

I turn him around, rubbing my breasts on his back. His back
is warm, and a moan escapes, startling us both. He pushes
his ass back against my crotch, as I wrap my arms around
his belly.

Winc: ::sighing::
Scratch: ::sliding my hands down to your hips, pulling
you against my crotch, pushing you hard, bending you
over::
Winc: ::lifting my hands above my head, against the
wall::
  ::turning my head to face you . . . questioning::

I push him into the wall, crotch pressed against his ass.
  "Questioning what, boy?"
  He gasps, shakes his head: "What are you doing to me?"
  "Gonna take you boy, are you complaining?"
  "No . . . not complaining, no."
  I pull away from him, lean against the wall, next to him.
And suddenly look at him, a grin on my face. I have my hands
across my chest.

Winc: ::breathing hard . . . looking in your eyes::
  ::softly:: I want you . . . please.
Scratch: I know . . . stand up.
Winc: ::standing up . . . shakily::
Scratch: ::coming over to you, putting fingers on top of
your jeans::
Winc: ::cock throbbing in my jeans::
Scratch: ::Pulling first button slowly, plup!::
  ::watching cock::
Winc: ahhhh. ::not moving . . . watching you closely::

Scratch: There, all free now? ::Smirk:: Or do you need more buttons undone?
Winc: ::head of my cock peeking out over undone top button::
Scratch: ::pressing against you, feeling tip of cock on my belly::
Winc: M-m-more, I think.

His tentative desire makes me laugh. His arms go up around me, I grab his hair with one hand, buttons with the other. Plup, plup, plup, and he's free. The odd thing is, while I'm typing that, he's typing this:

Winc: ::cock springs free from my jeans::

It keeps happening, this kind of "simulpost" where despite the delay of online time we're in synch.

He leans forward, burying his face into my neck. I grab his cock, squeezing gently. I feel the hair around his balls. He sighs happily, licking my shoulder and throat. I slide my hands around his ass, under his jeans, pressing against his cock, squeezing his ass. His hands work up and down my bare back. My crotch is throbbing, the wetness warm against my clothes.

He pushes his hips hard against me, I pull his hand to my breast. I slide my hand back around to his cock, pushing his jeans down. He's squeezing my breasts softly, kneading. His jeans are to his knees. I push him to the floor.

Winc: ::startled . . . falling back::
Scratch: Yeah. I like that. Don't move.
Winc: ::looking up at you . . . hungry::
Scratch: ::Walking around you, stopping behind your head, looking down at you::
Winc: ::wiping hair out from in front of my eyes::
Scratch: ::Pulling off my own jeans::
Winc: ::moaning::
Scratch: ::Standing straight up, straddling your head, bending over from the waist::
Winc: Oh yes!
Scratch: ::Cunt hair wet::
Winc: ::pushing my face forward, inhaling you::
Scratch: ::placing my hands on either side of you, I lower my mouth down to your cock::
Winc: ahhhhhhhhhhhhhh

Scratch: ::Licking, once twice, a few soft swipes with my tongue::
Winc: ::licking up and down your cunt lips gently::
Scratch: ::Lowering my cunt to just a few inches from your mouth lower, lower, moaning as I feel your tongue, licking your cock::

I suddenly stand up, walk away from him; he cries out.

Winc: ::falling back onto the floor::

I walk back to his side, grasping his cock with my hand, bringing my mouth to it.

Winc: Oh!
Scratch: ::Other hand on my pussy, rubbing juices around. Rubbing juices on your cock::
Winc: ::my hands go to your breasts . . . tweaking your nipples, pinching harder::
Scratch: ::moaning::

I bring my mouth back up to his . . .

Winc: ::hungry mouth meeting yours::

. . . slap his hand, kiss him hard, bite his lip.

Winc: ::crying out, tasting my own blood::
Scratch: ::Pulling your jeans all the way off:: Turn over.
Winc: Huh?
Scratch: Turn the fuck over.
Winc: ::mumbling, confused:: . . . OK. OK . . .
Scratch: You want a bed or something? Turn over.
Winc: ::turning over:: ::looking at you over my shoulder::
Scratch: ::Pressing you into the floor. Straddling you::
Winc: Oh!
Scratch: ::Sitting on your ass, my cunt on your butt-bone:: ::Rubbing, rocking back and forth::
Winc: ::pushing my ass back to meet you::
Scratch: ::moaning::
Winc: ::moving my ass side to side against you::
Scratch: oh, gawd . . . yes . . . ::pressing your cock into the floor::
Winc: ::pushing back harder, twisting against you::
Scratch: Does it hurt, does it hurt, boy?
Winc: ::crying out:: YES!
Scratch: ahhhhhhh

Winc: Hurts realllllll good!

I bite his neck, pushing against him.

Winc: ::tears spring to my eyes, twisting against you::

I rub my juices on my hand, rubbing his ass, squeezing. It's so nasty, this wetness all over him, not caring what it does to him. I can smell myself, sweet and tangy, wafting up to me. I circle two fingers closer to his hole.

Winc: ::gasping:: ::clenching my asshole tight::
Scratch: ::Teasing, entering just a little, coming back out.::
Winc: ::shuddering::
Scratch: ::Sliding one finger all the way in, wet with my juices.::
Winc: ::moaning:: ohyesohyesohyes ::pushing up against your finger::
Scratch: ::Reaching around you with my other hand, grabbing your cock.:: That feels good in my hand.
Winc: ::moaning:: ::clenching, unclenching around your finger::

I can feel his own wetness on the tip of his cock, as I slide another finger in hard, deep.

Winc: ::whimpering::
Scratch: ::Pushing both fingers deep inside you.::
Winc: YAHHHHH!

I slide his cock up and down in my hand.

Winc: ::rotating my ass back against you:: ::shuddering:: oh geez
Scratch: ::Sliding around to the side of you, turning you slightly::
I want you, I want you, boy. ::Pulling fingers out slowly:: ::Turning you over again, on your back::
Winc: ::looking into your face . . . tears in eyes, bloody lip::
Want you to take me, grrrl.

I rub his blood all over my breasts.

Winc: Want you real bad.
Scratch: Want more of that.

I watch his cock, swelling at the head. He pushes forward,

hungrily, licking his blood off my breasts. I squeeze his balls
in my hand, pinching his nipples, kissing him with my teeth.

Winc: ::leaning back, arching my neck back:: Bite me . . .
bite me hard. Please!

At the same time, I type what he's just said:

Scratch: ::biting you on the nipples hard, feeling blood
on my tongue::
::biting you up to your neck, bites all the way up your
chest::
Winc: ::crying, laughing:: Oh yes!

I pin both his arms to the floor.

Winc: ::startled . . . looking up at you::

I slide up his body, straddling his cock, just above it. I dangle
my cunt hairs, teasing his cock.

Winc: ::lifting my hips up to meet your cunt::
Scratch: uhhhhhh . . . ::pushing your cock against my
clit::

End Scratch Entry<<

Toobe Entry con't

Scratch is easily confused. The rest of the entry wasn't transmitted right, which happens
with about half hir files. I keep trying to explain how you save files and send them but . . .
anyway, ze's doing better these days. Fortunately, this was one of those times Winc had sent me
hir own transcript of the same thing, so I'll just go on with it from hir point of view.

>>Winc Entry

It wasn't my first round of cybersex, not by a long shot.
But it was the best. No matter what Scratch says, and no matter how out of control all the stories about us have gotten,
this is what really happened. Well, with one or two extra
words from me . . . ::grin::

Winc: ::wriggling my cock back and forth against you::
Scratch: ::sliding in a little, then back out to my
clit, rubbing::
::moaning:: yessss
Winc: ::moaning:: oh yes!
Scratch: ::sliding down hard on your cock, taking it
deep inside me.::

Winc: ::urgently pushing up against you::
::gasping . . . feeling you wet and hot around my cock::
Scratch: ::Feeling you stirring inside me::
Winc: ::pumping my hips hard into you::
Scratch: ::sliding off you abruptly again, bending down
to your cock with my mouth::
Winc: ::crying out:: OH!
Scratch: ::sly smile:: Whatsa matter, huh?
Winc: ::shuddering:: Pleeeeeeeeease!
Scratch: Please what? What do you want? Say it. Say the
nasty words, boy.
Winc: Want you so bad!
Want you on top of me . . . fucking me . . . please!
Want your cunt swallowing my cock!
Want you dripping juice all over me!
Scratch: Good boy, good good boy.

Yup. Good boy, that was me! She grabbed my cock with both
hands, pulling it hard, up and down. Then, just as suddenly,
she stopped and said:

Scratch: No.
Winc: Ohhhhhhhhhhhhhhhhhh!
::tossing head side to side frustrated::

So then she stood up again, walked around by my head, and
pulled me across the floor by my hair. I got to my knees quick
enough to scramble along as she pulled me. She straddled my
head, dipping her cunt to my face.

Scratch: Not ready yet.
Winc: ::on my knees in front of you . . . looking up
into your eyes::
::cock throbbing::
::precum glistening with your juices on my cock::
Scratch: Whatcha gonna do for me now, huh?
Winc: ::swallowing hard:: I . . . I want to lick your
cunt . . . want to taste you, fuck you with my tongue.
::breathing hard::
Scratch: Lie back down . . .
Winc: ::not moving, looking at you::
Scratch: ::Straddling your face . . . pressing my pussy
into your mouth, hands on floor on either side of you::
Winc: ::moaning into your pussy::

Scratch: ::dropping my body down onto your chest::
Winc: ::kissing up and down your lips:: ::lapping you with the broad of my tongue::
Scratch: yessssss.
Winc: ::swallowing your juice:: ::flicking your clit with the tip of my tongue:: ::over and over::
Scratch: ::pulling on your cock, squeezing your balls::
Winc: ::gasping::
Scratch: ::tugging on your hairs::
Winc: ::pushing my tongue up inside you::
Scratch: ::Knees pressing into floor, hurting, sending pain straight to my cunt::
Winc: ::lapping at you like a dog::

And that's when I started to get these private messages from FoolsGold! Of course, Scratch couldn't see them, but I ended up still in the scene with Scratch, while flirting with FoolsGold at the same time. Hey, don't get down on me. It happens all the time.

Private Message to Winc

FoolsGold: Look upon my garden gate a snail that's what it is.
Winc: ::gasp:: What a lovely note to send. *So* much better than "what are you wearing"!
FoolsGold: Well, I like the song and that's what I could remember of the lyrics.
Winc: ::laughing:: And what song is that?
FoolsGold: By the way, what are you wearing? Only joking.

Scratch: ::bringing my mouth to the tip of your cock. lapping at you::
Winc: ::shuddering:: ::hips pumping against your mouth::
Scratch: ::grasping your tongue with my cunt, letting my body fall completely down onto you, taking your cock all the way into my mouth::
Winc: ::moaning:: oh yessssssssssssssss
Scratch: ::Juices pour out of me::
Winc: ::wrapping long arms up around you::

Private Message to Winc

FoolsGold: An old song by Donovan. First there is a mountain . . . is part of the lyrics. As is the snail part.
Winc: That's right, he made a song out of that!

FoolsGold: I'm showing my age, I fear.
Winc: <--- has a penchant for hippies.
FoolsGold: Kind of a Zen feeling to it. Or Taoist.
Well I used to be a hippie . . . I reckon ::wink::

> **Scratch**: ::throat contracting around your cock. Moaning, building, pulling away from you.:: ::panting:: Can't, can't stay there . . .
> **Winc**: ::crying out:: NO!
> **Scratch**: ::Sweat on my back, sliding your hands around my back::
> **Winc**: ::trembling fingers kneading into your back::
> **Scratch**: ::Coming back around to gaze at you, still playing with your cock::
> **Winc**: ::licking my lips . . . your juice and my blood::
> **Scratch**: ::sliding up to it, lowering myself slowly down on it, looking at you, not flinching::
> **Winc**: ::looking at you, adoring you::

Private Message to FoolsGold

Winc: The phrase "first there is a mountain, then there is no mountain, then there is," is part of an old koan. That's in the song, too. ::grinning:: I know you, don't I?

> **Scratch**: ::holding your arms, rocking up and down, closing eyes, throwing head back.::
> **Winc**: Yesssss.

I thought this guy FoolsGold mighta been Jabba! But no, I don't think it was. ::grin:: Not J's style. Still . . .

Private Message to Winc

FoolsGold: Relating to the spiritual growth of the student and his/her perception of reality.
Winc: ::eyes widening:: Yeah . . . I *do* know you, don't I?
FoolsGold: I don't know, perhaps in a past incarnation. We might have been possums in the same pouch.
Winc: Or fishies in the same pond. Snails on the same garden gate?
FoolsGold: In fact I seem to have a vague memory of something like that, but maybe it's just the mushrooms.
Winc: ::snapping my fingers:: Shrooms! That's it! Golden Gate Park!

This double conversation is doing a number on my head. Not a bad number, mind you, but a number nonetheless. ::grin:: Meanwhile, back in Apartment 3G . . .

Winc: ::lapping at your shoulder, pumping my cock into you:: ::my balls slamming up under your cunt::
Scratch: ::Juice gushing down onto your cock, not caring what you do, just rocking hard pumping, using your cock in me, using you::
Winc: ::hair on my stomach rubbing against you:: ::tossing my head from side to side . . . out of control::
Scratch: ::putting a finger in your mouth:: Suck it, boy, Suck your ass . . .
Winc: ::sucking your finger my ass your finger::
Scratch: ::Cunt tightening:: ::gasping::

It was getting a lot harder to pay attention to FoolsGold, but I left off being myself and . . . *splattered* myself between the two simultaneous identities I was creating: the sexpassion with Scratch, and the mindspirit with Foolsgold were spilling into each other.

Private Message to Winc

FoolsGold: I don't know if we have indeed met before, but I have the feeling that I would like to be acquainted with you, if that's not too forward.
Winc: ::grinning:: To be honest, I thought you were someone I know from Seattle. She surfs as a guy sometimes.
FoolsGold: I'm assuming that you are a woman, but you might be a guy. Still you seem to be a friendly creature. And I am not a woman, I'm glad to say. I have all the respect in the world for them, but wouldn't want to be one.
Winc: ::blinking:: Why not?
FoolsGold: Well, they have to put up with a lot of crap, some of it biological, and some from men.
Winc: ::nodding:: For sure!
FoolsGold: Are you a woman?

Winc: ::tasting myself on you, licking sucking::
Scratch: ::Reaching under, grasping your balls, squeezing::

Winc: ::thighs trembling:: oh yesssssss . . . yesssss
::cock throbbing inside you::
Scratch: ::feeling you swelling bigger inside me, clamping down on you::
Winc: ::balls tightening::
 gonna . . .
 wanna . . .
Scratch: I'm gonna . . . I'm gonna, don't you dare youmotherfucker I'm gonna
Winc: p-pp-p . . .
Scratch: ::Legs shuddering rocking against you—frenzy::
Winc: ::groaning::
 I
 need
 to . . .
Scratch: Higher higher, Cccccominggggggyou fucker you comeyoucome
Winc: YAAAHHHHHH!
Scratch: ::shaking, shuddering:: ohhhhhhhhhhhhhh
Winc: ::pumping hot cum up inside you::
Scratch: yeah.
Winc: yeaaah.
Scratch: ::Rocking slower, slower, digging my hands into your chest::
::throbbing, cunt raw, sore::
Winc: ::panting, gasping:: ::reaching up around you::
::pulling you tightly against me::
Scratch: ::my hand sliding up to your throat . . .
tightening:: ::leaning over to kiss you deep, my hand around your throat, tight, squeezing::
Winc: ::kissing you deeply . . . no breath::
Scratch: ::Biting your lips again::
Winc: ::can't breathe, world is slowing down . . . kissing you . . . tasting more of my blood::
Scratch: ::rubbing my clit, contracting again and again around your cock::
Winc: ::relaxing into your hand around my throat::
Scratch: ::releasing your throat, putting both hands on your chest, falling down on you, sliding your cock out slowly:: ::panting:: ::sweat all over us::
Winc: ::gulping air::

I was a goner. Love isn't the word, and even though nowadays Scratch says I say I love you way too much, that's just how I felt. But deeper than a casual I-love-you. How could that happen in such a short space of time? ::shaking my head:: I thought I was gonna really die. I love that. Some day I wanna die in Scratch's arms.

Scratch: ::pulling your hair gently::
Winc: ::wrapping long arms around you:: I . . . I could die like that . . . happily.

Private Message to Winc

FoolsGold: You haven't answered me. Are you a woman?
Winc: ::blinking:: Isn't that a rather personal question? ::laughing delightedly at your need to know::

Scratch: ::smile:: ::Playing with hairs on your belly:: No hairs on your chest?
Winc: ::laughing softly:: Yeah . . . hair on my chest . . . soft hair.
Scratch: ::you could be a girl here ::touching:: and here.
Winc: yeah . . . could be.

Private Message to Winc

FoolsGold: Well, I'm enjoying the conversation regardless of your sex or sexual orientation.
Winc: ::laughing:: As am I!
FoolsGold: Just trying to form a mental image.
Winc: <--- tall, copper hair, green eyes, waterfall tattoo spilling down from under my right eye. Rose tattoo on right thigh (rose has a whip curled up around it).

Scratch: But not there: ::patting cock::
Winc: ::gasp:: No, not there . . . not . . . well . . .
Scratch: ::rubbing hands all over sweaty bodies:: ::rubbing my juices all over you::
Winc: ::licking your neck and shoulders::
Scratch: Shit.
Winc: ::taking your face in my hands:: What?
Scratch: Want you real time.
Winc: ::smiling::

Private Message to Winc

FoolsGold: Is that how you keep guys in line? With a whip?
Winc: ::grinning:: Perhaps. Is that your interest?

Scratch: Real hands on real crotch right now. Hate this part. I mean, real time hate this part.
Winc: Where are you? No! Don't tell me.
Scratch: What?!
Winc: Can't say stuff like where and who . . . I keep forgetting.
Scratch: Nope, you can't.

Private Message to Winc

FoolsGold: Well, I do enjoy it at times when a woman takes control, but I have my limits.
Winc: ::purring:: Everyone does, darlin'.
FoolsGold: Gee, and I thought that I was strange or something.
Winc: ::laughing:: Without limits, S/M would be limited to one session, then *poof*.
FoolsGold: Are you into the S&M scene then?
Winc: S/M, or SM, not S&M darlin' . . . Yeah, guess I am.

Scratch: You're a nice guy. Too bad.
Winc: ::kissing you all over your face:: ::chuckling:: Tonight I'm a nice guy, yeah.
Scratch: What? Nice or a guy?
Winc: ::eyes sparkling:: Both. Neither.
Scratch: Hey! You fucking with me?
Winc: Always. Never!

Private Message to FoolsGold

Winc: ::grinning:: Yeah, I really think either/or questions should be answered yes or no.
FoolsGold: LOL, you seem to maintain a bit of an air of mystery, but that's an attraction too. You're keeping me guessing.
Winc: ::blinking:: Mystery? Moi?
FoolsGold: What can I say.
Winc: ::biting my lip, thinking of a *lot* of things he could say::

Scratch: ::grabbing pants, stepping a few feet away from you::
Winc: Hey! Hey, wait. I'm sorry . . . I . . .
Scratch: ::coming back to you, giving up::
Winc: I . . . this . . .
Scratch: ::pulling you up . . . climbing into your lap::

Winc: mmmmmmmmmmmmmm.

Scratch: ::sitting facing you:: ::rocking with you::

Winc: ::touching your cheek:: I like you. A lot.

Scratch: Winc . . .

Winc: mmmmm?

Scratch: Don't. And no I can't get email.

Winc: ::face falling::

Scratch: Well, do you get email? How long do you stay at an address?

Winc: Wait . . . you signed on with a bypass, didn't you?

Scratch: Maybe I did, maybe I didn't.

Winc: Are you CRAZY?

Scratch: OK, OK, I did.

Winc: ::fiercely:: Grrrrrl . . . you make sure of it next time. I don't want them arresting you, and me having to bring you a file baked into a cake.

Private Message to Winc

FoolsGold: I'm 6'1" with brown hair (what's left of it) and about 190 lbs, and a full beard.

Winc: ::laughing delightedly:: Now tell me you live in Bolinas!

Scratch: How did we know neither of us were Registered? ::smiling::

Winc: Whoa. True. Just assumed.

Scratch: Hey, you ever get it on with an Eye?

Winc: Huh??

Scratch: Did it with a guy who turned out to be an Eye?

///7990F0 909I///

Winc: No, I hate them. You can always tell when it's an Eye.

Scratch: Oh, yeah? Well, I did it with an Eye once.

Winc: Oh shit. You see that garble? YOU DID?

Scratch: That's not me, you know . . . line's frazzing.

Winc: ::carefully:: Not so sure about that.

Scratch: Anyway, I fixed him up, though, threatened to go public, he's never bothered me since.

Winc: ::laughing, shaking my head:: That is so cool! So who are you? I want to know.

Private Message to Winc

FoolsGold: I'd guess that you are a bit younger, early 20s (a wild stab).

Winc: ::leaning forward, kissing you gently on the cheek:: You're really sweet . . . but I've made a solemn vow not to talk gender or age online. ::grin:: Makes life interesting! ::brushing my lips with my fingertips from where your beard tickled::

Scratch: I'm a me. What the fuck is it to you? Who are you?
Winc: Me? ::straining brain to come up with best description::
Scratch: Wait! Don't tell me.
Winc: Huh?
Scratch: I don't wanna know. It doesn't matter. But I know you're a guy.
Winc: ::laughing:: Oh do ya, now.
Scratch: ::shy:: well, yeah . . . We could be anything.
Winc: ::reaching down to between my legs, stroking my cunt:: Yes, we could. ::impish grin::

Private Message to Winc
FoolsGold: Would you care to exchange email?
FoolsGold: You still there??

I couldn't tell FoolsGold I was on an illegal bypass, or that I had just had this great sex with someone else, and that we were starting to lose contact. He could have been an Eye, though why I trusted Scratch is a mystery . . .

///3¶999 –– 444///
THIS LINE IS_¶¶ SECURE. •ª¶¶¶THIS IS NOT A PUBLIC LINE.
YOU ARE WARN¢_¶76§____
Scratch: Is your numbers key stuck?
Winc: I didn't write that!
///SAFE PASSAGE IS NOT ABL¶¶¶///
Scratch: I didn't either! Outta here.
Winc: Wait! I wanna see you again! I like you!

Private Message to FoolsGold
Winc: Eeeeeeep . . . sorry, I was super tied up . . .
FoolsGold: ::chuckling:: Literally? I thought I'd lost you.
Winc: Not a chance, mister! Anyway, there's lots of places, especially in the Bay Area, that are filled with opportunities to explore S/M.

FoolsGold: That is not my only interest in you. It only came up late in our conversation, but it is an interest of mine, I fear.

Winc: ::putting my hands on your shoulders:: I know it's not your only interest. And there's nothing to fear . . . well, almost nothing. ::wicked chuckle::

Scratch: We'll meet up again, we will, I know it. ::giving you a real look:: Feel it. Bye.

Private Message to Winc
FoolsGold: You still there? Are you getting my messages?

///JI U9K JIOPJH]\///
Scratch has left "Apt 3G".

Winc: Noooooo! Oh major, rats.

Toober, I never did find out what happened with FoolsGold, but that was it with Scratch. ::sighing happily:: Was it ever! Scratch says it took "her" longer, but I don't believe hir. I think ze was as in love as I was. It can happen. ::grin:: Cool, huh?

End Winc Entry<<

Toobe Entry con't
That's how they met. Pretty good for a first date, eh? Their accounts of it arrived to me within a few minutes of each other. They do that. They're both such loners in a way, but they were on the same wavelength from the first meeting.

End Toobe Entry

Narrative Entry, Jabbathehut
And in what some might call a green office, a message flashes on the screen:

To: Bureau of Census & Stats From: Jabbathehut Date: (transmission garbled) Subject: Sex, Sex, Sex—is that all?? Re: file <u>Scratch and Winc</u>

> You're reading their sex logs? *These* are the ones you're calling outlaws? ::rolling my eyes:: Surely you jest!
> —J.

Sucking at his teeth, Wally Budge mutters out loud, "Son of a gun. Does this joker know everyone I'm lookin' for?"

Source: persLOG/budge/harddrive

[To this bit of expected incredulity I cannot help but add: Of course I do, I am all-powerful, nothing escapes my notice.]

End Jabba Entry

‹HAPTER TWO

Toobe Entry

I just found a Chinese wall, a bathroom stall, a place everybody writes random stuff in no particular order: an electronic graffiti board. I use a "skim" program to grab anything new that's popped onto the Net. It's completely disorganized when it arrives on my machine, then I arrange it like a collage. Some of the postings are like a bulletin board, some more urgent, like the walls in a ghetto where you can see lines being drawn, rage or sorrow vented. I'm gonna include them in this journal, along with everything else. This one just appealed to me.

E-ffiti of the day:

Where are the baby pigeons? Has anyone *ever* seen one? No!
You just see grown-up ones . . .

—P.

That's all there was today. I didn't say they were real deep or anything, although it's true, I've never seen a baby pigeon.

I'm not sure I've mentioned Jabba before. Jabba is a genius, and although I always thought ze was a guy, hanging around with S and W I realize how stoopid that was. I have to admit I've never seen a pronoun. I'm gonna say she, just to balance it out. I've never met her face to face, but I've known her for a long time, through my dad. As far as I know they used to know each other a long time ago.

Jabba never comes out of her hole, and has banks of computers all over the place. It's freezing inside, and that's why she has fish. They can take the cold. The lights from the computers weave a magic stream through the tanks, rippling patterns all over the ceiling and walls. The water bubbles through little chugging pumps in the tanks, scattering ultraviolet and dark green pockets around the room. And the computers hum, of course. It's really cool. Feels like a safe, green cave with water escape routes.

I saw it only once, when I went over a long time ago to pick up a disk, but I always picture it when I write to Jabba. Jabba was there, but she didn't come out of the other room until I left. Here's something I got today.

>>To: Toobe
From: Jabbathehut
Subj: Handwriting

My quick little friend, I need a favor of you. A distribution point, if you will. I won't begin to tell you my thoughts on the proud forces of government and their interaction with the "Information Superhighway," as they call it, but you may have been following the news re: Registration. Where there is a new rule there are rule breakers. Our men in Washington are attempting, in their usual slipshod way, to organize that which cannot be organized. But what they do have on their side is the slowness of Time, an ever-present factor in any of their undertakings. In other words, those who don't go along with the program will simply be put in a category called Other, where they will languish until they figure out what to do with them.

As it stands now, if you don't Register, you don't get to go play where you were able to play before. In an unusual spurt of compassion, I have come up with some bypass codes. They are quite simple and easy to use. Anyone can make them up, and will, but as usual, I am the first as far as I know. You, who seem to have a twenty-four-hour clock and the attention span of a gnat (at fifteen, you can be forgiven this, but not for long), are the perfect letter carrier for me. You may never light long but you do light everywhere. If you would, please offer your acquaintances these codes (discreetly of course) in your wanderings. Would much appreciate.

Fighting God,

—J.<<

[No, I don't know what Fighting God means, and I'm afraid to ask.]

>>To: Jabbathehut
From: Toobe
Subj: On the wall

"Spurt of compassion" my nuts. Just how much are you charging for these, may I ask? Don't tell me you've put a virus on them so they stop working if people don't pay?<<

>>To: Toobe
From: Jabbathehut
Subj: Exactly

Of course, my little schmendrik. At least I don't require real names, as the Registration mavens do. Will download package within the hour. You, of course, may simply fill out yours with your screen name, and may have one free of charge.<<

>>To:Jabbathehut
From: Toobe
Subj: Ah, I see
   Gee, thanks. No, seriously, does this mean I can go anywhere?<<

>>To: Toobe
From: Jabbathehut
Subj: Indeed
   Yes, but do Register anyway. You won't be bothered again by cheap govt suits. As a result, they will spend the rest of the next millennium trying to undo this action, for of course, they haven't been thorough, and refuse to see the inevitability of the mess soon to be on their hands.<<

Toobe Entry con't

So I went to all these rooms like I always do, handed out Jabba's bypass codes like candy. Can't believe how many people didn't want them, they were worried about breaking the law. The majority of people actually said no. Scary. Everybody's having Reg parties online and offline like it's some goddamn gift they've been given, like they don't get that this is the equivalent of willingly signing up for all the junk mail you've ever received, and your neighbor's too.

But the government's working with business on this one, I mean Bizness. People are all stirred up, deep in their cyberbones. Here's a good one: if you don't have a computer, the govt will *give* you one when you Register. Who could resist? And then these dweebs can't even navigate around the Net; they're totally overwhelmed with all the choices.

I got a hysterical note from a law freak who found Lexis (a deep law library). He's racked up hundreds of dollars looking through tits and torts, and he claims he didn't know he'd be charged for all that time. Poor doode ended up having to pay anyway. He's what you'd call a typical consumer, this whole plan's *made* for him.

Bet if I wait a week Jabba's little toyz are gonna look a lot better to these folks. But here's another twist: When you fill out all the profile crap, you'll start getting advertisements and product samples just for you! How exciting. This one friend of mine went on as a girl in the lesbian room (he's a guy—they always figure him out, but he keeps trying) and he got tampon ads. His mail's flooded with them. If he tries to get out of it, they'll give him menopause stuff. Cracks me up. But if you Register right, you'll get just what you "need." It's seductive. Of course, I'm interested in computer toys and skateboard gear. I could be flooded with catalogs if I'm not careful. Here's an electronic zine excerpt; a few people are figuring things out:

>>Zine: PISSED OFF, NOT GONNA take it anymore

Some of us have noticed that we're not all getting the same information since Registering. Oh, it's not anything serious, this or that product isn't offered to everyone, this reporter almost missed a concert he wanted to attend because he wasn't in the right demographic to receive the invitation. This reporter went anyway. Next thing you know you won't be allowed in to such concert if you weren't prescreened in the first place.

<<

Toobe Entry con't

This all started cuz the businesses cooperated for once (I think a phone company's behind it), and people are believing anything, and panicking. They're really freaked about missing out. There's just enough differences in what Registered people get, and what you miss if you don't Register. It's like cable TV, people without it miss all the cool movies, so after awhile everyone thinks they should have cable. Here's what came out today:

>>Registration Will Curb Criminal Activity

by **Thomas Fulton**

The Internet, and the so-called 500-channel television have become out-of-control monsters. So said spokespersons for the Triumvirate Association of Businesses at a press conference yesterday. No one can find what they want on the Net anymore, consumers complain that they can't buy the brands they want because they can't find them; indeed, the choices are too many to justify the exhaustive hunt-and-peck a simple "shopping trip" has become.

Although the government's Registration plan will ultimately make the process smoother, at present there are suddenly several million more users of a highly sophisticated information system with no clear way to figure it all out. Veteran Net users are skeptical that an interface can be created to accommodate the average computer user, but plans move forward to organize.

Add to this mix the goals of Internet Intelligence, and the need to organize the system becomes crucial. "The criminal element has made inroads into most of the major electronic bulletin boards," says Federal Bureau of Census and Statistics

Undersecretary Margaret LaBouchere. "They are distributing illegal information, false advertising campaigns, and worst of all, porn, all over the Internet system." Once everyone is Registered, says LaBouchere, only criminals will be unregistered. It will be virtually impossible to conduct illegal activity, "because all the users can be traced back to their Registration numbers."

While it is doubtful all criminals will be forced offline, the effort so far is working, and has met with no real resistance. New Registrants agree their Net sessions are easier to manage. As consumers indicate their preferences for certain information systems, those preferences are made into a permanent file, so that with each use the computer does the work of choosing the consumer's point of interest.

What's more, each time a consumer buys something, his or her preference will be noted, so that the range of services offered to them will grow narrower, thereby thinning out the traffic on the Internet.

Matching the consumer with his or her interest will become a quick and easy process for the new, streamlined and technically savvy marketing departments of the private sector, with little interaction needed by the consumer at all, says the Triumvirate. Users will simply point and click to their interest icon, and the information will appear.

Toobe Entry cont'd

Yeah, right. But if you want to try something new and different outside of what they package for you, you have to wait forever. So for most people, it's easier to stick with what you got and not explore. Which *I* think is the point. Old Net users are furious, the ones who started it some time in the '70s, when it was an exclusive Pentagon system. But they seem to agree that at least the traffic won't be as bad in the areas *they're* in, cuz nobody knows how to get there.

Oh, got some email this morning. Scratch thinks too much.

>>To: Toobe
From: Scratch
Subj: Not gonna

Hey pal, option means option. I'm not Registering for the same reason I don't have a driver's license. I don't need paper to travel around, especially on the Net. I can't even get past the first few questions on that signup thing (like "Sex") they have. I tried to fill in "yes," but it will only take one answer or the other. I tried to write "N" for neither but it wouldn't take that either. Look at this #ə!×&%!!&×:

>>Sex? (M) or (F)?
Yes

```
Very funny. Sex? (M) or (F)?
  No
Very funny. Sex? (M) or (F)?
  ?
Very funny. Sex? (M) or (F)?
  WHY?
Very funny. Sex? (M) or (F)?
  EXIT
Very funny. Sex? (M) or (F)?
  CANCEL
Very funny. Sex? (M) or (F)?
  QUIT
Do you really want to quit the Registration Process?
  NO!
Sex? (M) or (F)?<<
```

Doesn't anyone see this is an invasion of privacy? What the hell does my gender mean in cyberspace?

I know you think I go in for conspiracy theories too much, and you may be right. It's habit. But people who create forms don't think about the questions they ask. This is a computer form; you can't go to the next question unless you fill it out right. That's scary, Toobers. I mean, there isn't even a human to argue with. I'll stick with my bypass.<<

Toobe Entry con't

Of course I'll delete the bypass part. Dumb shit. Like I'm gonna leave reference to that in a file. Sometimes Scratch is so paranoid, and sometimes not paranoid enough.

Here's a small part of the form. Ever since Scratch and Winc have been talking to me I can't look at it without seeing what they mean.

```
>>Registration Information
Name:
Credit Card #:
Sex:
Social Security #:
Income Level (round off
    to nearest ten thousand)
Address:
Phone:
Age:
Spouse's name:
Spouse's work phone:
```

```
        Ethnicity (choose one):
        Caucasian/Black/Hispanic/Asian/Other
        Sexual Orientation (choose one):
        Heterosexual/Homosexual
        Number of children, and their ages:
        Computer:
        Occupation:
        Employer's Name:
        Work phone number:
        Number of people in the household:
        Names of other residents:
        Brands:
    (Registrants must fill out the Product Survey Questions
    1–125 .)<<
```

That isn't even all of it! Doesn't that strike you as a little weird? That's a lot of info; where's it going? There's more on the form, like what kinds of toothpaste I use, how much I watch TV. It took me almost an hour to finish the whole thing. If I try to skip a question, it says I haven't completely filled out the form. I emailed Jabba again, and she said to put fake answers in as many boxes as I can. I wonder if she's Registered.

Winc just sent me something. If I were talking to hir right now online I'd write "::shaking my head::"

I'll excerpt it, but first let me explain why ze sent it first. I'm trying to understand Winc's thing about losing your gender. Or rather, choosing it. Consciously. Ze sez everybody's obsessed with guessing what people really are, behind their screen names. Ze sez ze's found, without exception, that once people's covers are blown they can't seem to keep going, as people. It helps when ze sends me examples. Here's one Winc sent. Ze was being a tough grrl. Ze calls this "a perfectly good conversation ruined by gender."

>>12:33:11 a.m. Chat Log

Private Message to Winc

Daisy: Hello.
Winc: Hello yourself, whassup?
Daisy: Just looking to get off*, you could say. I'm slowly hiking my skirt.
 [*That was my first hint, Toobe]
Winc: ::slowly lifting aviators off my eyes to see you better::
Daisy: ::slowly rubbing my clit::
Winc: ::twirling the stem of my sunglasses on my tongue::

41

Daisy: ::panties at my ankles:: ::wishing u were under my desk::*
[*that was my second one, hon.]
Winc: ::chuckling:: If anyone is gonna be under anything, darlin',
it's you. Keep talkin'.

System will go offline in 30 minutes for maintenance.

Private Message to Daisy

Winc: hmmmm . . . we have thirty minutes. Want to go to a private
room?
Daisy: ::rubbing my hard nipples:: Yes. Which one?
Winc: ::slow smile:: What place would be the most embarrassing for
you to have sex in?<<

I thought that was a way good question, it embarrassed me just to read it.

Private Message to Winc

>>**Daisy**: My grandparents' room . . .
Winc: ::nodding approvingly:: Good girl. I'll be in private room
called Grandparents Rm.
Daisy: ::getting wet::
Winc: Tell me . . . what kind of sex or position would be most embar-
rassing for you?
Daisy: I like it all, baby . . .
Winc: That's not what I asked.
Daisy: My ass.
Winc: What about your ass?
Daisy: I like only certain things there.
Winc: What *wouldn't* you like?
Daisy: Thick dicks.*
[*Needless to say, that was my next clue, dear.]
Winc: ::laughing softly:: I think you're a guy. It doesn't really mat-
ter, OK? But I appreciate a good acting job, and there are some flaws
in yours, that's all.

**Online Host: ***You have just changed to room
"Grandparents Rm."***
System going down in 20 minutes.**

Daisy has entered the room.

Winc: ::tapping my foot:: You kept me waiting. ::walking
over to you slowly::
Daisy: :shrugging:: Sorry.
Winc: ::purring:: Don't move . . . wanna look at you.
Lift your skirt for me.
Daisy: ::wanting to touch you::
Winc: ::smiling, sensing your needs::
Daisy: Here you go baby slowly.
Winc: ::taking your chin in my hand:: ::shaking my head::
Winc: No . . . I'll tell *you* where we're going,
right?
Daisy: Don't have a skirt, I like it nasty.
["She" forgot she had a skirt on . . .]<<

Winc just asterisked the next clues, which I'm glad for, cuz I was beginning to get it.

>>**Winc**: ::laughing:: Describe this room for me.
Daisy: Which one?
Winc: Your grandparents' room.
Daisy: Lots of old dressers, six-shooters*, a trunk,
family portraits staring at u.
Winc: mmmmmm . . . nice. ::taking you in my arms::
::leaning you back, kissing you hard on the mouth::
Daisy: ::slowly using one finger right now:: What are you
wearing?*
Winc: ::suddenly letting you go, walking to the other
side of the room:: ::lighting a cigarette, staring at
you:: So, who are you? Describe yourself to me. ::inhal-
ing slowly . . . eyes never leaving you::
Daisy: 5'8, 34-24-34, aerobics instructor, firm ass,
great tits and love to play.*
[::laughing:: that whole sentence is a clue!]
Winc: ::blinking:: I see. ::blowing smoke rings:: And . . .
a guy?
It's OK with me if you are . . . I'm just curious.
Daisy: Nope I'm legit. Are you?
Winc: ::chuckling:: Like I said, it's OK if you're a gal
or a guy . . . cybersex is cool, but you come across as
a guy. Am I what?
Daisy: A guy.
Winc: ::laughing:: nope . . . not this lifetime.
Daisy: lol.
Winc: Where are you on your cycle?
Daisy: Nope. Are you?*

That was this person's undoing . . .

Winc: ::chuckling:: Reread my question. It wasn't a yes
or no.
Daisy: No.
Winc: ::softly:: no . . . what? What do you think I'm
asking?
Daisy: YOU ASKING IF IT'S MY TIME OF THE MONTH RIGHT.
If not I'm lost.
Winc: ::shaking my head:: Nope.

System going down in 10 minutes.

Winc: I asked *where* on your cycle you are, not if
you're bleeding.
 ::glancing down:: I'm bleeding now, though. Just curious where on your cycle you are.<<

I thought that was pretty bold ...

>>**Daisy**: 2nd week.
Winc: ::blinking:: You're a guy. ::running a finger up
inside me, then licking my blood off my finger::
Daisy: OK, how figure?
Winc: ::smiling:: First off, no woman I know knows her
measurements.
Or if they do, they don't give them out.
Daisy: Got it flaunt it baby.
Winc: ::shaking my head:: nope . . . men do that. ::lean-
ing back, watching you::
Daisy: Us Californians are like that . . .
Winc: Do you like being a woman online?
Daisy: We think we have it all.
Winc: ::shaking my head:: you forget, I'm from
California too.
Daisy: I know. Read your profile.
Winc: Women *know* they don't have it all, darlin'.
Daisy: This one does.
Winc: ::mild applause::
Daisy: How's that finger?
Winc: ::sniffing:: Nice.

System going down in 5 minutes.

Daisy: You think you know it all, hon.
Winc: ::laughing:: I know I don't!

44

Winc: System's gonna go down any minute. Sigh. Wish you'd open up a bit.

Daisy: OK, OK, I'm a guy, happy?

Winc: ::nodding:: Yep. ::softly:: Thank you so much. Really. ::leaning forward, kissing you gently::

Daisy: You're god. Whoops, I mean good.

Winc: ::laughing:: nice slip there, mister. ::wrapping my arms around your neck:: you make a pretty girl.

Daisy: Guess my age.

Winc: You really want me to?

Daisy: Yeah.

Winc: 14.

Daisy: No.

Winc: ::laughing:: then ya got me!

Daisy: 17. Close.

System will go down in 2 minutes.

Winc: ::smiling:: you're very sweet. . . . Thank you for being honest with me.

Daisy: You're good, what can I say?

Winc: ::smiling:: I've just run into so many guys being girls, it gets easy . . .

Daisy: I'm really known as "dabug" onscreen.

Winc: In the future, don't put all the emphasis on sex, rather, get to know people. That's what girlz do . . . ::grin:: *then* we have hot sex! ::laughing::

Daisy: Steven Langley from Madison November 27th.

Winc: Pleased to meet you, Steven. My name is in fact ::grin:: Winc.

System closing, all contact terminated.<<

Poor guy just wanted to get off.

Here's an excerpt from a Gay Pride meeting sent to me by—oh, I shouldn't say that, confidentiality and all. It's a transcript, so there's a Private Message scene embedded in it, too.

>>Minutes: The Coalition
Meeting: Registration
Attendees: Approximately 100

Participants principally concerned with Registration. Majority in agreement that the Reg process serves to divide us. Many are refusing to fill out the sex pref. box, are confused as to whether to list spouse for Significant Other, etc. Excerpts as follows:

Digqueer: Cooperation = Death!

Tom: That's Silence, you turkey! This is just about whether to list our partners in the spouse box!

Sharina: Look, the point is, do we make our stand by refusing to fill out the form? Or do we infiltrate by Registering along with everyone else?

David: Good point. If we Register now we'll be showing them we're just like everyone else.

Sharina: I'm sorry, but I, for one, am not! I am so sick of that phrase being used by queers. What an insult.

David: I'm not either, but for the purposes of Registration we can be.

Private Message from Digqueer to Luvboyz:

Digqueer: *No*body's like anyone else. They act like they're on the outside looking in.

Luvboyz: ::sadly:: True. What made you PM me?

Digqueer: Your name. At least you seem to be out of the closet.

Luvboyz: ::laughing:: Oh, that I am.

Vina: OK, OK, let's think about it for awhile. Meanwhile, if anyone wants to go ahead and Register, do so, and let us know at the next meeting.

Private Message from Digqueer to Luvboyz :

Digqueer: Here we go again.

Luvboyz: Yup.

Digqueer: ::laughing:: splittin' hairs.

Luvboyz: Yeah. Maybe it's just a phase?

Digqueer: ::smile:: Let's hope so.

Luvboyz: Maybe this is the only way we grow?

Digqueer: I'd rather see something else grow.

Luvboyz: ::blushing::

Digqueer: Oh how sweet!

Luvboyz: Not as sweet as you think. Wanna go private?

Digqueer: Sure. I have the feeling you're not big and hard and hairy, and right now that sounds really good.

Luvboyz: You mean that's your usual M.O.?

Digqueer: Yeah, gets boring sometimes.

Vina: We must resist the attempts of government to legislate our lives.

Tom: They're not fucking trying to legislate, they're trying to organize! If we cooperate, we'll be represented!

Private Message from Luvboyz to Digqueer:

Luvboyz: So you do this a lot?

Digqueer: When I can't sleep, when I can't get off. I can say I'll try something new, but certain things are just tried and true.

Luvboyz: Yep. Right now just "hard" sounds good.

Digqueer: Hard, urgent, maybe a little sweaty.

Luvboyz: I wanna stand up with you, cup our cocks together in our hands.

Digqueer: Yeahhhhh. It's warm, arms wrapped around each other's waists.

Brknstock: You guys and your foul mouths. Goddess!

Tom: ::rolling my eyes::

Private Message from Luvboyz to Digqueer:

Luvboyz: My hair is long, I rub it all over your back.

Digqueer: Mmmmm. I bend over to feel you against me.

Luvboyz: I turn you around. Kiss you hard, feel your beard against mine.

<<

Toobe Entry con't

That's all for now. I found a memo from the cops! Actually it's the cop division of the Bureau of Census and Stats, called Internet Intelligence. Scratch sez that's an oxymoron.

>>To: All Staff, FBC&S
From: U'Sec L
Subj: Registration Evaders

The Registration period will be over one week from today. All those not Registered must be warranted and contacted no longer than ONE DAY after this date. This will send a message that the department is organized and efficient, and that Registration is mandatory.

—Margaret Labouchere
Undersec'y, FBC&S<<

End Toobe Entry

Narrative Entry, Jabbathehut

Budge brings his seat back down hard, feet flying off the desk. What the hell are they thinking up there? Have they forgotten the Reg is supposed to be optional? We can't even track down parking violators, how the fuck do they think we're gonna track computer users?

Source: persLOG/budge/harddrive

End Jabba Entry

Toobe Entry

Ohfuckohfuck. The memo's really cool but I think I blew it. I mean, I scan police messages, just like an audio scanner, only it's the online one from the Central electronic bulletin board. It's never really deep content, cuz they would have it protected, but with Jabba's toyz I can get a little further in. She gave me extra codes, not stuff she gives to other people. I think she likes me even though she calls me names in Yiddish. Could she be Jewish? Concentrate, Toober, concentrate.

Anyway. I was so excited, I mean, here's this memo about the Reg, and I knew they were being real anal about catching people who didn't comply, so I downloaded it, but I was too long in that area and I think my screen name was spotted! If they wanted to play back activity in that area some time, my stupid name would be right there! Okay, maybe they won't play it back. Why should they play back a day's worth of cybermessages? They won't play it back. So who do I call? JJJJJJa-a-a-aba . . .

>>To: Jabbathehut
From: Toobe
Subj: Trouble

Answer me something please? If I was reading messages on a police bulletin board and I was live, and I downloaded something, could they trace me?

—T.

To: Toobe
From: Jabbathehut
Subj: In River City

Absolutely. However, chances are they won't because they have no reason to go over logs every day. As far as they know it's a Bulletin Board Service for gendarmes only. (You do know "BBS" is the abbreviation for such a service?) I'm certain I don't have to remind you, but you surprise me constantly, so I will: do NOT go live into their BBS. Download all

the messages or use one of my bypasses so it's not traced
back to your computer, but for geek's sake do not go live.
::muttering::
    Fighting God,
    —J.<<

Toobe Entry con't

Nope, didn't make me sleep easier. And I couldn't tell anybody, I didn't want to worry them.
Then this comes out today:

>>Registration Process Nearly Complete

by Thomas Fulton

All is well with the Registration process. Government spokespersons report that people are registering at the rate of 650 an hour, 24 hours a day. Officials of the Triumvirate Association of Businesses (TAB) are also confident that the Reg process will be completed soon. In addition, government sources are pleased with what looks to be an Instant Census, wherein all citizens of the United States are not only Registered, but their information is more current than any other form of Census that has been undertaken in the past.

In related news, the Coalition for Freedom of Expression indicated at a press conference today that the Reg process is "unconstitutional" and not representative of all citizens.

"Not everyone has a computer," said Vina Damon, spokesperson for the Coalition. "They say they'll give people free computers but they don't mention that you have to qualify to get one," Damon said. She then referred to "the disenfranchised and the homeless, who do not qualify for various reasons."

Damon also claims there are some citizens who actually own computers but refuse to Register. These are also "the disenfranchised," says Damon, but they are joined by a new group of "Vaders" who simply refuse to Register.

Damon would not go into detail about these so-called Vaders, but TAB officials have dismissed the claims as " . . . business-bashing and fear-mongering."

"The number of people choosing this route is negligible," continued a TAB spokesperson. "They would only be shooting themselves in the foot. At any rate, such people account for less than 1% of the population."

<<

Toobe Entry con't

Just got another letter from Winc. Ze digs deep into this stuff.

>>To: Toobe
From: Winc

Subj: Curiouser and Curiouser

Hey, my friend, here's an interesting log for your growing pile of trivia. I'm sending you excerpts because it was an hour's worth of chat, a lot of it goofy. They invited me to talk, Toobe! I picked the name "Gyrl" ::sighing:: it was either that or "Boyy." (::standing on top of the wall of Two Choices:: Hmmm, looks more interesting from up here!)

Have fun!

—W.

8:02:56 PM "ONSTAGE Transcript" is now open for recording. There are 17 people in the room.

Webster: Hey, gang, remember I invited someone this week? She's going to talk about her experience as a phone sex hostess.

Lisa321: No duh, Webster, why do you think the whole group showed up?!

Webster: Hah! Writers Anon. has never had such attendance.

Gyrl has entered the room.

Gyrl: ::rushing into room, out of breath:: Phew! Howdy!

Webster: Had a flat on that old info highway, love?

Lisa321: "Gyrl?" I thought Webster was kidding.

Gyrl: It's me name. ::glancing down:: And let's not talk about flat here, OK? ::rueful grin::

Webster: LOL

Webster: *Good* to see you Gyrl.

Gyrl: ::purring:: Good to see you too, hon.

Genuine1: Gee, Webster, just how *did* you meet this Gyrl?

Gyrl: Ah, so we discover the first pitfall of writing, class. ::glasses slipping down nose:: The stereotype! ::glancing over at Webster, giggling::

Webster: While I have no problem with the possibility of having met Gyrl for phone sex, the truth is we ran into each other as blood drinkers in a Sim room.

Lisa321: Simulation room?

Webster: Yep. OK, let's start!

Webster: Welcome to ONSTAGE. Our guest tonight is Gyrl. She'll be taking questions relating to sex and gender in fiction, on the phone, and in life . . .

[Toober, I'm gonna skip the standard stuff: this came later.]

Lisa321: If you're saying a man can be a female phone sex hostess, are you also saying a man can write a woman's character?

Gyrl: Well, I think that "Man" and "Woman" are only two of many possible genders . . .

Pico: Wow.

Gyrl: . . . and gender is simply another facet of identity, not unlike age, race, state of body, etc. So, of course a man can write a woman's character. If he does the work. ::bracing myself for onslaught::

Tale2Tell: Gyrl, I don't know if *you* are a man or a woman.

Gyrl: ::chuckling:: I like to keep it that way, too.

Mythter has entered the room.

Tale2Tell: ::laughing:: OK: Do you believe that gender in fiction is now passé?

Gyrl: I believe gender in the *world* is now passé. Fiction will follow or lead, whatever.

BillJo: Gender is passé? Does that mean gender was once a trend?

Gyrl: I think so, Bill. Gender may have been important back when we had to breed & only breed. There're more options now, maybe we don't need gender?

BillJo: You'd do away with biology?

Gyrl: We definitely need biology! But biology is not gender.

Mythter: Wait a minute. . . . Gyrl, are you a man or a woman?

IrishEyes: Good question!

BillJo: Right on, Mythter!

Webster: Can't dance your way out of *this* one, hon.

Gyrl: Well, the answer is . . . ::impish grin:: Both. Neither.

Tale2Tell: Coolness.

Private Message to Gyrl

Mythter: Do I know you?

Gyrl: ::eyes sparkling:: I dunno. I say that to lots of folks.

Mythter: I bet!

Gyrl: How many folks here have surfed in other genders?

Vick TF: ::raising hand::

Mythter: ::raising hand::

Private Message to Mythter

Gyrl: I figured you were a surfer.
Mythter: Sometimes.
Gyrl: Cool! ::batting eyelashes:: Wanna talk a bit after this chat?
Mythter: Maybe. As what?
Gyrl: Both! Neither! ::ducking::
Mythter: Ha!

IrishEyes: I try to keep gender out of the issue online unless it's forced.
Gyrl: Has anyone ever gotten caught? In another gender, that is? Caught by the person you were "fooling"?
Vick TF: Yep, I did. ::studying fingernails:: I think I played BigBob69 a bit too broadly.

Private Message to Gyrl

Mythter: ::leaning back against the wall, thumbs through my belt loops::
Gyrl: ::walking into the schoolyard:: Young man! Recess was over 20 minutes ago!
Mythter: ::looking up lazily:: Don't you recognize me?
Gyrl: ::going pale:: You! ::sputtering:: You were expelled two months ago!
Mythter: Hee hee. Hey, you're good.
Gyrl: Takes one to know one. ::wide grin::

Vick TF: Oh, I got caught because I was being obnoxiously bubba . . . ::scratching crotch::
Gyrl: ::cracking up::
IrishEyes: Actually, that seems to be the problem acting the other gender . . . over-broad play.
Gyrl: Definitely! Maybe that's the first step, going over-broad. Necessary perhaps. After a while, you learn to tone it down. The boys who work the phone line do!

Private Message to Vick TF

Gyrl: Hey, darlin' . . . who's this Mythter?
Vick TF: ::chuckling:: What do I look like . . . Cupid?
Gyrl: ::wheedling:: Pleeeeeeeeze?
Vick TF: Mythter is good people. In fact, Mythter just asked the same thing about you!

Gyrl: REALLY?

Vick TF: ::clearing throat:: Your audience awaits you, darlin'.

Gyrl: Eeep!

Genuine1: Are we operating under the belief that your personality has something to do with or derives wholly or in part from your gender? Or . . . are we operating under the belief that every human being is first a human being and second a male or female?

Gyrl: Oh, I think there's danger in thinking "we're all human." Or saying "we have no gender" (which I do think can be true). The danger is that we overlook all the very real violence done in the name of gender . . .

Genuine1: But . . .

Gyrl: . . . it's the danger of any humanist philosophy.

Genuine1: I don't believe that gender has any role in violence.

Mythter: Aw, come on!

Gyrl: ::turning slowly to Genuine1:: You're a guy, right?

Catch 22: Maybe the point is that gender just IS— biologically and culturally—but we don't have to be stuck with its nuances.

IrishEyes: I like that one, Catch.

Private Message to Gyrl

Mythter: You seem to have a lot of answers!

Gyrl: ::flustered:: Uh, no . . . not by a long shot! I chew on the questions. A lot. That's all.

Mythter: I like that in a gyrl/boy.

Gyrl: ::shy grin:: Thanks.

Webster: Gyrl, you have some questions waiting for you. You still there?

Gyrl: Ummmm, I'm lost. Sorry.

Private Message to Mythter

Gyrl: Bad bad bad bad bad! See what you made me do? ::laughing::

Mythter: ::chuckling::

Catch 22: I've begun to realize that I need a definition of "gender" from Gyrl.

Gyrl: ::laughing merrily:: Yes. How about: gender is a category. A classification. Nothing more.

Catch 22: Am I the only nut here who *likes* the distinctions of gender?

Gyrl: Oh, I like distinctions in gender, Catch. . . . I just think there's more than two to like, that's all.

Mythter: <---loves distinctions, just wish they were "cross" genderal, so we all could have more fun.

Private Message to Mythter

Gyrl: Cross genderal . . . way cool term!

Mythter: Something *I'm* chewing on.

Gyrl: So, you're a writer?

Mythter: ::ducking my head:: Nah, I just tell stories sometimes.

Gyrl: Tell me a story. Please.

Tale2Tell: We need more fuzzy thinkers!

Mythter: Yes, Tale2.

Private Message to Gyrl

Mythter: Once upon a time . . .

Gyrl: ::settling down at your knee, listening::

Mythter: . . . in a faraway land, there lived a very beautiful gyrl.

Gyrl: ::resting my head in your lap, listening::

Mythter: Only no one knew she was beautiful because she was invisible. They only knew her voice.

Genuine1: I believe that every human being is FAR too different . . . has met with FAR too unique circumstances . . . to be able to know the mind of any others.

Gyrl: Gotcha, Gen, and I think that by calling ourselves MEN or WOMEN, we deny ourselves the uniqueness you talk about.

Private Message to Mythter

Gyrl: ::softly:: So this gyrl, all she had was a voice?

Mythter: Uh huh. And they all loved her until . . .

Gyrl: Until?

Mythter: Until one day, a child asked, "Is that a boy or a girl?"

Gyrl: Oh geez.

Tale2Tell: Actually, I've always thought that the poles of gender were like chaotic attractors, anyway . . .

Gyrl: ::wincing:: I think we need to do away with the image of opposite poles when it comes to gender.
Tale2Tell: Chaotic attractors are different: You can orbit them, never touch, whenever or whatever. Binaries will always exist. Some people will always need labels. The rest of us just won't care.
Gyrl: Whoa! Cool concept, Tale2. Thanks!

Private Message to Mythter

Gyrl: And no one could see her.
Mythter: Right.
Gyrl: And she liked it that way.
Mythter: Right.
Gyrl: But everyone in the town *wanted* to see her.
Mythter: Hey, who's telling this story?
Gyrl: ::clamping hands over my mouth::
Mythter: They wanted to know if she was a boy or a girl.

BillJo: So, Gyrl, why do you suppose gender is such a big deal, nowadays?
Gyrl: Because maybe it's time to question, and it's gonna get worse before better.
Webster: Worse?
Gyrl: When folks in power find out that those of us who have no gender are talking . . . there's gonna be a mighty big backlash . . . and it's not gonna be pretty.
Genuine1: {{{{{Gyrl}}}}}
Webster: I fear you're right. Backlash enough already.

Private Message to Mythter

Gyrl: Sorry, I had to jump in there big time. You were saying . . .
Mythter: You're really good, carrying on with me and with them.
Gyrl: Both are fascinating. Go on . . . please.

Gyrl: ::gently:: Genuine1 . . . do you have a gender?

Private Message to Gyrl

Mythter: The mayor and the town council convened to do something about it. They brought her to trial on charges of sedition.
Gyrl: Eeeep!
Mythter: "You are disturbing the natural order," they said to her. "You must tell us if you are a boy or a girl!"

Mythter: On the day of the trial, a fool happened to walk into town.

Gyrl: ::softly:: And this fool stood up to speak?

Mythter: ::nodding:: Uh huh. And the fool asked the townspeople what all the fuss was. And the townspeople said "This gyrl is an abomination."

Gyrl: ::wincing::

Mythter: "This gyrl is disturbing the natural order," they said.

Mythter: "How?" asked the fool. "She will not tell us if she is truly a girl," cried the townspeople.

Gyrl: ::curling up closer to you, listening::

Mythter: "We cannot see her!" cried the townspeople.

Mythter: And the fool said, "What's a girl?"

> **BeenThere**: I have a comment, um, kind of long, do you mind?
> **Gyrl**: Go for it!
> **BeenThere**: I think binary thinking is a tool to control folks by limiting their choices to only two. If I do that, I control what you choose. I may even create a dilemma in which you feel you have no choice.
> **Tale2Tell**: Amen, BeenThere!

Private Message to Gyrl

Mythter: "A girl is obedient to boys," proclaimed the Bishop.

"A girl bears children" said the Doctor, quite sure of himself.

"A girl is not a boy!" proclaimed the Lawyer.

"A girl does the housework," cried the Merchant.

"Well," said the fool . . .

> **Gyrl**: Gen: what box do you fill in on govt forms?
> **Genuine1**: I fill in the ones that have the little "m" next to them, OK?
> **Mythter**: Gee, what a surprise.
> **Gyrl**: Right, Gen . . . so you have a gender.
> **Genuine1**: I have a physical gender--not a mental gender.
> **Gyrl**: ::raising an eyebrow:: As you say, Gen.
> **Genuine1**: :)

Private Message to Gyrl

Mythter: "It seems to me," said the fool, "That if you cannot agree on something as simple as what exactly a girl *is*, . . . then how can you agree to charge or sentence this person?"

Gyrl: And the mayor, who was quite wise after all, agreed, and everyone lived happily ever after?
Mythter: ::softly:: In the story, yeah, they all live happily ever after.
Gyrl: And in real life?
Mythter: ::shrugging:: In real life they listen to the herd's loudest voice, lynch the gyrl *and* the fool.

IrishEyes: All gender tells me for sure is how I'm gonna have sex with them if the spark catches. ::smile::
Mythter: Right *on*, Irish!
BillJo: Imagine if there were only one, rigidly defined "Blue" in the world.
Gyrl: ::listening intently to Bill::
BillJo: We don't want to wipe away "Blue," we want to go further in describing the shades, right?
Mythter: Yes!

Private Message to Gyrl

Tale2Tell: Ummm . . . do you want to go private after this?
Gyrl: ::purring:: Thanks, darlin', but ::glancing over at Mythter:: I think I've got other plans.
Tale2Tell: ::chuckling:: Ah, yes. Scratch is a dear.
Gyrl: HUH? SCRATCH?
Tale2Tell: Whoops. I thought everyone here knew Mythter was another of Scratch's screen names.
Gyrl: Ah.

Webster: We're outta time! Damn! I think we're gonna have to ask Gyrl back! A round of applause!

[Toobe, there were sound effects! Real clapping in my computer speakers!]

Private Message to Gyrl

Mythter: Hello? OK, so my ending was a little cynical. Sorry. Is that why you didn't answer?
Gyrl: Um, no, hon . . . I . . . oh shoot.
Mythter: ::grinning:: What?
Gyrl: It's me, Scratch. I'm Winc.
Mythter: WHAT??

Private Message to Mythter

Gyrl: Scratch? You OK?

Mythter: This is too weird.

Gyrl: ::softly:: Way good story. Really, way.

Mythter: Winc/Gyrl, whoever, I'm outta here, again, OK? Our encounters seem to leave me looking for the exit signs.

Gyrl: Sorry!

Mythter: No! I mean, I've been thinking about . . . look, I'll see you again, OK? Just need some . . . ::no words::

Mythter has left the room.

Private Message to Mythter

Gyrl: SCRATCH! WAIT!

Mythter: ::muttering:: space. That's the word, space . . .

Gyrl: What's the *matter*? This is *lovely*!

AutoHost: "Mythter" is no longer online and did not receive your last message.

> **Genuine1**: I'd like to know how the topic strayed from phone sex to the role of gender in fiction to gender, period.
>
> **BillJo**: Inevitable, Gen.
>
> **Genuine1**: Yeah, probably was.

Private Message to Gyrl

Vick TF: Hey, what happened to Mythter? You two have a fight?

Gyrl: ::wailing:: I don't *know*! I thought it was all going so *well*!

Vick TF: ::wry grin:: Hey, don't take it personally. You probably got way close, right?

Gyrl: ::sniff:: Uh huh.

Vick TF: Don't worry. Mythter takes off fast. A trademark.

Gyrl: Oh, goody.

Vick TF: But comes back. Really. Just has to think. Hang in there.

Gyrl: ::squaring my shoulders:: I *intend* to!

Vick TF: ::chuckling:: You go, Gyrl.

> **Gyrl**: ::getting to my feet, shakily:: Gotta go.
>
> **Vick TF**: Gyrl, you were brilliant.
>
> **Gyrl**: Awwwww, Vick . . . you just see yourself in me.
>
> **BillJo**: Mind-boggling, Gyrl. Still don't know if you're a man or a woman.

Tale2Tell: Um . . . Mythter's not online. Do I stand a chance?

Gyrl: ::softly:: You're real sweet, hon, I'm just not there right now.

Tale2Tell: ::kissing Gyrl's cheek:: Goodnight, then.

Gyrl: G'nite.

9:07:47 PM Closing transcript file.

[Awww, Toobe . . . where did I screw up?]<<

Can you believe it? Ze does this amazing interview with people asking questions I never in a million years would think to ask, then beats hirself up for Scratch leaving.

Scratch just does that. I'm glad Winc sends me stuff, but I gotta say I don't get what the heck that room was talking about.

I don't know if you can tell, it's obvious to me, but those two were Scratch and Winc. When Scratch emailed it to me, I could tell right away.

Still worried about that memo I snarfed from the law. Jabba sez since I save everything I could have a hefty file to blackmail people with. She's bizarre that way. I wouldn't even know how to set it up. But maybe I should go back *in* to the police bulletin board and get some dirt! Ugh . . . my stomach just answered that one. No way.

End Toobe Entry

Narrative Entry, Jabbathehut

Out of habit, Wally Budge of the Federal Bureau of Census and Statistics, does his hourly, albeit usually fruitless, scan to find any newly-created alternate screen-names for Scratch and Winc.

Search Results

- 0 hits on search criteria "Winc"
- 2 hits on "Scratch"/ = Mythter, O'Bere

A smile spreads across the craggy face of the cyber-gumshoe, as he happily adds the names "Mythter" and "O'Bere" to his database. So, he thinks to himself, Scratch is the careless one.

Source: persLOG/budge/harddrive

End Jabba Entry

59

‹HAPTER THREE

Toobe Entry

E-Pitti oP the Day

Isn't This a Rerun? The cable television company that serves
Columbia. S.C., aimed a camera fulltime at an aquarium to
occupy a vacant channel while awaiting the start-up of the
Science-Fiction Channel. When the Science-Fiction Channel
replaced the "fish channel," complaints were so numerous that
the cable company was forced to find another channel for the
aquarium, which it ran 24 hours a day.

(That one came from *Offbeat News Stories of 1993, The World Almanac and Book of Facts
1994,* but someone posted it today online.)

End Toobe Entry

Narrative Entry, Jabbathehut

Shaking his head in disbelief, Wally Budge reads the article one more time.

> **WASHINGTON**—Sources inside the Federal
> Bureau of Census and Statistics today con-
> firmed reports that "a number of warrants"
> have been issued for the arrest of Registration
> Evaders. "The only people who aren't register-
> ing are people who have something to hide,"
> said Undersecretary LaBouchere, "and we have
> the full cooperation of the FBI and local law
> enforcement agencies to find these people and
> bring them to justice."
>
> All that extra muscle may not be neces-
> sary—the FBCS has been slowly building up
> its own enforcement arm over the past few
> years in preparation for yesterday's
> Registration deadline. Bureau officials have
> declined to disclose details, but officials agree
> "arrests are imminent."
>
> **See Registration Benefits, p. 3**

Budge puts down his paper noisily. He drums his fingers on the table, blinks once, and a smile breaks across his face. Set a thief, catch a thief. Maybe it's time to get a little help from somebody who knows the cyberstreets better than I know New York City. A hacker. Nicotine-stained fingers tap happily at the keyboard as Budge hums "London Bridge Is Falling Down." Good for Budge. Trouble for Scratch and Winc.

Source: persLOG/budge/harddrive

End Jabba Entry

Toobe Entry

Some of the "rooms" online are structured. They're like a play, with stage directions and everything. A host tells you what to do and what the scene is and all that.

>>***Online Host: You have entered the public room "A.R." ***

Private Message to Toobe

A.R. Host: Welcome to the Anne Rice room. You see an assortment of mostly grey people seated at tables. They are dressed in clothing that situates them in feudal Eastern Europe. Some are peasants, some nobility. Some are involved in lively discussions, others sit quietly and mutter to themselves. Have fun, member Toobe.

<<

Remember there's no censoring, no PG-17 rating or anything. You're responsible for your own gag reflex. In this room, there's a woman carving on her own arm with a *knife*. She's posting about her bones and muscles and stuff, out there for everyone to see. I asked her publicly why she was doing that. (I didn't want to get into Private Messages with her.)

>>**Leilia**: ::snarling:: I'm conducting an experiment, impudent one.
Toobe: Uh, OK. Just checking.<<

After that I shut up for the most part.

>>Karn has entered the room.

Karn: ::a tall youth enters the room tentatively, dressed like a stable boy. His flesh is not grey, but rather tanned and healthy::
::squaring his shoulders, brushing the straw from his jerkin, he makes his way across the room to the bar where the mistress of the establishment is preparing drinks::<<

Part of the "rules" in game rooms like this is that even though your name shows up for everyone to see, you're not supposed to *know* the name of the character talking to you unless they tell you during the dialogue. And you're supposed to be one of the characters, too.

>>**Orlio**: ::seated alone at my table, staring unblinking at the young stranger::
Karn: ::transfixed by the nobleman's stare::
Orlio: ::pleased with the effect of my mere glance, rising to my feet::
Karn: ::a chill runs up my spine . . . thinking to myself where on earth am I?::
Orlio: ::softly, with a well-bred accent:: Boy, you seem out of your element.
Karn: ::stammering:: I . . . I . . . I've traveled far, Sire.
Barnabus: ::laughing:: He has manners, Orlio . . . good breeding belies his rough clothing.
Orlio: ::turning a withering glance at Barnabus:: I'm well aware of our young stranger's contradictions, fool.
Karn: ::coughing to cover my embarrassment::
Barnabus: Oh, ho! The lad is pleasing to your eye then, eh m'lord?
Orlio: ::with a low growl:: Perhaps he is, Barnabus.
Leilia: ::popping small wedges of my flesh into my mouth, chewing thoughtfully as I watch the conversation::

<<

I tried not to read too much of what Leilia was posting. But Orlio's a friend of mine from the teen room.

>>Private Message to Karn

Orlio: hello? M/F?
Karn: ::grinning:: Oh come on, you can do better than that!
Orlio: I just want to know if you're male or female.
Karn: ::shaking my head sadly:: And I just want a better opening line!
Orlio: Then I'll try again.
Karn: ::smiling, waiting patiently::
Orlio: Hello Karn, how are you on this fine night?
Karn: ::blinking:: Just lovely, Orlio, thanks for asking. And you? Are you enjoying a cyberstroll?

Orlio: Oh fine. What's a cyberstroll?
Karn: ::laughing merrily:: It's what we're doing!
Orlio: Oh. Then yes, I am.

Orlio: ::raising the back of my gloved hand to touch the boy's cheek::
Karn: ::shivering, pulling back slightly::
Leilia: ::muttering to myself:: The old fool's gone on young blood. Pah!

Private Message to Toobe

Orlio: Hey Toobe, my main man!
Toobe: Hey yerself . . . who's the kid?
Orlio: Karn? Not a clue. Cute, though!
Toobe: I thought you weren't "out" online.
Orlio: ::shrug:: It's a game. Who cares?

Orlio: ::gently stroking the lad's neck and shoulders::
Leilia: ::cackling::
Karn: ::clearing my throat:: Sire, a question, please?
Orlio: ::turning slowly to the madwoman:: Leilia, you know mine ears can hear a dove's tailfeather brush the earth . . . have you something you wish to tell me?
Leilia: ::cold fire in my eyes, I slowly shake my head:: Not for the moment, Sire.
Orlio: ::satisfied, turning back to face the boy:: A question?

Private Message to Karn

Orlio: Hey, I must say you are the nicest person I've talked to all night.
Karn: ::wide grin:: The same back at you, Orlio. Really . . . a lot of folks just want to do the nasty from the word go. Eeeeeep!
Orlio: Well, I'm not like that (I hope).
Karn: ::slow smile:: You're a perfect gentleperson.

Karn: ::nodding:: A question, please. Know you the merchant, Darius?
Orlio: ::smiling, revealing long canines:: Darius? Perhaps.
Karn: ::eyes go wide at the sight of long, sharp teeth . . . stammers, but proceeds gamely:: It is he whom I seek.

Orlio: ::crooking my finger under Karn's chin, lifting his face to mine:: And if I *did* know this Darius? Then what?

Karn: ::gasping at Orlio's touch:: I . . . then . . . I . . . would you tell me how to find him? My father has instructed me to . . . ::knees going week at Orlio's insistent stroking::

Barnabus: ::arching an eyebrow:: I didn't know you craved boyflesh, Orlio.

Orlio: ::to Karn:: I might find him for you, lad . . . for a price.
::turning:: Barnabus, it is not that he is a boy . . . it is his youth.

Private Message to Karn

Orlio: How about *that*?
Karn: ::laughing:: Way cool!

Leilia: ::murmuring softly:: Youngflesh . . . my blade *wails* for youngboyflesh.

Karn: ::innocently:: A price, Sire? What might that be?

Barnabus: ::snickers in his knickers::

Leilia: ::crooning to my maimed and bleeding arm:: Youngflesh, youngblood, that's what this dam needs.

Private Message to Orlio

Karn: Pull off my hat.
Orlio: OK, you got it!

Orlio: My price, m'lad, is *this* ::reaching forward suddenly, pulling off the stableboy's slouch hat::

Karn: ::crying out . . . long chestnut hair falls to my shoulders::

Leilia: ::looking up, interest rising::

Barnabus: Oh, HO!

Orlio: ::smiling appreciatively, reaching out to undo the "lad's" vest and shirt::

Leilia: Young *girl*flesh!

Karn: ::clasping my arms over my chest, protectively::

Orlio: ::chuckling::

Toobe: Is that you, Winc?
Karn: Maybe it is, maybe it isn't.
Toobe: Sorry, I—
Karn: ::laughing softly:: Yeah, it's me. What're you doing here?
Toobe: You told me to check out the Vampire room, I'm here.

Leilia: I want you. Will you be taken?
Karn: ::startled:: Excuse me?
Leilia: ::impatiently:: It was a simple question. What's your answer?
Karn: ::slowly:: Yes, ma'am.
Leilia: ::smiling, revealing fine sharp teeth:: I like that. Back to the main screen with you, little one.

Orlio: Would you stop talking to me if I told you I'm using my dad's computer and I'm only 14? I am 6'2, though!
Karn: ::smiling happily:: Wouldn't stop at all.
Orlio: Thank you. How old are you?
Karn: Ahhhhhh . . . two things I don't talk about . . . age and gender . . . more fun that way.
Orlio: That'll work, I can see why it would be more fun.
Karn: ::nodding:: We can be anything this way, non?
Orlio: Yeah!

```
Leilia: I've never cut living flesh before. If she wants
to meet this lord badly enough, let her pay for him
with her flesh.
Orlio: Not so fast, woman. I've not decided what to do
with her myself.
Leilia: ::slowly, menacingly:: Some decisions are not
yours to make . . . my lord.
Orlio: ::glaring at Leilia, taking the young girl in my
arms::
Karn: ::melting into his embrace . . . confused::
```

Orlio: I've never seen this Leilia before. You OK with her?
Karn: ::smiling:: Yeah, thanks. It could be interesting

Orlio: OK, just checking. I gotta go. Take care of yourself!

Karn: ::chuckling:: I always manage to do *that*. Stay in touch, OK?

Orlio: Really?

Karn: Yes, really, way. ::warm smile::

Orlio: Great! Then I know what you really are!

Karn: Which is? ::grin::

Orlio: *You* are my ladybuddy!

Karn: ::smiling softly:: As you wish.

Private Message to Karn

Leilia: I don't have all night.

Karn: Then come and get me.

Orlio has left the room.<<

So *then* Leilia starts gazing at Karn/Winc's arm. And she looks *hungry*. Really glad my pal Orlio got out of there. ::retching noise:: Leilia pulls Karn/Winc down into a chair next to her. Winc loved it!

>>Private Message to Toobe

Karn: I think I'm about to be taken, big time.

Toobe: You slut. Enjoy!

> **Leilia:** What a bold girl. I do not repulse you?
>
> **Karn:** ::hesitantly:: No . . . no, not really.

Private Message to Karn

Leilia: Why did you arrive in this room as a boy?

Karn: ::shrugging:: I like plot twists.

Leilia: That's noncommittal. Did you read my profile?

Karn: Nope. I like what you're doin' though!

<<

So I had to pull up Leilia's profile. Big help.

>>

Member Profile: Leilia
Member Name: Leilia
Occupation: Blood-drinker
Quote: Doppelgängers know how to find one another.

Leilia: That's funny. Most people run screaming from the room when they see me cutting myself. They don't mind suffering contusions themselves, but when you hack your *own* body . . . ::shaking head:: Watch this.

<<

I'm gonna spare you. Let's just say they got into it. Leilia starts slicing into Karn's arm. Karn's loving it. . . . One of these days I'll ask Winc about it but right now I don't want to know. It grossed everyone out, they all left except me, Karn, and Leilia. I think they forgot I was there. Happens a lot to me.

>>**Leilia**: ::chuckling:: See what I mean? They scurry like rats.

Karn: I like it!

Leilia: I'm still curious . . . why bother arriving as a boy, then change to girl? Did you tell Orlio to do that, or did he just know?

Karn: I told Orlio to take off my hat. I had no idea what would happen next. ::smiling:: I . . . I like to play back and forth across the line.

Leilia: Ever get any weird reactions? I've found some can't accept me as a *female* predator.

Karn: Ummmmm, so, are you a woman?

Leilia: ::laughing:: Not so fast, young'un. Who cares, anyway?

Karn: ::squirming:: I hate that I even asked! I just got curious. ::laughing:: OK, be a mystery!

Leilia: Do you realize that I don't take either of the genders you presented for granted?

Karn: ::slowly:: Now, that is a breath of fresh air. Been wondering lately. People try to guess the "real" person behind the persona, but it *doesn't* matter.

Leilia: That's all very well, but one builds barriers to keep people away. To stave off . . . ::throwing the back of my hand to my forehead:: the pain of it all.

Karn: ::shyly:: Are you really a blood drinker?

Leilia: Heehee. I neither cut nor drink unless I can feel it . . . deep within myself, and in the other person too. Sometimes I feel it deeper as a "woman," sometimes as a "man."

Karn: ::slowly:: Did you feel it deep in you . . . with me?

Leilia: Indeed, I did. Rather surprising; so fast. But I can tell one thing about you:
Karn: Oh?
Leilia: You're young, aren't you?
Karn: ::smiling:: Right now I am.
Leilia: Ah, good point. And what do you think *I* really am?

Orlio has entered the room.

Karn: ::turning, noticing the nobleman in the room::

Private Message to Orlio

Karn: Hey, darlin'. Back for some fun?
Orlio: Not *this* kind of "fun!" You OK? Just wanted to check.
Karn: You're *very* sweet. Yep, having a good time.
Orlio: ::sigh:: OK, I'll be off.

Leilia: ::to the panting and ragged girl seated across from me:: Have the courage to look at me while I draw your blood. It runs as red as I had imagined.
Karn: ::gasping:: It sings to you, ma'am.
Leilia: ::gentle smile to Karn:: We are bonded now. Do you know the significance of *that*? ::turning in triumph to Orlio::

Orlio has left the room.

Karn: Wow. I think you're good at what you do, I'm tempted to say you're a woman. But there's something else there I can't put a finger on.
Leilia: So to speak.
Karn: ::squirming happily::
Leilia: Something is familiar. ::thinking:: One meets so many people online. It would kind of ruin it if someone knew, for instance, that I was a 6-foot guy with pimples and bad breath and straggly hair, so myopic that he tends to stare at people, eh?
Karn: ::taking that in:: Yeah, maybe I'm 5'2" . . . wide . . . sitting here cuz there's nothing else in my life to do. On the other hand . . .
Leilia: ::sly grin:: yes?
Karn: I may be at my computer with a group of friends. Maybe they're looking over my shoulder, egging me on. One never knows. ::grin::
Leilia: Yes. Agreed.
<<

Then I get this message from Orlio, who's way over in another part of the Net.

>>Private Message to Toobe

Orlio: Hey, you find anything out about Karn?

Toobe: Karn is not your type, man.

Orlio: Sigh. Wanna join me in the Teen Room?

Toobe: What's the topic tonite?

Orlio: Online friendships.

Toobe: Nah. I'm being a fly on the wall here. {{{{Orlio, my friend}}}}

Orlio: {{{{Toobe}}}}

Leilia: What's the strangest/best encounter you've had online?

Karn: ::shyly:: Apart from this one . . . with you?

Leilia: Oh, yes, flatter me, do. Perhaps your life will be spared at the end of this scene. Yes, apart from this.

Karn: Once I was with someone . . . it was sex. I could feel it. Every bit of it. We went way beyond the "opening my legs" or "take my firehose, baby" stuff.

Leilia: Ha! You do the online sex thing, then, do you?

Karn: Of course I do. This time, though, I felt connected. This person used text the same way I do, during cybersex. Never ran into that before.

Leilia: Rare.

Karn: Ummmmm, do I know you?

Leilia: I don't think so. Why?

Karn: ::shyly:: You *are* good, at lots of things.

Barnabus has entered the room.

Barnabus: I just want to say you two are *really* fucked up.

Karn: ::rising slowly, turning to Barnabus, raising my arms, torn and bleeding, muscles hanging loosely off my bones::

Barnabus: SERIOUSLY FUCKED UP!

Karn: ::blowing a kiss to Barnabus, blood spraying across the floor::

Barnabus has left the room.

Leilia: ::laughing:: You're pretty good yourself.

Karn: ::tossing hair out of my eyes, smiling:: Back to sex. Please?

Leilia: I had sex online once. It was weird.

Karn: Do tell!

Leilia: Oh now . . .

Karn : <--- wants to know every lurid detail! ::grin::

Leilia: ::snort:: Let's just say I wasn't being myself, but it was hot, and that confused me.

Karn: Good point. Online, what exactly is your
ʷᴛ·±>®©ÿ…"v₤» ÷úÎ"?®õ"9˜d−_; |qᴦôzç\Oɣ

Leilia: What the hell is that?

Karn: ::warily:: an insecure line, I call it. I mean, the line's not secure. Sorry about that . . . I thought my bypass was foolproof. Guess not. ::growling::

Leilia: You're on a bypass? Where do you get such a thing? The garble was probably from my end.

Karn: You're not on a bypass? Whoa! Live dangerously, don't you?

Leilia: Well, what's the alternative?

Karn: Geez, um, I don't think I can say. Sorry. You understand?

Leilia: Sort of. I haven't Registered yet, but I've got to one of these days. I'm on the old system. It's weird, I can't go into places I used to. So why would *you* need a bypass if you can go anywhere after Registration?

Karn: Tell you what. Registration isn't all it's cracked up to be. Once you sign up, places get blocked off , but bypasses get you around that . . .

///Are we all doing OK in here?///

Leilia: Fine, Eye.

Toobe has left the room.

Karn: Way fine, Eye.

Private Message to Toobe

Karn: Why you outta here?

Toobe: Long story. Nervous around Eyes just now.

Karn: Who isn't. OK, check you later.

<<

But Winc/Karn sent me the rest of it, bless hir little furry heart:

>>Private Message to Leilia

Karn: What did you mean, you were playing dumb?

Leilia: ::shrugging:: I can see what's happening is what I mean. Sometimes I'll talk in a private room with someone about computers, the next day I'll get computer advertisements. And they're *not* from the person I was talking to.

Karn: Wow.

Leilia: I wonder if actual Private Messages are monitored. Why wouldn't they be? I figured the govt wouldn't bother, but they're getting pretty nosy lately.

Karn: Yeah, but there's so much babble going on, so much "M or F?" or "How old are you?" or "what are you wearing?" I figure anything we say will be lost in the shuffle.

Leilia: Good point.

Leilia: Let's go to a private room named Vamp. That way we have a better chance at being unmonitored, y'know?

Karn: Cool!

Leilia has left the room.
Karn has left the room.<<

So, off they went. Winc wouldn't give me the password into their private room, but sent me a full text of it later (just like I knew ze would).

I should tell you, I actually got to talk with an Eye once. I asked if they could go into private rooms, uninvited. The creep wouldn't answer me.

>>***Online Host: You are in private room "Vamp."***

Leilia: Truth is, Karn, I didn't want to keep cutting you onscreen. It makes the desire rush up in my throat . . . brings more frustration than pleasure.

Karn: Ah, and I was so enjoying your knife.

Leilia: You have quite the ability to "morph," don't you?

Karn: ::blushing:: I do.

Leilia: I like that, I was going to say more . . .

Karn: ::grinning:: And *I* was gonna say more along the same lines . . . 'bout this sex thing you did with someone, you said you weren't being "yourself" . . .

Leilia: Yeah.

Karn: Question: . . . ::drumroll:: Online, what *is* your "self"?

Leilia: Oh, christ, there's the question of a lifetime.
Karn: Uh huh. Why so for you?
Leilia: I really become that person online. That's the scary thing. I really believe my fiction. Used to feel bad about it, but obviously there's truth in those fictions.
Karn: ::murmuring:: Know what you mean.
Leilia: I went online that sex time as somebody I *used* to be. Someone I thought I hated in myself. But I got very turned on, I fucked somebody I thought I'd never fuck again. Does that make any sense?
Karn: Umm. OK, here's something: Do we really compartmentalize who we are from all the "who"s we've ever been? It's easy to do that online. But what about life?
Leilia: Depends where I am. (1) I've learned to kinda avoid big, dumb guys. (2) I have a problem with authority, so I avoid cops. I have reasons for compartmentalizing, in other words. I make snap decisions based on what somebody looks like. I hate that, but sometimes you gotta . . .

Private Message to Toobe:

Karn: Leilia's a woman!
Toobe: Why you say?
Karn: She's going on about being intimidated by big goons.
Toobe: I'm not exactly safe around 'em either. Tend to give them a wide berth.
Karn: Oh, right. True.

Leilia: I know what you're thinking, too! Have you ever seen a small guy in a sports bar? It's not a pretty sight. Women think they have a premium on feeling threatened in the street.
Karn: Good point. But . . . do you think we can compartmentalize gender?
Leilia: ::thinking:: I've never had a discussion like this. Oh, it's hard to talk about without a context, I mean, of who I am, and my experiences. Do you know what I mean about hating a part of who you used to be?
Karn: ::slowly:: Yes I do.
Leilia: Hmm, sounds like a story there. Let's put it this way: sometimes I think who I've become was like a sex change. I mean, that big a shift. Like I'm a completely different sex than how I grew up. And I still

don't identify as one or the other very much, until
somebody *else* nails me.<<

There was a pause at Winc's end right after that.

>>**Leilia**: Are you OK?
Karn: Yeah. PM storm . . . sorry . . . hang on.
Leilia: PM storm?
Karn: <--- flooded with tons of Private Messages.
Leilia: Hate that.
Karn: Don't get what you mean, sorry. You hate . . . ?
Leilia: I hate waiting through someone else's PM
storms. Makes me want to flounce around like a drag
queen and walk out.<<

That sent Winc into another pause.

>>**Leilia**: Hello?
Karn: I have to ask you . . . You have a problem with
drag queens?
Leilia: NO! Whatever made you think that?
Karn: ::shrugging:: Sorry, sorry, it's hard sometimes to
read tone of voice.
Leilia: The drag queen remark?
Karn: Yeah, I guess.
Leilia: <--- loves drag queens. Think they're very
brave boys. Wish I had that persona at my fingertips.
Karn: It's easy! ::handing you a feather boa and purple
eyeshadow::
Leilia: ::snorting:: It's a *lot* more than that. Wait,
another dangling thought, let me scroll up to see what
I wrote earlier.
Karn: Oh, good, I have to pee anyway.<<

Meanwhile, I'm still online and Orlio catches me:

>>Private Message to Toobe
Orlio: Gotta go. My dad's home and needs the computer.
Toobe: See ya around!
Orlio: ::smooch:: Bye!
Toobe: ::laughing:: Cut that out!
   <<

He's such a good boy. Said all his good-byes:

> **>>Private Message to Karn**
>
> **Orlio**: Bye, Ladybuddy. I gotta sign off. Will I see you again?
> **Karn**: ::softly:: Anytime you need a Jadybuddy, I'm here.
> **Orlio**: I *like* you! Bye!
> **Karn**: I like you too, darlin'.
> **AutoHost**: Orlio is no longer online and did not receive your last message.

Leilia: Gender change thing: I don't like the way men and women are supposed to be. I would just remake myself into another gender 5-6 times a day, if I could.
Karn: Remake yourself?
Leilia: Well, I'd never want to go as far as surgery. Just getting a tattoo was agonizing. I couldn't stand the thought of an "always" on my body.
Karn: ::nodding:: I agree with changing personas. It's what I do online all the time, but don't you think that some folks need to be one thing or the other, in real life?
Leilia: Yes, their whole identity is wrapped up in it. That's the island on which they have to stand, in order to function.
Karn: If we can change, the way we do online, over and over, *can* we do that in--what can I call it--"the real world"?
Leilia: ::sadly:: I don't think so. The only feeling I can come close to is when a context is real clear. Here's an example:
There's this civil rights march in my neighborhood once a year. All of us, black and white, march in it. Suddenly people smile at me who won't give me the time of day otherwise. The colors of our skin don't matter then, because it's *that* day, that march.
Karn: ::rocked:: Side note: I hadn't even considered your race. Ouch.
Leilia: Exactly. You probably assumed I'm white, right?
Karn: ::wearily:: Yeah, sorry.
Leilia: ::also wearily:: It's OK, happens all the time. One of the cool things for black folks online is they are assumed to be white, too. Not that they want to be white, but they're assumed to be "in the club," without having to prove credentials at the door.

Karn: ::slowly:: What do you think *I* am?

Leilia: Don't know. Was focused on gender thing earlier, but I don't care now. It's great! It's that moment
I wait for online, where I no longer care, where (I
believe, anyway) I'm truly relating to the inner, formless being of someone. ::doing Snoopy's happy dance::

Karn: ::laughing delightedly:: Right! That's where I got
to when I did this sex thing I was telling you about.
::muttering to self:: How did I know exactly what you
meant by Snoopy's dance?

Leilia: ::smiling:: Hmmm, I just realized something. My
body, my real one, mind you, in the sex scene *I* had,
got into it right away. But my head didn't. It snagged
on what that would *make* me. My whole sexuality would
have changed in the real world, but my body didn't give
a damn.

Karn: ::excited:: Right. Now take the principle of what
you're saying, and apply it to the real world. What
would we have?

Leilia: Pansexuality?

Karn: And more! What we do online is an extension of what
we *could* be doing in the real world. All this change,
freedom, including sex, including, maybe, gender.

Leilia: Hah, you just nailed yourself in an age group,
and so will I by saying this. Curious?

Karn: ::squirming happily:: Nailed myself, you say? I
love/*hate* to get caught. Pray tell.

Leilia: Hippie!

Karn: <--- *adores* hippies!

Leilia: ::snort:: They have their good traits. And *you*
did a good job of ducking out of owning up to what
you are.

Karn: ::smiling::

Leilia: Maybe being online is like being drunk at a
party, getting to do whatever you want, then not being
responsible the next day.

Karn: Good point, but why wait to be drunk? Why only
do it online? ::wistfully:: Why not do that in the
real world?

Leilia: I think I have this deep fear that one day I'll
be boffing my bigoted-ass neighbor, that's why. I just
couldn't live with myself. (If I boffed him, we'd have
something to talk about . . . Yeccccchhhh . . .)
Karn: ::laughing:: I like the way you grab things and
shake them. Ideas I mean.<<

That made "Leilia" get silent.

>>**Karn**: Hello?
Leilia: ::quietly:: I think I just figured out who
you are.
Karn: Yeah?
Leilia: Gonna chew on it awhile.
Karn: ::sassy smile:: Is that like chewing flesh?
Leilia: ::surge of eros:: oh, you, girl-guy-fool-child.
Karn: ::blinking, surging, too::
Leilia: Exactly. Time to exit now. You're getting in
way too deep.
In me.
Karn: ::softly:: It's good to see you again.
Leilia: You fuckhead! Majorly vulnerable now. Outta
here.
Karn: WAIT!
Leilia: Yeah, what.
Karn: I didn't know it was you . . . really . . . I
mean not until just a second ago. I'm sorry if I
stepped over some line. But I didn't know.
Leilia: What you hear is the sound of crashing walls.
Winc, you permeate me. I've been thinking of you. I got
to go. I . . . ::frantically scrolling up:: There's a
reason for my identity shifts, you know, and now I feel
like Superman naked in the phone booth.
Karn: ::gently:: Ain't watchin' you in the phone booth,
hon. No kryptonite here. A bit stunned myself.

Leilia has left the room.

Private Message to Leilia

Karn: Scratch . . . ?
Leilia: Bye. Who the fuck *are* you?
Karn: ::softly:: like you said, question of the year.
AutoHost: Leilia is no longer online and did not receive
your last message.

<<

Toobe Entry, cont'd

Poor Scratch. Says ze has a very tenuous hold to the ground, but I don't believe it. Pretty darned grounded, but I do think ze sees too much. Has hir eyes wide open like that scene in *Clockwork Orange* where the guy couldn't close them if he tried. Feels guilty a lot, but not like Catholic guilt or Jewish guilt. More like a person who knows too much.

I was trying to remember how I met Scratch. It was online, I don't know hir in real life like I do Winc. You make so many "friends" online, mostly by writing letters, or seeing something cool they said. I think that may be how we initially met. But I told hir to fuck off after a few letters cuz ze wouldn't tell me how old ze was, or what sex. I didn't know that was kind of a point of honor with hir, but I had my own reasons for being cryptic. Then ze ran into me in a teen chat room and figured it out. "I'm no predator after your ass, Toobe," ze wrote. "I'm sorry I was so insensitive." I liked that about Scratch. Ze apologized right away and didn't try to explain it like most people do. Ze also added that ze was in the teen chat room by mistake. I believe hir. You wouldn't believe how dumb Scratch is about getting around online.

Ze said that within 10 minutes of being in that room ze saw all of us get harassed by older men. Scratch, being Scratch, did a little investigating. Checked out all their profiles one by one, sought them out every time ze got online, and cross-referenced them with other rooms. About a third of them hung out in the Christian room, all of them were married men, and a whole bunch also hung out in rooms where there were women. Rooms like "Married but Restless" and "Horny in Omaha." I told Scratch not to jump to conclusions about all that cross-referencing. They were probably making up the Christian part.

But of course Scratch forwarded some of these conversations to the powers that be, and got a couple of them bounced off the service. Hard to do on a private service where they're more interested in your money than civil rights. Ze didn't tell me any of this, I heard it thoo da gravevine. Jabba had heard it too, so I know it traveled far and wide.

Scratch gets pissed easily. Righteous anger is hir best suit.

I just emailed Scratch asking where we met online, and ze couldn't remember either. "Left-handed Lithuanians for John Lennon, probably," ze wrote back. Thanks, Scratch. That helps.

So here's a classic Scratch list:

>>To: **Toobe**
From: **Scratch**
Subj: **Gender roles**

    Tripped out by my online adventure last night. Ran into that Winc character again. You say you know this person? Any insights into why I want to head screaming for the hills every time I run into hir? In a good way, though. I get all calm with hir one minute, hysterical a minute later. Gets me thinking, and you know how much I need to do more of ˣthatˣ.

I should really keep a journal, but I just write you! Hah! I got another letter to the editor published, too; I can't remember which one. One day when I'm famous they will turn them all over to the press, and I will be tragically ruined, or the toast of the talk show circuit. Worse, I'll be ignored.

A list has been plaguing me lately, a little startling.

Songs My Parents Taught Me

Each of mine, like all parents, hoped for a better likeness of hirself reflected back in their child. I don't suppose it occurred to either of them that they could have tried to stretch the borders for themselves, rather than stretch the child. Still, I'm grateful, I know how to do most everything.

Things my father taught me	Things my mother taught me
How to paint a picture.	How to paint a house.
Wipe down the whole kitchen (including the stove!) after doing the dishes, otherwise it doesn't count.	Take the part you need with you to the hardware store, so the new part fits exactly.
Buy Brand X, and look at the ingredients.	Buy two of something if they're cheap.
Smile.	Grin.
Watch people; they're entertaining.	Watch women.
Cry; it purges the soul.	Never cry, you'll look like a wimp.
Never mix dark loads with white ones.	Hold the hammer at the very end of the shaft, not up by the head, like a girl.
Read great literature.	Read about people who made something of themselves.

Be nice to people.	You can't trust people.
Let women vent.	Let women vent.

My father made our lunches, my mother drove us to the bus stop. I would watch his fingers float over the bread, the mayonnaise, the bologna. Delicate, handsome fingers, floating in the air like a storyteller. A few times a guest grown-up would remark on the novelty of a father who fixed lunch for his kids. They never saw my mother's sandwiches (Daddy's sick! Daddy's been kicked out!), which always consisted of hunks of cheese and bread, no sandwich, and no napkin. "Eat like a peasant," she would say. "It's good for your character."<<

Toobe Entry con't

The simultaneity of their writings was a little spooky. I'm certain this one was written right after that online encounter with Scratch. I don't even think Winc meant me to have it. Ouch.

>>Winc Diary

Rode my bike past a group of old men today. Smiled and waved to them, long legs pedaling. They loved it, I could see it in their faces how much they loved my smile, my long legs, they smiled and waved back. Maybe right now they're thinking about me, maybe they're lying in bed next to their wives and they're thinking about my smile floating past them, a butterfly they'll never catch. Some of them saw the young boy of their dreams. Some of them saw a girl.

They never see me when I sign off and sit here naked with a cockroach floating in my teacup. And I wonder. How do some people just get off their bikes and laugh with a stranger who seems nice? How do they move their heads just so? How do they know when to smile? Is there some secret code I've never been taught? Is it in the genes? What's wrong with my genes, then? How do they drink their tea?

Me? I'm a flash of long legs, pedaling. A lipstick trace on a teacup.

Scratch: what if I'm not the right one on the bike this time? What if you need the long-haired Winc with the

79

urgent cock, and you're that nasty riotgrrl. What if you need that boy because you're a sweet young boy too, what if I could be your strong woman, the one who would love you for your strong woman self?

End Winc Diary<<

Toobe Entry con't

Here's something from Jabba:

>>**To**: Toobe
From: **Jabbathehut**
Subj: **Files**

Your propensity for saving is going to get you in the end, my friend. But thanks for the reading. Are there really people who spend their time in a fictional vampire room? Boggles the mind.

Fighting God,

—J.

To: **Jabbathehut**
From: **Toobe**
Subj: **Vampire room**

Well, fuck me, you weren't supposed to get that vampire file. I knew you'd make fun of it. Guess I'm a little nervous lately. But I haven't had any fallout yet from that police snooping incident. Yes, it's fun to play with other people, and not have to chat about the weather or their dog.

To: Toobe
From: **Jabbathehut**
Subj: **Re**: **Doggy vampires**

Yes, I can see your point. Interesting that you would "accidentally" send that file, when the Registration snake wends its insidious way through our circuits. Don't delude yourself, I can get any file I want to access.

To: **Jabbathehut**
From: **Toobe**
Subj: **Re**: **Any?**

What do you mean, I don't get the connection.

To: Toobe
From: Jabbathehut
Subj: Connection

Stretch your 10-second brain, my little cybergnat. This Registration process is sucking the life out of otherwise imaginative people. Perhaps not so imaginative as I would wish, but they have potential. Interesting that you would find yourself in an online metaphor, if you will, for bloodsucking. The Registration process is taking everyone's time.

I noted your report as to the reluctance of people to receive the bypass codes. The fear of missing out is predominant, it guides some people's every action. Ironic, because as they are struggling so hard to fill out the blanks, they are indeed missing the far reaches of their own adventures, if they only had the courage.

Pardon my philosophical bent, perhaps you bring it out in me.

To: Jabbathehut
From: Toobe
Subj: Philosophy

I think it's cool! Never knew you gave these rooms two seconds of your time!

To: Toobe
From: Jabbathehut
Subj: Vague warning

I dare not even ask. When you filled out your Reg card did you put in your real age? You will be snagged so fast your ears will freeze-dry. Note this, from one of my clients:

>>Forward msg. from XXXXXXX

Dear Jabba:

Thank you so much for helping me "lock" my computer. You have no idea the numbers of children using their parents' accounts. My eleven-year-old had been approached by several older men within the first few weeks of our using this service. I've had to keep her completely away from the thing, but of course, this wasn't satisfactory to me. Thank goodness for the Registration process, you can state your preferences immediately. But the system withholds many rooms from her that her mother and I have no problem with her using. It's either all or nothing, I've discovered with the Reg restrictions. But your lockout code lets my daughter use *my* account, and now she doesn't have to bother with being assigned one of her own by the government.<<

Tell me, dear Toobechild, that you are still among us as an adult.

To: Jabbathehut
From: Toobe
Subj: Not that dumb
    I yam. But I gotta tell ya, I'm thinking about holding one of those endless workshops for my li'l peers on how to avoid the perverts. You can't have a teen room without all of them flocking.

To: Toobe
From: Jabbathehut
Subj: Know you're not

And what would your advice be?

To: Jabbathehut
From: Toobe
Subj: Uh uh
    I can't even tell you, Jabba. With my luck (lately) the message will get intercepted and all your stupid clients will find out.

To: Toobe
From: Jabbathehut
Subj: Clients
    I believe I resent that remark, but do as you wish.<<

Damn, I'm sitting here reading this way later. When I see that exchange now I wanna cry. I was so stupid! If only I'd found a way to erase myself right then. I would have saved everybody a lot of trouble, and then Winc wouldn't have gotten—whoops, all in good time, I guess.

End Toobe Entry

CHAPTER FOUR

Narrative Entry, Jabbathehut

The roach slowly makes its way across Wally Budge's desktop, looking for all the world like a miniaturized Jules Verne battle contraption intent on some unknown task. Budge shakes his head in disgust, causing the roach to stop its forward motion and neatly blend in with the coffee stain on which it hovers.

"If I ignore it, it'll go away," he thinks to himself, returning to his latest memo.

> **To: Investigations**
> **From: Undersec'y L.**
> **Subj: Cough Up**
> Wally,
>
> I think you'll agree I've given you more than enough time to test out your theories about Reg vaders. Well, where are they? Do you have any leads? I have the Secretary himself breathing down my neck on this one. I need some names. Give me what you've got, and I'll keep the dogs away from your door.
> —L.

Raising his hand slowly, Budge makes to swat the invader from his domain, but with that inexplicable foresense they seem to possess as a species, the roach dashes for cover down the back of his desk.

Rich, dark phrases of disgust escapes Budge's lips as he stabs three digits into his desk phone.

"Yeah?" comes the smoky, familiar voice into his ear.

"Shelly, I got me an infestation up here."

"You talkin' about your office or your brain, Wally?"

"Har-de-har, Shel. I got me some roaches."

"Yeah, well everyone's got roaches, Walls. They'll die."

"Huh?"

"They'll die. My guys put out a poison last week, great stuff. Roaches eat it, carry the poison in their bellies back to their nest, then they die. Then the little cannibals eat the dead roach, and *they* die. So don't sweat it. If you saw one roach, you saw Typhoid Mary heading back to wipe out her nest."

"Typhoid Mary . . .

"She was the woman who——"

"Yeah, yeah. I know who she was. Shelly, you are an amazing woman, and if the girls and boys down in Programming can build it for me, I owe you a steak dinner."

"Build you what, Walls?"

But Budge just chuckles as he hangs up. Rapidly, he types:

To: **Development**
Via: **Records, Assets, Materiel**
From: **Investigations**
Subj: **Not So Common Cold**

   Booker: Remember you were explaining computer viruses to me the other day in the cafeteria? And you said those things can be built to search stuff out on the Net? Do me a favor: Put your head together with Shelly Dunlap, ask her to describe Typhoid Mary to you. Then see if you can come up with a little virus for yours truly?
—Budge

He presses SEND, and it's not five minutes later that he receives:

To: **Investigations**
From: **P_Booker**
cc: **S_Dunlap**
Subj: **Your wish . . . etc, etc . . .**

   Shel and I have been talking about this for weeks. I have a prototype you might find interesting, but you'll need some new hardware to accommodate it. Shel's arranging.

   By the way . . . you're still using your generic department account? Haven't you Registered yet? You'll need a private account in order to work this thing I'm sending you.
—Booker

Register, huh? They told him it would take about 35 minutes, but he'd never found the time. Add it to the list. Right after he answers her ladyship's memo. He types:

To: **Undersec'y Labouchere**
From: **Investigations**

84

Wally Budge is putting it all together. His favorite task. What had Shelly called him? A garbage hound? Yeah, and two of his wives had been slightly kinder with "pack rat." Wally Budge has his ways. Collect, think, catalog, muse, compare, review: information. He loses himself happily for the next few minutes or so. It's a shock when he hears a voice come from behind him, and the clock says it's five hours later.

"Lieutenant Wallace Budge?"

Budge's bloodshot eyes swivel themselves onto the workman standing in the doorway. "Yeah?"

"This stuff is for you, where do ya want it?" The workman wheels in a dolly loaded with sleek dove-grey boxes, a huge monitor, and a keyboard that would have sent Gene Roddenberry into fits of ecstasy.

Budge narrows his eyes. "Whassat?"

The workman shrugs, "New work station. Merry Christmas, I guess."

"Hold on, hold on, lemme check this out first."

The man by the dolly eyes Budge's archaic desktop computer. "Sure thing, Boss. You fond of antiques or somethin'?"

Ignoring him, Budge punches numbers into his phone.

"Yeah, Walls?"

"Shel! What's with the new computer?"

A husky laugh, then, "It's for Mary."

"Huh?"

"Typhoid Mary . . . hell of a sophisticated search engine for the Net."

"Huh?"

That chuckle. "Your virus, Wally. She's got a graphic interface, so she won't live in your old Unix box. She needs Windows at least, and a Mac at best. So I got ya a Mac. Merry ..."

"... Christmas, yeah yeah yeah. I *like* my old box, Shel!"

"Oh hush. This stuff is top of the line. Wait'll you see what you can do with it! Full color, video. Trust me, you'll thank me."

"I trust *you*, Shel. I've just never trusted a computer that smiles at me when it boots up."

"Get over it. Who knows, maybe you can download some dirty pictures and bring them over to my house some night, and we can check out the pixelation."

Budge flushes despite himself. "Awright, awright. And if whatsername ... Mary? ... does her job the way she's supposed to, dinner's on me."

A deep chuckle, then, "Enjoy, Wally."

Hanging up the phone, Wally looks up at the man still standing in the doorway. "Umm, I guess you can put it here, next to the old one."

The man snorts, "Not a chance. That box of junk is headed for the dump. How could you stand looking into that green screen all day, anyway?"

"I *like* green," sniffs Budge.

Source1: persLOG/budge/harddrive
Source2: bckupfiles@FBCS.gov
Source3: diary.sdunlap@FBCS.dov

Narrative Entry, Jabbathehut (con't):

It is appallingly easy to purloin files, and if I had the lack of character assigned to most code crackers, I would idly scan the world's computers. I must note that the term for such folks has been completely misnamed by what passes for media today, who inanely devised the word "hacker." This is so fitting, albeit insulting for the *cracker* craft.

While I do so enjoy playing Dashiell Hammett, it's time to turn my attention to other sources. The only behavior that astounds me any more about the human race is its continued gullibility. The following is a memo about to be sent out to the general public. I like to see these things before their official release date:

>>Dear Service Consumer:

Please note you are about to be given an extraordinary opportunity. The members of the Triumvirate Association of Businesses have generously donated their time and expertise to a new Registration bonus which would allow you complete access to any area of the computer online world you may desire. Simply Register as you normally would, but be sure to select the "Special Options" item provided. This will allow you access not usually afforded to Netusers, and will cost you nothing in additional fees.

[Add closing paragraph]

—T.A.B. etc.<<

This was sent to *all* computer users, no special demographic required. Attached for interoffice use only is the special options goodies, which, predictably, are the supreme privilege of being assaulted with a myriad of electronic mail order catalogs. This is the only advantage to the option. ::yawn:: Response to the offer? Hysterical, and 100% return.

Source I: TABfiles, interoffice memo, Confidential

Meanwhile, back in a certain green office:

Lt. Wally Budge is making his beefy paw guide a small plastic "mouse" which somehow attaches to the cursor on his computer screen. Now he's supposed to be able to navigate through a shifting sea of endlessly cute Macintosh icons. He clicks once, and on his screen appears:

> **You are now ready to open your online account.**
> **Please, enter your name in the highlighted spaces.**

Budge frowns, and maneuvers the mouse gently, he thinks. The result sends the arrow skittering to all corners of the computer monitor. The memo now repeating itself on his screen helps neither his mood nor his coordination.

> **You are now ready to open your online account.**
> **Please, enter your name in the highlighted spaces.**

"I heard ya the first four times," Budge mutters darkly. "Is *this* what people go through every day just to use their computers? No *wonder* they try to be someone else online."

> **You are now ready to open your online account.**
> **Please, enter your name in the highlighted spaces.**

With a self-satisfied snort, Budge manages to land his mouse in the little glowing box, where he enters his name.

> **Thank you, now enter your age.**

Grumbling, Budge enters 48.

> **What is your sex? (M) or (F)**

Budge laughs ruefully, trying to think back to the last time he got laid. He types "None," receiving a disapproving beep for his efforts.

> **Very funny. What is your sex?**

Budge laughs again, peers over his shoulder to make sure no one is looking, and types "Hopefully."

> **Very funny. What is your sex?**

"Screw this," he mutters under his breath, positioning his mouse to move on.

> **I'm sorry. Your signup sequence will fail to complete
> unless you completely fill out the form.**

"What the *hell* do you need to know all this for, anyway?" says Budge aloud as he tries to maneuver his mouse to get the cursor back into the SEX box. Just as he lands in place, though, a roach peeks its armored head over the edge of the sleek, new, dove-grey monitor. For a moment, neither officer nor insect moves a muscle. Then Budge begins to whistle "London Bridge Is Falling Down," in an effort to convince the roach its ugly carapace hasn't been spotted.

"I'm just doin' what I was doin'," says Budge aloud in a cheery voice. "I'm just signin' myself onto this online service, that's what I'm doin'." His left hand moves slowly toward the roach, while his right hand goes though the signup motions, filling in boxes indiscriminately. This continues for a full fifteen to twenty minutes: left hand closing in on the immobile roach; right hand filling in boxes, until the dialogue box opens on his screen...

> **You have completed the sign-up process.
> If you wish to use your new account right away,
> please click OK now.**

Budge's index finger clicks OK at the same time his left hand crashes down on top of his monitor, missing the roach by inches.

"Damn!"

> **Thank you, Ms. Budge, and welcome to your Online World.
> Would you like to look around a bit,
> or would you prefer to take the guided tour?**

"Huh?"

The message repeats itself.

"*Ms.* Budge?" Budge says aloud with a half-laugh. Sure enough, when he clicks his online profile box, FEMALE is entered firmly into the SEX box. "Damned roach," he mutters, and makes to change the designation.

"Huh?"

Source: persLOG/budge/harddrive

End Jabba Entry

Toobe Entry

I think Scratch is starting to relax a little. Keeps running into Winc, but maybe ze's getting used to it. At least, unlike real life, when ze gets freaked out, which is a pretty regular thing, ze can just jump offline, never to be heard from again (if ze doesn't want to be). Hir Spoiler persona's working pretty well for hir lately. Ze actually stayed 'til the end. They ran into each other in some Star Trek room. Winc plays in there all the time. Weird, though, Scratch never goes into those rooms:

>>**Spoiler**: Hey, whats a nonspacey like me gotta do to get a little attention around here?
Lt. T Yar: Oh, something like that'll do.
Spoiler: ::slow grin::
Lt. T Yar: Why "Spoiler"?
Spoiler: Oh, you'll find out.
Lt. T Yar: Will I, now?
Spoiler: Actually, main mission in life is getting you off . . . ::ducking::
Lt. T Yar: ::slow smile, folding my arms:: Is that right? And why would that be?
Spoiler: You space aliens are so repressed. Always shooting down ships when you'd be better off fucking . . .
Lt. T Yar: ::swinging, missing:: Who you callin' an alien? ::growling::
Spoiler: Don't want to get off?
Lt. T Yar: ::walking over to you, fairly ominously::
Spoiler: Hmmm, thought all you space things liked girls in every port. Oh, I guess that was before you became a nun, eh? ::dancing sideways, real fast::
Lt. T Yar: That did it! ::lunging at you, tackling you at the knees::
Spoiler: Eeeeeep!
Lt. T Yar: ::pulling you closer, the two of us on the ground::
Spoiler: ::Muffled:: My, what big muscles you have . . .
Lt. T Yar: ::grinning:: All the better to do what must be done, my darling!

Spoiler: Ooh, your scent, it's so seductive. Wish I could see you better. ::muffled:: But your sleeve's across my face, and ::grunt::

Lt. T Yar: ::straddling you, looking down into your eyes:: ::smiling::

Spoiler: Yes?

Lt. T Yar: ::leaning down, my face against your neck:: ::biting gently::

Spoiler: ::squirming:: Mmmmmmmmm

Lt. T Yar: ::sitting back up:: ::whispering:: Next time, it's for blood.

Spoiler: ::batting baby blues:: Did you say blood?! If you say that again I'm afraid you'll wake a sleeping beast.

Lt. T Yar: ::grin slowly spreading across my face:: Oh, I'm real scared. "Blood."

Spoiler: ::batting some more:: You wouldn't want to do that, would ya?

Lt. T Yar: ::holding your wrists out at your sides:: Do what, darlin'?

Spoiler: ::shoving leg over yours, flipping you over:: ::lower voice:: Bring out the bloodlust.

Lt. T Yar: ::yelping at sudden move::

Spoiler: ::jumping up, grabbing phaser::

Lt. T Yar: ::still holding on to your wrists, struggling::

Spoiler: :stopping dead still:: ::Looking down into your eyes::
Ah hah . . . ::struggling with inner demons:: Perhaps we are at an impasse.

Lt. T Yar: ::looking up at you:: No . . . no impasse ::struggling as well, then falling into your eyes::

Spoiler: ::watching pulsing in your throat::

Lt. T Yar: ::watching pulsing in your throat::

Spoiler: ::slow blink:: Would you like to get up?

Lt. T Yar: ::breathing hard:: I . . . I'm not sure.

Spoiler: You do look awfully nice there, lying on the ground with your hands on my wrists . . . ::soft chuckle::

Lt. T Yar: ::snarling, trying to flip you over::

Spoiler: heeheehee. You forget I have the phaser . . .

Lt. T Yar: ::falling back, panting:: You'd use that?

Spoiler: ::soft murmur:: Ah, no, let me just use my words then . . .

Lt. T Yar: Uh oh.

Spoiler: ::smiling:: If you provoke the blood lust in me, you will surrender, for your blood sings loud in my ears, and you need it to break free . . . for me . . . ::soft, soft, voice:: Don't you darlin'?

Lt. T Yar: ::mesmerized, slowly loosening my grip on your wrists::
Yes . . . yes . . .

Spoiler: ::low::: You are such a tempting morsel . . .

Lt. T Yar: ::lying back, arching my throat::

Spoiler: ::murmuring nothings, mesmerizing. chanting::

Lt. T Yar: ::whimpering:: please . . .

Spoiler: beat, beat, beat, beat, beat . . .

Lt. T Yar: ::softly:: Please.

Spoiler: Please, what?

Lt. T Yar: Please take my blood. Please open me. Please!

Spoiler: It's awfully late ::looking at cyberwatch:: Perhaps a little nibble . . .

Lt. T Yar: ::holding my breath::

Spoiler: ::snick:: A light nick on your upper shoulder, my head flashing beyond quickness to drink . . .

Lt. T Yar: ::crying out joyfully::

Spoiler: ::drinking the little trickle from your shoulder:: ::rocking back on my heels:: ::wiping my mouth::

Lt. T Yar: ::small happy noises::

Spoiler: ::Eyes glowing red, then green, then amber, then blue again::

Lt. T Yar: I . . . am . . . taken . . .

Spoiler: Yesssss.

Lt. T Yar: ::eyes flashing:: This time!

Spoiler: Of course this time. Next time, we start all over again. . . . And you didn't lose at all, you know.

Lt. T Yar: ::nodding, with sideways grin at you:: Oh yes, I know.

Spoiler: My intent was to drive you crazy . . .

Lt. T Yar: ::squirming:: How perfectly wonderful.

Spoiler: ::demurely:: Did it work?

Lt. T Yar: ::taking your chin in my hand, lifting your eyes to mine:: Yes . . . but only because I wish it . . . Spoiler.

Spoiler: ::flushing:: Whatever you say, dear.

Lt. T Yar: ::narrowing my eyes:: A gag would do you wonders.

Spoiler: If you wish it . . . but wouldn't you miss my tongue? ::stepping back ever so slowly:: And now I really must say goodnight.

Lt. T Yar: ::chuckling:: I can think of some very good
uses for your tongue . . . but none you'll discover
until you've been very very good.
Spoiler: ::never letting my eyes off of you:: Good
night, sweet Yar.
Lt. T Yar: Good night.<<

End Toobe Entry

Narrative Entry, Jabbathehut

She's dressed in a granny skirt and moves coquettishly across his screen. Budge slaps his hand over his eyes and groans, "If this damned computer gets any *cuter,* I'll feed it to the roaches." But gamely he types, "Who are you?"

The onscreen coquette turns, winks at Budge who, in turn, lights another cigarette despite the two already burning in his ashtray.

"Hi there, Missy, my name's Mary. What's *yours?*"

Budge rolls his eyes. He'd *have* to remember to get Shelly to change his sex. He groans inwardly at the conversation that would entail. "My name is Budge," he types, "and you're *Typhoid* Mary?"

The flirt curtsies prettily and nods her head.

"Okay, then, I've got a . . ."

Budge's screen suddenly flashes ominous dark violet. The sound of a preprogrammed gong sets him coughing. Onscreen appears:

To: FBCS Inspections
From: DevilsOwn
Subj: YOUR DISCARDED MEMO RE: REG. VADERS

So, you're the folks looking for prowlers on your weeny
BBS, huh? (That's Bulletin Board Service, newbie.) Thought
you might be interested to hear someone picked up a memo
you discarded. I'm enclosing the perp's tag (Screen name:
Toobe) in case you want to put some sort of tail on him.

This one's on the house. I work on retainer. Wanna talk?
—Devil

Toobe? Toobe? Where'd he heard that name before? He glances up to his wall charts tracing the movements of suspects Scratch and Winc. Swiveling his head back toward the screen, he types out a memo from his generic department account. Damned if he's going to write some hacker as a broad, he thinks.

```
To: DevilsOwn
From: FBCS Inspections
Subj: You're Hired
     Good work, mister. Consider yourself on retainer. Email
me specs on how to get $$$ to you. Don't need you at the
moment, but want to know you'll be there when I do.
—(And I may be a "newbie," but it's Lieutenant Budge to you)
```

Grinning, he lights a fourth cigarette. Sure enough, every other encounter between Scratch and Winc is marked by a meeting with the Toobe character. He tries not to get excited, but if this is a good day, he has them. Glancing back down to the screen he sees another memo flashing:

```
To: Inspections
From: Undersec'y Labouchere
Subj: NAMES!
Wally: Names. I need names. Or we're both out in the cold.
We won't let it out of the bag, I promise you.
—L.
```

Damn! Quickly he types:

```
To: Undersec'y Labouchere
From: Inspections
Subj: TOP SECRET
Ma'am: OK, as close as I can tell, "Scratch" and "Winc" (see
attached ident summaries) will be our first collars. They've
been everywhere, I mean everywhere, and neither of them
have Registered. Please keep this Eyes Only.
—W.

          ◎  click here to read attached file: S&Widsum.doc
```

Returning to his online screen he scans again the hacker's memo:

"...in case you want to put some sort of tail on him."

Yeah, he thinks to himself. Some sort of tail indeed. Off to one corner of his screen, the hippie chick in the granny dress waits, endlessly patient.

"Mary," he types, "I have someone I want you to meet."

Sweating profusely, Budge makes his way through the arcane series of icons on the screen, programming Typhoid Mary to search. Mission: to find the Toobe character, stick to him like glue, and regularly send information back to Budge. At last, a flashing red window appears on Budge's screen with the words: SEND? YES or NO. He chews his lip for a moment, then punches a series of familiar numbers into his phone. Before he can even say hello, she starts talking.

"What's up, Walls? More insects?"

"Shell, how'd you know it was me, I . . . No, don't tell me, I don't want to know."

Her throaty chuckle in the receiver almost wakes something inside him. But he presses on, explaining the steps he'd taken to program the computer virus, Typhoid Mary.

"So all I do now is hit "YES," and it goes and looks for this character? Is that right?"

"Nail on the head, hot stuff. And when it finds whoever it's looking for, it'll tag this person for you nice and pretty so they can't get away from you."

"Shel," he says beaming broadly, "you are a peach."

Putting down the phone, Budge turns back to the screen. He takes a deep breath, then his thick finger darts out and stabs at YES. The hippie chick icon on his screen turns to him, winks once, and practically dances off the screen.

"I'll be damned," he mutters.

To: Inspections
From: Sgt. Harrison, Bureau Demographics
Subj: Your Request re: "Scratch" and "Winc"

Lieutenant Budge: Enclosed please find our pattern profiles on the two . . . people you named. This is an odd collection of information. I must confess to a professional curiosity regarding your methodology. In short, where did you *find* these two? I would be most grateful for a speedy reply. People like this could make the lives of people like me quite miserable, thank you.

It is not all clear to me at this point, but there are *other identities* that go with the cross-factors you asked me to look up. In other words, usually with a request I come back with one name. But there are several names for each main identity, and each of those names has an identity as well. Add the following to your file, Lieutenant, and I think you may share my consternation:

SCRATCH: aka Luvboyz, MarthaW, Chicanita
WINC: aka Digqueers, Katchoo, Deth.

You may be interested to know these multiples is why I somewhat less than politely informed the powers that be that we cannot let people sign on as anything but their own names. You can imagine the possibilities. Not a pretty world, Lieutenant.

—Your Obedient etc. etc.

D.H.

    ◎ click here to read attached file: perpWinc.DOC
    ◎ click here to read attached file: perpScratch.DOC

Budge smiles around his cigarette, the smoke curling up into his well-watered eyes, and reads the attached profiles:

>>Citizen WINC

According to product interest area frequency, Citizen is a young senior white Native American female male earning between $6,000 and $500,000 annually. Objects of regular perusal include, but are not limited to, *Vogue Online* catalog, *True Romance, Scientific American, Mondo 2000, Urban Sportsman,* and *Girlfriends* magazines, and *National Enquirer Online*. Citizen also frequents multiple university libraries, searching for information in the field of Ethnomethodology, is a regular subscriber to several Vertigo comic book titles, and to a small press comic called *HotHead Paisan: Homicidal Lesbian Terrorist*. Pattern indicates Citizen is a heterosexual, homosexual, bisexual male ages 12 through 58 or heterosexual, homosexual, bisexual female ages 23 through 72.

Note: Account window shows activity in sectors clearly counter-Registrational. Name is Registered, but no feasible profile corresponds with the name. This indicates the user has some sort of bypass "worm technique" which inserts a name into the database without the required demographic information.<<

Budge takes a long satisfying suck at an old familiar missing tooth, and scribbles down the words "Ethnomethodology," and "HotHead Paisan."

"Damnedest thing I ever saw," he chuckles to himself.

Flipping to the next page, he reads:

>>Citizen SCRATCH

According to product interest area frequency, Citizen is a middle-aged senior female male African-American Caucasian of Irish descent, living on several welfare programs, alternately earning up to $75,000 annually. Objects of regular perusal include, but are not limited to, *Black America, Rolling Stone, Wired, Ms., On Our Backs, Off Our Backs, GQ, Interview* and *Mother Jones* magazines. Citizen also frequents multiple university libraries, searching for information in the fields of Psychology of Mind, Goddess Culture, and Weaponry, the latter with a focus on knives. Citizen regularly subscribes to both *Time* and the *New Yorker,* indicating the citizen is a heterosexual homosexual bisexual male ages 12 through 58 or heterosexual, homosexual, bisexual female ages 23 through 72.

Note: Account window shows activity in sectors clearly counter-Registrational. Name is Registered, but no information exists, indicating use of bypass "worm technique" which inserts a name into the database without the required demographic information.<<

Budge writes the words, "Goddess Culture," "Psychology of Mind," and "BLADES," the latter underlined several times.

"In all my years," he muses aloud, "I've never had to locate someone without at least knowing *something* about them. Like age, maybe? Maybe you could tell me what sex or color, hmm?" His laughter dissolves into a series of coughs.

Source1: persLOG/budge/harddrive
Source2: bckupfiles@FBCS.gov
Source3: TAB.confid/pers.com

End Jabba Entry

Toobe Entry

So then Scratch and Winc had their first cyberdate. I mean, they actually *planned* to run into each other. Scratch was in hir "Fuck your gender" profile and Winc was in hir ain't life grand mode, and they went on a little cybersurf. When they started they were really pissed off—the whole intent was to flame everyone who got in their way. Flame's a term for sounding off at somebody, which some people do a lot, just to be mean.

But they're total suckers for dialogue, and Mean just faded out as Lust (for words) rose. I followed them, logging the text in their wake like a little dinghy. As usual, the Private Messages were where everything happened, and they were kind enough to supply them to me later. Okay, I begged a little.

This gets a little dizzying, but the kick in cyberspace is everything happening at once. Someone could "pop in" to your screen at any moment. Feels like anyone can read what you're doing, when in fact, at least with the Private Messages, no one has a clue what you're up to, or who you're communicating with. Say you've got a "room" going, with various bits of dialogue by 20 people spider-legging down your screen. Every time you look up at the screen, someone has entered a comment, and bam, it's immediately followed by someone else, who's responding to something a couple of lines back. It gets hard to follow, if you're one of those everything-has-to-be-in-a-straight-line-one-after-the-other folks. Different parts of your brain fire.

More of those windows pop up over everything else! And of course you jump into a room in the middle of a conversation, so the whole effect is like some kind of tone poem. So I, Rap Master Toobe, "sampled" what they did that night. They started with the Christian Room (two rooms full on any given night).

>>**Online Host:** ××× **You are in "Christian Fellowship."** ×××

Scratch: This is my first time in this room. Can I ask a question?
Eccle: Go for it.
Ruth: Ask away, Scratch!
Scratch: I'm sure no one here is like this, but, what do you think of your fellow Christians who are so intolerant of others? Kind of bad PR, don't you think?
Luke: You're right Scratch.
Eccle: Don't have to answer to God for others . . . Just me.
Winc: ::muttering:: It wasn't God who asked for an answer, Eccle, it was Scratch.
Matthew: Scratch . . . its' just the way some peepl deal with there own lack of self esteme . . . attack others so you don't have to look at yourself.<<

[I didn't say they were especially articulate. In fact a stickler would go absolutely nuts in a chat room. Some people spend hours correcting other people's grammar and spelling. Then there are fights about *that*.]

>>**Scratch:** But they do so much damage. Maybe "real" Christians oughta try to help?
Ruth: Yes, it's bad to be intolerant. Have you heard "love the sinner, hate the sin?"

> **Eccle**: It is hard to help someone when they know every-
> thing, Winc.
> **Scratch**: Yes, Ruth. But I guess I think it's up to God
> to hate the sin, too. Who are we to judge?<<

That went on forever, with both of them trying valiantly for a little dialogue. But we all drowned in a sea of scripture.

Private Message to Toobe

Scratch: Whoa! What a trip. Let's go to a "queer" room or something! Anything!
Toobe: Gotcha.

Private Message to Scratch

Winc: You were good in there.
Scratch: ::heavy sigh:: Right. Thought we could talk. Out of 19, there was only one who was open. Feel like I need a shower.

<<

[So they changed rooms, but remember, they jump into the *middle* of a conversation.]

>>Online Host: ××× You are in "Gay and Lesbian Room." ×××

CJ: Age, sex check?
Sniffer: Escondido, CA.
Baubles: And you? Where were you born?

Private Message to Winc

Winc: Uh oh, Age/Sex check!
Scratch: Yeah, sameolshit.

> **Sniffer**: This is scary. So many people.
> **CJ**: Sniffer: What an unusual name.
> **Sniffer**: Gracias.
> **Scratch**: What are you scared of, Sniffer?
> **CJ**: Female, 25.
> **Sniffer**: Scratch and sniff!
> **Meds**: hi from boston; 26 m lifeguard/grad student look-
> ing for cyber-playmates.
> **Winc**: ::boppin' into the room, shakin' rain out of my
> hair:: Evenin', all!
> **Baubles**: Evening, Win. Raining where you are?

Winc: East Coast, Baubles. An' it's Winc. Not Win.
::grin::
Scratch: Hey gang, I just went into a Christian room.
Scary!
Born4luv: Why scary?
Scratch: Does anyone ever converse in here, or is it
all just cocktail chat, hmmm?
Born4luv: Scratch, go ahead. Ask us about quantum theory.
Sniffer: Quantum? A particulate matter, I think.
Scratch: Oh, hah. Just wondering if anyone had ever
tried to "dialogue" with our Christian friends.
Baubles: I've never tried. What did they say?
Scratch: They retreated into the Bible, and never
came out.
HardGuy: Hi all from the big Eazy.
Sniffer: Hey I've been to the Big Easy! Great town.
HardGuy: 'Specially around Mardi Gras!
Sniffer: To hell if we don't change our ways—isn't that
what they talk about?

Private Message to Winc

Scratch: I'm outta here. Disappointing.
Winc: Way. From mindless chatter to mindless chat.

Private Message to Scratch

Toobe: How bout the Women's Room?
Scratch: OK, why?
Toobe: Either it's full of boyz trying to be girls, or it's got real women
in it and the talk is good.
Scratch: We're there!

<<

But first we went to a private room for a minute.

>>Online Host: ***You are now in room "Morph."***

Toobe: Hey, what are we gonna be?
Scratch: Good question.
Winc: Do we have to be anything?
Toobe: No, I just figured you guys always want to be
something else.
Scratch: Well, do you go in there as a woman, Toobe?
Toobe: Maybe, sometimes. I dunno.

>Winc: ::eyes twinkling:: Perhaps that's too personal a
question, Scratch.
Scratch: Let's just try being a nothing, I mean no gender.
Winc: Right!
Toobe: What the heck is that?<<

But they had already left. So I just watched and keep my mouth shut. Nothing—what does that feel like?

There were endless screens about where people were from, what the weather was like there, and how old they were. We're talking $5 an hour and people are chatting as stupidly as they would in study hall, when the teacher's not looking. So I saved highlights.

>>Online Host: *** You are in "The Women's Room." ***

Private Message to Winc
Scratch: There's a guy named Holiday in here, I think he likes me!
Winc: Cool!

>Holiday: Hey let's talk about pussy, anyone game?
Debbie: Go away Holiday.

Private Message to Winc
Scratch: Duh, something tells me I was wrong about Holiday . . .
Winc: What are you *doing* to get all these PMs? <<

[People call the Eyes when they start getting unpleasantness from assholes, but it usually makes for the only good stuff all night.]

>>Scratch: Gee, Holiday, no men in here I thought.
Holiday: So what, vibrator-head, you need one!
Emily: Maybe we should call an Eye for Holiday.
Princess: Aww, just ignore him.
<<

Private Message to Winc
Scratch: Honey I'm in a PM storm.
Winc: What's happening?
Scratch: Dunno. I called Holiday a man, maybe?
Winc: LOL! Dastardly thing to do, m'dear.
Scratch: What is?
Winc: Calling a man a man when he's in the women's room, darling.

Private Message to Holiday
Scratch: Gosh, Holiday, you must be about 17.
Holiday: 17 or not, you donut bumper, you have to buy a plastic electrical device to get off.

100

[I don't believe Scratch followed up that conversation, but I was falling off my chair laughing.]

>>**Private Message to Winc**

Scratch: Holiday called me a donut bumper! What exactly is that on the anatomy?
Winc: ::Looking down:: no donuts here! ::smiling:: Nice pie, though.
Scratch: No, seriously, I--aw, forget it.
Winc: Mmph!

Holiday: Are you scared to talk about our sexuality?
Emily: What's the topic tonight?
MizMaid: Never mind. Holiday, are you provoking?
Winc: "Our" sexuality, Holiday?
Debbie: Well MizMaid, I think he's trying to.
Slim: Any bi women out there?
Emily: Any single mothers here?
Minn: Any bohemians here?
Emily: All of the above!
Princess: Anyone in love out there?
Emily: I'm in love with Glenda the Good Witch.
Princess: That's a start. Age, sex check?
Winc: Fine/yes.
Minn: I'm in love with the air witch.
Emily: I think I'm going to see if I can generate some conversation about pathological assholes. (That's not a commentary on anyone here . . .)
Holiday: hey i heard that too much cold air dries the pussy out. is that a common problem?
Princess: I bet Holiday is young. Least I hope so.
Emily: I'm looking for some practical advice on how not to put up with men just because I had a child by one.
Princess: Homicide?
Emily: I love that suggestion!
MizMaid: LOL, Princess.
Princess: I want my ex to have PMS. That way he would be an asshole only once a month.
Emily: Am I the only woman here who had a child with a pathological asshole?
Janis: Does everyone in here hate men?
Emily: I don't hate men.
Princess: Some are OK.

Private Message to Scratch

Winc: <--- having way cool PMs with MizMaid about lies and cyber-space.
Scratch: Just realized my name changes its meaning in different contexts. E.g., in this room I would be a yeast infection.
Winc: STOP THAT!!
:X

<<

[That's a gag symbol, as in Winc's laughing so hard ze has to cover hir mouth. And the arrow at the top of the box, points back to Winc's name if you follow it. Winc loves cute stuff like that.]

> **Minn**: To call an asshole an asshole does not = hate.
> **MizMaid**: Right, Princess.
> **Janis**: No one said they hated men. I just came in and every one is griping about them.
> **MizMaid**: Trash is trash, doesn't matter the gender.
> **Minn**: If you can't hate an asshole, then who can you hate!
> **Emily**: No, we're not griping about *men*, we're griping about assholes.

Private Message to Winc

Scratch: And in the gun room it would be . . .
Winc: Winc . . . chester?
Scratch: Uh huh.
Winc: ::Wince-ing::

Private Message to Scratch

Pubes: Touch me.
Scratch: Well that's a weird one, never heard that one before . . .
Pubes: I'm surprised. With a name like that?
Scratch: Like Pubes, or Scratch?

> **Scratch**: Question: how many here are PMing right now? Fess up!<<

Scratch and I pulled up Pubes's profile, just to see how "she" wants us to see "her."

```
┌─────────────────────────────────────┐
│        >>Profile of Pubes           │
├─────────────────────────────────────┤
│  Screen Name: Pubes                 │
│  Member Name: Rita Mae              │
│  Location: Madison, WI              │
│  Birthdate: 5-1-69                  │
│  Sex: Female                        │
│  Computers: 386                     │
│  Hobbies: rafting                   │
│  Occupation: flowers                │
│  Quote: Love the one you're with    │
└─────────────────────────────────────┘
```

MizMaid: Why do you ask how many are PMing, Scratch?
Scratch: Just curious, Maid.
Winc: ::liftin' head from PMs:: Howdy, Scratch!
Scratch: Well, hell-o there, Winc! OK, Winc fessed up, anyone else?

Private Message to Scratch

Winc ::laughing:: I think I'm having fun! MizMaid is busting gender-typing online. I like hir!
Scratch: Me too! Now ze's "challenging" me! Muhahaha.

MizMaid: Yes, Win is very busy, aren't we?
Winc: ::blushing:: You could say that, Maid, yes.
Scratch: Ah, brave Maid's confessed.
You call her Win? Hmm. I call her Winc.
MizMaid: Scratch, how do you know Win is a she?
Winc: ::grinning:: Maid, right!
Scratch: Well, Maid, she's fairly clever. That's one clue. And in this room that's what you get to be. A She for a day.
MizMaid: Non, mon cher, You get to be you.

Private Message to Winc

Scratch: I think your Maid's a guy, tho. Don't you?
Winc: Yup. I asked her about favorite books. She listed dead white boy authors all.
Scratch: All? Shew-w-w. She appears to be holding court right now. Bet s/he's over 50.

Winc: ::sadly:: I think so . . . how do they do that?

Scratch: "They?"

Winc: ::muttering:: men, grabbing center stage.

Scratch: I dunno, I thought it was pretty graceful.

Winc: Funny, I didn't think it was graceful. Ze prefaced going back on to the main screen with "Watch this," then took over.

Scratch: Huh. You are so hard on men sometimes. Do you realize when you're being a "straight girl" that you're not as hard on them? ::ducking::

Winc:: : eyes going wide::

Scratch: Uh huh.

Winc: That is weird. True. And weird.

Scratch: But you're neutral tonight, aren't you? Or at least a queer gal. Actually, what are you?

Winc: I have no idea, Ollie.

MizMaid: Win, read Scratch's profile, you'll like it.

Winc: Nice profile there, Scratch.

Private Message to Scratch

Scratch: Heehee. ::blush:: you know, I'm playing darling little boy to Maid's benevolent mother. Happens every time. Feel embarrassed.

Winc: We go into familiar roles, time after time. How do you know Maid's not playing you as darling little gay girl?

Scratch: Whoa.

Winc: Uh huh.

You have left "The Women's Room."<<
End Toobe Entry

Narrative Entry, Jabbathehut

I have issued a warning, as I do from time to time, to my young, energetic friend. Perhaps he will actually retain the thread of this conversation.

>>To: Toobe
From: Jabbathehut
Subj: Patterns

I wanted to make you aware of a stirring, my friend. Certain elements within some troops of the police persuasion are wending their way towards some truths. I put it so languidly because I have no faith in their detective powers, nor in their ability to interpret should they find themselves with evidence in hand.

But, they are starting to realize that many of us are not what we appear. I've been monitoring some memos and know that one division in particular does know how to crunch numbers to find some answers.

All this means they will be making quite a show of those who masquerade. You, of course, will not be so silly as to lose any bypass skills and lead them to your lair.

In short, do not for a moment sign on casually without bypass codes; even if these detectives don't catch any aberrations, their computers automatically will.

—J.

To: Jabbathehut
From: Toobe
Subj: Whoa!

What's the big deal? So what if we sign on as different people? Jesus, don't they have anything better to do?

—T.

To: Toobe
From: Jabbathehut
Subj: Patterns

How quickly you forget your little dance with an elder pervert of some months back. This is ostensibly what they're after: those who would break laws in cyberspace, particularly crimes directed toward children. But you'll learn from this point on in your short little life that threats to children are always the sword held up as the first weapon of invasion. No, they're after much bigger fish, and many of us will get caught in the net, purely by accident, not by design. They will not simply "act first, ask questions later." (They don't even know what questions to ask.) They shall simply arrest people in their typically blind fashion.

—J.

To: Jabbathehut
From: Toobe
Subj: Goofy patterns

   I've never seen you so ominus, however you spell it. But I think I could take your warning much easier if I could get around like you do. How the heck did you intercept those memos?
—T.

To: Toobe
From: Jabbathehut
Subj: Not so fast, Bub

   (May I remind you that every software program has a spellcheck tool?) Of course you would be interested in an intercept toy, cyberbug. All I can tell you is that you, like Dorothy, have had the power all along. But as your recent brush with the law's bulletin board service should have told you, unless you know how to cover your tracks, don't go anywhere you can't immediately get out of.

   Fighting God,
—J.

To: Jabbathehut
From: Toobe
Subj: Paranoid

   Hey, don't worry. I wouldn't. Talk to you soon.
—T.<<

One can hope, at any rate.

Source: myfiles

End Jabba Entry

Begin Toobe Entry

   I just did a bunch of memos with Jabba about this police thing and assured him everything was cool just like with my dad. Then I promptly turned around and started messing around with Jabba's whole package of bypasses. What's wrong with me? I started charting her movements with them, working up to cracking just about every area on the Net. It was so much fun! There were Pentagon files, AT&T networks, universities, the works.

   But did I stop there? Nope. One simple little code I had completely overlooked turned out to be this magic lamp, and boom! I was into the files of TAB, the Triumvirate Association of

Businesses. Then into this 2nd level police bulletin board, not the one I fell into before but another one, at a deeper level. And that's where I acted like some addict going through a dumpster. I was just soaring around that place, reading memos and shit. Leaving a trail that might as well have said, Go find Toobe, he lives right there, and he works right here, and his friends are A-Z, and his dad does this, and everything except, thank gawd, my connection with Jabba. Of course she has a shield that protects her from such mistakes. But my connection to everyone else; I handed it all over on a fucking platter.

But let me continue the saga of S and W.

>>**To: Winc**
From: Scratch
Subj: Talking

I have been thinking about you a lot. Thinking and reading Gertrude Stein if you want to know you know. You know. Thinking when there is no thinking I think of you. Thinking about talking to you which makes me want. Makes me want to ask you questions makes me want to just meet you real time as real as we can get I mean online. Not in real time but in real time with no personas. Online. A room has been created that is I have created this room. This room is called "Woods" to which you might go.
—S.

You have entered Room "Woods."

Scratch: ::Soft carpet of needles, sunlight filtering through trees::
Winc: ::kicking the leaves ahead of me as I walk::
::inhaling pine scent from the forest . . . happy::
Scratch: OK, so my mind's been spinning. I gotta know.
Winc: ::settling down into a large pile of leaves, listening::
Scratch: In my rush to draw you into me, I have gone a lot into the male and female roles, for lack of a better model. If you were being a girl, I stressed a lot of girl stuff. In you I mean. And yet you refer to a "third space," . . .
Winc: Well, actually, I read that some place.
Scratch: OK. I realized I *have* made a third space, for many people, not just you. And I wonder if I've

made the girl space too big, gone too far the other way
I mean.

Winc: ::listening::

Scratch: If you're a guy, maybe you feel rejected that
way. That part of you. When we're online, that third
space seems huge, you and I both are all things. Like
when I call you dude, it's not something I usually call
girls.

Winc: Yes, I make that third space for you, too.

Scratch: Ahhh. Toobe brought up a chat you two had re:
the boy in you. Point is: I don't want you to repress
any of that! I mean, third space should be everything
and nothing, as they say.

Winc: ::letting my fingers trail along the edges of a
dead leaf . . . listening::

Scratch: Maybe you feel you have to "bring it down,"
restrain yourself. Am I correct? Like maybe you think I
wouldn't like you as a boy? Because I'm a het man, or a
lesbian?

Winc: ::pulling my knees up to beneath my chin,
thinking:: I agree with you that the space we share,
like right now, is very much "third" space . . . genderless as it can be . . . where each of us is talking.

Scratch: ::listening, watching you::

Winc: Yet when it comes to love, romance, sex, perhaps
a little S/M . . .
::breaking leaf into little bits:: umm . . . This is
hard . . .

Scratch: Yes, hon, go on . . . I'm with you. I can take
it . . .

Winc: ::smiling:: no, it's hard on me . . .

Scratch: OK, I can take *that*.

Winc: ::laughing:: You asked for it. All my life I never
really fit into "girl" or "boy." Always felt outside,
y'know that one?

Scratch: ::chewing on blade of grass, nodding::

Winc: For so long, I've *wanted* to be just one or the
other, some gender I can hang with full-time, but now
that I *can* be whatever, here online . . .

Scratch: ::gently:: Let me guess . . . why bother choosing?

Winc: ::chewing lip, nodding:: It's dizzying to me,
still. I know I don't want to get stuck in *any* of
this, don't want to freeze into either. Don't want to
lose any sense of myself as boy or . . .

Scratch: So you *are*—

Winc: Wait a minute. ::curling toes inside my boot::

Scratch: ::going quiet, looking up at you, soft eyes::

Winc: ::looking back, grateful:: You're still trying to find out what I "really" am, but I'm *being* who I really am! Right now I mean. We're talking about all of us being boy and girl inside, not what we live as in the so-called real world.

Scratch: Right, sorry.

Winc: But at the risk of breaking out into song, I enjoy being a girl.

Scratch: ::softly:: What is boy? What is girl? Heehee.

Winc: Right, good point, but I'm just getting into exploring something, a softer strength, and that's *amazing* to me.

Scratch: Yes. You mean not just the sex of girl, but a femme kind of girl?

Winc: Yes. ::softly:: I always thought I was too tall, awkward to be femme, that it'd be really, really stupid. ::looking off into the forest::

Scratch: Wow. I just realized that if you really are a girl, that sentence would fit. And if you really are a boy, it would, too.

Winc: ::shrugging:: Yeah . . .

Scratch: Is there more?

Winc: Don't think so.

Scratch: OK. See, what really gets me about these lines drawn in the sand is that people might miss out on how wonderful you are . . .

Winc: ::blushing::

Scratch: Maybe some of them will miss you because of the packaging. We all miss each other that way.

Winc: ::gently:: You can't prevent that.

Scratch: This *is* hard.

Winc: ::laughing delightedly::

Scratch: Me: I feel stuck in my real-time persona, but I love exploring the variations. It's so heady. I never got to be this particular form of human until now, online.

Winc: You mean, you're a guy, but you're being a particular kind of guy for once? Or you're a girl, and you're being a particular kind of girl right now?

Scratch: Yes! I can be androgynous, but I'm exploring something more specific.

Winc: ::looking up at you, questioning::
Scratch: I'm not trying to be coy. I just want to keep the discussion more abstract. As soon as we know each other's sexes, it limits us.
Winc: You mean genders.
Scratch: Oh, yeah. Sex means something else, eh?
Winc: Right, I use sex to mean fucking. Gender is a category, to put people into.
Scratch: Sex is fucking . . . gender is . . . wow. Gonna have to think about that one.
Winc: Uh huh. So what are you discovering?
Scratch: That lots of people respond *sexually* to it, to this form of me. Some of them wish I would be more yang, some more yin, but there's still a sexual response! From different levels within one gender, and from different genders.
Winc: Whoa!
Scratch: Yeah! I get more yang when more yin types are around. It's weird.
Winc: ::settling back against a large tree, listening, fascinated::
You mean, if you're being a hippie boy, you get more response from hippie girls, and if you're being a gay man, you get responses from other gay men.
Scratch: Yes. But it goes deeper. Within the gay men's group, there are maybe 100 other more ways that yin and yang are expressed.
Winc: ::a bit confused:: You mean like some '50s sitcom idea of man and woman?
Scratch: Exactly! Like that people have to go yin and yang, they can't help it! Even if they're really macho with one kind of person, if they met up with another macho person, they'd get more yin.
Winc: So gender is interactive.
Scratch: Oh, fine, you sum all that up in one perfectly succinct sentence.
Winc: ::blushing:: I've been working on it.
Scratch: ::laughing:: It works. We are who we are in *relation* to each other, even in expressing our genders!
Winc: ::smiling at you:: And your conclusion?
Scratch: Well, I read some of your . . . umm . . . opinions, the ones you posted online on something called "alt.bellybutton."

Winc: Oh geez. I didn't know you knew about those. ::blushing again::

Scratch: Yes, they're great! When I read them, I felt I was truly coming to understand genderless space. But the more I read, the more I got panicked: whoamIwhoamIwhoamIwhoamIwhoamI. To you, to others, to me . . .

Winc: Oh hon.

Scratch: If you can change, then what does that make me? If I'm talking to a guy and all of a sudden he becomes a girl, what does that make me? Especially if I'm attracted?

Winc: ::softly, slowly:: Talk about summing things up . . .

Scratch: And then I go to the store, to the park, the bar, to work, and I'm told: you are _____ you are_____ you are_____. Even though I was born as a male/female, I'm *supposed* to belong to one gender.

Winc: ::nodding, listening intently::

Scratch: I have exactly the same fluidity in my mind that you describe. But haven't been as willing to push, and let go, and just float ::looking around:: out here . . .

Winc: ::murmuring:: yes yes yes.

Scratch: . . . and if our two genderless spaces are attracted to each other, as they clearly seem to be, no matter the package . . . why did *we* of all people . . . immediately put them into such tight extremes of male/female?

Winc: Yes, good question. ::leaning over, kissing you gently:: Because we're frightened? Human? Because we recognize that we have to take that journey and we want to lay in provisions?

Scratch: Yeah! And because one needs traction in order to make any movement at all?

Winc: Traction. I like that one.

Scratch: I know different people pull different things out in me. ::quietly:: I usually don't like when the woman in me is pulled out . . . by someone else I mean. Well, with some I do. I did it one night when I dressed up in drag. I mean, the whole "female package" of stockings and heels. But, I hate it being yanked out by aggressive women or stupid men . . .

Winc: ::not breathing . . . listening::

Scratch: I just don't feel it! What I'm supposed to, I don't feel it! But if I blend with someone, when I can

feel a give and take, even if I'm being very "girl,"
it's quite wonderful.

Winc: ::gently:: Maybe the chief thing going on with you
is that you're a dominant type.

Scratch: Dominant type?

Winc: ::very gently:: When we were playing het characters, when we were gay guys, you took the "lead"
both times.

Scratch: True. Then that disappoints me. I feel like
such a shape shifter in other ways . . .

Winc: ::fingers moving through the leaves::

Scratch: ::bewildered::

Winc: ::speechless::

Scratch: Don't like being dominated.

Winc: Like when I was Yar and starting to dominate you?

Scratch: Right . . . ::wriggling uncomfortably:: Makes
me claustrophobic. But I don't want to smother *you*!

Winc: But you wanted to take me down . . . as Yar?

Scratch: Right.

Winc: And once you did?

Scratch: In the best of all possible worlds?

Winc: Uh huh.

Scratch: Then I'd set you free, so you could move
again. Literally and figuratively.

Winc: Do you like playing the top?

Scratch: Emphasis on top, or playing?

Winc: ::smiling:: yeah.

Scratch: A lot of the time it's unconscious . . .

Winc: Jeeze, we're so similar, I like playing the
bottom . . .

Scratch: Ah. No matter the gender?

Winc: ::nodding:: No matter the gender. I spend so much
of my days being warrior, fighting off labels, being in
third space, I *like* the traction you and I create.
::blinking:: at-traction?

Scratch: Hah!

Winc: I mean it. Needing traction to realize desire =
attraction.

Scratch: That's what I meant earlier! Maybe you need a
place to *stand* in order to act on desire, to feel
desire.

Winc: ::smacking my forehead with palm of my hand:: DUH!

Scratch: We were initially drawn without roles/gender,
but then chose personas to act out in, like ghosts who
choose bodies to be in.

Winc: But most people don't play from a third space either. ::shivering:: Scratch . . .

Scratch: I can't think of one sexual connection where I haven't chosen some kind of role. What?

Winc: Whenever I post something about this genderless space, there's inevitably one person who's *really* worried that I'm saying we shouldn't have *desire*. That *does* worry me. What was that great Pogo line? We have met the enemy and it is us?

Scratch: ::smiling:: When I fucked you online, I mean, when it got deep, so to speak, it was the closest thing to being in genderless space, while being sexually intimate.

Winc: YES . . . when you fucked me . . . I was . . . I was me.

::softly:: And I knew you were you.

Scratch: I didn't want to move or talk or breathe, I didn't want to change anything. That's why I was so quiet at the end there. When you were boy and I was girl.

Winc: Wow. Desire in a third space.

Scratch: Oh, great, *now* you can explain it on *Geraldo* . . .

Winc: ::cracking up::

Scratch: Guess what . . .

Winc: ::smiling:: what?

Scratch: I have to go . . .

Winc: ::small voice:: no.

Scratch: Ulogdis?

Winc: ::nodding:: yeah . . . I'm logging it all.

Scratch: Um . . . I'm excited!

Winc: Oh, Scratch, I am too. ::blushing:: Excited at what?

Scratch: These ideas! We should make a copy of all this for Toobe. I should write up all the fucks I've had online. Particularly the way I feel afterward (kind of cheap, even as a boy!).

Winc: ::drumming heels against the forest floor, kicking leaves up in the air::

Scratch: What do you see when you "see" me? ::bracing::

Winc: ::smiling:: Puck.

Scratch: From *Midsummer's Night*?

Winc: Yes.

Scratch: Oh good! That's exactly who I often feel like!
Sometimes I just go "child" as a character, so I don't
have to be so heavy into boy or girl.
Winc: ::smiling, pulling a loose grape leaf out of
your hair::
Scratch: I could talk with you for hours.
Winc: ::looking up at the sky through the treetops::
Ever think about being dominated, topped while you were
more in yin space?
Scratch: Oh, yes. And it's happened sometimes. But it's
short-lived. Scary.
Winc: ::nodding:: As it would be if you topped me while
I was more in yang space.
Scratch: So, forget your actual gender, you're saying
you are more inclined to the yin?
Winc: Yes, and you to the yang.
Scratch: But I don't want to be trapped in that either!
Winc: You can't solve everything at once.
Scratch: Frankly, the first time I thought of your boy-
space I wanted to top that. And now I don't want to
always have to top everything, like some rutting pig
pissing on every tree.
Winc: ::shiver:: Some of us *really* like that!
Scratch: ::shaking head:: I know. I've discovered that.
Winc: ::softly:: It's time.
Scratch: Yes, was just gonna write that! Good-bye.
Winc: :X
Scratch: Heehee. OK, we go on the count of three . . .
 One
 Two
Winc: ::sniff::
Scratch: You say three!
Winc: thr . . . thr . . .
Scratch: You little . . . Why I oughta . . .
Winc: thr . . . eeeeeeeee!
Scratch: Bye doll.
Winc: Doll? Isn't that a particularly female term?
Scratch: &*(_(*&%$$#
Winc: ::waving::
<<

That was a heavy one. I'm still trying to sort it out.

End Toobe Entry

Narrative Entry, Jabbathehut

Wally Budge is reading a full page ad in his favorite taggleblat, the *Daily News*. It reminds him of his old days as a beat cop in NYC. Nowadays, he rides his cyberhorse from a desk, in whatever race they sign him up for. He was a lot happier, he realizes, when the only pressure he got came from upstairs. Now everyone's getting into the act.

A Public Appeal
from Concerned Citizens

In June of this year a 12-year-old child was repeatedly assaulted via electronic mail by men interested in exploiting her youth. The nation's security is being compromised by the dissemination online of top security documents. We are endangered continually as terrorists obtain access to electronic files. Yet the government, and its all-too-willing sponsor, the Triumvirate Association of Businesses, do nothing.

We concerned citizens have formed a grassroots network: Family Values Above All. We call for the immediate apprehension and severe punishment of these criminals, and a tightening of restrictions regarding the Network. And so, we pray:

Almighty God, Lord of all life, we praise You for the betterments in computerized communications that we command in our time. Sadly, there are those who are littering Your information superhighway with unclean, indecent, and injurious pornography. Virtual but virtueless reality is creeping into Your United States of America through the most perverted, diseased misuse of sexuality. Those who would watch over us, O Lord, are aware of these activities, but so far have chosen to do nothing.

God, help us care for our children. Give us wisdom to fashion regulations that will protect the innocent. Guide our Government when they consider ways of controlling the pollution of online intercourse and how to preserve one of our greatest resources: the minds of our children and the future and moral strength of our Nation. Amen.

Wally Budge shakes his head wearily as he scans a list of approximately 500 individuals and organizations, in 8-point type. As if that weren't enough, a fat packet of documents awaits the intrepid lieutenant—hard copy no less, no onscreen memos this time—replies, at last, from the advertising companies regarding his queries about some consumers. Approaching perhaps his first break of the day, Budge flops his bulky frame further back into his squeaky chair and reads the first one.

>>Dear Lt. Budge:

In response to your department's request for persons who fit the demographic profile of conflicting consumer patterns I have the following match:

Onscreen name: Noh
Online Service: Commercial
Income: $35,000/yearly

This person is a white male, 25 years old, frequents Young Christians, Married but Restless, and Trivia II approximately four times a week. Mr. Noh has requested information regarding retirement funds, hemorrhoid medication, subscriptions to *TV Guide*, *PC Computer*, and *Time*. A number of adjacent advertising products have been requested having to do with consumer products targeted to elder black females, which we can forward to you if you are interested, but each seems to fall outside the parameters of your search. We are having our database checked for a programming error, as this is clearly impossible. Our apologies. Within the narrow bands of your department's request, we have come up with this name and one other. The other person's income was below $10,000 and unfortunately, we discard such persons after 3 months.<<

One cigarette smoking away in the ashtray, another wedged between tight lips, Budge is not pleased. Noh? Never heard of him. He scans the next memo, and the profile it contains:

>>**Onscreen name: Deafkid**
Online Service: Commercial
Income: unknown

Subject is 17, orders a wide range of Home Security products, frequents the deaf-disability forums only, and is a frequent user. We are certain this is the candidate you were seeking in regards to the profile you requested. Will you be staging a sting operation to apprehend him? We can release more information, if you like.<<

"Someone's been reading too many action adventure novels," he mutters outloud. Deafkid, huh? Well, at least that's something. He shuffles a few memos, and plucks out another at random.

>>**Onscreen name: Miss Thing**
Online Service: University
Income: $55,000/yearly

Miss Thing buys a wide range of products not consistent with her profile. In addition to the usual feminine hygiene products, she also requests information about tools, lawn products, and geriatric goods, rarely buying anything at all to date, but we feel confident that the target advertising will result in increased consumption shortly. Although in some ways this is an ideal consumer for us, as we sell items in each of these areas, Miss Thing came to our attention for the inconsistent profile you yourself are looking for. We find it hard to believe that she is who she says she is. In addition, she has listed her occupation as welder, which is highly unlikely.<<

Unlikely, but consistent, Budge thinks ruefully. With one eye covered, he makes himself shuffle through the rest of the memos. As he has begun to suspect, his perp is black, female, disabled, young, old, Asian, male, gay, straight, a cross-dresser (why would you even put that down? he wonders idly), a child, an old woman, and white.

"How the hell am I supposed to find someone like that? How am I supposed to find someone who *thinks* like that?"

He slams down the sheaf of useless paper. "Oh, we're hot on that old trail, now," he says aloud.

Idly, he flicks a dead cockroach off the edge of his desk. Shelly's poison is working.

Disgusted, he glances at his own screen, hoping to find word from Typhoid Mary. Nope. The little hippie chick is still off on her mission. Instead, another inter-office memo flashes:

To: Inspections
From: Undersec'y L.
Subj: Profiles

We got a note that you've received several profiles. This is wonderful news! Please begin procedures to apprehend the perpetrators, in connection with fraudulent misuse of Internet service. If we move swiftly and publicly, we can make an example of them, and the govt and the FBI liaison can go back to their real jobs.

Good work; that was fast!

—L.

P.S. Why are you still using your department's generic account?

Wearily, Budge puts his feet up on the desk. He wads up a memo, throws it at his screen, watches it bounce off and, in a perfect trajectory, land in the wastepaper basket beside his desk. But his eyes remain fixed to the screen, on which is written:

WELCOME, MS. BUDGE. YOU'VE GOT MAIL

Slowly, almost despairingly, but with great determination, like a man who hasn't seen the sun for years and who now has had enough of it, he says aloud, "Ms. Budge." He closes his eyes, wearily. "Have to figure these guys out," he continues. "Gals. Whatevers. Why they keep doing this . . . this . . . dance of theirs."

"Maybe the Toobe character will lead somewhere."

Source: persLOG/budge/harddrive
Source: chaplin@senate.gov

End Jabba Entry

Toobe Entry

E-Pitti of the day:

My writing is as clear as mud, but mud settles and clear
streams run on and disappear ...

—Gertrude Stein, *Lectures in America*

I don't see how monks wrote down everything in history without freaking out all over their scrolls and spilling ink all over the place. No wonder history is all screwed up and certain things never got recorded. This was in the paper today; it tripped me out and if I were a monk there'd be this big blot of ink messing up the screen:

>>

"Vaders" identified by Net Police

by Thomas Fulton

An unnamed official high in the administration has indicated that the Federal Bureau of Census and Statistics is rapidly closing in on two Registration evaders. Long known to have abused the convention of the Internet, the individuals, whose real identities are not yet determined, are known through various commercial communications services as "Scratch" and "Winc."

Bureau Undersecretary Margaret LaBouchere said today at a press conference that the two Vaders came to FBCS attention because they use the Internet extensively, but are not Registered. In addition, Scratch and Winc are not the only names used by these individuals, but in fact are two of many used by the pair.

"Of course, that in itself is not a crime," said LaBouchere, "but it is what tipped us off. The multi-persona factor is a dead giveaway to the types of flagrant abuse of the Net we've been concerned about. When we discovered none of these aliases was Registered, we knew we had a criminal profile.

"Such profiles are almost always linked to criminal activity on the Internet, the undersecretary said, because aliases are needed to traffic in pornography, computer fraud and harassment of minors.

<<

Jesus fucking Christ! Do you see what the crime *is?* No! As far as I can tell it's that they fit some frame and the police just poured them in! *Hundreds* of people must fit that profile. How'd S and W get so lucky? I'm Registered, but I use different personas too.

End Toobe Entry

Narrative Entry, Jabbathehut

His tie is looser than usual, his hair even more disheveled. He has been staring into the screen for the past five hours. He has landed in a room entitled, "Don't Send Me Private Messages," in an attempt to learn how to "Netsurf." Unfortunately for Wally Budge, he's not alone.

> **GoodGuy:** I just want to get to know you, that's all. I won't hurt you, really.
>
> **Ms. Budge:** Dammit, I am *not* a woman, knock it off, will you?
>
> **GoodGuy:** I'm not like all the rest of the guys you meet online, honest.
>
> **Ms. Budge:** ::evenly:: And what if I told you I was a cop. A *male* cop, and you could be arrested for . . . *harassment*.
>
> **GoodGuy:** ROTFL! That's a good one, baby. Even if you were a cop, how do you think you'd make it *stick*? Speaking of stick . . . ::chuckle::
>
> **Ms. Budge:** Look, I have work to do, so piss off.
>
> **GoodGuy:** Stupid bitch! You're probably a dyke!

GoodGuy has left the room.

He lights a cigarette, searching for a sign of Typhoid Mary. The little imp has yet to reappear on his screen with news of having successfully "infected" the Toobe character with an unshakable tracer. A memo flashes on his screen.

To: Ms. Budge
From: Shel
Subj: Have you read the news today? Oh, boy!

Your line was tied up, so I thought it might be easier to drop you a note onscreen. ::chuckling:: You're getting addicted to the online world, aren't you?

I thought you might appreciate Tom Fulton's column in today's paper. You're after Scratch and Winc, huh? Ha! My sister's kid has a T-shirt with their names on it!

::quietly:: Did you *want* their names in the paper, Wally?

Call me.

—Shel

P.S.—I'm assuming *Ms* Budge is an undercover thing?

He stares at the memo for a moment, then punches "No Reply." Swiveling in his chair, he picks up his unread newspaper, opens up to the prolific columnist, and reads. And reads again. And a third time. A chime sounds from his computer, heralding a Private Message.

Private Message to Ms. Budge

RamStud: What are you wearing?
Ms. Budge: Can't you read? The name of this room is DON'T SEND ME PRIVATE MESSAGES!
RamStud: Oh bite me!

The world is full of perverts, he thinks to himself, and taking a deep breath, carefully composes an interoffice memo.

To: Undersec'y L.
From: Ms. Budge
Subj: Scratch and Winc
    Ma'am: Have you read the news? We may need a plumber. Seems someone leaked names to the media. This is going to make my job a lot harder. Any idea how they got those names? You and I were the only ones who had them, as far as I know . . .
—Wally

And in less than five minutes . . .

To: Ms. Budge
From: L.
Subj: Re: Scratch and Winc
    Wally, I told you before: we had to give them *some-thing*. I'm sure you'll do your usual, excellent work in apprehending the perpetrators. Say, 72 hours?
—L.
    P.S. (*Ms.* Budge?)

That chime once again, and . . .

Private Message to Ms. Budge

SubRobert: Hello! I hear you're a police officer. Will you put me in handcuffs, please? I've been a very naughty boy.

Ms. Budge: If you heard I was a cop, you heard I was a man. Buzz off, faggot.

SubRobert: ::shivering:: Yes ma'am, I adore women who play men. Thank you for the insult, ma'am.

Ms. Budge: LEAVE ME ALONE!!!

SubRobert: Can I sniff your panties?

Ms. Budge: No!

SubRobert: Fucking CUNT!

Wide-eyed, and perhaps a shade paler than usual, he stares at the text sitting on his screen.

"I don't get it," he says aloud to no one in particular. "So, you let both our cats out of the bag," he murmurs, "and now you want me to catch them."

Source1: persLOG/budge/harddrive
Source2: bckupfiles@FBCS.gov

End Jabba Entry

Toobe Entry

So I panicked all over the place, wrote a bunch of hysterical messages to Jabba which I didn't send, tried to key in the whole newspaper article, but got bored, and then got the bright idea to ask Scratch and Winc what's going on. Haven't heard back yet.

>>To: Winc@e-world.com
From: Toobe@eor.com
Subj: You guys!
CC: Scratch@eor.com

Have you seen the papers? What the hell did you guys do? I'm sorry. I know you didn't do anything, but what the hell is going on? You're not Registered either, Scratch? Why? Why do they even care? Let me know what's going on, please.
—T.<<

But they were as usual, oblivious. That night they sent me their latest email to each other, which I'm putting right here cuz it fits in with how the day went. Right now it seems logging stuff as close to real time as possible is important. I can't believe they're doing this while Rome fries.

>>To: Scratch@eor.com
From: Winc@eor.com
Subj: Wait'll you see this!
 Scratcher,
 I was prowling the bulletin boards last night, not much else going on, it was way way late, and I was, well, it was late. Anyway, I found this whole section called Lesbian Boards. *Finally* some intelligent conversation! I was blown away. But that's not the best part. Inside this section, there's a message board called Butch/Femme. Have you ever heard of this? I swear, it's the best! Look at this message:

>>To: Brknstck
From: Fembot
Subj: Imitating the dominant paradigm
 Dear Brknstck,
 Oh fiddlesticks! Butch/femme is no more an imitation of the "dominant paradigm" than girl/girl sex is an imitation of hetsex. Really, girl, get a life, will you? Butches (at least the ones *I* know, and I know quite a few) don't want to be men, as you intimate in your last posting. Nor do femmes want to "pass for straight." I am *not* interested in attracting any men, dear heart. I can't speak for butches, but let me tell you what *I* see is the soul of this thing.
 Courtship ::slow smile:: and flirtation. When a butch is gallant on my behalf, it just makes my knees go weak. And if I can make a butch's eyes spin just by wearing a tight dress, you'd better *believe* I'm going to have more than a few choice tight dresses on hand!
 Butch/femme is an expression of *equality*, Brknstck. In heterosexual terms, the man has all the power, and the woman is subordinate, at least that's the default setting, and nobody usually bothers to change it. Butch/femme is a consensual sharing of strength. I mean, hey, I call myself a high femme, but I know how to change a tire, and I do! ::laughing lightly:: I don't mind that you personally don't want to take

on the roles of either butch or femme, but don't censor me or any one of my brave butch or femme sisters.

LIPSTICK FOREVER!

Fembot<<

Is that cool, or what? Can we try this one? Come play with me! ::wriggling happily:: Guess what *I* wanna be? heehee.

Lipstick Forever!

—Winc

P.S. Do you know someone named Jabbathehut?

P.P.S. Have you seen some postings recently about us? I haven't, but some folks have said there's stuff popping up around the Net. Have you seen anything? ::giggle:: Wouldn't that be cool?

To: Winc
From: Scratch
Subj: Femme/butch

::feigning a snarl:: Don't ever call me Scratcher, hon. It's Scratch. Besides, one letter off and you could be sending email to your next-door neighbor. Muhahaha. Maybe I *am* your next-door neighbor.

Femme/butch, huh? (I reversed the names for a little equality.) Man, you get into the weirdest things. Isn't that kind of tired? I mean wasn't it the norm for lesbians in the '50s, and now it's just kind of embarrassing?

What is it exactly that compels you? And if we're gonna do this, do I have to get an ugly haircut and never smile?

—S.

P.S. Jabba? Nope, never heard of hir. Should I have?

P.P.S. Postings about us? What the fuck for? Probably Toobe screwing around.

To: Scratch
From: Winc
Subj: Snarls of all sorts

Dear SCRATCH (not Scratcher, I would *never* say Scratcher):

Tired? You're asking *me* if butch/femme is tired? ::laughing merrily:: I don't know. Sounds awfully refreshing to me. Like it's an in-your-face response to a world that would have even the outcasts homogenized.

And listen, I *dream* about your smile, so you'd better keep it! ::tossing long hair off my face, looking up at you through lowered eyelids:: And if you get a bad haircut, the trip is off.

—W.

P.S. Jabba's just someone I know, that's all, just wondering.

P.P.S. Yeah, probably Toobe screwing around with our names. Sigh. But it *would* be cool to be . . . notorious, don't you think? ::winning smile::

To: Winc
From: Scratch
Subj: Butch and femme

Hmm, maybe this is another take on the gender thing. Provides another kind of traction? Funny you mentioned it a day ago. Since then I ran into that bulletin board and found a posting from a woman who calls herself a butch. Thank gawd you want to be femme, the butch one made more sense to me. Does this mean that in real life you're a woman and I'm a man? Sigh.

—S.

To: Scratch
From: Winc
Subj: Femme and butch

Re: your wanting to be butch. I'm so glad! Because I don't understand half the butch posts on that board. Maybe you can explain them to me. Like what's a "stone butch?"

You *then* proceed to say, >>Does this mean that in real life we're a woman and a man?<<

::stepping lightly away from you, moving toward the window where the soft breeze blows the gossamer curtains lightly into the room, ze begins to dance à la Isadora Duncan, and speaks while dancing:: I'm a woman? You're a man? I *seem* to recall a certain riotgrrl who had her way with a certain skateboard dude. ::ze stops dead still, looking at you deadpan:: Or had you forgotten our first evening of bliss? ::resuming hir dance:: Besides, I thought we didn't think it mattered.

Are we on, butch?

—W.

P.S. I went to the corner store about 30 minutes ago, and the T-shirt guy who's always on the street now has one that says "Scratch Here for Electronic Freedom/Wink If You Know What I Mean." I'm not making this up. Coincidence?

To: Winc
From: Scratch
Subj: Are we on

Hmm, well can we at least put a spin on it like Bogie and Bacall? I like my role playing multisomething or other.

Stone butch? I think it means "very butch" or, it refers to the one who just pleases the other one but never gets off herself. Kind of blows me away, because they say butch lesbians are imitating men, but I don't think you'd see many men doing that for women. Nice contradictions there, let's do it.

—S.

P.S. I don't live in any kind of metropolitan area right now, one of the reasons being those stupid T-shirt kiosks selling the latest nonidea. Don't wanna hear no more about it. ::shudder::

To: Scratch
From: Winc
Subj: Bogie and Bacall

I love Bogie and Bacall! You *know* they started out as onscreen lovers, then fell in love and got married? Well, they did.

What was the butch post you liked? I am *so* intrigued by this.

—W.

P.S. OK, hon. T-shirts = :X (gagged mouth, in case you forgot)

To: Winc
From: Scratch
Subj: B. posts

The post I saw was this:

>>Yeah, I tend to hide my emotions and go for girls who wear theirs on their sleeves. And men's clothes are just more comfortable for me. But it doesn't make me male, any more than straight women who started wearing pants in the '60s were trying to be men. That's too simple. The way I relate to women isn't about conquest, or trying to dominate her (unless she wants it ::grin::), but celebrating who we are: strong, proud butch, and strong, proud femme.

There just aren't words yet in this culture. I know, and my woman knows, how I mean strong and proud differently when describing her or me. But it's hard to explain.
—Spike<<

Kinda got to me, know what I mean?
—Scratch

To: Scratch
From: Winc
Subj: Ohhh, if *"that"*'s butch . . .

. . . then I like butches. You're kind of like that, you know? ::smiling:: Wonder what you would call yourself, if anything. ::raising a finger to your lips:: I'm not really asking. Well, maybe a little. But if you like what you read there, and you're ready to try it out, then let me set the scene a bit:

::Stepping back quickly, ze draws a hand across hir face, as though ze were lifting a veil into position. Hir features lose their focus, soften, and blend. A well-practiced smile forms on hir lips, the smile of a girl who's been around the block one too many times. Another motion of her hand, and the waterfall tattoo beneath her right eye disappears. In its place, her hair falls in taunting copper waves. She stands facing you, close enough for you to feel her breath at your shoulder. In her heels, she's almost as tall as you, but not quite. She smoothes out her skin-tight dress, looks up at you. When she speaks, her husky voice goes right into your heart, to a place you thought you'd walled off years ago:: "Let's go to a Private room called Key Largo. Name the time . . ." ::she turns to leave, but stops, and looks back at you over her shoulder:: "You know how to name the time, don't you? ::laughing softly:: You put one hand *here*, and the other hand *here*. I'll do the rest."

  ::The door clicks shut behind her, you hear the sound of her heels retreating down the passageway::

—W.

To: Winc
From: Scratch
Subj: Key Largo

  ::groan:: Um, okay:

She glances up toward the mirror over the bar. She's got a stern, serious face, the kind of face that looks good to a certain kind of woman. She stopped wearing anything but men's clothes years ago; these duds fit her like a glove. Wide-brimmed hat pulled down over one eye, baggy pants that keep a lot to themselves, and two-toned shoes, her favorite pair. She sees the broad in the corner, and shakes her head, grinning up at the bartender. "Why didn't you tell me she walked in the door, Jack?" The bartender just shrugs and goes to wipe a glass. "I knew you'd notice her sooner or later, pal." She lifts her drink in a cheap salute, wishing right away she hadn't, and in spite of her better judgment, she lifts her hat, and says in a low voice, heavily inflected with the state of New York:

"Key Largo, tomorrow, noon. Don't be late."

(P.S. Someone told me there were buttons floating around out there that say "Scratch This." Tell me it's a coincidence, dollface.)<<

Toobe Entry con't

Oblivious. They'll probably send me the log of *that* scene tomorrow night. Meanwhile, I did get one of those T-shirts, and wear it sometimes. This "outlaw" thing is spreading like wildfire. I never saw it before today, but all of a sudden it's everywhere. How did I miss it? I'm random-surfing and I go to alt.newsgroups as usual. These are the famous newsgroups that started all the interest in the Net in the first place. They began as purely information files, but now they're like bulletin boards for everything from people who like movies, to about 50 million permutations of sex folders, to car mechanics, to public radio lovers. It's where I get a lot of my e-fitti. So I went to alt.parents.concern, and it lets me know what to be careful of, and I see this. It was posted a few days ago, I can't believe I missed it.

>>Folder: alt.parents.concern
From: JanStanM
Subj: Cults?

We just wondered if anyone else has noticed their kids getting involved in what we fear is a cult around so-called "vaders." Our daughter goes online every chance she gets, and hangs out in different personae as she's always done. Of course she's Registered, but we're concerned: A new teen group has popped up since she signed on, and as far as we know it's not being monitored. In it, teens trade news and graphics of two vaders in particular, who call themselves "Scratch" and "Winc," speculating on their whereabouts, etc. Harmless enough, really, but we're concerned that too much attention is being focused on people who are, after all, breaking the law. Apparently at the malls kids are connecting with each other by scratching, or winking, to indicate membership in this club.
Jan and Stan Margolis<<

There were about 25 postings in response, about half of them saying their kid was in this cult. What a mess. Nobody's checking anything out!

I've been playing with Jabba's toy and I think I can get some goodies. I'm going to hack into the internal communications lines of some of these services. Let's see, I need a list. Now I see why Scratch makes them. Delphi, America OnLine, Prodigy, the Pentagon (just kidding), some universities, CompuServe. . . . Okay, that's enough for now.

Toobe Entry con't

Oh, I'm real glad I did that. Now I can read other people's mail. It's like this one time I read my best friend's journal (I wanted to see if he wrote anything about me). Well, he didn't write about me, but he wrote about his parents fighting and how there was broken glass all over the floor and I was really sorry. Then do you do something now that you know, or do you just pretend you don't know anything? Which is really not possible.

Anyway, a little sampler:

>>**Delphi intercom**
General memo:
(Classification: no discussion outside your department, none outside the company.)

The advertising reps are not happy that the multipersona phenomenon is so rampant. They cannot target demographic groups successfully because users are not representing themselves accurately. They're recommending very strong action. We will be calling a meeting to discuss options about the situation. Please bring some examples of multipersona users in your areas, for use in spotting/handling simulations.<<

There were memos like that in practically all the services, and I only did a random check. The Triumvirate Association of Businesses (TAB) must have sent a press release to all of the services at the same time. But not one of them defended what they were doing. Nobody seemed to think it was weird that this was being called a problem. I mean, don't they have enough money from people paying by the hour, without having to target them for ads, too? I don't get it.

I saved the scariest memo for last:

>>**Interoffice Memo, Hyperlink Communications Services**
To: Mark Shrine, CEO
From: Tom Braga, VP Customer Data
Subj: Customer "Scratch," Customer "Winc"

Yes, in answer to your question, the names you sent are those of Hyperlink Comm Services customers. They each have been seen on this service since spring of 1995, and use a variety of names. Due to infrequent activity use, I would not say this is the main service they use. They link up for approximately one week, and do not return until an average of 18 days later.

One, customer "Scratch," used the service almost exclusively up until three months ago, at which point communications with customer "Winc" seemed to become more frequent. After that point virtually all correspondence was directed at "Winc" or his or her other screen names.

We are monitoring the situation carefully in light of today's newspaper announcement. At this point, we have adopted a wait-and-see attitude, as they have not violated any of the terms of our service.

Between you and me and the lamppost, I think the reactions are pretty strong. Perhaps the FBCS has no idea how virtually all customers use at least two personas, and most use more. As for criminal activity by any of our clients, we have witnessed only one case in the history of the service, and the incident was dealt with swiftly at that time.<<

So then I went to the bulletin boards, randomly, again:

>>Alt.sex.fetish

I think they're cool. They hang out here ALL the time. One time Winc got Scratch on all fours sniffing her shoes. It was great!

Alt.teen.chat

They're in the teen chat live room now! They're using other personas, but I know it's them!

Alt.deaf.bbs

I know Scratch from chat rooms. Nice person. I never found out what sex she or he is because no response when I asked. Knows about deaf community and writes a lot of letters to the editors of various magazines, especially about the movie *Children of a Lesser God* and how it hurts Deaf Culture.

Alt.bellybutton

Winc posts right here! Under his own name! I think we should make this a closed list, and charge admission!

Alt.movies.action

Of course they're not women. They're both guys. Nobody else could come up with that many sick personas. There's a Conan type, and a damsel type. I've seen them.

Alt.dykes.inyerface

Oh, sure, I've had sex with Winc. I screen my partners real carefully, too many guys come in here. I can always tell. My first clue was she didn't ask my breast size. It was great, by the way, very imaginative.<<

Okay, fine, except I checked the dates and the locales on these, and there's no way it's them. I mean, they may have been in those places at some time, but not all at once. Not to mention that I really doubt Winc could get Scratch on all fours. False sightings. The Fugitive syndrome. The bulletin boards are like a small town, everyone gossiping about nothing they've really seen. The Net is cool but you can't be two places at once, not yet anyway. Check this out:

>>To: Toobe
From: Jabba
Subj: simultaneous being

Even the most bungling newbie could be in two, 20, or 200 chat channels at the same time. *If* the managers of those channels allow them to be. However, they would always have the same screen name in each room which, if I catch your drift, is not the case with these two. Of course, my mind-fettered friend, one *can* create a program which acts as a loop, if you will. It's called a virus. Normally that word is associated with infection (like so many Net terms, it's a misnomer). But the chief nature of a virus is its replicating nature, which *is* in keeping with the poorly chosen name. You would write a virus program attached to a bulletin board posting, for example, send it out with instructions to replicate every time it has been read, then send it out to other bulletin boards of your choice. Perhaps you instruct it to stay in one area forever. But in most cases the message would remain the same, although some can change the nature of their own messages. The result is that you, or your message, would appear to "be" in several places at once. This is simple. For me, yes, for the majority of Net users, impossible.
—J.<<

I don't doubt it. Maybe Jabba invented one and used it to post as Scratch and Winc? Naw, she wouldn't waste her time. Besides, they refer to cybersex sessions, and that couldn't be a virus. So they're legends. Oh, goodie.

End Toobe Entry

Narrative Entry, Jabbathehut

"I'm out of the loop, Shel," Budge says flatly. "I'm gettin' lots of "you-can-do-it," from upstairs, but not what I need to do my job. And they're goin' around my ass directly to the press."

"Oh, so that's why you're not touching a perfectly good plate of calamari fra diavolo," she retorts. She dabs a napkin to her lips and nods at his plate.

He takes a stab at the circles of sliced shellfish swimming in the sluggish sauce and looks up at her morosely.

"It's no surprise Upstairs cut me off; I've been expecting that," he shrugs. "I'll do what I have to do, but that's where I run into a wall. I'm out of my element here, Shel. This Scratch, and this Winc. I can't get into their heads."

She studies him for a moment.

"I've known you for many years, old pal," she says softly, "and I've never heard you say anything like that. Not once. What's going on?"

He stares down at the table in front of him, at the crumbs of garlic bread ringing his plate, idly wondering how restaurants keep the roaches away.

"Wally?"

He looks up into the face of his closest friend.

"I don't know what to make of this, and I have a feeling it's got something to do with . . . them, with this whole online mess."

Reaching into his jacket pocket, he withdraws several neatly folded pages—hard copy text logs of his online adventures earlier that day—and hands them across the table. As she unfolds them, he continues.

"What's with this 'stupid bitch,' and 'bite me,' and, well, worse, you'll read it."

Read she does.

"I'm a regular guy," he continues in a voice almost plaintive with true consternation. "I'm not one of your perverts or frustrated psychos looking to hurt someone online or off."

Then, he quietly concludes, "Every one of those people was downright mean to me. And for no reason, Shel. For no goddamn reason."

"Every one of those *men* was downright mean," she says, her voice slow and even. "And the reason is, you weren't one of them. You were a woman."

His obvious befuddlement brings a familiar crooked smile to her lips. But she's not saying any more. She's enjoying this too much.

The soft clinking of silverware and muted conversation in the background seems to him a perfect sound track for this moment. Maybe that's why he's a detective, he thinks to himself. Life is so much like the movies.

"I don't get it," he says finally. "You know me. I've been voting for the Democrats ever since Mondale. I'm as liberal as they come, but I can't wrap myself around this one."

She reaches across the table and touches the back of his hand. Why does this simple movement seem to comfort him down to his bones, he wonders.

"You are one of the good ones. That's the trouble, there's not that many like you." Her voice gently challenging, her fingers still resting on the back of his hand. "But you still haven't got a clue, have you?"

He grins despite his discomfort. "Aw, c'mon. All men are creeps, is that what you're gonna say? G'head, I can take it. I'm a big boy."

"All right, Wally, all right." She looks at him evenly for a moment.

"What do you suppose it would be like," she says, "if every time you signed online, no, every time you walked out your front door, you were expecting that kind of treatment? And you'd never know where it was going to come from, or when, but you're always ready for it. You'd know that under the smile, under the come-on, even under the greatest words you've ever heard, someone's waiting to catch you up if . . . if you don't do just what they want you to do . . ."

She can see him strain to grasp it. He's working hard, maybe that's why she likes him. He does work at it.

"Still with me?"

He shifts uncomfortably in his chair.

"So what you're saying is that Scratch and Winc . . . they're women, is that what you're tellin' me? That's why they keep on changing, running . . ."

". . . playing," she finishes his thought. "They're playing."

That smile of hers.

"They're free. That's what they are."

"Huh?"

She continues, absently stroking the back of his hand.

"I don't know if Scratch and Winc are women or not. No one does, maybe that's why everyone's talking about them. And you better believe me, Mister stuck-behind-his-desk, everyone is talking about them. It doesn't matter if they're women. They could be black, Latino, the little guy in the wheelchair outside our building. The Asians getting off the boat in California. Gays. Lesbians. Children. Anyone who can't speak up because they were always afraid of being put in their place."

He loves it when she talks like this.

"I don't know who they are. For me, I'd like them to be women. But whatever they are, they're showing the rest of us that there's a place where there's no fear."

Their eyes meet. He's dizzy, and she knows it.

"I wanna know more about this," he says slowly. "If I'm gonna find them, I have to know more about this. To get into their heads. Will you . . . ?"

She chuckles. Gets him every time.

"Sure. But first," she lifts a forkful from her own plate to his lips, "try the mussels. They're amazing."

Source1: persLOG/budge/harddrive
Source2: diary.sdunlap @ FBCS.gov
Source3: persLOG/sdunlap/harddrive

End Jabba Entry

Toobe Entry

Sure enough, when I got back from snooping there's this log from Scratch. And then an identical one comes from Winc. Hello? Are you home? Do you have any brains? I think I just got that tree falls in the forest thing. Nope, if you're not hearing it, it's not falling.

>>***Online Host: *** You are in "Key Largo." ***

Johnny: ::tropical breezes . . . chichi drinks on the table::

Frankie: ::ceiling fans slowly rotating::

Johnny: Just another day in paradise.

Frankie: ::to no one in particular:: Phew. ::fanning face:: Hot out there.

Johnny: Hey, dollface. What'll ya have?

Frankie: ::turning:: You talkin' to me?

Johnny: Yeah, I'm talkin' to you. You see any other good-lookin' broads in here?

Frankie: ::giving you a long even look:: And how many times have you used *that* line? ::lazy smile::

Johnny: How often you give a slow turn like that? ::small twitch of lips::

Frankie: ::slow smile:: Only when I'm expectin' to see something I like.

Johnny: And did ya?

Frankie: ::nodding:: Oh, yeah.

Johnny: So, whaddya drinkin'?

Frankie: ::pulling out a cigarette:: Comfort and coke. Light on the coke.

Johnny: Comin' right up.

Frankie: ::looking deep into your eyes::

Johnny: ::looking into your eyes, lighting cigarette::
So what brings you to these parts?
Frankie: ::shrugging:: Maybe I heard the ponies are run-
nin' sweet . . . then again . . . maybe I'm the one
who's runnin.
Johnny: You got a weakness for ponies? Or runnin'?
Frankie: ::throwing my head back laughing:: Right now,
I've got a weakness for good looking butches.
Johnny: ::ducking head:: is that right? ::sly smile::
Kinda bold, ain'tcha sister?

///Good Evening, Everything all right?///

Johnny: Oh, sure sure, it's all right.
Frankie: ::turning:: Hello, Eye . . . yeah, me and my
. . . escort, we're fine.
Johnny: Nothin' doing here, Eye.

///Fine . . . Have a nice one . . . love that movie!///
EYE HAS LEFT THE ROOM.

Johnny: Movie? Oh, the room name . . . Jesus! Must've
followed ya in.
Frankie: Scratch?
Johnny: Yes, Winc?
Frankie: That's scary! ::moving closer to you, shaking::
Johnny: Yeah. Since s/he came *in* to ask, maybe the
Eyes can't monitor us from outside the room.
Frankie: ::quietly:: Maybe, maybe not.
Johnny: You know, sweetheart, I might be bad news for ya.
Frankie: ::looking up into your eyes:: I've had my share
of bad news.
Johnny: I bet you have.
Johnny: But I'm on the run, see. You might say I got
myself lost.
Frankie: ::arching an eyebrow:: Why ya runnin'?
Johnny: I got my reasons. What about you? [My screen
just froze, Winc. Careful.]
Frankie: ::offhandedly:: I had a run-in with a . . .
[huh? You signed on with a . . . you-know-what, right?]
Johnny: ::cupping your chin in my hand:: Maybe if it looks
like an ordinary love scene, they won't bother us.
Frankie: ::pressing softly against you:: Yes.
Johnny: ::talking real low in your ear:: What's that
perfume you're wearin'?

Frankie: ::laughing softly:: It's called Trouble. You like the smell of Trouble?

Johnny: No, but I can guarantee the scent will follow me.

Frankie: ::softly, almost to myself:: Trouble, spelled B-U-T-C-H.

Johnny: Maybe you should just be quiet for a minute. ::kissing you hard::

Frankie: ::struggling:: ::pulling back, breathing hard:: Pretty sure of yourself, aren't ya?

Johnny: No. I'm not. You're a new kind of trouble for me.

Frankie: ::wiping my mouth with the back of my hand::

Johnny: Damn. Sorry I got fresh.

Frankie: ::laughing low:: What did you say your name was?

Johnny: I didn't.

Frankie: ::sizing you up::

Johnny: Ladies first.

Frankie: ::smiling:: Some folks call me Frankie . . . and you're . . . ?

Johnny: Well, wouldn't ya know it? They call me Johnny.

Frankie: Just my luck.

Frankie: You know that story, don'tcha?

Johnny: There's a juke box here. Maybe they got the song.

Frankie: ::turning, spotting the juke against the wall:: Play it, Johnny. Go ahead.

Johnny: Dance?

Frankie: Sure . . . why not. ::tugging my skirt down:: ::moving close into you, pressing my breasts against you::

Johnny: ::breathing in your scent above your head:: ::pressing close to you, not speaking::

Frankie: ::pressing my lips to your white shirt, softly, leaving just a trace of red::

Johnny: Hey . . . aw, forget it.

Frankie: I can forget a lot of things . . . but not you, handsome. What is it?

Johnny: ::feeling the softness of your dress:: Nothin'. You dance real good.

Frankie: ::tears springing to eyes, averting my face quickly::

Johnny: Hey, sweetheart, what is it?

Frankie: ::softly:: Damn. ::shaking my head:: It's nothing. Just keep holding me.

Johnny: No problem, doll. ::dancing out to the patio slowly::

Frankie: Maybe you're all right, Johnny. Maybe you're not like the rest of 'em.

Johnny: Oh, I probably am, sweetheart. But it looks like we got the same amount to lose.

Frankie: Tell me, Johnny . . . ::breaking away from you, gently::

Johnny: Yeah?

Frankie: You stone? ::holding my breath::

Johnny: ::stiffening:: Why ya gotta go and ask a question like that?

Frankie: ::softly:: Oh baby, c'mere. ::holding my arms out::

Johnny: What's it to you? ::slowly moving back close to you::

Frankie: ::softly:: Had to know, Johnny. It's OK.

Johnny: ::relaxing into you again:: Depends. I don't plan it, but it usually works out that way.

Frankie: ::running my fingers through your hair gently:: It's OK, Johnny.

Johnny: I ain't got no bones 'bout being a female. If that bugs you, you better buzz off now.

Frankie: ::pressing myself hard against you, taking your face in my hands:: ::kissing you hard::

Johnny: ::holding you tighter, kissing back:: ::Looking around:: Think we're really alone here?

Frankie: I hope we are. We have to run, you know that, right?

Johnny: ::smiling:: Yeah, I know. But I want somethin' real bad, Frankie. Want it now.

Frankie: ::lazy smile:: What's that, handsome?

Johnny: You, dollface. We ain't got much time, so . . .

Frankie: ::nodding:: So . . .

Johnny: ::moving my hand lower:: So one thing I noticed about both of us bein' female . . .

Frankie: ::gasping, smiling, putting my arms up around your neck::

::breathless:: What's that, Johnny?

Johnny: We can go to the can together.

Frankie: ::pulling back, looking at you, shocked::

Johnny: ::whispering:: Come on, just for a minute.

Frankie: ::bursting out laughing:: The can?

Johnny: ::laughing with you:: Sorry to be crude. You just . . . you . . .

Frankie: ::rueful laugh:: I bring it out in ya, right? I always seem to do that with the good ones.

Johnny: ::moving you to Ladies Lounge::

Frankie: ::holding you back:: Hey, handsome . . .

Johnny: Come on, doll, let's do it one more time before we gotta go.

Frankie: You sure you wanna go in there?

Johnny: Why not? It ain't polite to do what I wanna do in public.

Frankie: ::shrugging:: I saw some straight girls go in earlier, and . . .

Johnny: Yeah. They do get jumpy. Damn. ::moving my hands over your breasts:: Patio's deserted, I guess.

Frankie: ::whispering:: I just don't want you hurt, darlin'. Patio's fine.

Johnny: You like stone butches?

Frankie: ::small smile:: I like butches. Stone or otherwise, I like 'em.

Johnny: Too many femmes . . . they're afraid. Don't want to touch us. Afraid we'll slap 'em down.

Frankie: ::nodding:: So then they don't touch you.

Johnny: Yeah . . . ::nuzzling your neck:: ::sliding hand down your thigh::

Frankie: ::bringing my hands up to your breasts, my eyes locked on your eyes, asking::

Johnny: Yeah. Yeah, do that.

Frankie: ::closing my eyes, smiling, squeezing your breasts gently::

Johnny: ::sliding hand along your stockings, moving up under your dress:: ::turning your back to the lounge:: Oh, baby, you got a touch, you do.

Frankie: ::opening my legs a bit wider::

Johnny: ::sliding my knee in between your legs:: ::pushing you down on my thigh::

Frankie: Ahh! yesss.

Johnny: Ride, baby. Ride it for me.

Frankie: ::pushing down against your leg, eyes locked on yours::

Johnny: ::breathing:: You look so good. ::sliding hand in between your legs, dipping in::

Frankie: ::tossing my hair out of my face, riding your leg in time to the music::

Johnny: All nice and wet for me, baby?

Frankie: ::riding your leg, more urgently:: ::standing up suddenly, widening my stance::

Johnny: ::sliding my fingers over your clit, one finger, then two, inside you.:: What, baby, what?

Frankie: ::reaching up to your breasts, bringing my fingers around your nipples::
Johnny: [Oh, duh]
Frankie: Want you inside me . . . your hand. Now, please, baby!
[Scratch?? You OK?]
Johnny: ::Looking around, can't resist::
Johnny: [Yeah, just missed a cue. Go on, I'm stupid.]
::putting more fingers inside you . . . pushing hard::
Frankie: ::purring:: [You missed nothing. You are . . .
::gasp::]
Johnny: ::rubbing your clit hard, breathing into your neck::
Frankie: ::rolling your nipples in my fingers, harder now, hips back and forth on your hand::
Johnny: ::my own wetness warm . . . :: ::riding the seam of my pants::
Frankie: ::bringing my hand down to between your legs::
Johnny: ::rubbing your clit harder:: You gonna give it to me baby?
::pulling you to me, pushing my hand inside you::
Frankie: Everything I've got, Johnny. ::running my hand hard over your fly, squeezing down on your hand inside me::
Johnny: I'm not gonna lose it here, baby, but it sure feels good. ::dancing to the music, pushing my hand in and out::

///Sorry to interrupt, folks///

Frankie: What?
Johnny: What the fuck? What's up, Eye?

///There's a special announcement coming over the Net in 7 minutes . . .
We're supposed to alert everyone.///

Frankie: Thanks, Eye.
Johnny: Thanks.

///Have fun, you two. Hey . . .
which one of you is Bacall?///

Johnny: With all due respect, sir or madam, we'd like a little privacy.

///::shrugging:: Just trying to get into the spirit of things.
What a grouch.///
EYE HAS LEFT THE ROOM.

Frankie: ::breathing hard:: Maybe you shouldn't have—
Johnny: ::breathing hard for the wrong reasons::
Frankie: What's happening, Scratch? That isn't supposed to happen.
Johnny: Look, Winc, I don't want to sound paranoid, but . . .
Frankie: But?
Johnny: I think we gotta get outta here. I'll tell you by email.
Frankie: No, Scratch! Don't want you to leave!
Johnny: When the Net announcement comes, it'll stop all action anyway. ::pause:: I was so fucking turned on!
Frankie: I was so . . . you were?
Johnny: Of course! Weren't you?
Frankie: ::tilting my head, looking up at you through lowered lids:: Was I ever, handsome.
Johnny: Jesus! *Please* don't ever tell me who you really are! I mean *what* you really are.
Frankie: Umm . . . OK.
Johnny: Do you know what I mean?
Frankie: ::shaking my head, quiet::
Johnny: I can totally become these people with you!

> **ATTENTION ALL NETUSERS . . . A SPECIAL GOVERNMENT ANNOUNCEMENT WILL APPEAR IN 5 MINUTES.**

Johnny: Don't tell me we finally hit your real persona: a tart from the '40s . . .
Frankie: ::popping my gum:: And what if I was?

> **PLEASE STAND BY.**

Johnny: Christ. I've gotta do a complicated exit, through many byways, if you know what I mean. Give me your most obscure email address . . .
Frankie: ::uploading address to you::
Johnny: ::smiling at you, all rough and twinkley::
Frankie: SCRATCH!
Johnny: Bye, doll. ::Uploading my address to you:: Yeah?
Frankie: ::softly:: You make me crazy when you do that.
Johnny: I know, dollface. I practice.
Frankie: You . . . do . . . ?

Johnny: We girls got our secrets, you know.

Frankie: So you're . . . ?? NO! Don't tell me.

Johnny: Don't forget that boy scene. I've never been harder . . .

Frankie: ::closing my eyes, dizzy::
::your smile on so many bodies::

Johnny: ::chuckling::
::softly:: Does it matter, babe?

Frankie: Not as long as you're here with me, handsome.

> **THE NET ANNOUNCEMENT WILL COMMENCE
> IN 1 MINUTE, PLEASE STAND BY . . .**

Johnny: Let's go. It's rough to be kicked out. Better to saunter off on your own power.

Frankie: ::grabbing you, kissing you hard, sweet::

Frankie: Bye "Johnny"!

Johnny: Bye doll.<<

Toobe Entry con't

Told you they'd send that log to me. Wonder if they were being psychic by acting like they're on the run. My guess is, they just did it for the lark.

At least I don't feel so alone. Jabba's been doing a little cruising, too. This is all so confusing.

>>To: **Toobe**
From: **Jabbathehut**
Subj: **Them**

What have you been doing, mischievous one? Is this why you asked about the simultaneity of being? Surely you haven't mastered this yet. No offense to your computer skills, which are considerable, but you would have had to stay on one project for approximately 10 hours to have crafted a proper virus that did not fail. You haven't had that kind of time, have you? At any rate, is this your doing? These are some messages I've scanned in chat rooms in the space of a single hour:

>>Warrior Net:

Scratch Wincs, Winc Scratches, the coolest dudes in the universe. They Rule!

Cheating Husbands:

Scratch is the most popular girl in our area, I cannot believe she is being pursued by cyberpolice. I wonder if we can help?

Black Men for Black Men:

Of course Winc's been gone for awhile. Now I get it. Damn, what's he gotten himself into? Must have put it to an Eye ::evil grin::<<

This idol-worship is disgusting, to say the least, Master Toobe. Surely you are not trying to ruin your friends' sterling reputations. And again, I ask, do these "people" not have anything better to do than speculate on the whereabouts of persons of no import?

—J.

To: Jabbathehut
From: Toobe
Subj: My friends

They're important to me, Jabba, but I get what you're saying. No, it wasn't me. It's a fucking epidemic. It's all cuz of the newspaper announcement.

—T.

To: Toobe
From: Jabbathehut
Subj: Friends

Ah, I see. (Must your prose be so purple so often? There are other words--many, in fact--in our English language.) Thank you for the explanation. Another Net incident. How predictable

—J.

To: Jabbathehut
From: Toobe
Subj: Swearing

I'm sorry, Jabba, I'm just upset now. Catch you later.

—T.

<<

Well I am. I am way freaked out. I haven't heard one word from Scratch and Winc. That's not unusual, but they don't know a whole crisis has happened in the time they've been playing "getting to know you." I need a list.

End Toobe Entry

Narrative Entry, Jabbathehut

>>To: Investigations@FBCS.gov
From: Dgarner@hyperlink.com
Subj: Way sorry . . .

I'm a very private person, and I have my reasons for doing what I did. It's me, Winc, talking. I'd keep on doing it, but I can't take this kind of exposure. I mean, that whole newspaper article. Ouch! So I want to make a deal—I want to request amnesty, the witness protection program thing, or whatever you can give me. I sure hope it's like the movies, and you go easy on the one who gives himself up. I know how to get in touch with Scratch. I'd like to give you that information in exchange for some sort of leniency.

I hate myself for doing this, probably always will. And Scratch is going to hate me a whole lot more, but like I said, I have my reasons. So please, send an officer around to get me. I'll come peacefully, I swear it! My name is Donald Garner, and I live at 3624 Baltimore Avenue, Apt. 8, in Philadelphia. Only this time, send an earthling. I *beg* you. The last officers to come to my apartment were from Alpha Centauri, and I . . .

Wally Budge punches "Delete" in disgust. Kooks, how many kooks out there are going to show up now as "Winc," or "Scratch"? But something about that note rang false from the start. What was it? No stage directions! That's it! In all the verified chat logs he'd received, Winc almost always uses that double colon thing. He, or she, always draws some sort of picture. Why?

He types "Stage Directions" into his database. He's sifting through the growing pile of electronic recycling that's stacked up ever since the newspapers blew his leads. He's doing what he knows how to do, the way he has always done it: slow and steady. Some might say relentless.

Reading every bit of it. The countless confessions, the myriad sightings, and enough rumors to keep the *National Enquirer* happy for a decade—all as a result of one little newspaper article. To top it off, texts of alleged "conversations" keep pouring in to the bureau from good, upright, solid citizens who want to see justice served. Texts containing everything from recipe tips attributed to Scratch and Winc, to some grotesque scene involving a woman chewing on her own arm. Christ! They can't all be Scratch and Winc, that's obvious. Then it hits him, hard. If that's true, then there's lots more people out there doin' this stuff. And if that's the case . . . he shakes his head. Better stay far away from that one. Keep it simple. Do your job. Find your perps.

Source: persLOG/budge/harddrive

***

In the virtual pub known as "The Tavern," conversation is buzzing. The talk is of Registration evaders, bypasses, and random sightings of the rapidly escalating instant legend: the adventures of Scratch and Winc. The chat is idle. Boasts are made and discarded. Bets are placed, and removed. There is a sense of waiting, but in this idle corner of the Net, the waiting is for something official to tell them what they already know is happening.

The denizens of this online bar take little notice of two more characters stumbling into their midst. They're quiet, these two, seemingly shy of engaging in the desultory banter. The hour is early and lethargy is the mainstay of the day.

> **Fredman**: No, I never heard of them, but I've been hearing people talk about them.
> **Frankie**: Pour me a strong one, bub.
> **Bartender**: You got it.
> **Frankie**: ::winking at you:: Thanks.
> **Johnny**: Make that two, barkeep.
> **Frankie**: ::glancing over at the stranger::
> **Johnny**: ::scratching my head:: How ya doin' doll.

Private Message to Johnny:

Frankie: I am *so* discombobulated!
Johnny: Me, too. Feel like I just got out of bed.
Frankie: ::purring:: Well, you did.

> **Ted**: No, I ain't seen them. I don't know what all the fuss is about.
> **Barbun**: Oh, I dunno, I've had a few dealings with Scratch. He's a real cutie.
> **Johnny**: ::almost dropping drink::
> **Frankie**: Hey, steady there, handsome.
> **Johnny**: Thanks, hon.

Private Message to Johnny

Frankie: Scratch?
Johnny: What?

Fredman: What's the big deal, anyway? What'd they do?
Ted: They say trafficking in porn, but that's just a rumor.
Barbun: ::patting hair:: That doesn't sound like the Scratch I know.
Ted: ::quietly:: nor the one I know, either.

Private Message to Frankie

Johnny: Oh, gawd, Barbun. From some chat room . . .
Frankie: Uh, huh . . . and ::blush:: Fredman's somebody I know, too.

Barbun: I think it's just that they can't be nailed down.
Ted: Well, that and the fact that they didn't Register.
Barbun: True, a bad combo.
Ted: I'd hate to have everyone unmasked.
Fredman: Hah! That would be scary!

Private Message to Frankie

Johnny: Winc, we gotta ask.
Frankie: ::gulp:: Go ahead, you're the butch.
Johnny: ⸮ə*%!

Johnny: ::scratching chin:: What's all the talk?
Frankie: ::winking at Johnny:: Yeah, fill me in too.
Fredman: These Scratch and Winc characters, it's been all over the news.
Frankie: Yeah? Do tell.
Fredman: Doing what we're all doing, only they got caught.
Frankie: Sounds like a government with too much time on its hands.
Fredman: You got that right, cutie!
Barbun: Makes you want to show them how many of us "break the law."
Fredman: Yeah! What would they do if we all sent a letter to the brass, signed by all our other names!
Ted: A good idea, but I'm beginning to think they're tracing us all to our original accounts.
Fredman: ::snorting:: Like they have that much time, or that many brains?

Barbun: ::idly smoothing stockings:: Sometimes they get a little one-track, you know?
Ted: Yeah, I do know.

A soft chime interrupts the lazy chat, the special tone reserved for system and governmental announcements. All eyes revert to screens, in all sectors of every online service, commercial, educational, or private.

A Public Safety Announcement
from
The United States Government
Bureau of Census and Statistics
presented with the cooperation of your local Net service provider

◊

This is to alert all citizens
to the presence of two suspected criminals
and known Registration evaders on the Net.
Their most common aliases are "Scratch" and "Winc."

◊

Suspected activities constitute a grave threat to the safety of all Net users. As true identities are as yet unknown, an all-nodes, all-database government search is under way with the full cooperation of the private sector, to effect apprehension and questioning.

Your government requests your cooperation as follows:

•Forward exact date, time, and Net location of any encounter with "Scratch" or "Winc," under any alias.

•Forward any and all evidence linking "Scratch" or "Winc" with illegal trafficking of Net access bypass codes, child pornography, or copyright infringement.

•If you have participated in online commerce or exchange of any nature with "Scratch" or "Winc," forward details, and scan your hard drive for potentially damaging computer viruses.

◊

Any information, particularly access codes, and the text of any conversations with "Scratch" or "Winc," may be forwarded in all confidence to Safety@BCS.gov. Your anonymity in this investigation and subsequent apprehension and trial of this pair will be insured.

◊

We apologize for interrupting your service temporarily, and we thank your local service access provider for their assistance in making this public safety announcement available to you.

End: PSA: SAFETY #309

Fredman: Jesus, it *is* true!

Frankie has left the room.
Johnny has left the room.

Ted: Did it say to forward our own chats with these people?

Barbun has left the room.

Fredman: It did say that. Hey, didn't you say you'd met one of them?

Ted has left the room.

Fredman: Nothing exciting ever happens to me.
Bartender: Oh, I dunno, man. Didn't you notice two of those characters were scratching and winking?
Fredman: Whaaa?
Bartender: Scroll up your screen, man.

But there is no one in the room now but an indifferent bartender and a confused "Fredman," who squints at the screen, scrolling up and down, up and down.

Source: TavernLOG

End Jabba Entry

Toobe Entry

Back from some more surfing; it's all the same. Then that fucking govt announcement confirms it all, asking everyone to turn Scratch and Winc in. I couldn't log it cuz you have to have a special program.

But I finally got a message back.

>>To: Toobe
From: Winc
Subj: Natural born chillers

We know, my friend. No wonder you were frantic. We just heard/read the govt announcement. Confused here, Toober. Why me and Scratch? *What* is going on? Got to chew on this one, big time. But hey . . . ::bright smile:: Don't worry, dude. ::throwing my head back with a pirate laugh:: har-r-r-r! They'll never take us alive! ::savage outlaw grin::
—W.

P.S. Don't be concerned. We won't pollute your mailbox anymore with messages. But of course we'll get in touch with you . . . somehow. I'm sending *this* message via one of our mutual friend's bypasses (I am so glad you insisted I learn how to work it) but I probably won't use *this* name for awhile. ::snif::

P.P.S. About Scratch. Ze didn't use the bypass because ze said it's capitulating to the govt. Isn't that cool? Anyway, that's why *I'm* sending this. But Scratch knows, and will be careful too, and I'm setting hir up with a bypass over all hir (many and articulate) protestations.

P.P.P.S. Are people *really* scratching and winking? Have you seen that? Neat! ::softly:: I love you, and so does Scratch. More later.<<

Somehow I don't feel comforted. But I'm glad ze wrote.

End Toobe Entry

Narrative Entry, Jabbathehut

He's drumming his fingers on the edge of his desk. So they posted a Netwide warning. His electronic in-basket is overflowing, but it's worth it, he figures. He's getting the hang of it now. A pattern is starting to emerge.

Waterfall tattoo under the right eye. That's Winc, right? Right. Three out of five personas with the same tattoo. And Scratch is the one who can't seem to resist coming to the defense of some poor joker. It's slow work, but he's learning how to sift through it all. He's building a database, putting his pattern together.

A memo on his screen interrupts his methodical musings.

To: Ms. Budge
From: U'Sec L.
Subj: Good for you!

Wally, I hear you've got some hard evidence already. Glad to hear it. The clock is ticking, and the Media Relations people in the Bureau want to hand Scratch and Winc over to Justice on time. I know I can count on you.
—L.

(and do something about the "Ms."—people are starting to talk)

He laughs out loud, glad as always that they'd given him an office to himself so no one else could hear him laugh like that. He hates the way he laughs. So did two of this three exes. Evidence? She thinks I've got evidence? I've got bupkis. Oh, here's a good one.

>>To: Vina
From: GayMarket
Subj: Scratch and Winc

No dear, they're not gay men. They are a pair of dykes if I ever *saw* a pair of dykes! *No* gay man *I* know would *ever* do the wonderfully degrading things they do with ::rolling my eyes heavenward:: female genitalia, honey! And yes! I love your point. If we can get them to come out, admit they're gay, we've got a heavy wave of straight support on our side, and that *does* mean $$$$$$ in contributions, doesn't it! Can we work on their image though? PC-wise, that is? ::kiss kiss::

P.S. I've ordered the buttons—WE TAKE PRIDE IN SCRATCH AND WINC—with a little rainbow. Should sell an absolute *ton*. 20% of the proceeds to the Coalition, right? I can't afford to give you 50%, darling. The bills, oh the bills!<<

He leans his face against one hand, and types "Coalition," with the other.

He sighs. Is this the new "leg work"? Whatever happened to honest-to-god clues you could touch or smell? Leads, seedy informers in a smoky back room. Or fingerprints—that's going by the wayside too. He returns to the still-growing list of in-pouring bits and bytes.

"You're in there somewhere, I'm beginning to taste you," he mutters, and lights another cigarette.

End Jabba Entry

Source: persLOG/budge/harddrive

Toobe Entry

Turn them in? No way. What if they access my files and just make the connection anyway? What if they trace that stupid bulletin board memo I excerpted? This is what Scratch is always yammering about. They make it so easy to panic, and then the worst enemy you have is your own paranoid friends. Nope. Not going to do a thing. But I'm taking everything off my drive that could be accessed by somebody else's computer. Gonna go online again and search for sign-on sites that could be traced back to me. Don't want to be online for so long, but I'll do it late, when no one else is awake.

End Toobe Entry

Narrative Entry, Jabbathehut

If you were walking outside the Federal Bureau of Census and Statistics Building that evening, very late, and you looked up, you might see a lone office light burning.

He thinks, as he manipulates fields in his database, about that sex scene with Scratch as a skateboard kid, and Winc as a Generation X girl, or was it the other way around? Getting hard to tell who's what. But it was legit, maybe traceable, but probably too old. File it away, though. Could mean a pattern. Light a cigarette.

A too-cute giggle from his computer screen interrupts his thoughts.

Looking up, he sees Typhoid Mary sashaying across his screen, her eyes positively aglow with a cyber-rendition of triumph.

"Hel-l-l-l-o-o-o-o-o-o, Missy Budge," she says brightly. "Look what *I* found!"

Before he has a chance to reply, the hippie chick opens her duffel bag and withdraws a . . . magic wand? She waves it over her head and giggles. "Presto," she says, and Budge's screen is suddenly filled with a graphic image: the unfortunately bad high school photograph of Toobe.

And at the same instant Budge is staring at the unbelievably young face of his only perpetrator, he knows a similar staredown is happening on a teenager's screen. Halfway across the world, or is it only across town, he can just picture Toobe swallowing hard, gawking as suddenly into his own screen. For there he will see the automatic insertion of his own cyber "signature," the unforgiving federal photo ID of Lieutenant Wally Budge.

Neither stirs. They stare at each other's photos, the detective and the kid, their hands frozen over their keyboards.

In the background, Typhoid Mary hums "Do Not Forsake Me, Oh My Darling," and on two computers the old town clock slowly tolls twelve.

As one, two hands flash out toward two keyboards. The nicotine-stained finger wins, punching "Capture" before the younger hand reaches "Escape."

And two photos vanish from two computer screens, leaving Budge with his jaw hanging open, and an unsmoked cigarette burning between his fingers.

"He's a little kid," says Wally Budge aloud to no one. "Just a scared little kid."

"Got him, Boss," says Typhoid Mary. "Tracking sequence initiated and sustained. He can't get away now."

End Jabba Entry

Source: persLOG/budge/harddrive

Toobe Entry

>>To: **Jabbathehut**
From: **Toobe**
Subj: **Disappearing**

Jabba, you were wrong. Please send a memo very carefully to my friends: Orlio, Scratch, and Winc. Route it so no one
can trace it ever. I can't explain, but I got to go offline now.
I'm using a very complex bypass I stole from you. It's the
Shimomura one, so if you hear anything, or you can help me,
send me email to that node, cuz as far as I know it's untrace-
able still. You can use your own Shimo to trace what happened to me.<<

End Toobe Entry

Narrative Entry, Jabbathehut

In a green office, a very tired detective stares blankly at the screen.

The onscreen hippie is singing a little ditty as she packs up her duffel bag. "Pray for the
dead," she sings, "And the dead will pray for you."

"Sonata Number 2 in B-flat Minor, Opus 35," murmurs Wally Budge absently, "Chopin's
'Funeral March'."

Typhoid Mary smiles coyly, then switches her tune to a mangled version of "London Bridge
is Falling Down." She then steps lightly through an onscreen "door," leading her back through
cyberspace to "Perpetrator Toobe." She knows how to reach him now, wherever he goes.

"Bye, Missy. I'll keep you posted." And she's gone.

Wearily, he types a memo and sends it off.

To: **Henderson, Enforcement**
From: **Investigations**
Subj: **Top Priority / Scratch and Winc**

Phil, I'm attaching an electronic signature to this memo.
Follow it down, will you? He's hooked into this whole Scratch
and Winc thing. He's a minor. Keep me posted on every step.
I'll have a warrant by the time you've got him.
—Wally

◎ click here to read attached file: toobe.sig

Lt. Wally Budge, senior investigator for the Office of Internet Intelligence, Bureau of Census and Statistics, Federal Government of the United States of America, watches his message vanish from the screen, and whispers,

"A little kid."

End Jabba Entry

Source: persLOG/budge/harddrive

‹HAPTER SIX

Narrative Entry, Jabbathehut

I have the distasteful business of involving myself in the narrative at this point. What began as idle documenting of certain events as they occurred has now necessitated a small amount of intervention on my part. The surprise is that I have broken my own rule of remaining as neutral as the Swiss. I should mention my longtime friendship with Toobe's father, and admit my affection for the boy. At any rate, Toobe acted admirably in the face of his gross error by taking himself completely offline. I have set forward a chain of events that should keep him safe, but I had not anticipated the terrierlike quality of the law in matters cyber. As always, I had underestimated the amount of time on the hands of those who enforce where no enforcement is needed. Meanwhile . . .

***

Wally Budge listens to the terse voice of the undersecretary coming through his phone. Idly, he wonders what color her office is. He's never been in there, he realizes.

"Vanished, ma'am," he's saying. "Not a trace of him since we tagged him with the bloodhound virus five days ago."

"Yes, ma'am," he manages from time to time, phone cradled to his ear. He's heard it all before, pressure from the brass, duty, perseverance, national security. Reality check, he thinks to himself, this is the Bureau of Census and Statistics, right?

Such a promising beginning—the hunt, and then the onscreen tagging of the perp. But the kid went offline, and regardless of the complicated web of electronic Eyes and memos, if a person is offline, he or she is unreachable.

"I'm personally supervising every step of the way, ma'am," he states flatly. "Henderson's boys are on hold until they hear from me." Out of habit, he taps in "LOCATE," through his keyboard.

"Yes indeed, ma'am. Absolutely," he says into the receiver. The onscreen graphic icon in the granny skirt shrugs at him, as she was programmed to do when her quarry cannot be found.

"For now, ma'am. For now, that's right." The sound of the undersecretary hanging up her phone does not give him the comfort he'd hoped for. If only the kid would sign on, just for a second.

Source1: persLOG/budge/harddrive
Source2: bckupfiles@FBCS.gov

End Jabba Entry

Begin narrative entry, Gwynyth
Gwynythmydiary.logenterpassword *****:

Diary Entry: 12th of March, Dark of the Moon in three days
I got a message from Jabba out of the blue. "Expect 'a friend' to stay for some time." Must be dire or I would never have seen hide nor cyberhair. I've made up the spare bed. Hope this visitor isn't allergic to pusscats.

I must send a message to my Guides to aid Jabba, struggling technowiz and wounded healer, in finding some peace. Yang to my yin, near as I can tell. Aw, yang my sage pot. There's no reason or rhyme in "fighting god." Guides, let the wound be embraced. So be it.

Ninkip fares much better. Tossed a colossal hairball right into the center of my altar (good omen) and looked at me as though to say, "Fine now, Mom." Told the rest of the cats to steer clear, but would they listen? No, they want to eat it.

Have implemented worm code hecuba.antivir. Should do the trick for those ailing folks on the Well. And they can afford the hefty bill I sent them. Time to hit the thrift shops in search of some frippery and finery. Loot's on the way. Ha!
autoescape: Gwynythmydiary.logclose
End Gwynyth Entry

Narrative Entry, Jabbathehut
The cyberwitch is solitary, uninterested in the events of real time, online or off. She is a brilliant thinker and engineer, albeit eccentric and entirely self-taught. Her claim to fame is in "housekeeping" (a nasty word), where she is not only expert at cleaning up files, but at rendering links to and from various sources inoperable, retroactively. She was the logical one to turn to when requesting virtual succor for our two scalawags, and tangible haven for my persistent young charge.
End Jabba Entry

Begin narrative entry, Gwynyth
Gwynythmydiary.logenterpassword *****:

Diary Entry: 12th of March, Dark of the Moon in three days
Second diary entry in the same day. Two letters from Jabba in the same day. Blackbird perched on the thrift store awning. Found the perfect straw hat for the coming Equinox. My Guides are having a field day.

Jabba has requested I look out for one Scratch and Winc, and use my Craft and Code to protect them if need be. No questions asked when the large one requests, it's infrequent enough. Still, I am curious. On my way home, I passed several street vendors selling Scratch and Winc paraphernalia. What am I getting tangled up in? Must poke around a bit. I need to find a way to lure this Scratch and Winc into the safety of my Spot. Have modified my cyberland power spot; it's now ready to both welcome them, and ward off intruders. Modifications as follows:

Autochat installed. hiya-how's-the-weather-where-you-are? Bores the pants off me. Should discourage snoops.

• Autoalarm sensor sensitivity turned on high. Banshee wail will alert me to increased activity on the board. Ha! As if the cats need any more noise to deal with.

• circe.anti-Eye installed.

• autolog set to monitor all chat

Jabba, dear, if you are asking me to disturb my hermitage, your own lair must be getting compromised. I do not take this lightly.

autoescape: Gwynythmydiary.logclose

End Gwynyth entry

Narrative Entry, Jabbathehut

The sorcery of the cyberwitch came into play quite recently, when she was asked by a powerful technowizard to delete any traces of a young boy and his links to friends, government agencies, and the law itself. Under her care, the boy's whereabouts, either electronically or physically, will not be traced. Winc, Scratch, Orlio, and Jabbathehut are safely uncontaminated now, although the latter was never in much danger.

End Jabba Entry

Narrative Entry, Gwynyth
Gwynythmydiary.logenterpassword ×××××:

Diary Entry: 13th of March, Dark of the Moon in two days

The young charge has arrived, now firmly ensconced in the spare room. As I recall, that room is beneath the primary gearbox, so I've issued him earplugs.

He had a particularly virulent trace attached to each of his log-ons. I removed them, of course, he's quite safe now. But who would seek a child so thoroughly? He has more intelligence than I gave him credit for: He asked to see my hardware. By the time we reached Room Five, his tongue was hanging out. I showed him one or two arcane log-ons, sweetie that I am.

Note to myself: This new trace (who in heaven's name called it Typhoid Mary?) is more virulent than I suspected. Must crosscheck my detox codes. Must also warn that pup to stay away from logging on for the next day or two.

autoescape: Gwynythmydiary.logclose

End Gwynyth Entry

Narrative Entry, Jabbathehut

Unfortunately, people who are being protected often continue to act in the very manner that necessitated their protection, and my former protégé has slipped his bonds for a fatal moment.

> **>>To: Orlio**
> **From: Toobe**
> **Subj: absence**
> This is a quickie, my friend. I'm safe, offline, but I have
> run into the coolest technology I've ever discovered. It's as
> cool as my friend Jabba's, but it's set up really weird, and
> you have to invoke all these strange incantations as pass-
> words, so all I really got was this quick way into the Net for a
> second before this program called "Safesmudge" will force
> me offline again. (Don't ask, some protective device.) Just
> couldn't resist getting a message to you, pal. Don't worry
> about me.
> —T.<<

End Jabba Entry

Begin narrative entry, Gwynyth
Gwynythmydiary.logenterpassword ×××××:

Diary Entry: Who cares what day it is, the bloody moon is dark!

The child logged on without my knowledge or permission, using Safesmudge. Cute little tyke. If it weren't against my principles, I'd chop him up and feed him to the cats. Guides, I hope he used the most current Smudge version. Running a logcheck now, which should take a few hours to determine what he did exactly, and what havoc, if any, he wreaked. Jabba owes me, and I shall collect.

Note to myself: buy cat food.

autoescape: Gwynythmydiary.logclose

End Gwynyth Entry

Narrative Entry, Jabbathehut

My accomplishments over many years are legend, and I have no need to doubt perfection. I have read, however, that in every Persian carpet there is a flaw, and that this flaw is intentionally woven in, lest the carpet be perfect, and thus be an affront to the gods. If every last Persion rug-weaver can allow for humanity, then it seems fair, if galling, that I do as well. Perhaps I've erred in sending Toobe to the cyberwitch, as she was so gracious to point out to me:

>>To: **Jabbathehut**
From: **Gwynyth**
Subj: **Hope your karmic debts are paid in full**
Young, troublesome male is living with me and is, despite his mischief, safe for the time being. I think. Will know for sure in a few hours. You might have told me he has a propensity for not listening to warnings. We shall discuss repayment at a later date, when services have been fully rendered. If it were not so good to hear from you again, I would perhaps consider a small spell just to bug you.
—Gwyn<<

The following note arrived soon after:

>>To: **Jabbathehut**
From: **Gwynyth**
Subj: **Karmic credit card solid gold?**
It seems your two adventurers actually stumbled onto my board of their own accord. Their email to one another is routing through my server. It won't be long before they're using my cyberlair for their live chats. Oh, there's magick afoot, no mistake. My autolog follows, at no extra charge to you (I'm working on generosity).
Gwyn<<

I am vindicated for my decision to send the child to the cyberwitch, perhaps to the point of reconsidering my musings upon rug-weavers. After all, why not seek perfection if one can?

End Jabba Entry

Begin narrative entry, Gwynyth
Gwynythmydiary.logenterpassword ×××××:

Diary Entry: Dramadrama

Both my cyberlair and my real-time hobbit-hole have become hostels to the flotsam and jetsam of the digital seas. I have agreed to supply email logs (and chat-logs, when they occur) to my large friend.

AutoMailLog:

>>To: Gyrl
From: Razorfun@"encrypted"
Subj: Contact

You once told me when all else failed to find you under your simplest name. I hope I have found it. This is a contingent name. Although it is not my simplest, it is my most primitive persona. It is where I go when in danger. Please be aware of my need to don this persona, as I am fighting to keep my wits about me and to remain in contact with you, despite our peril.

There is a small area on the Net called Tree, which I created many months ago, and as recently as this morning, remains private. You are to leave messages for me there. Answer me the name of our mutual friend, and I will know it is you.

—RF.

To: RF
From: Gyrl@famtree.eor.com
Subj: Our friend

Tree? Like . . . here?

Um . . . name of mutual friend is Oobtay. Cool?

Is that really you? ::warily:: How'd you learn to encrypt your address? I'm trying to figure out what you mean by "cold persona," and I'm picking up *something*. I want to respect it but I'm *so* happy to hear from you.

—Gyrl

To: Gyrl
From: Razorfun
Subj: Coldness

Excellent. It is you. I am no one, I am merely essence. I cannot be baited, scared, or caught. There is no feeling in this place, only vengeance. I will not tolerate weak-egoed flackeys for the law following too closely from behind.

I would suggest you look to friends who have technical skills. We need assistance.

You look lovely tonight, naked and waiting for me. As I am simple, so must you be.

—RF.

To: Razorfun
From: Gyrl@famtree.eor.com
Subj: Our friend

::shiver:: I think I *like* this new persona. Scary, but intriguing. I blushed at your words!

Quick note: Remember me asking you about a friend of mine, J.? Remember? Ze's cool. More than cool. Ze's our life-line. For real.

Okay, this may sound weird, but we need to role play. Although I guess you don't need to be told that. ::glancing up at your note:: I have no idea who's reading what these days, and a role play won't get us as much attention if our letters are snagged and read, okay? It needs to be very . . . different. We need to build a world that's safe to talk in.

I've said enough. Love you way big, and *so* glad to hear from you!

"Razorfun"? I need more on that. Please? I'll read and reread yours for clues.

Also, just wondering, have you heard from our little friend lately?

—Gyrl

To: Gyrl
From: Razorfun
Subj: Coldness

You are mine. We are connected by blood and isolation from others. That's all you need to know. I will begin to work on another persona, as this one is too volatile for play.

And no, I haven't heard, but that's not unusual. Is it for you?

—RF

To: Razorfun
From: Gyrl
Subj: Yes

I await your requests of me. I am simply,
—Gyrl

To: Gyrl
From: Razorfun
Subj: Paris

We are in the French city, near Montmartre, where the flower stalls and booksellers spill their wares happily into the streets. Our mutual friend Jobert runs a bakery, where we will meet from time to time to receive hir assistance.

You are mine, little one, slave to my blade, to my will, to my cold need of you. You will refer to yourself only as "this one," for you have no name, as I have taken it from you. And I, Razorfun, am neither he nor she. In my despair at the vagaries of the world, I have retreated into a safer place inside myself. For it was our adventures afoul of the cages of gender that has apparently put us on the run.

To: RF
From: Gyrl
Subj: If it pleases

::she stands quietly at the entrance to small grove of trees, her heart pounding:: From the leftmost limb of the nearest tree flutters a small, square, black handkerchief. Trembling, she withdraws a paper and, looking over her shoulder to be sure she was not followed, she slips it into the neatly concealed hole in the branch. Were you to search and find her note, you might read the following: Thank heavens I've heard from you and you're safe. I've done as you instructed, praying this is the correct place.

I . . . this one . . . hears the coldness in your voice, and respects its depth with the deepness of her own heart, which she lays before you in hopes of providing some comfort in this hour.

This one has constructed a world to honor your Tree, understanding your desire for safety. And here, this one waits for her beloved Razorfun. She sits by her window, gazing at the sunrise as she hears the morning vendors in the marketplace. Some days, she threads her way through the stalls, a familiar sight in the earlier hours. Other days, she is so distracted by her longing that she goes barefoot, wandering where she will. In her distraction she finds herself at a small patisserie and café where she knows she will find their trusted friend: Jobert, the smiling, rotund, proprietor of the establishment.

Each day, she asks Jobert if ze has heard from . . . from the one who holds her heart with fingers like polished blades. "Non, mademoiselle," comes the answer, accompanied by a sad smile and the offer of café au lait. But she is patient. She will appear at the bakery each morning just after sunrise to learn of the one who knows her more deeply than she has ever been known before.

—G.

To: Gyrl
From: Razorfun
Subj: Old pathways

You have responded well. Now, little one, we must seek clues. You must carefully visit your old haunts, through a confusing series of twists and turns, for there you will find word from Jobert. Bring word from hir to me, as I have similar communication from hir. Together, we will determine the best path for us.

I gaze at you kneeling at my feet, comforted by your obeisance, my thoughts distracted by the fate of our young friend. I stroke your hair absently, grabbing it gently, then cupping your face to mine. My gyrl, how I have missed you.

—RF.<<

These are the nation's leading scofflaws? America's most wanted? Is Jabba's heart really beginning to thaw?

Note to myself: Thaw out the portobello mushroom steaks for dinner.

autoescape: Gwynythmydiary.logclose

End Gwynyth Entry

Narrative Entry, Jabbathehut

Lieutenant Wally Budge is a happy man. Pieces are coming together, slowly, as they always have. Those jig-sawed bits of information have positively linked the forlorn Toobe with this Scratch and Winc pair. It took a few hours with his computers and wall charts, but some theories are beginning to pan out.

"Gotta add corruption of a minor to the charges," he mutters almost protectively as he types his memo.

To: All Personel—Investigations/ Enforcement
From: Investigations
Subj: Scratch/Winc TOP PRIORITY
cc: U-Sec L

Hard evidence here now links suspects Scratch and Winc to suspect Toobe. Maintain all surveillance for Toobe, and my earlier directive that no direct action to be taken without my green light.
—Lt. Wally Budge, Sr. Ivstgtr

He smiles at his memo, pausing before he sends it. His files indicate these two are not merely accomplices. They're friends, which means they'll be in touch. He'll use the kid as a decoy for Scratch and Winc, plan 1-A in any police manual.

Before he can send the memo, another appears on his computer screen.

To: Ms. Budge
From: S_Dunlap
Subj: Good for You!

Walls, I'm glad you finally got your break! Everyone in the Bureau's been on edge, and now they all think you're marvelous again! I've made your reservations. There's an electronic key attached to this memo. Use it to pick up your plane tickets.

Celebration dinner when you return?
—Shel (can't get used to the "Ms")

© click here to download attached file: Cltix.KEY

Huh?

He stares at his unsent memo. What break? And how would Shelly know? Before he can reply, a third memo obscures the others on his computer screen.

To: Ms. Budge
From: Henderson
Subj: Perp Toobe

Wally,

We got lucky today. The kid signed on long enough for our automatic scanning tracer to catch him. (Didn't you get cleared for one of those? The Typhoid thing you have is cute, but it's really limited without the expanded access.) The perp is in New York. See attached confid file for details. You're not going to believe where we traced him to. We've got a network of 20 uniforms closing in, but we're going to need you to make the collar. Shelly has your flight reservations ready, check with her for details.

It's all coming down. Good work so far.

—Henderson

P.S. You might seriously consider losing this flakey screen name of yours.

◉ click here to read attached file: nymap.DOC

"DAMN THEM," he roars in his empty office. Furious, he punches in REPLY.

To: Henderson
From: Ms. Budge
Subj: Perp. Toobe

What the HELL is going on? I never authorized a close-in! This kid is connected to the whole Scratch and Winc thing, and you're sending UNIFORMS? What IDIOT authorized THAT? CANCEL CANCEL CANCEL the plans. We need to walk QUIET here, not broadcast everything. I'm PISSED OFF and SOMEONE's head is going to roll.

—ˣMisterˣ Lieutenant Wallace Budge.

He stares at what he's written.

Wally Budge finally gets it.

"They went right over my head. I'm alone on this one. Time to play the cards close to my chest. Real close." He deletes both his unsent memos.

"New York, huh?" he wonders aloud. "So the kid's in my old stomping grounds. But where, exactly? Where?"

Source1: persLOG/budge/harddrive
Source2: bckupfiles @ FBCS.gov

***

Private narrative, Jabbathehut (con't):

The cryptic remark from Henderson regarding Toobe's location is cause for some concern. I simply cannot risk leaving him where he is, endangering himself and my dear witch-friend.

End Jabba Entry

Begin narrative entry, Gwynyth
Gwynyth\mydiary.log\enterpassword *****:

AutoMailLog:

>>To: Razorfun
From: Gyrl
Subj: With utmost respect

::kneeling, head bowed, trembling:: This one begs your permission to speak freely and out of role, knowing as she does, the possible consequences and the hardship it would bring you. But this one assures you she feels it is necessary for both your safety and hers, and for the safety of our mutual friend.
—G.

To: Gyrl
From: Razorfun
Subj: Role

Of course, the safety of us all is the most important here. It does rattle me to leave the role, but it is necessary.
—RF.

To: Razorfun
From: Gyrl
Subj: Our pal

Sorry about the role-break (::shyly:: I ˣlikeˣ that role, and we need to talk later about it, if you'd like . . .) but we've got trouble. The following note came from our friend Jobert. I'm scared, it's a few days old. Leave a note in the tree ASAP, please!
—G./W.

>>To: Winc
From: Jabbathehut
Subj: Our friend

Do not contact me directly. Although I'm fairly impervious to inept governmental interferences, in the current climate of paranoia and panic I think it best to keep our channels clean. Please respond to me circuitously, using the tools supplied you long ago by our young friend. Enclosed you will find a sequence of events explaining his disappearance. You will see that at a crucial point in the exchange, his general whereabouts became known to the lawman at the other end of the exchange, a Wallace Budge, of the FBCS. This mid-space "capture" prompted our sprout to pop offline. But despite my efforts to cache his person in safety, he has risked discovery again and needs help. I hope that you are not so dizzy with your new (albeit unfathomable) fame that you have forgotten you can help him. I do not leave my own domain, for reasons perhaps he has explained to you. But I suggest you take yourself and your cyberfriend to meet him where he is. I dare not reveal his whereabouts online in any integrated form. A clue will follow for each of you.

Think of it like this: You each have a piece of the puzzle, and you cannot possibly hope to figure it out without each other. Rest assured I would not make the clues so dense that you could not understand them. Go live only when you're comparing messages. I have buried a protective agent for such exchanges. Do not, repeat DO NOT forward this message.
—J.<<

Oh, Scratch, I just shot this off to you before reading that last line! I'm scared. Do the cyber equivalent of eating this one. Meet me in Private Room "Scared" within alt.bbs.Farm Report, 6pm EST.
—W.

To: **Gyrl**
From: **Razorfun**
Subj: **Farm Report?**
    Where'd you dig this one up?
—S.

To: **Razorfun**
From: **Gyrl**
Subj: **Digging**

I did an all-Net search on user frequency and learned that that folder is almost *never* used, so it's more private.
—W.<<

AutoChatLog:

Online Host: You are in "Scared."

Winc: I picked a hopeful name, huh? ::gulp::

Scratch. Well, this is serious! From what you've told me of Jabba she wouldn't throw out warnings easily.

Winc: Exactly. Look, I got some kind of weird clue from hir. Did you?

Scratch. Yeah. But why did the message come from Jabba?

Winc: I don't know. She knows everything, and never misses a chance to share the fact.

Scratch: I'm beginning to see that.

Winc: Anyway, Jabba said we should go live when we're comparing clues from her.

Scratch: OK.

Winc: ::hurriedly explaining:: Each of us has a protected segment of the clue, and they need to be put together in order to be read.

Scratch: Whatever the hell "protected" means.

Winc: Steady, darling. Let's merge the files. One . . . two . . . three . . .

Scratch: ::uploading::

Winc::::uploading::

Scratch. Oh, fine. That makes a whole lot of sense.

Winc: Whoa! Funky shoe!

Scratch: ::rolling eyes:: That's *not* a shoe!

Winc: Maybe I should have picked "confused" for the room name?

Scratch: Because we have no idea what this means? What's this "clue" supposed to be revealing, anyway?

Winc: Toobe's location?

Scratch: Oh, yeah, right.

Winc: ::puzzling over picture:: Not a shoe, not a shoe . . . hey! It's an erector set!

Scratch: I'm glad that's what you thought, that's all I got, too.

Winc: But Jabba's smart, she's picked something she knows we know.

Scratch: How do you know this character anyway?

Winc: Oh, it's a long story. I strayed into one of her domains one day. She's--wait!

Scratch. What?

Winc: It's a close-up view of something.

Scratch: Close-up?

Winc: Something through a window.

Scratch: Why do you say window?

Winc: There's curtains.

Scratch: Pretty smart.

Winc: *I* know!

Scratch: Don't be so modest.

Winc: No, darlin', I mean I know what I can do!

Scratch: What?

Winc: I'm gonna go ask Jabba what it means!

Scratch: Uh, Winc?

Winc: Let's see, I have to get out of here so I can use the #2 bypass, ::muttering:: Be right back!

Winc has left the room.

Scratch: Winc, don't you think we ought to try to . . . and I'm just typing to myself right here.

Winc has entered the room.

Scratch: You could warn me with those disappearing acts, you know.

Winc: Oh, I'm sorry! I was excited!

///Anything I can help you with, cyberfolk?///

Private Message to Winc

Scratch: Christ! It's an Eye! Go back out for a minute. I think I may know this one.

Winc: ::jealously:: That guy you boffed before, eh?

Scratch: No, darlin', it's a woman. Not many say "cyberfolk," so I think it's her. Go hang out somewhere for a bit. Please?

Winc: OK.

Winc has left the room.

Scratch: No thanks, Eye, just trollin' around a bit. I think I know you, don't I?

///An Eye is an Eye. What are you trolling for?///

Scratch: A bit of company, I guess. Do you know *me*? You're not Marie, are you?

///That's my name off duty. I'm an Eye, and you are Amazon38. You were in communication with another one, may I have that name?///

Private Message to Scratch

Winc: SCRATCH! Just realized you're on with your real name! GET OUT!

Scratch: No, no, that's what's weird. The Eye thinks I'm somebody else entirely.

Winc: ::purring:: Well you are, dear. But how is *that* happening?

Scratch: Dunno. I'll let you know when I find out.

Winc: ::dubious:: Just be careful.

Scratch: Sorry, Marie, you have a distinct, memorable style. See you later.

Amazon38 has left the room.

///Retrieve Amazon38 and Hold.///

Private Message to Winc

Scratch: She's not reading my screen name right. I thought we were dead meat!

Winc: I know, I'm finding stuff out about that!

///Sorry to be so gruff.
Eyes have to stay pretty upright you know.///

Scratch: Why'd you call me back? Are you really "holding" me or were you just showing off?

///You make me laugh. I get off in about 10 minutes, want to hang out? You *are* a woman, aren't you? Did we meet in the Women's section that time?///

Scratch: Yeah, of course I'm a woman. That was me!

Private Message to Winc:

Scratch: I believe I got a Sapphist here, friend, and she thinks I'm one too.
Winc: Go for it, if it gets us by, but hang on, I've found some really cool stuff!
Scratch: Send it on, pal. I'll distract her, if I can, and I'll let you know when it's all clear.
Winc: Oh, the sacrifices you make for li'l ol' me. heehee.

Scratch: I'll hang out, but 10 minutes is so long . . .

////Well, I don't really have to be in another sector. Shall we go to a private room?///

Scratch: That'd be great, but do you think you could . .

///What? Go ahead.///

Scratch: No, never mind.

///Tell me. Really, it's OK.///

Scratch: Do you think you could become Marie first?

///::laughing::///

Scratch: Kinda like taking off your holster I guess.

///No problem.///

Marie: Better?
Scratch: Wow. You don't even have to leave the room.
Marie: Of course not. Let's go to 13Lounge.
Scratch: OK.

Private Message to Scratch

Winc: You aren't gonna believe this, hon, but there's a reason she hasn't forwarded your little butt to the cops.
Scratch: ::sweating profusely:: and the reason is?
Winc: She's not seeing your name. It appears as . . . checking:: "Amazon38."

Scratch: I know! Why?

Winc: Hang on. I'll forward an automatic message I just found.

You are in 13Lounge.

Scratch: What's the significance of "13Lounge"?

Marie: Just an Eye lounge. It's secure.

Scratch: More secure than the private rooms the rest of us use?

Marie: Let's not talk about work.

Scratch: No problem, lady.

Marie: You know, maybe this wasn't such a good idea.

Scratch: Why?

Marie: I'm kinda in a hurry, and I . . .

Scratch: I pulled you off duty?

Marie: No! I mean I'm . . . eager. And I don't like to stay . . .

Scratch: . . . in uniform?

Marie. Exactly! I like to be able to let down a little.

Scratch: Or a lot?

Marie. ::eyes down:: Yes.

Scratch: I'm thinking of you on your knees in a bathtub.

Marie. Oh, that's a very good start.

Private Message to Scratch

Winc: OK, here it is. There's a "safespace option," so it'll come to your screen but no one else sees it! Weirrrrd!

AutoForward to Scratch

Automatic Host: You have reached the domain of Gwynyth, either by accident or by choice. As a protective measure, a Circe device has been placed on your communications, rendering your onscreen name "invisible" and replaced with another more suitable for this area. This is a safe haven, by Code and by Craft, and all rules *will* be respected. *So be it.*

Scratch: I don't have much time, I want you now.

Marie: ::softly:: good.

Scratch: I'm running a little water in the tub, I'm supposed to be lovingly drawing you a bath, but . . .

Marie: I'm being bad.

Scratch: I'm taking--right. You're a bad girl. I grab

you around the waist, half lifting you up, grabbing for
your cunt.
Marie: Y-y-y-ess.
Scratch: You're wet already, little girl.
Marie: I'm sorry.
Scratch: You've been thinking nasty thoughts.
Marie: Yes.
Scratch: My hand is rubbing your clit, my other sneak-
ing around behind you, teasing your cunt. But I refuse
to go in.
Marie: ::whimpering::
Scratch: I put two fingers just inside, but you want it--
Marie: Deeper.
Scratch: Yes, but I won't, you know, not until you open
way up.
Marie. ::Opening::

Private message to Winc:

Scratch: You won't believe what's happening. Guess what the "way
powerful" want?
Winc: ::dryly:: To be dominated?
Scratch: Yep.
Winc: As Jabba would say, how predictable.
Scratch: I think we're gonna be OK, if you can just hold on a little
more.
Winc: Scratch? Make it short, OK?
Scratch: Aw, don't be jealous.
Winc: It's not that. Darling, we're in the middle of rescuing
someone.
Scratch: I haven't forgotten that! Do you know how weird it is to be
having sex at a time like this?
Winc: ::patting your little head::

Scratch: Not yet. You writhe in the water, spreading
your legs as far as the tub will let you. How dare you
lift your ass that way!
Marie: I'm sorry, I . . .
Scratch: I climb into the tub with you, clothes and
all, my boots tromping on your bare feet, trapping you.
Marie: Please—
Scratch: I lift your ass against me, lift you high, my
hand working furiously on your clit. Your cunt begins
to open. I take my hand away.

Marie: Oh!

Scratch: I slide it up to your breasts, pinching.

Marie: Yessss.

Scratch: I'm straddling you, lifting your ass against me, pushing my crotch into you. I dip your head down into the water.

Marie: I'm choking.

Scratch: Yes. I lift your head out, then dip it in again.

Private Message to Scratch

Winc: My name isn't being seen either! An Eye just strolled by and called me Diana!

Scratch: ::struggling:: That's incredible!

Winc: We've got a guardian angel, Scratch!<<

Guardian angel my bony ass. It's all done with mirrors and Code.

>>**Marie**: My cunt is pouring, opening.

Scratch: I slide my hand down your back, around your ass, to your cunt. I plunge in with three fingers.

Marie: Yes!

Scratch: I turn my hand, and slide in another, then cup my whole hand, pushing.

Marie: ::very still, lifting my ass::

Scratch: Slowly, I lower you down back on your knees. My hand makes slower circles on your clit. I push my hand, turn it, cup it, reveling in the juices. And then, quickly, I slide my whole hand in.

Marie: Yes, please!

Scratch: I close my fingers together into a fist.

Marie: Ohhh, pain!

Scratch: Yes. I hold my hand very still.

Marie: Please, yes just a minute. Hurts. Deep, but touching me so deep.

Scratch: My thumb is tucked inside my fingers. I expand just a little.

Marie: Oh yes, just a little . . .

Scratch: My other hand concentrates on your clit. The water is getting deeper, up over the top of my boots. It starts lapping up your thighs, warm, touching you everywhere slowly as it rises.

Marie: Your hand moves inside me.

Scratch: ::laughing:: yes, moving.

Marie: It feels so good.

Scratch: ::gritting my teeth:: This isn't for you, girl, it's for me. What're you doing with your ass up in the air like that? What kinda horny girl are you?

Marie: ::whispering:: Very horny. All day, keeping it inside.

Scratch: I start pumping my fist in you, turning it around inside you, fast, then slow.

Marie: Oh, god, no don't.

Private Message to Scratch

Winc: ::Brightly:: How ya doin', Scratch ol' pal? ::doing a little Snoopy dance on top of your computer:: Having fun, are you?

Scratch: :X

Winc: ::gleeful chuckle::

Scratch: I'm . . . sorry. To be doing this, I mean.

Winc: ::softly:: Darlin', if it's keeping us safe, go for it. This "protective device" might not hold out forever. Later this Eye may be asked if she saw us. If you're as good as ever, I think our passage will be safer now.

Scratch: ::softly:: That's so cool of you. Thank you.

Scratch: Yes, I will. Pushing inside, rubbing your clit. Feeling it expand and jump under my hand. My fist is sliding around in your wetness, pouring out of you. I push harder . . .

Marie: . . . and contract around your fist, tighter and tighter, so you can hardly move.

Scratch: I circle my other hand harder around your clit, moving all up and down your lips, and back again.

Marie: I press down, my ass hard against you, I'm tightening . . . my legs shuddering.

Scratch: I can feel you start to come. I lift you up higher, the water splashing around us.

Marie: I'm coming . . .

Scratch: Spasms against my hand, almost crushing my fist inside you.

Scratch: Marie? Fuck, are you gone?

Marie: I'm here.

Scratch: I am too.

Marie: No tenderness, just bye, OK?

Scratch: You sure?

Marie: Yeah. Bye.

Marie has left the room.

Scratch: But, but! ::muttering to self:: It's not like you want to see her again . . .

Exit Amazon38. Room closed.

Scratch: Hey! I was kicked out! What room am I in now?

Private Message to Winc

Scratch: OK, you can come back now.

Only I'm not sure where I am.

Winc: That good, huh?

Scratch: No, I mean, there are no names here, no name of the Eye, nothing.

Winc: Just go back into the room we were in.

Scratch: OK.

Online Host: You are in "Scared."
Winc has entered the room.

Winc: Jabba answered within an hour--this is a record! How was your little, umm . . . delay?

Scratch: Kinda weird. Quick, like I said, Eyes can change their screen names, and enter a room without your knowing it.

Winc: Yeah?

Scratch: I'm not sure she even knew she was in this "Gwynyth domain" at all. I think all she thought was "Farm Report," and that it was urgent.

Winc: ::chuckling:: Are you *trying* to get me jealous?

Scratch: No, I mean, I think I feel kind of used.

Winc: ::nodding:: So, is she gone? Are we safe?

Scratch: Yeah.

Winc: OK, I'll just retype what I got from Jabba here onscreen, no forward. Here goes:

alpha%^&*#$%(anon

Scratch: Do you know what that means?

Winc: ::helpfully:: That she's pissed?

Scratch: ::laughing:: It's a code! Do you know the translation?

Winc: No. Actually, it's what she always sends me. It's a way she has of saying "recipient is stupid."

Scratch: And you put up with this?

Winc: Like I said, it's a long story. There's that one word: Anon. Is she trying to say it's anonymous?

Scratch: No. ::thinking:: Maybe it means "soon." Like Shakespeare language, soon. As in "See you anon."

Winc: Right! Ze talks like that! So there's more?

Scratch: Yeah. I think. Check your mailbox again.

Winc has left the room.
Winc has entered the room.

Winc: ::bursting into room, out of breath:: OK, here it is. Retyping now:

> "Got to see a man about a horse. Two men and two horses in fact. And if I don't see them I'll just spin around by a river."

Winc: ::brightly:: OK, do *you* know what that means?

Scratch: Oh sure. Hmm . . . ::thinking::

Winc: You've read more, I bet it comes from literature.

Scratch: Literature's kind of a big area, my love. How long have you known Jabba?

Winc: A few years maybe. She's weird, but I like her.

Scratch: So she's definitely female?

Winc: ::laughing:: Oh, it's Toobe's game. He was trying to show me how much he'd been thinking about the pro-noun thing, so he thought he'd balance out the "default masculine pronoun."

Scratch: By calling Jabba a she?

Winc: Right. But I really don't know, and neither does Toobe. I do know that "she" doesn't go in for "hir" and "ze." Thinks it's stupid, like everything else.

Scratch: Stupid?

Winc: She spends a whole lot of time being disgusted with people. But one thing I do know, she's huge. That's why "Jabba." There are little hints I get, like she doesn't fit in the world so well.

Scratch: Kind of like us.

Winc: ::wincing:: Yeah. Anyway, she's smart, so she-- Wait! ::staring at picture::

Scratch: Yeah?

Winc: I got it! That's the Eiffel Tower! Well, a teeny, tiny part of the Eiffel Tower. What a strange view! Step way back from your screen and you'll see it!

::thinking:: WHOA! I'm sure it's the Eiffel Tower . . . there's statues of two guys on horses. Right next to a carousel by the Seine!

Scratch: Huh?

Winc: Spin by the river! That's it! The carousel!

Scratch: You're stretching now, pal.

Winc: It's way close up. Really, way.

Scratch: The Seine, as in Paris?

Winc: Yep. It's the view from some hotel right next to the Tower. That's the keyword! That hotel!

Scratch: Um, Winc?

Winc: I'm sure of it! J. and I were talking one day and she knows I've been there. Because I was so tripped out that there were *hotels* so near to the Tower! Isn't that amazing? I mean, you'd think that there'd be *nothing* next to the Tower, but . . .

Scratch: ::tapping my foot::

Winc: ::pouting:: OK, I'm typing in the name of the hotel now.

Scratch: How'm I gonna know what you see? Don't we have to put this together?

Winc: Oh, right. ::brightening:: Wait! I've got a program of hers, called Jabbawindow. Uploading now. It'll go through two bypasses, then to Farm room. Retrieve it from Hog Reports, no one goes there.

Scratch: ::sighing:: OK.

Winc: ::gently:: Scratch, please trust me? It's not hard. You'll be able to find it.

Scratch: ::Trusting, trusting:: ::downloading:: Got it. Wow!

Winc: Now you should be able to see what I'm doing!

Jabbawindow

> >Hotel Andrean\enter.
>
> **Incorrect password.**

Winc: Oh, darn!

Scratch: Well, leave off the hotel part.

Winc: No, that's part of the name.

Scratch: Don't the French have all those du's and de's? Is there a . . .

Winc: Right!

JabbaWindow

> >Hotel d'Andrean\enter.
>
> **Entering Jabbaworld**

Winc: Yowee!

Scratch: Good job! ::shyly:: Good thing we had Paris on our minds.

Winc: ::smiling at you:: Yes, good thing.

Jabbaworld Message

> If you're reading this past 10pm, you're either in trouble yourselves or you're lacking imagination and/or education. My guess is the latter.

Winc: ::dryly:: I've got 10:30, how about you dear?

Scratch: 10:30 here, too.

Winc: ::shyly:: That means we're in the same time zone. I like that.

Scratch: Uh huh. New window opening up. Read on.

Jabbaworld Message

> Toobe has no access to the Net, repeat none: not email, not bypass, not any of my special "fixes," etc. He is safe at present, but there is the slight possibili-

ty that the law knows exactly where he is and is
closing in.

Scratch: Poor little shit.
Winc: Yeah.

Jabbaworld Message

He needs your help in real time. Real . . . ::spelling it
out for you:: You-have-to-go-in-person-to-get-him.

Winc: Right.! Let's do it! ::heading for the door::
Scratch: How?
Winc: Oh. ::turning, sheepish::

Jabbaworld Message

Should you be wondering why *you* need to go, I
will take the trouble to explain once again. If you
would use your obviously fertile minds for something
more than cybersex, you'd realize that the young
Toobe is just that: young. If the media gets a whiff of
his age, there will be "CHILD PORN RING" written over
all your foreheads. *But* for some reason incomprehensible to me, *you* are the only ones he will trust.
Sigh.

Winc: Child porn?! Us?
Scratch: That is ABSURD!

Jabbaworld Message

Please grow up and smell the public sentiment. It's
bad enough that you're connected to the youngster. I
have him staying temporarily at a friend's home, and
he needs to be taken from there to a more permanent place until all this blows over. Do you understand?

Scratch: Hey, how is Jabba able to contact us?
Winc: Read on.

Jabbaworld Message

The reason I can contact you is because you got
into a new bypass. However, the arbitrarily efficient

> cyberpolice are decoding almost as fast as I can cre-
> ate these days. They've put lots more geeks on this
> case and I'm actually having to get tricky. It's usually
> amusing, but I may be a bit rusty. Be careful. Anyone
> related to Toobe is being checked now. Not all of the
> gendarmes may know that the famous S & W know
> him, but they will.

Scratch: Winc?
Winc: Mmm?
Scratch: Where is Toobe? Did I miss something?
Winc: Oh, right. ::scrolling through entire chat session::
Scratch: Maybe we're supposed to keep putting our mes-
sages together. Let's each check our mail again.
Winc: ::purring:: You're so smart!

Winc has left the room.
Scratch has left the room.
Winc has entered the room.
Scratch has entered the room.

Scratch: OK, I'm uploading my coded message to
Jabbawindow.
Winc: Right, dear. Me too.

Jabbaworld Message

Island
Coney

Scratch: island coney?
Winc: Coney Island! New York!
Scratch: ::doubtfully:: That's where he is?
Winc: Gotta be. And that makes sense. It's skateboard-
ing heaven, of course he would go there.
Scratch: I don't know if that's why, Winc. But let's
go!<<

Gwyn.mydiary.cont.

There is no indication of their plan, as enthusiastic as they may have seemed. There was no more communication between them, but they seemed bent on taking off . . . for here! Not that they know where here really is.

Snagged this out from under the govt three minutes ago:

>>To: FBCS All Hands
From: Henderson, Enforcement
Subject: Child abduction?

ATTENTION: We have an unconfirmed report that perp Toobe is a juvenile, and may be under the influence of a cult of mind-control hackers, or victim of an East Coast child pornography ring. Arrangements have been made to transport perp to Bellevue Psychiatric for investigation upon apprehension.
—H<<

autoescape: Gwynythmydiary.logclose

End Gwynyth Entry

‹HAPTER SEVEN

Begin narrative entry, Gwynyth
Gwynythmydiary.logenterpassword ✕✕✕✕✕:

E-FFiti of the Day
Comedy = Tragedy + Time.
—Laura Love, Musician

Diary Entry: I'm Beginning to Enjoy All This

Toobe asked me to post one of his e-ffiti messages. Dear child. He's got them stored away like acorns. I have allowed him to send a piece of email just now, heavily encrypted of course:

>>**To: Winc@"encrypted"**
From: Toobe@"encrypted"
Subj: Help?
cc: Scratch@"encrypted"

Guys, I gotta tell you, I'm scared. I'm safe at the moment but you wouldn't believe a memo I saw—about me!—from the cops. They're saying I could go to the looney bin. I don't get it, how did it come to this? I'm one of those Most Wanted doodes . . .

I've been trying to get through to my dad but they've got his house and work BUGGED! There's no way you can answer this, but I hope I get to see you *soon* for real.

—T.

P.S. Just so you know this isn't some govt trick and that it's really me—Winc LOVE your belt buckle!

◎ click here to read attached file: ABDUCT?.DOC<<

I'm working on a way to reach Toobe's father without being traced. If he gives his permission for Toobe to be "away from home," the authorities can't pursue. The little one is safer here than he knows, but if it gives him some comfort to reach his friends, then more kibbles to him.

His friends certainly responded quickly.

AutoChatLog:

>>**Frankie**: ::arriving in room, out of breath:: You get T's message?

Johnny: ::nervously looking around for cops:: Uh huh. Think it's real?

Frankie: ::groaning:: I wouldn't let anyone else see that belt buckle . . .

Johnny: So we definitely go? What can we *do* for him?

Frankie: I don't know what we can do, but yes, we definitely go.

Johnny: Don't we need a plan?

Frankie: ::eyes sparkling:: Oh yes, definitely. I'm working on it, handsome. We gotta beat it right now, ::popping gum:: but I'll send you some mail.<<

AutoMailLog:

>>**To: Razorfun**
From: Gyrl
Subj: Morphin' USA

Got it! They're gonna be looking for our friend the surfin' teenager, right? Let's morph him into something else, something completely different! Real time, in life! Let's make him a girl, and we'll be his parents! We'd blend right in, no one would notice us, waltzing right out of there, just a happy little family. (I'm assuming you're the right age to morph as a parent of a fifteen-year-old.) You up for this?

—W.

To: Gyrl
From: Razorfun
Subj: Parents

::narrowing eyes:: Who's playing whom? I'm NOT saying I'm going along with this, I just want to know what you had in mind.

—S.

To: Razorfun
From: Gyrl
Subj: Depends on . . .

. . . your height. I'm 5'10", how about you? ::innocently::

whoever's tallest is the father, the shorter one gets to be mom, was what I was thinking. Got a mustache? Going to shave it off? Grow one? Go to a costume store, hmmmmm?

    ::eyes twinkling::

—W.

To: Gyrl
From: Razorfun
Subj: You're *how* tall?!

    Sigh. I guess I'm the mother. How did I *know* it would lead to this? I'm 5 . . . never mind what height I am.

—S.

To: Razorfun
From: Gyrl
Subj: You're so brave

    ::gently:: I'm sorry if it's difficult for you, dear. It was just an idea. Although your reluctance is giving me a big hint as to who/what you are!

—W.

To: Gyrl
From: Razorfun
Subj: ::eyes twinkling::

    I doubt it. Oh, what the hell, it's too outrageous to fail. Gawd, can you just see it?

    I tell ya, "drag" is a good name; the prospect doesn't appeal to me at all. But you're right, they won't be looking for that. I'll be at the roller coaster, sliding around reluctantly on high heels and tottering toward a tall man with a mustache, possibly accompanied by a young female teenager. Then I think of our little Toober: Surely he won't go along with this.

—S.

To: Razorfun
From: Gyrl
Subj: Amurican

    He doesn't have much of a choice. He'll be our shining

daughter, full of hope and promise and mascara. We are simply waiting to meet Mom! Can't wait to see you, and of course, what you will wear! ::ducking::
—W.

To: Gyrl
From: Razorfun
Subj: IHOP

Oh, groan. Okay, let me put a bland, midwestern wash over the whole thing: I'll leave behind stylish and you do the same with dapper. We've got to be practically invisible. You take a cab or something, okay? Me, I can't use my car (long story) so I'll rent something for our getaway. Gawd knows I won't be able to walk far in the kind of shoes I'm going to need.
—S.

P.S. You know, this is just another role. I mean, I'm nervous about meeting you in real time and all, but I love that we're going in drag. We won't be any different than hundreds of people facing the day. Right? ::shudder:: I just hope this morph is as hard for you as it is for me.

To: Razorfun
From: Gyrl
Subj: This role

::smiling gently:: I'll get there safely, hon. You do the same.

This role *is* hard for me, my love. ::softly:: I'm scared, but also relieved. We can put our theories to the test, non?
—W.<<

>>To: Razorfun
From: MailerDaemon
Subj: Returned Mail, Undelivered to "Gyrl"
The following mail is being returned to you unopened. Error # -97

xxxxxxxxx

Test, that's a good word for it. I've run down all the scenarios and realized it's fine whoever *you* are, I mean

185

whoever you are is okay with me. But the idea of what each of *you* would make *me* is still tripping me out. Without revealing yet who I am, what I'm fretting about is that depending on who you are then I'll become a queer, a straight person, or a freak in some way that may not be how I was a freak before. You know? The hardest thing would be if you were a man. That would be the biggest stretch for me.

Also, I can't seem to get my mind around the fact that nothing about the content will change, but the form will be changed completely. Something I didn't think I cared about (disappointing realization). But the world is not that "better place" I used to dream about when I was figuring out who I was going to love. I guess none of that makes sense, maybe it'll just be moot when we finally meet.

::shakily, but determinedly::

—S.<<

Oh, what fun! Time to get out the old paint pots and froufrou.

autoescape: Gwynythmydiary.logclose

End Gwynyth entry

Narrative Entry, Jabbathehut

The interior of this commerical airliner is a nice soothing shade of green. Speeding northward, Wally Budge isn't noticing any particular color just now. But soothing is what this federal gumshoe needs at the moment. It's not the wailing child in the seat across the aisle. It's not the overlarge man next to him, who seems to be perspiring a particularly vile cologne. It's the text currently scrolling on the screen of his PowerBook laptop computer.

To: Investigations@FBCS.gov
From: DevilsOwn
Subj: We're IN!

Okay, we've got access to one of the maildrops. It belongs to Winc, and that's the only name attached to it. No address, no phone. I've got three of my best working on it, but I recognize a familiar access-blocker here. If it's the cracker I think it is, this one's a blind alley.

To answer your question: No, I've never heard of any "mind-control cult of hackers." Pardon my saying so, but maybe you should lay off the Michael Crichton?

I was able to extract Winc's unread mail for you. This character sure gets around. Thanks for the prompt payment. A pleasure to do business with you.

—Dev

◉ click here to read attached file: WincMail.DOC

Yes, the geek minions of the Federal Bureau of Census and Statistics have hacked their way into the private online mailboxes of one of the suspects, Winc, and Lieutenant Budge always cringes at this part of investigations. Never mind the obvious fact that he's been dumped in at the very tail end of an investigation, that he started! Shaking his head to clear it, he begins reading.

>>Dear Winc,

Do you remember me? We met a long time ago in the Disabilities Forum. We had a good talk. My father says that if you are half as good as the police say you are that you'll get this message even if your mailbox is bugged. Well, I sure hope you're reading this, and I also hope you are what I think you are, a boy in a wheelchair like me, because you give me so much to look forward to. I really think it's fun to be other things online too. I am Registered, and so are my parents, but none of us believe the pornography or child abuse stuff they're saying about you because you never tried anything like that with me so thank you.

Your friend who likes you,

—Emilio Saldarriaga<<

According to DevilsOwn, Winc had not in fact retrieved this or any other message that Budge is now reading. On to the next missive.

>>Dear Winc,

Hey babe, remember me? ::wicked chuckle:: We got it on a couple of months ago. ::dangling long-handled spoon in front of your eyes to jog your memory:: Look, I just wanted to see if I could help--somehow. I know you're a dyke, even if those stupid cops can't figure it out. First time lesbian invisibility came in *handy*, huh?

Keep on doing what you need to do, girl. We're all proud of you for taking the heat. Speaking of heat, something's cooking and I can't go into it, but someone from the Coalition is going to probably contact you soon. ::curling my finger between your collar and your throat::

Until we meet again.

—MstrssBoot<<

"What the *hell* did they do with the long-handled spoon?" muses Budge aloud. He reads another:

>>Dear Winc,

You are going right to HELL! That is where you are going to spend the rest of your eternal life you are so sick you make me and every good person I know want to throw up. And if you ever show anyone the log of the filthy things you made me do online with you, I will tell them the truth that you did it not me so you might as well throw that log away and never show it to anyone ever.

—NCJes333@sen.gov<<

Amused, Budge makes a mental note to check the senator's email at a later date, but he figures *no one* deserves this next one . . .

>>DIE YOU FAGGOT WINK ASSHOLE-SUCKING HIPPIE SHIT, I HOPE THE COPS FUCKING TEAR YOUR FINGERS OFF<<

. . . and probably no one really deserved this one either . . .

>>Dear Mr. Winc,

We'd like to speak with you and Mr. Scratch concerning a made-for-television movie we're thinking of doing. No promises, of course. But I think the climate is right, and you could walk out of this deal a very rich man. Please contact me soonest.

—John Lancer, assistant to Barry Dillard

Paramount Television<<

Wally Budge stares out the window at the clouds. "Maybe they'll make *me* a very rich man for being the cop who catches them," he muses. One hour into the flight, one hour more to go. Then it's a half-hour helicopter ride to Coney Island? Budge has finished Winc's mail, and is reading his own, which isn't much better.

>>Lieutenant Budge,
　　My twelve-year-old son came home today with a tattoo under his right eye. My wife fainted when she saw it. If you don't catch this Scratch and Winc duo, and fast, I will personally come down to your DC offices and . . .<<
Budge presses DELETE, and scans the next letter.

>>Lieut. W. Budge—
　　As legal liaison for Family Values Above All (FVAA), I wanted you to have an advance copy of an article we hope to have released in the *Washington Post* this Sunday. We stand behind you, Lieutenant. Please call on us, and God be with you.
　　—Amos Rafferty, D.D., esq.

◎ click here to read attached file: ChilPorn.DOC <<

Budge grunts once, and scans the document:

FAMILY NEWS
Hard-Core Child Porn Hits Internet

By Matt Holloway, staff writer for
Concerned Parents Digest
　　　　This week's revelation of the crimes of "Scratch" and "Winc" is more than a routine unearthing of a Dirtybooks distributor. "Scratch" and "Winc" are currently at large, transmitting obscenity through interstate phone lines via their computer bulletin board system on the Internet. The case, which is currently being investigated by the Investigations Department of the Federal Bureau of Census and Statistics, served to open the eyes of both the computer network industry, Christians, and

> other concerned parents to the growing availability
> and acceptance of sexually explicit images over the
> emerging information superhighway and the erod-
> ing control of parents over the information their
> children take in.

Sheer frustration overcomes his natural repugnance, and Wally Budge turns to his unsuspecting, freely-perspiring seat companion, ready to launch a particurlarly vile invective. He
stares at the startled man who's trying to open his fifth bag of free peanuts, and decides,
reluctantly, against such an indulgence.

Source: persLOG/budge/harddrive

***

Jabba Entry, con't

There is what I call The Craze.

Flip any channel on radio or TV and it's Scratch and Winc, who are responsible for
bringing rain to the desert, driving children away from parents, solving the problems of quantum physics, or operating a huge contraband ring. In other words, no one knows anything, but
everyone is talking. Even *60 Minutes* has resorted to using "unnamed sources" and "it has
been reported that." That detestible tabloid *Hard Copy* has a fractured photo of Toobe which
they use for their opening teaser every night: "Have You Seen This Child?" No matter what the
truth, the Net is buzzing, the real world is tittering, and the vast wastelands of boredom are
being filled by the latest pop-cult phenomenon.

Speaking of the devils, I have received yet another entry from a coprotagonist, inexplic-
ably forwarded to me in hopes of getting it to our young fugitive. Of course at present that
would be unwise, but I will save it with the others.

—┤.

>>Scratch letter to Toobe

I don't know about you, dude, but I can NOT go out into
the world in a dress! I don't know how to shop for stockings,
and there's no way I'd ask my friends who do. For one thing
most of them are online and I don't want any of them to have
a hint of what we're about to do. Will this work? I've got to
admit if there really are cops bearing down, which I'm still
not sure is true, they won't be looking for a man, a woman,
and a young girl. But I've seen drag queens and they're way
obvious. On the other hand, a bland floral print (gagging

noises) and sensible shoes and my hubby in tow . . . pretty
unnoticable. So Winc's tall, eh? Damn, I'm short!<<

Meanwhile, aloft, Wally Budge has discovered a new toy: the air-phone in the seat-back directly in front of him can be hooked into the modem on his PowerBook. He's typing a memo, sucking away happily at the remains of the turkey breast sandwich (too dry) they'd served him for lunch half an hour ago.

He makes himself read the rest of the Family Values article:

> Sexually explicit discussion groups on the Internet,
> a "network of computer networks," are regularly
> logging the greatest number of messages by
> Internet's 40 million estimated users.
>   The difference between the red-light district of
> the past and the home cyberporn connection of
> today is the tolerance that has grown with the relax-
> ation of public attitudes and prosecutorial zeal.
> After a decade of high-profile convictions of people
> such as major pornography distributor Charles
> (Chuck) Winsl . . .

Shaken, Budge once again pushes DELETE. He types:

To: Mobile Enforcement
From: Mobile Investigations
Subj: URGENT: SEARCH PARAMETER MODIFICATION
    Henderson: Have reason to believe that juvenile suspect Toobe
may be in the company of . . .

He pauses. Give it away that Toobe is linked with Scratch and Winc? Not yet. He contin-ues typing.

    . . . in the company of two adults, or slightly older juveniles.
Accomplices may in fact be of any age, any race, any physical pre-
sentation. These adults or older juveniles are to be detained for questioning along with the kid, Toobe.
    No reason to believe there is any porn or mind control going on
(where did you *get* that?), so advise you call off the men in the
white coats.

Repeat, you are looking for a threesome, or one lone white juvenile male. I'll be there in less than two hours. Hold for questioning any, repeat *any* suspicious-looking threesome that includes the suspected perp until my arrival on site.

—Budge

He pushes SEND, marveling as the indicators at the top of his screen flash away—his memo is now in the hands of the search squad at Coney Island. Quite satisfied with his mastery of telecommunications, he leans back in his seat and ponders his real problem. It isn't catching the buggers. It's what to tell them they're charged with.

Source: persLOG/budge/harddrive

***

Narrative Entry, Jabbathehut con't

Scene: Coney Island
Time: Afternoon
Purpose: Unknown

A number of hysterical accounts of the Coney Island Rescue have been forwarded to me for some reason, I think because they are in the habit of forwarding their most intimate and unpublishable thoughts to one another, and in the absence of that conduit, dumped their diary scribblings off on me. The report:

It was one of those typically prespring, sunny afternoons in Coney Island.

A man in a checkered sport coat, with a mustache and unbearably cheap shoes stands with a young girl. She looks pouty, as most young girls do in the presence of their parents. They gaze out at the sea, and appear to be waiting for something. Soon they are joined by a plain, worn-looking woman. Apparently the man had spotted her from far off.

[And here I will lift a section from the missive Winc so graciously offered me]:

>>"How did you know it was hir?" Toobe asked me.

"I just knew," I said, and it was true. Ze was clearly a female, but looked like ze was in drag somehow. Awkward, the gait not quite right, the clothes seeming to fit funny. I could see hir tottering on hir shoes, even though they were almost flats and quite sensible. I wanted us all to hug, but as usual ze was aware of what was happening around us, while I was only aware of the rush of emotion in knowing we were safe, at least for the moment, the three of us. In the hysteria I realized crazily, "This is my family," and wanted to join hands with the two of them and swing round and round right there on the boardwalk. I laughed out loud, and guess what? Scratch was laughing, too.

"Look at us," ze said. "The people I care about most in the world are right here, in real time! I didn't expect us to look like this!"

It was like a simulpost, when we both would type the same thing online. Only there was no delay, and I was standing there, completely willing to stay like that forever. Toobe was grinning, innocent like the child he is, as if he believed that as long as we were literally surrounding him he was safe. But the moment ended so soon, and Scratch's eyes kept darting around, and sure enough, it did look like a number of dark-suited men were prowling, although none of them had looked our way, yet.

"We gotta go," Scratch said then, jolting me out of the reverie as surely as if an Eye had come onto my computer screen.

"We're just a family at Coney Island, and now we're going to the car, okay?" Scratch said.

I felt this thump inside, that we were nowhere near out of danger yet, and any minute we could be surrounded by the Bad Guys. I was so glad for Scratch right then: I couldn't begin to sort out whether ze looked like what I had imagined, but the feeling was the same; ze was making plans and I believed in hir and it was going to be all right.

But of course I had to play with hir: I put out my arm and ze had no choice but to hold on to it, while I took slow, measured steps that were just a tad too long for both hir and Toobe. I could hear hir grumbling all the way. Toobe was laughing quietly, and although I'm sure he felt awkward as hell in the (rather nice) pantyhose Gwynyth had supplied him, and (thank gawd for modern fashions) heavy combat boots and a backward baseball cap, he was a very pretty grrl. A little too much make-up, but Gwynyth was pretty smart with the application, all things considered.

We were walking out the main gate, I was nudging Scratch to show hir all the stands selling T-shirts with our names on them, when we got stopped by one of those men in the dark suits.

I nearly panicked. I remember turning to Scratch to find out what to do, but instead of Scratch, this sweet woman looks up into my face with all the warmth and confidence a . . . a man could wish for. So I did the only thing to do: I went into being Dad.

"Yes, officer?" I said, and I think "convivial" best expresses my performance. "Anything I can do for you?"

"The little woman" held on to my arm, and by this time, Toobe had no trouble at all looking like a very uncomfortable teenage girl.

The officer explained: a routine check. He was sorry to bother us, but it had something to do with—he lowered his voice so as not to offend the wife and child—the porn industry. They had orders, he said, to question any suspicious-looking threesomes. My brain is screaming, "Threesomes? They know?" But I got quite grave with him, nodding at him with this silent signal of thanks for not speaking too loudly.

My knees were shaking inside my baggy trousers.

Then this guy, the park's security guard, apologizes and says he needs to check my ID. You know about my driver's license, right? I figured that was it—we were caught—but just then, I see Scratch pinch Toobe's arm! And Toobe goes Ow. Then Scratch, smooth as silk, glides up to the guard and in this hushed voice, says, "Officer, I'm so sorry, but my daughter is having her first . . . well, you know . . . her first little visitor." The guard stared at Scratch, uncomprehending. So Scratch lowers hir voice again, but it's still loud enough for all of us to hear, and ze says, "It's her first period, Officer. She's having her monthly time, and we need to get her to a bathroom. Now."

Well, the guard goes pale, and Toobe goes even more pale. I'm staring at Scratch with a mixture of pure disbelief and admiration, and I turn to the shaken guy and look kind of apologetic and embarrassed and say "Sorry, officer . . ." and he shrugs back at me, real fast, and waves us on through.

We found the car (Scratch had rented one); Toobe dove into the backseat and started peeling off his pantyhose immediately, yowling about the shackles of the opposite sex or some such thing, and I said, how do you think I feel, peeled off my mustache, and wiped off the makeup that was concealing the tattoo under my eye. We were all hysterically laughing, relief and joy and tension spilling out of us. I was so . . . happy.<<

[I think it best to put Scratch's narrative here, as ze busies hirself with more of the details than Winc, who trailed off into some incomprehensible yammering.
—J.]

>>What a trip to see Winc take off that hat and see long hair spill down, and the mustache off, and wise, wise eyes. Ze's taller than me, and has the longest legs, I think that's what made hir look almost like a colt, kind of awkward. Then ze did that classic maneuver women do of reaching under hir dress to undo hir bra, but of course it was actually a roll of ace bandages that were keeping hir breasts down, and the juxtaposition of hir in that man's shirt with breasts all soft underneath them was sexy, like I like it. I thought, oh, good, two women, that's what we are. And started tripping on all that would mean, to me and to hir. But neither one of us knew the half of it.<<

Source 1: ScratchLog
Source 2: Winc Diary

End Jabba Entry

Toobe Entry

We were sitting in the rental car. Winc was driving, Scratch was in front with hir, and although it felt like we should be acting out some car chase, we weren't; no one could trace us. Then Scratch sez, and somehow I knew ze would be the one to bring it up: "Okay, what are we all really? I mean, in real life?"

Impatient as ze always is, Scratch wants revelation time.

"Okay, okay," says Scratch, "Here's what I am." Ze took a deep breath, but it was like the breath had nothing to blow. Ze started to smile, like ze could have said a bunch of things all at once and it wouldn't have answered hir own question.

"Why would this be the big question now, anyway?" ze said, more to hirself, looking out the window. "Not 'am I Jewish,' or 'where do I live' or 'do I like to ride horses'? Why would the biggie be what sex we are?"

I felt my heart sink. I was sitting in a car with my best friends and they were about talk about the gender thing. There was no way to leave. When just one of them starts in on it, my mind glazes over. "What does it matter?" is what I wanted to say, about what gender they really were, and now I wish I'd said it. Maybe it would have made a difference.

Scratch felt me fidgeting and thought it meant for hir to just get on with it.

"Okay," ze finally said, all the breath pushing out of hir in a whoosh. "I'm a girl, woman, crone, maiden, chick, bitch, cow, dyke, babe, sweet-pea, female person. This week I wanna look like Johnny Depp and last week it was Garbo. I wish I were black because I hate my skin and probably next week being a wolf would be even better."

Ze kept looking down, but the words kept pouring out.

"I'm not afraid to walk down the street alone because I am all those things inside without thinking about it; then somebody calls my name or rather, my sex, and I feel like I'm in a borrowed body, the body I was born into, easily recognizable, to other people, not to me. They want to sculpt it and dress it and reduce it and extend it but it's worked against me a lot or has had itself worked against.

"I'm a female," ze finished in a lower voice that trailed off. "And now my freedom's over." Ze looked over at Winc, who was quiet now.

"I haven't worn a dress in about twenty-five years." Scratch said. "I'm thirty-eight and in the last few years I've grown to love my face and my tits and for some reason my feet. I've heard 'ugly chick' in my head for so long it has no meaning anymore."

[No way ze's ugly! But in a flash I could see how ze does appear to Them, as ze put it.]

"Pushing forty, I started dressing and acting how I felt and realized it's my life and I'd been wasting a whole lot of time acting like it's someone else's."

Ze paused. "Do you know what happened when I started doing that?" But ze wasn't really waiting for our answer. "Nothing. Except," and Scratch started blushing, "I got a whole lot more dates from women."

For some reason I blushed, too.

"I feel I'm finally in my body," Scratch went on. "Which is funny because the second I went online I started being in a whole lot of other bodies, too."

"And how!" Winc said very quietly to himself, but Scratch heard it and kind of shifted like ze was uncomfortable.

Winc took a deep breath and said, "Okay, since you're being so honest. Um . . ." and then ze looked at me.

"That's all you're gonna say?!" Scratch asked. "You don't even want to know anything else?"

"Well, maybe who you like to sleep with." I looked at Winc like I didn't know who ze was.

"I like to sleep with my teddy bear and my modem at this point," Scratch snapped.

"That's not what I mean," Winc replied. But Scratch talks in paragraphs.

"I think I've slept with more men than women, but I'm not sure. I'm not sure of what I am or who I sleep with, I'm in transition right now. Not that I'm some fence-sitter, but right now, touching someone else's body whether it has a dick or cunt is equally scary to me. I prefer the company of women but sometimes it's as a man, so what does that make me? I have a mustache—I keep in a jar—and an old felt hat. Sometimes I go downtown and signal drinks from one end of the bar for people. Most times it's for women, sometimes it's for men. Gay men, mostly, but the point is I do it silently like there's a contract between me and the bartender that's as old as men drinking in a bar. Then I go home and take it all off and stare at my body and am shocked that I don't look like James Dean or don't have a tail. It kills me sometimes that I don't have a tail . . ."

Scratch looked up at Winc with a huge gape on hir face.

"I can't believe you asked that," Scratch finally said. "I can't tell you what I'm about sexually; I just arrived at being female. My kind of female," ze muttered.

"It makes a difference to me, that's all," said Winc, and ze didn't add anything else.

Then I looked at Winc all astonished, cuz I've never heard that kind of thing matter to hir before. Ze was being persistent in this way I'd never seen, like ze'd decided something. I never thought about who ze had sex with in real life; all I ever heard was about online, and that's all I told hir about too. Come to think of it, we'd never talked about the kind of sex we had offline. I guess I just assumed ze didn't have any either.

Scratch looked at Winc, studying hir. "You're worried about how we'll fuck?" ze said, kind of shaking hir head.

Winc kept hir eyes on the road. "No! Yes! Look, this is getting too nailed down! Remember, we didn't want to meet in real time? I never would've thought that you . . . we . . . can't we just go back online now?"

Scratch smiled. They looked at each other. I felt like I was reading somebody else's mail, and should get the hell out of there.

Right then Scratch said to me, "I'm really glad you're here, dude. You're keeping me honest."

"Yes, exactly," said Winc, and they both looked at each other like everything was all figured out now. I was thinking, I'm more confused than ever.

"I asked that stupid question," Winc said at a red light, turning back to Scratch, "because I ran into that problem: Who we are affects how we will be with each other. I have my part to say now and I'm scared as hell. So can we just get it over with?"

I wanted to be funny because of all this tension so I said, "Hey, I'm a guy, and I'm fifteen! That's my story!" and they both laughed.

Winc took a deep breath and said, "I think the important thing is to know what to do with Toobe now that we're here."

Well, sure that was important, but Scratch and I looked at each other, both knowing Winc was stalling. But Scratch is cool, ze let Winc stall. Then ze said, "I think we just stick together here until Toobe's dad can step in and get the cops off his tail." I agreed, and we all went silent again.

I thought it was time for Winc to tell hir story, so I said: "Maybe you could start with how you know me, Winc?"

"Right. Okay," Winc mumbled. Ze took another deep breath. The light turned green, and ze put way too much attention on getting the car going. Finally ze talked again.

"Toobe's father and I went to college together. Matter of fact, we were in the same dorm room."

Scratch said "Uh, huh." Ze didn't get Winc's point, I don't think.

"Dorm rooms weren't coed then, Scratch," Winc added, eyes glued to the road. "I've known Toobe since he was born. I taught him to skateboard. We skateboarded all over the place. But I wasn't happy, except maybe when I was with him, because he never really cared what I was. When he came over to my house one day and I was dressed like I always wanted to dress, he didn't even notice, he just wanted to go skateboarding. He's always been like that. In some ways he saved my life. He didn't care that I decided to become a woman. I used to be a man, Scratch, up until about a year ago."

There was silence in the car.

Scratch didn't explode like I guess Winc thought ze would. "Wow," ze said. "This is funny. I mean, so ironic!"

Winc said kind of weakly, "Yeah. So, here we are, the all-American family."

Winc kind of touched hir own face like a girl, which I saw Scratch catch out of the corner of hir eye. Scratch was smiling and trying to say something, but it just sounded like wait a minute, give me a minute. Then all of a sudden Winc goes: "Could you drive, please?" And for some reason that set Scratch off, like a delayed reaction to what Winc had said earlier, maybe.

"Oh, right!" ze exploded, and later told me ze thinks with hir mouth instead of hir head sometimes. "Gonna really act like the girl, now?"

Everybody was stunned, especially me. But Winc was real careful.

"It's not what you think, Scratch. I don't have a driver's license. Ever since my change, I've kept meaning to get a new one, but they ask you for birth I.D., and . . ." ze shrugged.

Scratch was really embarrassed. "I'm sorry. I think I'm a little tripped out."

Winc nodded, stopped the car and they switched places. "So," Scratch said as ze pulled back out into traffic, "You're a woman."

"Well actually," Winc said, kind of pulling hirself closer to the door, "I don't think I can really say that either."

Scratch looked totally confused. You could tell ze would have said something if Winc had said, "Yes I'm a woman" but now ze didn't know where to go.

"So, um, what would you say you are, then? We came up with some cool theories, but you do have to choose something, don't you? Well, I guess you don't, if we're really going to reject the two sexes——"

"Scratch? Can I keep going?"

"Oh jesus, I'm sorry. Yes."

"All I knew was I was not-boy. In fact, I didn't know I had to choose something until kindergarten. They lined us up to go outside, and I stood with my friends, the girls, and everybody laughed at me and the teacher herded me into the boys' line."

Winc played with hir hair, and I wondered if ze would have twirled the mustache if it were still attached.

"It was like gravity pulling me, only I wanted to float in the air." Ze looked back at me, and I remembered the Drain.

"From then on I just knew I wasn't a boy. The more things there were to do as a boy, the more weird I felt. So, there being only two choices, I thought I must be girl."

"That sounds familiar," Scratch said.

Winc turned in hir seat to look at Scratch for a minute. There was a question in hir eyes. "I didn't realize women went through it too."

Scratch looked like ze was about to fire something off, but Winc held up hir hand.

"Please. My story. So about a year ago I had the surgery, and . . ."

"We're kinda jumping the story a little, aren't we?" Scratch interrupted again.

Winc sighed almost impatiently.

"I went through a whole lot of painful years cross-dressing, feeling like a freak," ze said in a hurry, trying to rush through that part. "I met some transsexuals, I read everything I could get my hands on, I decided to become a woman. Snip snip. It was done. Then I went online, and realized I loved being everything. Including wolves and lions . . . and tigers and bears, oh my."

"So . . ." Scratch started slowly. Winc smiled a little.

"So now I'm saying I may be neither. Not a man. Probably not a woman. Seems like the most honest thing to say."

"Whoa. Okay." Scratch threw hir head back against the headrest.

"So you were socialized as a man, you have no idea what it's like to be a woman, except online you can come off as one when you want. This is textbook; I know everything about this conversation. But . . ." Ze started to shut up, but continued on, shaking hir head like ze had to go through with the thought.

"It's not going down real well, this story of yours. Because I'm making the wonderful discovery that I'm as bigoted and uptight as that next door neighbor I keep using as an example of a jerkoff."

"You're not bigoted, Scratch," Winc said. "This is hard, believe me." But Winc was already going someplace else, someplace just a little further away. I don't think Scratch saw it, but I did.

Scratch kept driving and shook hir head, putting hir hand in the air, the way you do when you're afraid a thought is gonna get away.

"Look, it's like this. All of a sudden it's like you're another species. Being female is its own thing, so is male. You say you're not a boy, but I have to say, you're not a girl either."

"I know that, Scratch, that's what I just said." Real calm, real quiet.

"Right, you did. I'm having a hard time relating to a not-gender right now."

Ze gathered up hir thoughts again like fish, you could almost see the net.

"If you're a woman trapped in a man's body then . . . then I don't know what that means. I want to ask you a million questions to see if you match some kind of internal test I've got set up for people like you . . ."

Ze shook hir head again, as if trying to bodily throw out the half-formed thoughts.

Winc studied hir fingernails, turning them this way and that.

"On the other hand I've never met people like you, not that I know of, anyway." Ze looked lost again.

"All the thoughts inside me, like that you're not a 'real' woman, like I am, are bigoted and ignorant . . ." Ze trailed off. Finally ze said, "I do NOT like what I'm thinking! How can I be thinking this!"

"Which is?" Winc said back softly. I thought ze was so brave, cuz even I didn't want to hear what Scratch said.

"Men can do any fucking thing they want to on the planet and now they even want to be women! Why the fuck do they have to take every fucking thing in sight?"

Scratch looked shocked at what ze'd said. "No, that's not what I mean. Let me try again. You're not a woman or a man and . . ." ze was muttering. "Talk about no traction. . . . How the fuck do I relate to you?"

"Like you always have," Winc said in that tone that sounds so reasonable.

Scratch winced before starting again. I was getting nervous that ze might be too into talking to drive, but I guess Scratch talks a lot whatever ze's doing.

"All right . . . now I'm looking at you, studying your face for clues of 'man-ness.' If we were walking down the street what would people think of you?"

"You mean what would they think of you?" Winc said real quick. "Isn't that what you're really concerned about?"

There was one of those terrible pauses that kept filling up the car with already-breathed air. "Look," Winc went on, "I don't have any answers . . ."

"I know that, goddammit! I know you're nobody else than the person I fell in love with online and there are no more surprises here than there were last week!"

"Fell in love with?" I knew Winc would never let that one pass, and ze didn't.

Scratch was sputtering. "Okay! Yes! I fell in love with a . . . with a . . . ze!"

We all kinda laughed a little, even Winc. Felt like there was more air in the car again. I just had to pipe up from the backseat: "You get used to it, after awhile."

"Oh easy for you to say, little person," Scratch said, but I could tell ze wasn't really mad.

"Look," ze said back to Winc. "Why are you presenting yourself as a woman then?"

Winc and I looked at each other and then down at our clothes. Winc fingered hir necktie, still trying not to smile. I held up my pantyhose.

"You know what I mean! Why are you—"

"But that's just it, Scratch," Winc said quietly. "Today I look like a man . . . tomorrow I may look like a cheerleader."

Scratch and I laughed a little again.

But Winc went on. "It's because I've had the chance to do all that with you——online——change from one thing to another to another to another . . . that's given me the courage to start doing it in real life."

Winc looked at Scratch in this really funny way, hir mouth all crooked and hir eyes kind of lit up, and she said real quietly, "I like it, Scratch."

Which made Scratch sputter again. "The point is, the point is . . . the point is that what I'm facing here is a monster of my own creation!"

Winc stopped smiling then. "Oh thanks, that feels real good," ze said.

"No, I mean I'm always mouthing off about how useless gender is and if we didn't have one we'd all be better off and now I'm sitting on a car seat next to someone whose gender is 'optional,' for lack of a better word. Freaks me out!"

Winc got that look back on hir face. "You're awfully cute when you freak out," ze said. "Did you know that?"

"I'm serious! What are you? What does that make me? If I thought I had to worry about that before . . ."

Winc kept smiling and I kept watching Winc. If ze wasn't worried I wasn't. But Scratch was still sputtering.

"This is just what I wanted. And I hate it! Now if I become a genderless person too then we can be a nice happy couple, but the fact is I'm not. I'm a woman, I was raised as a woman, I've made myself into a whole different kind of woman than I used to be. You were raised as a man, and then you became a woman, and now you're saying you're not either. Then of course the question is, what's a woman?"

"And what's a man?" Winc shot back, just like I knew ze would.

"I don't know!"

Winc looked out the window, away from Scratch and said, "Right." There was a long pause. "It seems to me that your consternation is about how you're going to behave now, with me."

"Yeah. Well, it's not just behaving for other people, it's behaving in a physical space with you."

"But wouldn't that be a problem for anybody after they meet in person? I mean, how do you feel about Toobe now that you've met him?"

Scratch sighed, pulling the car to a stop at a red light, and playing with the rings on hir fingers. Ze shrugged: "He's a guy. I mean a person with a gender, I can relate to him." Ze put hir head in hir hands. "I can't believe I said that."

The light turned green, and Winc went on in that voice. "Yes, but he's also very physical right now. You have to take that in: Maybe he has an annoying habit that you never had to deal with online."

I added helpfully: "Yeah, like I jerk my leg around, or click my tongue."

Scratch craned hir head around to look at me. "Yeah, he's so . . . near. You both are right in my face." Ze made a cross with hir fingers, between hir and us. "Not like I'm a hermit or something, but all the sensory input makes me a little crazy."

At which point ze pulled the car off to the side of the road. Got out and walked around. We sat inside, me fidgeting and Winc being very still. Finally Winc called out the window.

"Darlin', remember we're on the lam, here." Ze sounded like ze was online again.

So Scratch ambled back to the car and got in. Ze started talking like there hadn't been any break.

"Men have this privilege, they refuse to acknowledge they have it. They invade other people's territory like splashing into a still water and scattering all the sea creatures into oblivion. Then they look around and see the environment's changed and they say, what happened? They stock the pond with more creatures like themselves and the rest of the population disappears and then the pond dies and they wonder why. Not only that, a lot of the times they blame it on the creatures who left! Or if a sea snail wants to come back but it doesn't look like the man-creature, it gets eaten. Or at least it's given a lot of shit for not looking like a man-creature."

"I love how you stretch your metaphors, hon," said Winc, "Always have. And I agree. I hate that about men, too."

"Then why couldn't you just have been a better man! Why do you have to come over to this side of the fence and plow in this water?"

Winc finally looked over at Scratch. "That hurts. I'm really trying to stay with you on this, but it doesn't include your hurting my feelings just because you're angry. You're talking to me as if I'm Them, and the fact is—"

But I interrupted, cuz something finally dawned on me: "Nobody is."

Winc answered, "Well, dear, there are Thems out there. There really are. But I do know what you mean."

Ze turned back to Scratch. "The fact is I don't know about all of them, all I know about is myself."

Then ze did some more tugging on hir hair, and the car got quiet again. Scratch sat there while Winc composed hirself. Winc is kind of slow in real life.

"I never was happy, or felt like myself when I was stuck in Man. It wasn't that I was running wildly into becoming Woman, when I look back at it. I was running wildly away from Man."

Scratch's face got all soft and I could tell ze wanted to say something and so did I but Winc said "Please. You're asking if I could just be a better man. I guess, in a way, that's what I've done. This is it. The way for me to be a better man was to scrape off all the man stuff— the stuff we both cringe at—and become woman. Then when I found out *that* didn't work either, I've had to scrape off all the woman stuff and be . . . whatever the hell is left."

All I've ever heard Winc say was, "I need to be a woman." I couldn't believe what I was hearing.

Scratch covered hir head with hir hands, like ze was trying to crawl into a cave. Ze was steering with hir knees, which made me a little nervous.

"Wait a minute, go back, rewind, wait," ze said, hands back on the wheel. "Can we go back to this 'better man' stuff? I mean, why couldn't you change? Leave behind 'prick' or 'jerk' or 'arrogant asshole.' Pick one of those other options."

Scratch looked around for the words again. "What about sensitive guy, great father, loving husband, you know, them."

"Scratch, I'm well aware of the options in that category."

"So maybe you could make yourself over without . . . without ripping off women! Men can be great, it's when they take from other people that they get so obnoxious!"

"Like time and power and physical space, uh huh . . ." Winc was nodding hir head.

"Right!" Scratch shouted. "Women have redefined Woman. You can bet they got some shit for it, too. Why can't men do that?"

Winc sighed and nodded. "They should. Don't you think I've been wracking my brain about that? All my life? Here's all I know. Can you hear this for a minute?"

"Of course." Scratch turned to Winc and hir voice was all quiet. "I don't like feeling this way."

"That's a lot of why I love you," Winc said, but hir eyes were still sad. "Let me try this," ze went on. "Maybe it's just too hard for me to 'redefine.' Maybe the only solution was to join the other category, the one that's got some hope."

Scratch looked calmer than ze had for awhile. "You mean abandon the category altogether? Like maybe it isn't a category worth saving, the way it's defined now?"

"Yes, maybe that's it."

"Because it's such a fucked-up category and it doesn't even work that well for men themselves?" Scratch looked like a kid in my classroom.

"Exactly, dear," Winc said.

Scratch's expression was this weird combination of wild-eyed and calm at the same time. "That's really incredible," ze said slowly, eyes staring at the dashboard. I started staring at hir to see if ze'd look up at the road again. Ze did. Finally.

"That's subversive!" Scratch said, and started muttering. "That really blows my mind and I think I'm freaking out again."

Winc shrugged. "I can't imagine trying to work from inside Male again. I can't imagine what it would take. I couldn't do it."

But Scratch's eyes were lit up. "I always say when men get in my space that they're invading. But maybe they really want to be women. Well, not women, but not-men. It's traction again!"

Winc smiled for the first time in awhile, but ze still looked kind of distant. "So you're saying there should be only one category, or no categories at all?"

Scratch nodded.

"Yeah," Winc said, "That's a good one."

Right then, the car started to sputter and cough. Out of gas. Unbelievable. Scratch let fly with a string of curses I know I'll use some day. Then something really funny happened. . . . Scratch and Winc said to each other at the exact same time:

"I can't believe you let the gas run out. Just like a guy!"

They looked at each other and cracked up at the same time again, they said, "Simulpost!"

Scratch got the car off to the side of the road and I chose that moment to say I was hungry—it seemed as good a time as any. All I've been eating is tofu for five days! So we all trooped to this diner a couple of yards down the highway.

Winc realized we had to get back into drag. Scratch and I groaned, and I complained about having to put the hose back on, and thank gawd Winc said I didn't have to but told me to call them tights.

Back goes Winc's mustache; I could see how ze used to look when I was growing up but ze still looked like someone completely different and now I could also see how Scratch looked . . . funny . . . in that dress, something not quite right. I'm still not sure if it was cuz I knew ze was a woman who never wore that stuff or if I was still getting used to seeing hir in the flesh after imagining hir online.

Scratch has a very soft but sharp face, and intense eyes. I think under the bad wig ze had red hair; I saw a little wisp of it in the car. One time ze wrote me online that ze felt ze had carved hir own face from the inside, out of sheer will.

We went into the diner, sat at a table and looked at our menus. I had meant to tell them before about all the publicity on them but obviously there hadn't been a whole lot of time. I knew they wouldn't believe it and I was waiting for the right time to show them the key ring I had with their names on it. (They're selling them everywhere.) The waitress comes over and they both turned white and stared at her chest. She was wearing an "I Like Scratch and Winc" sweatshirt! I had to think of something cuz it was zombie-town at our table, so I whined "I'm hungry" in a high voice. It worked; they both looked up at the waitress's face and flapped their menus around. Then the waitress turned to Winc and asked hir what we're having, ignoring me and Scratch, right? And Winc, I can't believe this, Winc sat up straight, and cleared hir throat, and stroked hir mustache, and in this way deep voice, this grown-up guy voice, said to Scratch, "Honey, what are you having?" I thought Scratch was gonna pee right there, but then Scratch gets sweet and smiley and says to Winc, "Oh, you order for me. You always pick something nice."

Then Winc almost loses it. Ze's staring at Scratch like ze's never seen this person before, but I guess hir old guy stuff kicked in and ze did Dad ordering us breakfast, and the waitress walks away like nothing is strange. But everything was strange; the Drain thing was there, trying to suck everybody in, especially me. Watching the waitress leave, Scratch looks at me real serious and says, "Thank gawd this is a morph," and Winc says, "Amen."

Then it was silence again until our food came.

"I want to get back to something you said, Scratch," says Winc around a mouthful of waffles. "Something you were saying about sensory overload."

Scratch, who I swear looks one minute like everyone's mother, and the next like some guy in drag, and the very next minute, well, strong and proud, gets all quiet and nods, so Winc keeps talking.

"It ties in with something I was saying, about the courage you've given me——online. See, I did want to be a woman, Scratch. I really, really thought that was the answer for me. But when I finally did it, it felt like I was still acting."

It was weird hearing all this come from a doode with a mustache.

"All my life, I played at being a boy, and when I finally became a woman——and that's what I did, Scratch, I became a woman——I found I was playing at that too. It was too tight. Too many rules on both sides of that gender fence, and I just don't get along well with rules."

Scratch looked a little more like what I think ze really looks like then. "So online," ze says, "you got to escape?" Winc nodded, then Winc took a deep breath.

"I fell in love with you a lot of ways, Scratch. I loved being boy to your riot grrl. I loved being nasty gay man to your nasty gay man. I even loved you when you were a vampire and I was . . . um . . . food. I fell so deep and hard when we were Frankie and Johnny. And then Razorfun and Gyrl . . ."

I felt embarrassed but thought what ze was saying would maybe save this whole thing.

Hir voice trailed off, and Scratch's eyes got a little wet and ze just nodded some more. Winc went on. "What I'm realizing now," ze said, "is that I was falling with a safety net."

Winc was getting sadder and sadder, but ze kept talking. "I was finding a way to be all the different me's I could be, with you. But it wasn't with all of you, not really. A lot of it was in my head. It wasn't really you. It was the you I *wanted* you to be."

Ze just stopped and looked down, and took another bite of hir waffle, but I don't think ze was hungry. Scratch took up the slack.

"So you were becoming who I wanted you to be?"

"Sort of."

Scratch looked disgusted with hirself.

"It was always someone I wanted to be too," Winc went on. "I loved that no matter who we became, you were right there with me. We both had the safety net. I . . . I didn't have to worry about looking like a freak to other folks. You didn't know you'd be *with* a freak."

Right then, the waitress comes back and asks Winc if "the table" wants more coffee. So Winc says, in this girly voice ze usually uses, "Thanks, hon, yes please," and the waitress just stares at hir, pours the coffee quick and gets outta there.

"You're a freak?" Scratch said when she was gone. "You think you're the only one? Don't you know I'm one, too? Why do you think there's so many of us online. Not just queers either, but lots of people are freaks out there."

Ze looked around the diner. "I mean, out here."

Winc looked kind of surprised, but didn't say anything. Ze had a kind of "tell me more" look in hir eyes.

"You were trying to make me complete some kind of fantasy, right?" Scratch added. "Something to make you look more normal?"

Winc nodded, tears spilling out of hir right onto the waffle.

"You sort of used me, Winc," says Scratch, real quiet. Winc was crying now; ze just nodded and said ze was sorry.

Scratch didn't say anything, Winc excused hirself and despite what was happening I had this sudden gasp inside that I hoped ze would remember to use the right bathroom! When ze was gone, Scratch looked at me and asked if I thought ze was being a jerk. Scratch is so cool that way, asking me what I think, but I could tell ze was really confused, even hurt. Not just by what Winc was saying, but by what ze must be feeling.

So I said, "Nah, you're not a jerk. I freaked out myself, the first day I saw Winc in a dress. I mean, that was my buddy, and my buddy was wearing a dress."

"Yeah, I guess that's it," but Scratch sounded kind of doubtful.

Then Winc came back and slid back into the booth and started talking again.

"I don't want this whole thing to get into who used who, okay? It's a two-way street." It was like these walls had shot up around hir—spooky.

"I know that I fell in love with you. I learned a lot about who I am and how I want to be in the world. I learned I could be a lot of things with you, and figured maybe I could really be that way. Be anything, anyone, everything, everyone, all of me. With you. For real."

Scratch looked at hir; maybe something was about to happen or something but right then, I had filled up too much and I just busted out crying like a little kid.

Scratch was starting to say something but suddenly noticed me.

"Oh, man, Toobe, I'm sorry. Jesus, I . . . don't cry, Toobe!" Ze looked like ze was gonna join me. Ze looked at me, then looked at Winc, then put hir head in hir hands.

Winc reached hir arm around me and I thought I'd lose it right there. But we held still, just like that.

Finally Scratch said to Winc, "I don't see how it's going to work, in the real world, I wish I was bigger than I am, but there's so much involved. I guess I'm just not."

Winc got that other smile on hir face then. Someone else's smile. Ze sat way back in hir seat. "Then I guess I should say it's been nice to meet you," ze finally said, "and have a good life."

I felt like I'd been hit with a jolt from a million light sockets. But Scratch didn't move.

"Oh, that's very Ingrid Bergman, my friend, but this isn't the movies." Scratch said in a kind of drawl. Ze was grinning! And kept right on talking.

"Don't you realize that we're just getting started? Don't you realize we're at some kind of precipice, instead of stuck behind some theory!"

I didn't really get what Scratch was talking about, but I did like the grin. Winc looked surprised too, but ze still had a guarded face.

"What do you mean?" ze asked, kind of huffing up. "I wasn't being dramatic, I was—"

"I know, but darlin', you're not the only one with lines here. What about my freak status? My idea of a good time would be to walk off into the sunset with a woman, a wolf, or my computer. Not a husband. But probably not a wife, either."

"Oh, and now you can't because I'm not a real woman?"

Scratch winced big. "No. At least I don't think that's what it is. I came here ready to deal with your being a guy, to being straight and narrow all over again. I'm still stuck on what I'm going to be now. When the thought of being a straight anything makes me want to choke my food!"

They looked at each other. Then Scratch looked at me.

"Oh, Jesus, Toobe, I'm sorry. This must be awful for you, pal. I mean, Mom and Dad are fighting."

I got kind of mad then but I still didn't know why I was crying. "You're not Mom and Dad! You're Scratch and Winc. I don't know why that's not good enough for you!"

Scratch swung hir head back at Winc like a gangster. "He's hit it on the head again, you know dat, shweet-hawt?"

Winc said "Yeah," eyes all misty and clouded and really beautiful too.

They just sat there, a kind of truce, I think, or at least an agreement not to pick at this gaping wound that looked like it would spew all over the place again.

Then Scratch looked up at the TV, and there was a story about us! There was Coney Island, there were cops, there were walkie-talkies, helicopters, and an anchorman doing a standup and everything!

You wouldn't believe how fast somebody with a mustache can get his check. We were outta there.

End Toobe Entry

Narrative Entry, Jabbathehut

Lieutenant Wallace Budge crumples up the empty popcorn bag in his lap. "Tell me again," he says very patiently, the kind of patience that makes an underling nervous, "exactly what you saw. Just one more time for me, please."

The uniform in front of him takes a deep breath. "Our chief hadn't gotten your memo in writing yet sir, so all we had to go on was to look for a young white male, adolescent, or some threesome including a young, white . . ." His voice trails off.

"Yes, I understand. Go on," says Budge, almost oozing courteousness.

"So we go to Nathan's, like we'd been advised."

Budge is on him like a hawk. "Nathan's? Why Nathan's?"

"Umm . . . we were hungry, sir, and our dispatcher said it was the best . . ."

"Uh huh," Budge interrupts, "so you're at Nathan's, go on."

"There was a guy and his daughter buying a hot dog. That's all. Then later we get your memo and we start looking for—"

Budge nods his head vigorously, points his finger at something as if it were on a page of a transcript. "Right, that part. What did they look like?"

"At the hot dog stand? I don't know, just this guy, and his daughter."

"Fine. And how did you know it was his daughter?"

"He had his arm around her, and she called him Dad." The cop shrugs.

"Right," Budge says. "Go on. Please."

"Okay, so then we get word about your orders, so we switch to looking for three people. You said they could be anybody, so we're looking for two other people along with a kid—any two people with him."

"Uh huh, and was that a problem?"

"It's Coney Island, sir! With all due respect, there's lots of people here! I mean, any number of young guys, maybe two old people with one, two old black guys with another, two girls with a third . . . we were going crazy looking!" He places both hands out, palms outward, indicating the vast number of combinations he alone has thought of.

Budge takes a step back, steps forward again. If he were even more patient, it might have looked graceful.

"And did you see a threesome fitting the description they've got at the gate?"

"What? The guy, his daughter, and his wife?"

"Yes, those would be the ones."

"Yeah! But sir, you said they were criminals, and that the minor would be a young boy! We were going pretty fast, looking at all these people. There *was* a very suspicious looking threesome, let me tell you!" The cop rocks back on his heels a bit.

"Is that right? And why were they suspicious?"

"Well, one was young and the other two were older, and the young one was white, which was on the description, the other two were black, and they had sweatshirts on."

"I see." Budge wishes he had another bag of popcorn. Not for eating, for crumpling. The soft contours of the corn would crumble into tiny, teeny pieces, falling slowly to the ground . . . he interrupts his own reverie.

"Thank you officer, that's fine."

"I'm sorry, lieutenant, we just didn't—"

"Right, I understand," says Budge, the last drops of patience dripping out of him like hot oil from an overheated engine.

He turns and makes his way to the gate, where a nervous security guard watches his lumbering approach.

"Got it right here, sir, the tape of the last hour of people leaving the park," he says.

"Great, let's roll it." Budge slams into a chair.

Endless bad footage of black-and-white figures dances on the snowy screen.

Patiently, again, maybe even more patiently than earlier, Budge looks kindly upon the security officer.

"Is there any way to find a group of three?"

"Oh, sure, sir, I can get right to it."

He scans forward as Budge watches. And watches. And then sees them: the Scratch and Winc and Toobe family. One's playing the father, one the mother, and sure enough, there's Toobe under a young girl's guise. Looks uncomfortable as hell.

"Did you stop these three?"

"Well, as a matter of fact I did, sir." He starts to look pleased, then checks himself. He did let them pass, after all.

Budge can't believe his own good behavior. He simply looks up, eyes encouraging. "And?"

"Well, they looked normal enough and they were in kind of a hurry."

Budge swivels his head around like an old dog. "A . . ." he brings his voice down a bit. "Hurry?"

"Well, yeah. The young one was having her first time, you know? Her monthly. The mother says they got to get her to the bathroom. Kind of embarrassing. I didn't know if there was gonna be some kind of . . . accident or something."

Budge smiles for the first time that day, but it's not a happy smile, in fact it resembles something more like a grimace.

"I can see why you might not have pursued that line of questioning," is all he says.

"Yessir."

Budge crumples up the nearest thing to him. It's a paper ashtray, full of butts.

"Aw shit."

Source1: persLOG/budge/harddrive
Source2: bckupfiles@FBCS.gov
Source3: sec@coneyisland.com

End Jabba Entry

Gwynyth Entry
Gwynythmydiary.logenterpassword ×××××:
Diary Entry: As Seen on TV

Three bedraggled outlaws are now draped over various of my overstuffed furniture, their eyes glued to the television. We are watching instant replay coverage of the hunt in the park. Perhaps I was rash in my decision to carve my lair out of the warehouse space beneath the roller coaster. No, they've not found any of my doorways, and unless they have wizardry on their side . . . HA! . . . they won't find us here.

After Toobe left my lair, in search of Mom and Dad, I turned on my old television. My worst fears were confirmed when, on the screen, I saw a huge net of uniformed police converging on the amusement park, not thirty feet from my own home. They targeted the park due to the phone trace I've had rigged to the pay phone just about thirty yards away. Must do some serious rerouting.

In any case, the pigs at last fled the scene, leaving behind them the jackals of the press. There they were, their prey clearly my young charge, whose photograph they persistently flash every chance they get. Just when I'd despaired the whole ruse was up, the three of them came bursting through my door, looking for all the world like some sitcom from Hades. Cats scattered everywhere.

Why no one picked them up is beyond me. Their disguises had slipped considerably and they were flushed with the chase. They were laughing and crying and hugging me, though two of them had not met me before. None of them have commented on my beard. Perhaps they realize that at this point they've no room to cast stones.

`autoescape: Gwynythmydiary.logclose`

Toobe Entry

Awesome! All clear! Gwyn got through to my dad, and he ended up yelling at the govt jerks and they've had to back off completely! We talked for awhile and he actually sounded kind of excited. He says I can stay here for awhile, 'til the heat dies down. Gwynyth says I can be online again, I just have to use her bypasses and do a reroute. When we got to her house it was like some bizarre family gathering. Only I liked all of them.

We got a gallon of gas from the gas station next to the diner. Then we realized we didn't have to drive away from the park at all, we could have just walked over to Gwynyth's. But it's probably good we were away for awhile, cuz by the time we got back the cops weren't anywhere near the roller coaster anymore. In fact, they were all starting to leave.

The three of them and my dad decided I should stay here, which is cool, cuz Gwynyth's going to teach me a lot more about her "craft," as she calls it. She's a phone phreak too. She hooked me up with a new phone exchange so I could talk to my dad. Then he asked to speak to Gwynyth, like when I'd spend the night at a friend's house and the grown-ups had to talk it all over. Felt like a little kid but I was too happy to care.

We were on TV! These cops were swarming all over the place. Then the guy who's in charge of it all got on, the guy I saw in that photograph that time he caught me online. Must have been an old one cuz he looked grayer now, and his face was like some action hero, all craggy and pockmarked. Both Scratch and Winc said at the same time, "Kinda sexy."

They looked at each other in surprise for a second, hanging there in the air like two balloons. Then they cracked up.

But their fight started again. Winc pointed out that Scratch's theories about everybody just being human weren't working since ze obviously couldn't handle Winc. And Scratch saw that Winc was getting dressed back in women's clothes and said I thought you were going to be a neutral, a no-gender creature.

I was beginning to feel less scared and more tired of it all. They sounded like little kids! Gwynyth told me it was a good sign when that happened, but I didn't get it. "They're running out of steam, child," was all she'd say.

End Toobe Entry

Narrative Entry, Gwynyth

>>To: Jabbathehut
From: Gwynyth
Subj: Three Blind Mice

Now I know why I've been taking in strays all my life. It's all been in preparation to house the three you've sent my way. Not that I'm complaining.

The Mighty Morphin' Ninja Turtle Rangers (as Toobe calls them) have returned here as per their "Plan B." They are safe from any immediate danger. Thank you for your caution as to my privacy, but I am quite delighted at present.

Although I am pleased the child is out of reach of the law quite legally now, I'm concerned that the Police State has added "Kidnapping" and "Corruption of a Minor" to the growing list of noncharges of the other two. It's all over the media and the Net. It's best that the child remain with me for awhile (to which the rascal had no objections), but the other two must be on their separate ways. There were cameras, Jabba, and it would not be wise for them to be discovered in one another's company. They had no *overt* objections to this idea of spending time away from each other. They're more than a bit disillusioned with one another.

Poor children! I'm sorely tempted to intervene with a lovers' spell, but I've lived this long without resorting to one of those, as well you know.

Will write more as it surfaces.

—Gwyn

P.S. I won't be charging you for any of this. I haven't had

this much fun since the day we hacked our way into Fort
Monmouth and left them all those pictures!<<

Gwynythmydiary.logenterpassword *****:

Diary Entry: Tech Note to Self

Have rerouted my phone lines away from the park, through the Southern Georgia switch. I'll encourage my friends to log on so their signatures are "located" in Six Flags Amusement Park. That should keep the hounds at bay.

autoescape: Gwynythmydiary.logclose

End Gwynyth Entry

Toobe Entry

Gwynyth's got this cool beard! More than I can grow. I noticed Winc looking at it a lot. We haven't had a chance to talk in private yet, it's been too crazy.

Scratch kind of exploded at the idea of leaving me here, though. "You mean we did this rescue for nothing! Jabba said we had to go get Toobe!"

Gwynyth calmed hir down pretty well, explaining about the police memos and how Jabba "never deals in possibilities," only sure things. I finally told them I really had needed Scratch and Winc to be with me. I was really scared. That seemed to make them feel better.

Scratch and Winc are going back home but Gwynyth's giving them cool phone exchanges to go online with: all amusement parks! Every time they sign on, the call will trace to one of the hundreds in the country. I made the mistake of asking Gwynyth why amusement parks and she got this album with postcards and photos of every single fun park in it, and lots of close-ups of the roller-coasters. A whole albumful.

As they were getting ready to leave, Scratch was calmer again. "Okay, just tell me," ze said to Winc. "If you're big on not being a woman or a man, why do you wear women's clothing?"

"Look, Scratch, just how far do you think I'd get if I let my beard grow and walked around in a dress?"

Gwynyth snorted at that one, but she didn't say anything. Winc must've heard her, cuz ze went all red, but kept talking. I never knew Winc had to shave!

"Or maybe you'd rather I wore men's clothes and a mustache but you could see my breasts?"

Scratch looked like one of those surreal pictures where light shines down on somebody from out of the sky.

"Oh, man," ze said. "You speak truth, my friend."

Then Scratch told what it was like to walk around on the street in anywhere but a big city. Scratch was back now as hir normal self I guess, with jeans and a T-shirt and boots.

"They'd kill me," Scratch said, nodding. "And they'd kill you."

End Toobe Entry

*

CHAPTER EIGHT

Narrative Entry, Jabbathehut

Back in Washington, at the offices of the Federal Bureau of Census and Statistics, Wally Budge is on the phone.

"Shel," he says excitedly into the receiver, "These two are smart cookies. They've got me thinking they're *stupid*, they're so smart."

"How's that, Wally?" Guarded, noncommittal. Ever since he got back from Coney Island yesterday, he'd been oddly quiet, deep, she thinks to herself. What's with the sudden happy-face voice?

"Well," he says, a grin creeping into his voice, "Let me read you something." He taps a few keys and a memo surfaces. "Just got this one a couple of hours ago." He reads it out loud.

To: Budge, Investigations
cc: Henderson, Enforcement
From: Autotrace@hack.gov
Subj: WINC
    Winc/bcs.traceverifdblchk@sixflagsreverif.complete
    CONCLUDE:
    location.WINC = Six Flags. Confirmed.
close autotrace

Puzzled, Shel asks, "You mean you got a trace? On Winc?"

"Bona fide."

"How'd you get it, Wally? I mean, Six Flags? That's in Georgia, right?"

"Deep in the heart of Dixie. Apparently, Winc signed on, and triggered our trace. "

"What a great break! So there's a . . . an amusement park theme to all this?"

"Sure would seem so," sounding like the pusscat, claw's-length away from the canary.

"Is there . . . oh Wally, I hate to ask this, but . . . is there another sting going down?"

The pause on the other end answers her question, but she completes it: "And if so, why aren't you with them?"

With the same silence her answer is complete; she finally gets it. Then, rapid-fire, "Wait! You're not there because you don't wanna be there. You know something! Wally Budge——you know they're not there!"

"Have I ever told you how much I admire the speed of your brain? You should be heading up Enforcement, not Henderson."

"Uh huh, the day they give that job to a woman, I'll be dust in the wind."

Budge shifts uncomfortably in his chair, like he always does when she brings up stuff like that.

"Wait a minute, wait," she's adding, "Henderson is at Six Flags, right?"

"Uh huh."

"With all his men."

"Plus reenforcements."

"And he's there because you never told him that Scratch and Winc aren't there!"

"Nail on the head."

"Wally, you could get in deep trouble for withholding information."

"Shel, correct me if I'm wrong, but even you didn't seem to know about this Six Flags excursion."

Silence on the other end of the phone.

"Uh huh," he continues, dropping his voice to the pleased whisper of the cat holding the canary between his paws, toying. "I thought so. When Detective Henderson gets back in town, exhausted and looking like a fool, I'll have a few words to say to him about information, and the withholding of it."

"What words?" She's angry. She prides herself on being in touch with every facet of the division. Somewhere in her elaborate network someone should have told her about Henderson's little junket. But she keeps her cool right now. She knows Wally's got something.

"I'm just gonna say, 'Henderson, when you show me yours, I'll show you mine.'" He snorts for emphasis. "Then maybe," he continues, "maybe I'll have enough information to do my job!"

The two are silent for a moment, then both break into laughter. It's a warm and friendly sound.

"Aw, Walls . . . I was worried about you," says Shel when she catches her breath.

"I'm all right," he reassures her. "Save your worrying for Scratch and Winc," he says. "Because if anyone on God's green earth needs someone worrying for them, it's those two. See, I know how to get to them now. I know how to crack them wide open."

Source: diary.sdunlap@FBCS.gov

End Jabba Entry

Toobe Entry

Scratch and Winc just left. They didn't talk to each other the whole hour before they went. Scratch came over and said "Don't worry, we'll patch up our fight," like ze could read my mind, but I didn't feel so confident about it, and I don't think ze did either.

End Toobe Entry

Narrative Entry, Jabbathehut

Wally Budge is satisfied. If the brass were to know he's risking this, they'd go ballistic. But they don't know. And they're not *going* to know, even if this works. He surveys the memo one more time, and hits Send, using the bypass Typhoid Mary found for him. It's not a direct route, but it will get his message there.

0:53:07 EST
From: Ms Budge
To: Scratch
Subj: Greetings

Well, you certainly seem to be making the rounds of our nation's best amusement parks.

Your bypass is good. We've got no idea where you are. And yes, we're working to crack it. Eventually we will do just that, but it'll take some time, another week at best, from what my boys tell me.

So here's an offer: how about we talk? Just you and me. Live. Online. Can't hurt, can it? I've been reading a lot about you, and a lot *by* you, and frankly I'm interested. How does 11:30 a.m., Eastern Standard Time, Thursday sound to you? A Private Room: White Flag. Please note that I am unable to trace you live.

—Lt. Wally Budge,

Sr. Investigator

Federal Bureau of Census and Statistics

Ms Budge@fbcs.gov

P.S. Had an interesting chat with your friend, Winc, the other day.

He sends it off with a mouse click. Then copies it again for the same message to Winc, suggesting a meeting for the day after Scratch's. With the silence between them stretching ever longer these days, there's little chance they'll compare notes. Now Wally Budge waits.

End Jabba Entry

Toobe Entry

E-ffiti of the day

Toobe, Scratch, and Winc are living underground with an
entire computer node at their fingertips. They are safe, protected by a group of foreign legionnaire types prowling the
premises. They have managed to get messages out to all of us,
using various aliases. Be on the lookout for repeating patterns:
waterfall references, pronoun deception, and good sex. 54%
of the Young Libertarians have enjoyed congress with both
Scratch and Winc, and a few conversations with Toobe.
Please report all sightings to this node, as the Y.L . have
vowed to protect the fugitives if they can.

—Dennis

::dryly:: Guess *I'm* in it now. It's good that they're on our side, but it's all lies and they don't know what in fuck they're talking about. Wonder how they know about the rescue, and that we're safe? I guess the TV took care of the first part, but I don't feel so safe. The FBI's practically living at my dad's job and his boss is getting annoyed. We talk on the phone a lot cuz he still can't understand email. Despite Gwynyth's genius, I wouldn't trust him to be able to log on undetected anyway. On the other hand, he keeps telling me everybody at his job is wearing this button that's a flashing eye winking, openclose, openclose.

But Scratch and Winc are still not speaking to each other. It's been over a week. First I wasn't worried, like Gwynyth said not to be, then I got fed up, now I'm worried again. They've written to *me* plenty, but I'm not sure what to tell them. I can see why it'd be hard to get used to somebody suddenly being a he or she if you've been living in the free zone of ze. I've gotten used to it, and now that people are talking outloud about them it's strange to hear them use ze and hir.

Scratch blames hirself completely and so does Winc. Perfect for each other . . .

If they could meet in some chat room I think they'd be fine. But they refuse. Gwynyth still says not to worry, they need this time to think. I read somewhere that people fall in love with couples and then when the couple breaks up their friends get all angry and sad as if they were in the couple. I get that now.

Here's just one of the letters Scratch has sent me:

>>Toobe, my man, I'm an idiot. I asked for something, maybe even a long time ago, and now I'm running away from it. I hacked and clawed my way to a certain point only to have it all disintegrate before my very eyes.

Not to whine, but it ain't a great time to be unusual. I use the wrong computer and I wear big shoes, I sleep with whoever turns me on but mostly only online, and sometimes several times a night for some nice, empty electronic sex. There's more in my head than sex anyway. I'm in love with somebody who kind of looks like a woman but kind of looks like both. What a dream come true, eh? What did I do with that? Took a great big breath, and ran the fuck away.

Easier to be a freak all alone, at least you're carrying your own suitcases. When you got someone else with you it's less lonely but your feelers extend to them now, you get protective and repressive and anxious and worried. Like suddenly patting your hair down because now someone's going to be looking at it.

I never thought I cared what people think, but obviously I do. What a lovely discovery. I guess *that's* my own demon hammering on my head. Here's my chance: deal with a person who has shared both halves of a binary I don't even respect . . . great chance to breathe!

I'm back in my stupid apartment, just like I wanted. There's dust over everything, endless knicks and knacks of lives I lived years ago, stuff I keep moving every time I change apartments, but no longer has any real meaning to me except that it's mine. I've had eight of a set of nine photos ready to hang in three rows of three, waiting for the last one. I finally got it. Which doesn't fit, of course, not like the other eight: There is a wee bit of the cardboard backing of the frame showing, just enough to look incredibly tacky. I know, without even trying, that if I were to hang them up now, the last row would go crooked, lazing down the wall in a sly escape from the other two, out of obstinence, apathy.

Real-time sunlight streams in, illuminating all that is dingy. Instead of a happy spring feeling, it merely points up the pitfalls of the Real. And, I miss hir. I wouldn't have even noticed this crummy apartment last week. I would have jumped online and talked to my Winc, or gone cyberhunting.

We had a whole world, not just online, but somewhere above the ozone filled with all these strange people who were all us. They would take over and make sparkling the dinge of my dwelling. Even the bed—where I had fantasized taking and being taken by this creature—this bed is simply a rumple of covers with old socks and unread magazines, awaiting now-slaughtered fantasies. But like some cruel joke my cock is thick, my cunt pours wet and copiously, for something outside myself to provide the liberation of sex, the abandon to messy, gritty desperate fucking. I have to pee and let it build, feeding the thin wire of lust strumming inside. I could pee all over this chair and no one would know, and I wouldn't even notice, until I snapped back, like I always do. Disgusted by my own mess, sheepish at my lust in its aftermath.

Am I nothing without interacting with another? Me, who loves to be alone more than anything? Now that I'm *there* I don't truly know who I am. I am Scratch to the mailman, Scratch to the woman I buy cigarettes from, and Scratch to Winc. To you. To Gwynyth even. And without them I am Scratch to myself, whoever the hell *ze* is: stubborn, boring, unwilling to stretch, unable to make connections fire in my brain, unable to even pee without commenting on it.

Normally I would clean my place in a frenzy of new resolutions. But if all my stupid theories were tangible I would smash them onto the hardwood floors here, listening to them crack in stupid brittleness. *I* am scared of this person? Smoky eyes and a laugh like music even when it was shaking with fear? *I* am not willing to walk down the street with a creature whose gender slips like a failing clutch? Me, with the short hair and the wide hips and the mannish walk, the one who makes Them uncomfortable and the ladies curious? What exactly do I have to protect? What toehold in this life do I actually have that I would fight so hard to retain?

Or is it that ze scares me, that hir real face fixes hir permanently in time now, and ze can only be hirself, not Frankie, not the queerboy, not my fantasy of the week. Permanent.<<

End Toobe Entry

Narrative Entry, Jabbathehut

Typhoid Mary has brought Budge a Confirm message: Scratch has written back. He'd be excited but he has no idea how to proceed. Nevertheless, the appointed hour has arrived. Starting a good five minutes early, in order to master the chat rooms and log their conversations, he enters the onscreen chamber.

11:36:04 a.m. Opening "Chat Log" for recording.
Online Host: You have just entered the room "White Flag."*

Scratch: ::drumming fingers on tabletop:: You're late!

Ms. Budge: Let me guess: You're not really on the Santa Monica boardwalk, are you?

Scratch: What's it to you? What makes you think I wanna talk?

Ms. Budge: If I were you, I'd want to know as much about who's chasing me as I could.

Scratch: OK, here's a starter. I thought you were a guy.

Ms. Budge: Look, it was a screw-up with the way I Registered, OK? They only give us one account in the govt. I *am* a guy.

Scratch: Whatever you say, Miss Thing.

Ms. Budge: Ha ha ha. You haven't been hanging out with your pal recently, have you?

Scratch: None of your business.

Ms. Budge: Sorry, but it's very much my business. What's the matter, have a fight?

Scratch: I still have more questions. Why the hell are you after us?

Ms. Budge: Don't you read the papers? You're America's Most Wanted.

Scratch: I know we're wanted, but I don't know why.

Ms. Budge: All right, good place to start. I'll ask you a few questions about that, OK? I checked the laws on this, and no matter what you say, I can't hold you to it anyway.

Scratch: Oh, gee, now I'll tell you everything you want to know.

Ms. Budge: Hey, give me a break, will you?

Scratch: ::softly:: you're after me, Mister, why should I give you a break?

Ms. Budge: OK, OK, just answer me this . . . please.

Scratch: ::heavy sigh:: Oh, ga (deaf sign for go ahead).

He makes a private note: cross-reference "Deaf."

> **Ms. Budge:** Are you now or have you ever been involved
> in any kind of trafficking in pornography?
> **Scratch:** No!
> **Ms. Budge:** Thought not. OK, next question . . .
> **Scratch:** brb.

Scratch has left the room.

> **Ms. Budge:** Damn!

He looks up "brb" in his dog-eared manual. A stubby finger slides down the page to the definition. Ah, Scratch will "Be Right Back."

Scratch has entered the room.

> **Scratch:** bak.

That would mean "Back At Keyboard."

> **Ms. Budge:** Hey, where'd you go?
> **Scratch:** Just checking to see if this is being traced.
> Good cop.
> **Ms. Budge:** The best. I'm being straight with you,
> Scratch.
> **Scratch:** Uh huh. Next question?
> **Ms. Budge:** OK. Are you now or have you ever been
> involved in any kind of trafficking in the distribution
> of illegal access bypass code?
> **Scratch:** Define illegal.
> **Ms. Budge:** Ha! Good thief. OK, stuff that isn't autho-
> rized by the govt: bypassing Registration.
> **Scratch:** I refuse to recognize "Registration." Sodomy
> isn't recognized by the govt either, but it's done,
> isn't it?
> **Ms. Budge:** As you say. All right--last question, and
> it's the tough one. Are you now or have you ever been
> involved in hurting the kid in any way?
> **Scratch:** What kid?
> **Ms. Budge:** Toobe. The kid. The boy.
> **Scratch:** ::face steaming up, red as hell:: You guys got
> nasty minds. I'd do *anything* for that "kid."
> **Ms. Budge:** OK, calm down. I had to check.
> **Scratch:** Where the fuck do you get your info? Why aren't
> you going after real bad guys, like politicians and
> rapists?

Ms. Budge: Not my job to go after them. My job is to go after you.

Scratch: So this is my "crime"? You've been chasing us for something you "suspect"?

Ms. Budge: I can get you on illegal trafficking of code, but the laws on that are so fuzzy, you'll probably get off.

Scratch: And how do you get off, sir?

Ms. Budge: I don't understand your question.

Scratch: Forget it.

Ms. Budge: Look. No one can prosecute you, not with a conviction. Come on in.

Scratch: So your only job is to chase people you suspect of committing crimes on the Net?

Ms. Budge: Afraid it's better than that.

Scratch: Yeah?

Ms. Budge: We've got warrants out for you and Winc.

Scratch: Why?

Ms. Budge: You were the one in the cute flower print dress at Coney Island, am I right?

Scratch: No, I was the big black dude you're so afraid of in your dreams.

Ms. Budge: If you do keep hiding out, Scratch, I'm gonna have to add "Resisting Arrest." I won't like it, but I'll do it.

Scratch: Look, mister. Why are you talking to me if you have a warrant?

He doesn't have an answer to that. The screen scrolls blank after Scratch's question.

Scratch: I think you want to know something else.

Ms. Budge: You interest me. You're something/someone I don't have a handle on.

Scratch: What's so mysterious? brb.

Ms. Budge: Why do you DO this? Change all the time? DAMN! He's gone again.

Scratch has left the room.
Scratch has entered the room.

Scratch: bak. Good cop, no tracer.

Ms. Budge: Told you. It's just me and you.

Scratch: To your question I add mine: Why *not* change all the time? It's fun. You should try it. Ms, Budge.

Ms. Budge: Cut that out, will you?

Scratch: ::dry chuckle::

Ms. Budge: I have no interest in that.

Scratch: Tell me: Is there a crime in having different IDs?

Ms. Budge: There's no legal precedent for that, no.

Scratch: So why no interest in shifting yourself?

Ms. Budge: Too much around me changes all the time. I like things stable.

Scratch: That's why you're a cop. Good guys, bad guys, real clear lines.

Ms. Budge: Wait a minute. You think because I like things nice and slow and predictable I'm a bad guy?

Scratch: No, I'm saying cops love black and white. Sorry, pal. Some good people break the law, some bad people are real sweethearts.

Ms. Budge: Hey, don't start talking to me about criminals with hearts of gold.

Scratch: I don't think your heart is really in this investigation.

Budge pauses, as he notices they have both typed the word "heart" in their sentences at the same time.

Scratch: Hey, Ms. Budge, do you know what a simulpost is?

Ms. Budge: Huh? No. What is it?

Scratch: Forget it.

Ms. Budge: I spoke with your buddy just the other day.

Scratch: Which buddy?

Ms. Budge: I need to tell you, Scratch, he's not going to last too long.

Scratch: Who?

Ms. Budge: Don't play cute. Winc.

Scratch: What about Winc?

Ms. Budge: Winc's flighty, doesn't have the stamina to keep running. You know I'm right.

Scratch: We're not running. We're living. Don't you get that? Why does that bother you guys so much?

Ms. Budge: Your life is starting to run mine, and that bothers me.

Scratch: I'm so sorry.

Ms. Budge: Come on in, Scratch. Bring Winc with you. I'll get you a fair deal.

Scratch: A fair fucking deal for what? We did nothing wrong!

Ms. Budge: My point, exactly!

Budge cringes at the burst of honesty, cursing himself for typing it.

> **Scratch**: If you know we did nothing wrong, then stop the chase.

Again, he has no answer.

> **Scratch**: Your heart is telling you something else, pal.
> **Ms. Budge**: Look, this thing has gotten a lot bigger than you and me.
> **Scratch**: Uh huh.
> **Ms. Budge**: And if I don't bring you in, someone a lot nastier is going to. That's the fact.
> **Scratch**: They're gonna "bring you in" too.
> **Ms. Budge**: Huh?
> **Scratch**: If it's bigger than us, then you're a flunky for those "bigger powers."

There is another pause at Budge's end.

> **Scratch**: ::softly:: You don't believe in what they're doing, do you?

Budge is typing, but mid-keystroke, another window opens up on his desktop.

To: Investigations@FBCS.gov
From: DevilsOwn
Subj: Breakthrough!

Thought you might like to know we unraveled a major knot. Change that time estimate to four days. We'll have them pinned down by then, if not sooner. That's another $4K, right? $1K for every 24 hours before schedule?

—Devil

> **Scratch**: Just answer me honestly, and I'll trust you.

He deletes what he had just typed, and instead tries to get back to the point. The hacker's message can wait.

> **Ms. Budge**: I believe in justice. You broke the law when you distributed those codes. You're breaking the law by evading arrest.
> **Scratch**: You chickened out, bub. And I was never told, to my face, that I was wanted. I never evaded anything.

Ms. Budge: No, but the law says I can arrest you
because I suspect you and have evidence. The court system will get you off.

Scratch: You sound a little bitter, darlin'. Can I
point something out to you?

Ms. Budge: Go ahead.

Scratch: So why bother, dear?

Ms. Budge: Why bother with what?

Scratch: Don't you think the Reg process is just a wee
bit inadequate? Considering that you are currently
trapped in a female identity?!

Ms. Budge: Oh, I told you to cut that out. Of course
it's flawed. But if the laws fall apart, there's going
to be a lot of people hurting a lot of others.

Scratch: Oh, don't give me that law crap. I can tell
you have a bigger brain than that.

Ms. Budge: Gee, thanks.

Ms. Budge has another window open on his screen, and he's typing an answer back to
his hacker-for-hire. It's slow going, this two-things-at-once. Thank God Scratch hasn't noticed
anything amiss.

Scratch: Well, that's a pretty big flaw, getting your
identity "wrong." Do you realize when they check the
accounts for the office you're in, they'll report your
female profile? And send you the "appropriate" mail?

Ms. Budge: I know. You should *see* the ads I'm getting.

Scratch: ::sweetly:: I can just bet.

Ms. Budge: Tell me this. Since you don't like that
neighbor of yours. Why don't you just shoot him? Fuck
the law, right?

Scratch: Jesus fucking christ! How much of my mail do
you read?

Ms. Budge: All of it . . . dear.

Scratch: You fucker.

Ms. Budge: I don't like it, but if you stay out there,
you'll make a lot of people dig their heels in, get it?

Scratch: You motherfucker pervert, reading other people's mail . . .

Ms. Budge: Grow up, Scratch, you're in the big sandbox
now. It's the only way to find you.

Splattered, Budge thinks to himself. That's the word he's heard about this kind of online chat. Confusing enough to him that he doesn't even notice he's answering the hacker's note from his "Ms. Budge" account.

To: DevilsOwn
From: Ms. Budge
Subj: Breakthrough!

   $1K per each day before deadline is the deal. Great work. If you make it in less than four days, you can double the bonus. I want these two. I want them NOW!
—Lt. Budge

      Scratch: Look, let's cut the crap, OK?

The lieutenant hits SEND, and types his own next piece without reading Scratch's request.

      Ms. Budge: If you stay out, Winc is going to crack
      faster than you, and he's going to bring you with him.
      Scratch: You don't know shit about Winc, it's obvious.
      Ms. Budge: I know more about Winc than you'd like to
      hear.
      Scratch: ::waving hand impatiently:: You want me to go
      along with this program, to fill in the blanks of your
      investigation. But that just keeps it all going, like a
      juggernaut, hammering over people like me. And finally,
      people like you. The only ones left will be pod people.
      Ms. Budge: What are you talking about?
      Scratch: To follow a law just because it's a law is not
      good enough.
      Ms. Budge: I don't give a fuck whether you Register or
      not . . .

Once again, his memo window opens.

To: Ms. Budge
From: DevilsOwn
Subj: Breakthrough!

   Yes, ma'am! You get what we get and it's coming down soon. Uh, pardon me, but I always thought you were a dude. So what are you, some supergirl cop? I like your style! Send me a GIF!
—Devil

He looks up "GIF" in the manual, eyes still on the chat room with Scratch. Graphic Image Format? The guy wants a photograph! I should send him a picture of my ugly mug, mutters Wally Budge aloud. He deletes the message from his screen with a force that makes the Mouse button scream.

> **Scratch**: All I did was refuse to Register. And now you say you don't give a fuck?
> **Ms. Budge**: I AM NOT DISAGREEING WITH YOU!
> **Scratch**: Yeah, right, then the nice cops will listen. Huh?
> **Ms. Budge**: I'm not saying what you're doing is right or wrong. I'm saying right now it's against the law. And it won't be cops judging you, it'll be a jury of your peers.
> **Scratch**: My peers are too fucking scared of people like you. We all are.
> **Ms. Budge**: I know, and I really wish to hell you weren't scared of me.
> **Scratch**: You know what? I'm *not* scared of you anymore. It's liberating as hell. Maybe it's because you're less threatening as a "woman"!

If Budge could have typed what his own sputtering sounded like, he would have. The thought crosses his mind to send an all-purpose Private Message to everyone on the Net: "I AM NOT A WOMAN."

> **Scratch**: Look, Budge, here's the bottom line. If this is bigger than both of us, then you can't cut me any deals. You're impotent in this system, too.
> **Ms. Budge**: I've got connections with people who can help you.
> **Scratch**: I'm outta here. But it's been great talking to you.
> **Ms. Budge**: Wait, Scratch . . .

Scratch has left the room.

> **Ms. Budge**: Aw, great . . .

But he realizes he's typing into oblivion. He closes the chat log, not as proud of the conversation as he thought he'd be.

End Jabba Entry

Toobe Entry

Hand on the remote, I click the channel, to a letter from Winc:

>>**To: Toobe**
From: Winc
Subj: Oh, ouch

::softly:: Hey there. I'm on one of the last of Gwyn's bypasses; I wanted to know if you're safe and well. Please let me know right away.

Have you heard from Scratch? Don't tell hir I asked. Ze needs some space just now, space that doesn't include me. But if you could pass any word back, I'd appreciate it.

Wanna know something funny? I thought Scratch was going to be a guy! I was all set to be the little woman in his life. ::sigh:: Next time this sort of thing happens, slap me . . . hard!

The real world has become more and more threatening. Have you been reading *half* the stuff they're saying about me and Scratch? There's regular govt updates online. I start crying, it scares me that much. Which prison would they put me in, Toobe?

Not joking here. In England, they put gurlz like me into the men's prison, even after surgery. I don't know what they'd do to me *here*, because all my paperwork still says boy. I'm too freaked to go to the corner for Diet Pepsi and Cheez-Its, it's rice-cake city in my apartment. With peanut butter. Even the Pakistani family who runs the corner store is now asking if "Missy Winc" is the same Winc everyone's talking about. So . . . . ::deep breath:: I'm moving. Out of my neighborhood, out of the whole damned state. By the time you get this, I'll be "return to sender, address unknown."

Cyberspace is the one place I found to splatter into all of who I am--free--so I think that's where I'll stay for awhile. Been doing a lot of surfing these past few days, you might get a kick out of the logs. I've taken on every single identity I can think of, but never my own; that's under reconstruction.

This whole cops and robbers thing, I'm sure they'll find someone else to hound. And I can get on with my life.

I miss you. I miss Scratch. No . . . I miss what Scratch was to me, with me, online. I don't miss who ze turned out to be. But I miss something, someone.

Love you, hope you're well. Say hello to Gwyn for me, will you?

—W.

If they would just talk to each other. Winc thinks Scratch is rejecting hir when ze's only just thinking, and Scratch thinks Winc is all of a sudden just one person, instead of all the ones ze knew for awhile.

End Toobe Entry

Narrative Entry, Jabbathehut

Typhoid Mary makes another appearance on Budge's screen. Budge grabs the Mouse and enlarges the message. This better be a response from Winc, or pitting them against each other won't work.

"Confirm on the White Flag chat with Winc."

Budge looks at his watch. Not a moment too soon. A little more confidently this time, he heads for the chat room. Even remembers to record.

12:29:37 p.m. Opening "Chat Log 2" for recording.
***Online Host: You have just changed to room
"White Flag."***

Winc: ::standing outside the lion's cage, peering in at the strong handsome lion wearing a badge:: Howdy!
Ms. Budge: Thank you so much for talking with me.
Winc: Any time, darling.
Ms. Budge: You don't sound like a man.
Winc: Why *thank you*. I'm not being a man today. Are you?
Ms. Budge: I am a man.
Winc: Cute screen name. Get you many dates?
Ms. Budge: It was a mistake in Registration. I assure you I'm Lt. Budge, a man.
Winc: ::purring:: Oh I doubt that, but we'll let it ride. What do you want?
Ms. Budge: What do you mean you're "not being a man today"?
Winc: ::eyes sparkling:: You haven't done your homework.
Ms. Budge: Ah, I see. But why *do* you change around so much?

Winc: Please feel free to use your Private Messages, dear. They're so much more intimate.

Ms. Budge: I'll try if you'd like, but this is still fairly new technology to me.

Winc: ::slow smile:: How sweet!

Winc: Is *that* what you want to know? Why I change? ::laughing delightedly:: Try it yourself!

Ms. Budge: I'd rather hear it from you.

Winc: You men always say that. What is it you want to hear? What I'm wearing, right?

Budge, startled, jerks back from his computer. At least he knows what she's referring to now, giving the nature of his own Private Messages lately. He won't bite that easily, though.

Ms. Budge: No, no, no. I wonder if you know that the law is after you?

Winc: ::smiling softly, opening top buttons of my blouse:: The law? Whatever do they want?

Ms. Budge: Jesus, lady. That's not what this is about. I'm the detective assigned to your case. We've been talking with your friend Scratch.

Winc: ::rubbing a hand over my stubble, fixing my tie:: Hey, buddy, watch who you're callin' a dame!

Confused, Budge simply doesn't answer.

Winc: ::smiling gently:: Get your answer?

Weakly he types:

Ms. Budge: Hey, you're pretty good at that.

Winc: ::purring:: The best you'll ever meet.

Ms. Budge: I guess that's why you're so good at phone sex, right?

There is a long pause from the other end.

Ms. Budge: You're awfully quiet now . . .

Winc: When did you talk with Scratch, asshole?

Ms. Budge: Oh, the lady has a mouth. Recently.

There is another long pause. Budge worries he's driven him/her away.

Ms. Budge: Notice you two haven't been talking so much? Like I was saying, I had a nice chat with Scratch myself.

Winc: Well, good for you. Did you get hir autograph? Or a blow job?

There's that word again, "hir." Maybe Winc doesn't even know what sex Scratch is? He makes a note on his dog-eared manual.

Ms. Budge: What's the matter, have a fight?
Winc: Fuck you.
Ms. Budge: Look, let's try another tack.

Winc has left the room.

Ms. Budge: Damn!

He remembers the Private Messages.

Private Message to Winc:

Ms. Budge: Winc, please come back, I want to talk with you. I'm sorry.

He can't find the Send button for Private Messages. Frantic, he glances down the manual, and sends it. A Private Message back immediately follows.

Private Message to Ms. Budge:

Winc: Hold on . . . I'm checking something.

Winc has entered the room.

Winc: No tracer, huh? Good cop.
Ms. Budge: Thank you. Of course not, I told you in my letter you'd be safe. Can we start again?
Winc: ::sitting down across from you, blouse still open to reveal just a soft curve, leaning forward::
Ms. Budge: You can check a trace that quickly, eh?
Winc: ::softly:: I can do lots of things, darling. What do you want?

Budge feels the irresistible urge to call Shelly for help.

Ms. Budge: If we can just stick to the topic . . .
Winc: Things getting sticky, dear? How nice for you. Yes, let's stick.

Budge groans. She's persistent.

Ms. Budge: Are you aware there is a warrant for your arrest?

Winc: On what charges?

Ms. Budge: Well, they may or may not be true, but there's evidence enough for us to arrest you. So can I ask you a question or two, to clear this thing up?

Winc: ::laughing lightly:: Be my guest.

Ms. Budge: Are you now or have you ever trafficked in pornography on the Internet?

Winc: ::leaning forward, resting my hand on your knee:: As a participant?

Ms. Budge: Selling or loaning pornography to minors and others.

Winc: ::stroking your knee absently:: No, not that I can recall, officer.

Ms. Budge: Have you done any harm to the kid?

Winc: Excuse me?

Ms. Budge: Have you trafficked the kid Toobe in porn or otherwise corrupted him?

Winc: Oh fuck off, sewer brain!

Private Message to Winc:

Ms. Budge: Excusez moi?

Winc: ::melting into the floor in a writhing mass:: Yesssssssssssssss . . . talk French to me, you hot thing, you!

Budge rocks back in his chair violently. Recovers, then types again. He repeats the question, back in the "room" where he feels safer. In English. What compelled him to do that, he wonders?

Ms. Budge: I'm sorry, could you answer that question. We're concerned for his welfare.

Winc: Just a *little* question first? ::trailing my finger gently up your leg, and you feel it, right?::

Ms. Budge: First you answer: Did you hurt the kid?

Winc: Is your dick so small that all you can think of is hurting other people so you feel big? ::sweet smile::

Ms. Budge: I take it that's a no.

Winc: Bingo.

A new Private Message zaps his screen:

Private Message to Ms. Budge

SubRobert: ::shivering:: I *knew* you'd be online again, Mistress. I've been searching all over for you!

Ms. Budge: Huh?

SubRobert: Don't you remember me? I sure remember your hand-cuffs.

Ms. Budge: BUZZ OFF! I'M BUSY!

SubRobert: Oh . . . Private Room, huh? Can I lick up what's left over?

The trembling detective punches IGNORE.

> **Ms. Budge**: All right. What's *your* question? (I'm sorry for my poor typing.)
> **Winc**: (Typing with one hand always does that.)
> **Ms. Budge**: Cut that out! I'm being straight with you, sir or madame.
> **Winc**: ::laughing:: My question is simply this: What law have I broken?
> **Ms. Budge**: Have you ever distributed illegal bypass codes?
> **Winc**: Yes indeedy.

Winc has left the room.

Again Budge tries the pleading tone, but it's starting to wear thin.

Private Message to Winc:

Ms. Budge: Please, Winc, can we talk some more?

Winc has entered the room.

> **Ms. Budge**: Where did you go?
> **Winc**: ::smoky voice:: Maybe I slipped into something more comfortable.
> **Ms. Budge**: Look, I'm not trying to come on to you! I'm just trying to understand you.
> **Winc**: ::pouting:: Don't you find me a *little* bit attractive?

Private Message to Winc:

Ms. Budge: If I say you're attractive will you answer my questions?

Winc: Oh, you're so romantic, darling.

Now that sounded like one of his wives. What is it with women? Then, like a flash he remembers he hasn't got clue one about who or what this is on his screen.

Ms. Budge: Why don't you come on in, we can make a deal. I don't think any of the charges will stick if you do.
Winc: ::softly:: I'm waiting for an answer . . . don't you find this . . . me . . . attractive? Come on now . . . really, just a little?
Ms. Budge: Scratch has told us most of what we need to know. Now, we need some blanks filled in before we move in on you.
Winc: ::folding arms across my chest, mouth shut::
Ms. Budge: I see. You can make this easy. Just turn yourself in. I can make a deal for you.
Winc: ::sighing:: You're no fun at all. Ever get told that?
Ms. Budge: Yeah, I'm afraid I do. Sorry, not my job to be fun. Perhaps if we meet you could teach me.
Winc: ::laughing gently::
In
your
dreams,
copper.
Ms. Budge: I'm sorry, that was inappropriate.

Private Message to Ms. Budge:
Winc: ::purring:: Of course it was, darling. Don't worry your pretty little head about it. Way ahead of you . . . always will be.
Ms. Budge: Thank you. I think.

Winc: So what did Scratch say?
Ms. Budge: Funny, Scratch told us you would be much more cooperative. Guess you aren't speaking right now, huh?

He looks up at the two messages flashing on the screen at the same time. He remembers something, gives it a try.

Ms. Budge: I believe that was a simulpost.
Winc: Where did you hear that word?
Ms. Budge: Your mail is very interesting.
Winc: ::tossing my hair off my face, smiling:: You read all of it, huh?
Ms. Budge: Yes. All of it.
Winc: Did it get you hard?
Ms. Budge: Actually, no. Is sex all you think about? Is

that what this is about? You're sexually frustrated?

Winc: Uh huh. That's all I think about. That's all I am. What did Scratch say, exactly?

Ms. Budge: That you were weak and you'd tell us what we need to know because you're eager to please.

Winc: You're so full of shit.

Ms. Budge: Am I?

Winc: Scratch would *never* say anything like that.

Ms. Budge: You're that sure?

There is a long pause.

Winc: Tell me Scratch's words. Hir exact words.

Ms. Budge: It's over, Winc. Just come on in. Scratch has already cooperated. So you don't think he'd do that, eh? ⟨

Winc: ::smiling:: No, I don't think he would.

Ms. Budge: I don't have the transcript right here, but I assure you, he talked with us. We already have enough to bring you in, why not just do it voluntarily?

Winc: Well, you tell him from me that his dick is even smaller than yours, and that I'm outta here. Tell him I said that, OK?

Ms. Budge: I'm sure I'll pass that on.

Winc has left the room.

Private Message to Winc:

Ms. Budge: Winc, please come back. We were doing so well.

Winc: Oh, go suck your boss off like you've always wanted to.

Ms. Budge: Damn!

Just as he's beginning a probably futile trace on Winc, a message flashes onto his screen. URGENT, it says, ACCEPT ME NOW! Puzzled, he abandons the trace attempt, pushing the "Accept" button, only to have the following appear on his screen:

Paid Advertisement for MS. BUDGE:

This is your opportunity to make hygiene history!

******

Many career women **like yourself** have written us, asking for a new more absorbent, more easily insertable feminine hygiene product.

Ms. Budge has left the room.
12:59:21 p.m. Closing Log file.

1:01:36 p.m.: Wally Budge waits for Shelly Dunlap to answer her phone. He lifts his eyes
to his screen to catch the latest "Headline News Alert," for those who've forsaken newspapers,
television, and radio.

THEY'RE STILL FREE!

(AP) Enforcement agents of the Federal Bureau of Census and Statistics gathered at
dawn in large numbers today at Six Flags Amusement Park in Georgia, where a
"reliable tip" told them they could expect to find Scratch and Winc. The 75 lawmen
found some of the nation's best rides and tourist attractions, but no cyberfugitives.
Chief Enforcement Officer Phillip Henderson had no comment.

◎ click here to read related articles:

"Government Search: Roundabout, or Merry-Go-Round?"

"Nighttime Talk Show Hosts Rip into Government Hunt"

"Geraldo at 4:00: Identical Twins Who Have Had Cybersex with Scratch and Winc"

Lieutenant Budge is smiling now, despite his trembling hands. The voice in his ear brings
him back to the real world.

"Hello, Shelly here."

"Shel, it's me. You free?"

"I was just about to call you!"

"Simulcall," he chuckles dryly.

"Huh?"

"Nothing. What'd *you* want?"

"There's a *lot* of heat coming down on this side of the building. Everyone is pointing fingers, and when they find out you *knew*, those fingers are gonna point at you."

Silence at Wally's end.

"Wally, you okay?"

A deep sigh, then, "Yeah. Tell me this, though. Do you think I'm no fun?"

"Well," she answers carefully, "You have a . . . a unique sense of humor. I for one appreciate it."

"Okay. One more thing?"

"Sure."

"Would you ever tell a guy to his face that his ... um ... well, 'your dick is so small that all you can think of is hurting other people so you feel big'?"

Silence, and he winces, knowing deep down she's trying to keep from laughing. He's wrong.

"Well, I've *thought* that once or twice about some guys I used to know, but no, I'd never say it in person. Who told you that?"

"Winc."

She's stunned.

"Shel, can we have dinner tonight?"

"You got it, babe."

Source1: persLOG/budge/harddrive
Source2: diary.sdunlap @ FBCS.dov

End Jabba Entry

Toobe Entry

I know Winc's drowning hir sorrows but now *I'm* getting jealous!

>>**To: Toobe**
From: Winc
Subj: Surf's up!

Toobe, this is the sweetest guy. Great timing, huh? I knew there were some good ones out there! I'm Katchoo, hee hee.

—W.

You have just changed to room "Intelligent Desire."

Katchoo: ::walking into the hushed room, settling myself into an easy chair::
Aires: Well, allow me to initiate you . . .
Katchoo: ::looking up at Aires:: Initiate? ::swallowing hard:: Sure.
Aires: Anita?

Sexxxy has entered the room.

Katchoo: ::laughing:: Whoops . . . sorry, thought you were talkin' to me, Aires.
Prophet: ::watching from the back of the room::
Sexxxy: I'm back.
Aires: OK, Anita, I blindfold and undress you. You are on your back. I walk two wet fingers on the surface between your pubic hair and the underside of your breasts . . .
Sexxxy: (should we all go to a private room so the Eyes don't follow?)

238

Katchoo ::listening intently, but feeling eyes burning into the back of my head, turning to meet Prophet's eyes::
Aires: I now have a 1/4-inch-wide soft-bristled paintbrush (maybe a private room is advisable).
Prophet: Hi Sexxxy . . . you're back . . .
Sexxxy: Private room = "Sexxx."

Sexxxy has left the room.

Prophet: ::he sees ?her? looking back at him::
Katchoo: ::face flushing, realizing ?he? probably can't make out my . . . identity.

Aires has left the room.

Prophet: Well . . . the room is small. :) ::damn . . . I should have brought my glasses::

Anita has left the room.

Prophet:: Ouch! Who put that chair there?
Katchoo ::startled to see Prophet stumbling about the room, getting up to see what's going on::
Prophet: ::where is that damn switch::
Katchoo ::whispering:: We seem to be alone.
Prophet: Yes, I think we are. Is this good? he wonders . . . who is this person?
Katchoo ::grinning, quite aware of rather ambiguous appearance::
Prophet:: I just cannot get used to the '90s. Hi! ::with a grin::
Katchoo: Hi yerself! My name's Katchoo and I'm pleased to meet you. ::looking around:: Where do you suppose everyone went? Giving us a wide berth?
Prophet: Well, to the motel down the road I think.
Katchoo: The mo . . . oh!
Prophet: Well, Katchoo, it is nice to meet you. ::is she a she?:: ::muttering:: How are you this morning?
Katchoo: Fine thanks ::trying not to laugh out loud at his predicament:: What brings you to this room?
Prophet: Well, just surfing a bit this a.m. And you? ::he squints::
Katchoo: ::casually folding my arms in front of me:: Oh same, same. ::looking around the room::
Prophet: ::thinking to myself, what the heck. Seems nice. What is ?she? covering?::

Katchoo: So . . . ::clearing my throat::
Prophet: ::Looking up:: Well, maybe, we could, you know, have coffee sometime Kat . . .
Katchoo: ::eyes sparkling:: I'd like that, Prophet. Did you surf in here to listen or talk?
Prophet: ::blushing again:: I usually just listen.
Katchoo: ::purring:: That's fine, because I usually talk.
Prophet: ::regaining confidence:: Oh, that's good. ::still confused:: Well, Kat, I really do have to go, but maybe later?
Katchoo: ::turning slightly, moving into the shadows:: Well, enjoy your surfing, and if you're ever in Glocamora, look me up.
Prophet: ::trying to follow ?her? across the room:: Yes, see you sometime.
Katchoo: ::softly:: I'd like that.
Prophet: Bye . . . ::looking back over his shoulder as he leaves the room::
Katchoo: ::blowing kiss::
Prophet: ::big smile:: Oh well, another online mystery::
Katchoo: ::curling up onto the carpet, thinking about Prophet::
Katchoo: ::glancing up:: Alone again.
Prophet: ::peeking back in the door:: Uh, by the way, excuse me for asking . . .
Katchoo: ::blinking:: ?
Prophet: Are you a girl? :)
Katchoo: ::sighing:: -
Prophet: ::talk about extended foreplay::
Katchoo: Well, I sort of decided not to talk about that, because I really do enjoy the slipperiness of it all. ::turning red:: So to speak.
Prophet: :) Yeah, me too. What would your wife say?
Katchoo: ::laughing:: I'm not married!
Prophet: ::hummmm . . . did that answer my question::
Katchoo: ::laughing delightedly at perplexed expression on his face::
Prophet: Well, I really do have to go (real world), but it has been FUN.
Prophet: See you around this "room" . . .
Katchoo: ::rising to my feet:: ::walking over to Prophet:: ::putting my hands on your shoulders::
Prophet: ::standing by the door::

Katchoo: ::leaning forward and kissing you gently on the cheek:: Bye now.

Prophet has left the room.

Isn't he just the cutest?
—W.<<

Toobe Entry con't

Yeah, real cute. I'm thrilled. Oh, and THIS: I must get a few hundred a day:

>>**To: Toobe**
From: Blaze@Hardcopy.com
Subj: Article

We're very eager to hear from you, sir. We are prepared to go live on camera at a moment's notice should you give us an interview. I've gotten the go-ahead for $100,000, as you requested. We've got everything else, and as you know have been reporting on the Scratch and Winc story every night.

Please get back to me asap.
—Blaze Selder
Producer, *Hard Copy*<<

Man, these people are sly. I never requested anything! They just started with a $25,000 offer, then more. Jabba sez not to answer them at all, or they can claim I started negotiations. She also sez she's working on something that will help. An e-bomb?

Things have escalated, really spooky. Something I learned from all my dad's clippings of the '60s is that once somebody gets to be a hero they get shot. I don't want that. All I want is for my two friends to talk to each other again.

And for the law to find somebody else to fry.

End Toobe Entry

‹HAPTER NINE

Narrative Entry, Jabbathehut

With beefy hands folded behind his head, Lt. Wallace Budge stares out the lone window at the splendor of spring in Washington. He's replaying last night's dinner conversation in his mind, him and Shel at his favorite steak joint.

She'd said: "They have a point, you know. They haven't broken any laws yet, because they're aren't any yet."

"I know!" he'd said. "I just want them to come in, have their trial, become even bigger media heroes than they are now, get off scot-free, and let *me* get back to some real police work!"

"You *want* that?" she'd asked.

He'd slumped a bit in his chair, saying nothing.

Softly she'd added, "Sounds like a crisis of the heart to me."

What the hell had *that* meant? Before he can ruminate further, a message pops onto his screen. Better not be another ad for "How to Get a Man and Keep Him." It's not.

To: Ms. Budge
From: Undersec'y Labouchere
Subj: Good Explanation Ready

We have egg on our face over more than this Six Flags fiasco, and I hear you've been withholding information from Enforcement? What the HELL do you think you're doing? I'm waiting for your answer. —L.

It was time for a good old-fashioned meeting, time to mount the stairs to Ms. Labouchere's high-tech black-and-white office, and have a *mano a mano*. She'd agreed to meet—three minutes of her precious time. But she'd blasted him before he could even shove his big frame into one of her cold, chrome chairs.

"MS. BUDGE?! Do you KNOW that we've become a laughing stock over this? Did you KNOW that Letterman is intimating that you and I are LESBIANS? It hasn't been this bad since Reno took the oath of office with that awful haircut! Answer up, mister."

He didn't like the way she'd said mister. But he had practiced his counting to ten routine, and although it sometimes crept to eleven or twelve, he'd responded fairly well, he thought.

"I've heard all about it," he'd begun. "You know as well as I do that the media is gonna make a pig's ear out of any silk purse we give them. We can't get distracted." He'd looked up, expectantly, hoping that would wrap things up. She'd waited for more, so he'd pushed on.

"Ma'am . . . I'm *sorry* this is looking bad in the media. It's part of my plan to lull Scratch and Winc into a false sense of security. If they think I'm out of it, they'll slip, they're bound to. I can taste it. We're about three days away from locating them. Henderson will bag them. Four days, tops." As the words were out of his mouth, he realized Shelly had seen all this coming.

"Scratch was right," she'd said as he was chomping on his sirloin. "They'll take you down over this one if you don't deliver soon."

He'd sat, nodding, silent for a long time.

"And Winc was right, too," she'd said softly.

"Oh?"

She'd smiled. "You are quite handsome in a rugged sort of way."

But the undersec wasn't going to cut him any slack, and he could almost feel a searing heat coming off the very hair of his fearless leader. He winced at the memory. She'd stood up, drawing herself up to her full five feet four inches, which suddenly looked more like six.

"PLAN?" she'd exploded, and in a perverse sort of way, he'd been relieved.

"You don't get it, do you? Screw Henderson, this has got nothing to do with him. It's got nothing to do with Scratch or Winc either. There's an epidemic out there, Lieutenant. Scratch and Winc are *symbols*."

He'd whipped his head around at that one. He had begun to suspect the same thing, but had no idea she'd pegged it, too.

"They're catalysts," she'd sputtered again, searching in the air for something that would somehow get through to him. "For some reason—and we have our top shrinks working on it, believe me—everyone is falling into line, and they've *all* begun to resist Registration. Do you know what that means? Have you any idea *why* there's a Registration?

He'd starting counting again. All the way from the beginning. Of course he knew why there was Registration. That's what the Triumvirate demanded for dropping all that cash into the Infobahn in the first place. God knows the government was too broke to do it. So the name, rank, serial number, and preferred body odor antidotes were all handed over to Big Biz. He said as much, all but adding, "Yeah, so what?" at the end of his little recitation. Instead, he'd looked balefully back at his boss. He didn't like how calm she got, all of a sudden.

"We are letting down our end of the bargain, Lieutenant," she'd said evenly, her voice low. "All over the Net, ad campaigns are failing because you have let Scratch and Winc stay out there and stir up *shit!*"

She paused. Breathed. Continued.

"You catch them. You catch them *fast.* You add Conspiracy to Overthrow the Government. That's treason. We have a court order. If you have any doubts about how serious this is, you read the document. I just sent it to you. Find them. Catch them."

He'd tried to run with the "S and W are symbols" thing.

"If I catch them they'll be bigger heroes, you know. Maybe . . ." He had five seconds to save his own life. He ignored the little voice inside. ". . . maybe the Reg thing does need to be looked at more carefully."

"The Reg may be doomed," she spat, "but it's not going to be *my* fault, am I making myself quite clear? We catch the criminals, they go through the system, they whistle Dixie on one leg if they want to, but *we* won't have any shit on our hands, you get it?"

She came around from behind her desk. Stood just a little close so he had to look up at her. Oldest management trick in the book.

"Basic police work, or has it been too long since you graduated the Academy?"

He got up, looked her square in the face, and in his deepest voice said, "Yes Ma'am," turned on his heel, and left.

Seconds later there was a memo on his screen:

To: Ms. Budge
From: Undersec'y Labouchere
Subj: If you have doubts . . .

    . . . as to what I'm saying, read on . . .

—L.

                      ◎ click here to read attached file: "NoRegNo$.DOC"

Uh oh.

Source1: persLOG/budge/harddrive
Source2: bckupfiles @ FBCS.gov

End Jabba Entry

Toobe Entry

They finally sent me the questions they wanted to ask each other. It's a start. Never thought of them myself, but now I hope they show me their answers. This just popped up today. Pretty excellent.

E-fitti of the Day
Surgery happy USA

Don't you think it's kinda weird that if you want to have a
surgeon break your nose, suck out fat from your hips, stretch
your face tight over your skull, or add dangerous globs of
saline to your breasts you can go sign up and do it, but . . .

if you want to change your genitalia you have to live as
the opposite sex *before* the change (just a mite dangerous in
this culture), go to therapy, and play the nice girl/boy and get
permission?

I bet if I looked in Big Brother's closet I'd find stacks of
porno magazines . . .

Winc had to "live as a woman" while ze was starting hormones. Ze really looked kind of
"in between" for awhile there. That's like going out in drag against your will. It was a year of
doing that before ze could have the surgery. Then ze was told to make up an entire childhood
as a little girl, so when ze talked with people, they wouldn't suspect ze was once a guy. I
remember hir practicing that kinda stuff with me, way early in hir change. We both hated it,
ze only did it for a few days. Ze once said that being in therapy for being a seckshul (hir word
for transsexual, not mine) was the only therapy where they encouraged you to lie.

Everywhere I look there's the News, which Gwynyth won't let me watch much, and the Net
jumping all over the place with messages from everywhere. Brazil. New Zealand. Vienna. They're
all saying the same thing, mostly about Scratch and Winc. But also about other stuff, like cen-
sorship and greed. It's hard to follow, hard to figure out what people are so upset about. What
would they think if they knew Scratch and Winc were mad at each other, asking each other
questions like the ones I just got from each of them?

End Toobe Entry

Begin narrative entry, Gwynyth
Gwynythmydiary.logenterpassword *****:

Scratch is so desperate to find out about hir darling, ze asked me to help hir lurk online
without being detected. Scratch strays into the Farm Report daily, but Winc does not. My autolog
captured Scratch's journey as it always does.

Scratch did find Winc (HoneyLove) in a "spy" room, with just one other person. In Scratch's
state, I'm sure ze never noticed the desperate quality of the exchange. Winc lights from room
to room, never staying long enough to have a real conversation.

I want to shake them both! I'm about to side with the child, and tell them they've had enough time.

The boy does *not* like that I refer to him as "the child," and has taken to calling me "Girlie" in retaliation. Very well ... henceforth, I shall call him "Toobe."

Autolog entry:
Online Host: you are in room "007."

Bond007: Hey, babe!

HoneyLove: ::turning slowly so as not to give away any emotion:: James?

Bond007: ::inclining head:: Honey.

HoneyLove: ::purring, fingers wandering to spaghetti straps:: What brings *you* out on a night like this?

Bond007: ::gesturing to barkeep:: Heard you were in town. What other reason could I need? Buy you a drink, Honey?

HoneyLove: ::feeling the flush creep up into my face, resting my chin in the palm of my hand:: Yes. The usual.

Bond007: It's been a long time, Honey.

HoneyLove: ::arching an eyebrow . . . pointedly ignoring your hand on the bar::

HoneyLove: *I* wasn't the one who said "next week in Amsterdam" and didn't show up . . . beast! ::taking a cigarette from my case, holding it to my mouth::

Bond007: ::producing a lighter, touching the flame to your cigarette::
But I'm here now, Honey. ::reaching to take your hand between both of mine::

HoneyLove: ::inhaling deeply:: There's . . . someone else in the picture, James. ::squeezing your fingers gently with mine::

Bond007: I see. And so we're . . .

HoneyLove: ::bringing your hand up to my mouth, taking your fingers between my lips, then releasing them and smiling up at you:: We're illicit. James.

Bond007: ::tracing the outline of your mouth with my forefinger:: Well, then. Shall we Register under an assumed name? When the champagne comes, shall we answer the door in dark glasses?

HoneyLove: ::shuddering slightly:: Only if you promise not to use the glasses with the mustache and false nose! ::laughing delightedly::

Bond007: ::moving closer::

I promise, Honey. Something as tasteful as you are
. . . but not as beautiful. We'd be sure to be remembered then . . .

HoneyLove: ::low laughter:: There are still wait staff
in Tangiers who will never forget us, darling.

Bond007: Hey, gorgeous, guess what?

HoneyLove: ::sipping my drink:: What, hon?

Bond007: I ran into Scratch online today!

HoneyLove: ::slapping you hard across your face:: That's
for Venice, you pig! ::leaning forward and kissing you
hard on the mouth::

Bond007: ::kissing back, enjoying the taste of your
mouth and the softness of your neck under my hand::
I'll take my punishments, Honey, if I get my rewards.

HoneyLove: ::breaking free, running my hand through my
hair:: I've learned nothing about you if I haven't
learned *that*, James.

Bond007: ::chuckling:: I mean it about Scratch . . .
what a character!

HoneyLove: How lovely for you, dear.

Bond007: ::raising one eyebrow:: Don't you think that's
the most amazing thing?

HoneyLove: ::suddenly aware of my need to be held, looking up at you, eyes smoldering::

Bond007: Oh damn . . . I have to make *some* effort to
get to work. Can we make this for later? I'm really
sorry!

HoneyLove: ::laughing lightly:: Sure . . . no problem,
darlin'.

Bond007: ::nuzzling your ear:: I'll tell you all about
sex with Scratch then, OK?

End autolog 2:14 a.m.

Gwyn.mydiary.cont.

Curse me for my Virgo thoroughness and efficiency. The damn autolog is too vigilant. It pro-
ceeded to follow Scratch to another assignation: a private room. Apparently ze sought an old
friend for advice.

Autolog:
Online Host: You have entered the room "Butchbond."

Scratch: Hey girl.

Vicky: Scratch! Is that really you?

Scratch: Yep, it's me.

Vicky: ::blinking:: Just like that? How the hell can you be online as . . . you?

Scratch: Long story. But it's safe, OK?

Vicky: You're a celebrity! Wow, so much to catch up on!

Scratch: Um, if you wouldn't mind, I'd rather not talk about it. That's not really me anyway.

Vicky: ?

Scratch: ::waving hand:: It's all out of control. I got something else on my mind anyway. Just needed to talk to a dyke, knowhatimean?

Vicky: OK, honey, what's up?

Scratch: There's this person, let's say it's a her, for lack of a better term . . .

Vicky: Oh, I don't know, I'm enjoying hir and ze lately.

Scratch: You know about those?

Vicky: Scratch, everybody uses them. Where you been?

Scratch: ::shrugging:: So let's say this person's called Frankie. We play with gender. Splatter all into boy and girl, or something beyond.

Vicky: You and a million other people.

Scratch: Right. So just now I looked for hir online as that character, then donned mine, and found hir having this stupid romance novel-ish encounter with a dude . . .

Vicky: Oh, yes. ::knowing sigh::

Scratch: I feel stupid, this was supposed to be what it was about, but I got jealous! And of course, I've cyberfucked all kinds of people as all kinds of people. It's just the old fragile ego; I could kick myself.

Vicky: Oh, Scratch, I don't think it is just that . . .

Scratch: Yeah?

Vicky: I think you two have moved into tender areas of the heart . . .

Scratch: True.

Vicky: I mean, we're talking about Winc, right?

Scratch: ::blushing:: Uh huh.

Vicky: Cyberspace is real. The feelings are real. We don't want to lose what has become valuable . . .

Private Message to Scratch

HackDood: Whoa! Scratch? *The* Scratch?

Scratch: Sorry, Doode, I just copped the screen name. Scratch is a hero of mine.

Scratch: Yeah, real.

Vicky: And you care for hir deeply, I can see that . . .

Scratch: ::nodding head::

Vicky: There's an invisible line you can cross over, when it's not play anymore, and the heart is outraged. So tell me more about Frankie.

Scratch: ::grumbling:: We want to explore these characters, actually *be* them, not just play them, because why should it matter what we really are, you know?

Vicky: That's terrific!

Scratch: Right, but first time I see hir doing that with *other* people. . . . I gotta wonder how unique our thing really was. What's real, what's not, you know?

Vicky: Yes.

Scratch: I may pick all kinds of characters online, but I'm still an alpha wolf, no matter what.

Vicky: Alpha wolf?

Scratch: ::blushing:: A dominant type.

Vicky: Oh. ::big grin:: Me, too!

Scratch: But I'm evolved enough to know I should lose that trait . . .

Vicky: I don't think jealousy is about dominance . . .

Scratch: Mmm, but watching hir go under to someone else is hard. Especially to a man! Dominating someone else, no prob.

Vicky: ::smile:: Interesting . . .

Scratch: But if I can't walk my talk here, what good am I? ::muddled head::

Vicky: I don't know which would be harder for me. Probably watching my woman with a man . . .

Scratch: Right. That's decades of vintage dyke persona to lose.

Vicky: Well, damn, why should you?

Scratch: I hate the jealous shit. Thought I had it more together.

Vicky: Oh, right. Did you tell "Frankie"?

Scratch: No, we're taking a break just now.

Vicky: I see. ::wry smile::

Scratch: ::sheepishly:: Yeah. I'm getting over myself. When I do, I think we'll start up again. I hope.

Vicky: I'll be curious to see what happens.

Scratch: Thanks pal. You're great.

End Autolog 03:45 a.m. EDT

autoescape: Gwynythmydiary.logclose
End Gwynyth Entry

Toobe Entry

Later that day. (Always wanted to write that.) So here are the questions . . .

>>**To: Winc**
From: Scratch
Subj: Can I ask?

Okay, let's say I've got the music right: I love you, I want to be with you somehow, but the words are still fucked up, I have questions that are stupid but I have to ask them of *somebody*. It might as well be you since you're the reason I'm asking them.

—Scratch

To: Scratch
From: Winc
Subj: Questions

What do you mean, "I love you"? *Heck* of a thing to say. I guess I've got nothing to lose by answering as honestly as I can, and maybe even something to gain.

Your questions aren't stupid. Questions are brave. All that understood, here goes. I'm writing out the questions as you asked them.

Why do so many transsexuals wear too much makeup and look like they're about twenty years behind the time fashion-wise?

You should have seen me a few years ago, you would have gagged. I was trying so hard to be all the fashion models I'd grown up *wanting* to be. They became "woman" to me. They were literally my models. It's like that e-fitti about pigeons . . . you don't see the baby ones cuz they stay in the nest until they're fully grown, which happens in a matter of days, and then they *look* like grown-ups, only we don't see them. It's like that with transsexual women, only sort of in reverse: the "so many transsexuals" you see are the babies . . . the ones who are still trying stuff out. Once we find out it isn't all makeup and clothes, we settle into being ourselves, and we "pass." You don't *see* the "grown-up" seckshuls, we blend in.

Do you still have facial hair?
 ::groaning:: Yeah, I do. I have to scrape my face every day. It's a sore spot with me (literally!). But electrolysis, where they zap each and every hair with an electric current, is *so* expensive: $40–$80 an hour. And the average number of hours needed is around 200–300. I'm lucky, I'm on this estrogen stuff that seems to slow down the growth-rate of my beard. ::wincing:: Anyway, I seem to be able to go for a little over 24 hours.

If you were het before, are you lesbian now? Or did your sexuality change too and now you're a straight woman?
 ::slow smile:: Who wants to know? Are you flirting with me again? ::laughing lightly:: I've always been attracted to women romantically and sexually, and those are two differ-ent attractions. I've always been attracted to men sexually, but never romantically. What does that make me? When I was being Man, I figured I wasn't *really* a woman because I was *attracted* to women. I didn't have that heart-zing for men (like I did for you). But I *tried* getting involved with men. Spent a whole period of my life picking up guys, and I was a guy, right? I'd pick up these men, well, I'd let them pick *me* up, and they'd take me to their homes, it's late at night, and they'd lay down on their living room floors, and I'd suck them off. I liked doing that. A lot. But we always had to be quiet, because their wives were sleeping in the next room or upstairs. I'm not making this up.
 Am I a straight woman now? No way! I'd still like to boff a

guy with this new equipment I have (You do know I went ahead and had this genital surgery stuff, right?), but it's scary. Guys scare me. So, no, all that said, I guess I'm not straight.

Do you tell people you used to be a boy even though you weren't really, in your mind?

::gently:: Scratch, I *was* a boy. No in-the-mind about it. I was a boy, and later I was a man. I think that mind-body-spirit is so tightly woven that you can't say anything like "I wasn't really a boy, in my mind." At least *I* can't--it's just not my story. I was a boy, and I hated it. I was a man, and I hated it. I changed my body, and I changed my mind, and now my spirit feels so much more free! Yes, I tell people I want to be close to. And now you're going to ask why didn't I tell you from the start. Because we agreed not to say anything, and whatever you were being online, you kept bringing out the girl in me, the femme in me, and I loved that so much, and then I got scared again that you would freak if you knew.

Did you wear your mother's clothes when you were little?

::smiling:: What kind of transsexual textbooks have you been reading, hon? No, except for one time when I was about five or six. It felt really taboo to me, very wrong. I mean, that was Mom, not Woman. That was wearing Mom's clothes, not women's clothes. I made my own clothes to wear, though, from towels, old blankets, drapes, whatever, when I was a little kid.

Did you have to learn how to "be a woman" in terms of mannerisms and attitude, or was it already there?

Had to learn. It's all learned, isn't it? Look at how uncomfortable you were in being Mom at Coney Island, darling. That's how I spotted you from across the park. You never learned that girl stuff, and I'm so glad you didn't. But wait, maybe you did learn and you rejected it? That's a question for you. I'll add it to my list.

Do you miss your dick?

::hands on hips, tossing my head back defiantly:: And just *what* makes you think I don't have one now? I *do*, hon. The docs just cut it open like they were filleting a fish. Then they scraped out all the spongey stuff, turned it inside-out, and poked it up inside me, like when you turn a sock inside-out! So it's still there, technically, just in another, more, um, palatable shape. ::laughing merrily:: No, I don't miss it. I never hated my dick, though. I kinda liked it. It was sweet, in a vulnerable way. I loved making myself come with it. But I hated what it made me in the eyes of everyone else: a man. What I've been learning with you is that gender is as much how people relate to you as what you feel, and all these people were relating to me as a man, and it was all because of this thing hanging down between my legs, so . . . snip snip.

Do you have all female parts and do you come?

::eyes sparkling:: Female parts? When did we become such a prude, dear heart? I have a surgically-constructed vulva, vagina, cervix, and clitoris, if that's what you want to know. I have no internal stuff like uterus and ovaries. But wait a minute . . . what are female parts? Prior to my genital surgery, I was female. That cock and those balls were female, only I couldn't see it then. There are *people*, I think, not males and females, not biologically anyway . . . there are people with dicks, and people with cunts.

Do I come? ::softly:: Yeah, yeah. Do you think I faked it with you online?

***Hope these are okay. Part of the reason I'm asking is because the more I think of my questions, the more I recognize myself. I had to learn how to act female, too, and I was born one. Ask me some, too, okay?**

You answered my question about having to learn. Okay, I lied to you a little bit. I knew about butch and femme before seeing that online board. Here's how I knew: When I was first trying out my stuff, I would get myself dressed to the nines, way femme, right? And I would go out to lesbian bars. I was too scared to try to pick anyone up, or to let someone *pick* me up, but there was this one bar I used to go to and sit and have a drink, watch, study, learn. I couldn't really relate to all these young bar bunnies, not physically, but the *life* they had! The exuberance! I wanted that. But there I was, this tall gangly, older man/woman. They weren't very gentle with me. Can't say I blame them, not in hindsight. I was pretty defensive.

Anyway, I finally got up the courage one night to go upstairs, where the bathroom was. I walked slowly through the milling tank-topped girl bodies, and made my way upstairs where I'd never been before. There was this room— all these older women sitting there in shirtsleeves and ties— they were sprawled out in these chairs, and hon, their eyes lit up the minute I walked into the room. I'll never ever forget that moment. They were happy to see me. This one sweet butch said, "Hell-l-l-lo, sugar, come have a seat." And she stood up for me, so gallant. I sat there, and it was a dream come true They bought me drinks, we danced, I watched them play pool, they showed me how. I choked on one of their cigars, they laughed, but not *at* me. It's when I first realized I could be happy as girl, with butches. I went down there as frequently as I could. Then, like most of the girl bars in the city, that one closed down, and there was no place where they were hanging out, not that I knew of, anyway. That's around the time that Toober taught me about this online stuff.

—W.

To: Winc
From: Scratch
Subj: Questions

Wow. Great answers. Thank you. ::going back into the laboratory, or is that drawing board:: Don't feel bad about lying about the butch/femme stuff. I did, too, obviously. I know the outside world, and most lesbians, really smirk at the concept, but it's a yin yang thing more than anything. Fuck what people think, if it works. (Although obviously I'm not a classic butch, born too late and never got trained right!)

Okay, here's what you wrote me, and my answers to you.
>>You're surprising me again. You keep doing that, I like that
about you. But I'm just going to ask you my questions, and
see what that leads to. ::deep breath::
—W.<<

**Why do most lesbians have such short hair? ::gently:: Why
do *you*?**

The better question might be to ask a lot of men why they
don't have long hair. They'll probably tell you it's a pain in
the ass to keep up. Most straight men I know love long hair on
women, so straight women grow it. Me, I don't have to.

**Are you *trying* to look mannish? Pass for "man" in the
world?**

This is pretty funny coming from you! What's a man?
What's a woman? Nope, I love being a woman. There's more
ways for women to look like than they have in the fast food
machines. Sometimes I wear eyeliner because it looks cool.
Pass for a man? When we rescued Toobe, that was *you* trying to pass as a guy! When I get dressed in the morning, I'm
going for comfort, power, and sometimes armor, but never
disguise.

**Don't people stare at the way you look? Why do you do it?
Please don't get me wrong. I think you're *way* sexy and
attractive! But I've seen people stare at butches. Doesn't it
get to you?**

Lately I tell myself they stare because I look so damned
good. (Okay, this works about a tenth of the time.) Why would
I want to look like everyone else?

**Why do lesbians insist on "women only" spaces? Isn't that
really denying the existence of nearly 50% of the people in
the world? Isn't it just hiding away?**

Hey, I'm not the lesbian party line. I probably offend as
many gay women as I do anyone. It *is* hiding away and it
feels great. Any guy can tell you how fun it is to sit in a bar
with his buds and watch TV. It's a breather from dealing with
the "opposite" sex. He just doesn't have to go through a lot of
crap about it, and put up a bunch of flyers to do it. My ques-

tion is, why do men want to go into women-only spaces, or why are they offended by them? Why do they think it has anything to do with them at all?

What do lesbians do with their attractions to men (they have them, I know)?

Great question. The great taboo. The younger generation's doing better than mine on it. I still get very attracted to men. I used to go to bed with them even though I called myself a lesbian. But it was never worth it. The sex was always the same, I didn't care about them emotionally, they just don't interest me. Now I just enjoy my attractions, but don't act on them. To hell with people who think that's being attracted to the "wrong" sex. That's where all our crap started, right?

What was it like for you, growing up? Were you a tomboy? Did you hang with the guys? Play sports?

I was definitely a tomboy. Fortunately so was my mother, so I got to do it for a longer time than most girls. But then she got freaked out and thought I'd end up being a girl who couldn't get a guy. She started girl-ifying me. One day I went out to play kickball and only the boys were there! I looked around for the rest of the team and finally found them in the bathroom. They were playing with makeup and showing off their newly shaved legs. It was like some dog whistle had called them and I never heard it. I started doing it, too, so I'd be normal: stockings, skirts, high heels . . . which I hated but figured something was wrong with me. When I came out as a dyke, my girlfriend said if I didn't like it I didn't have to wear it; I haven't since. But there are lots of lesbians who wear skirts and lipstick, etc. Because they like it. They're just never noticed. It's a particular thorn in their sides, because they're always getting come-ons from guys; a lot of lesbians don't notice them either. They're caught in the middle.

Why were you attracted to me? What turned you off about me? Does it have to do with this butch/femme thing? Your identity as lesbian? Are you only attracted to "real" women? Femme women?

Who knows what makes people attracted. I seem to define my "type" and then fall for someone completely different.

I'm drawn to the femme, mostly in women, but sometimes in a good girl-guy, too. I'm drawn to the femme in you, online and live. But I was a little disoriented at seeing you physically for the first time. It was the idea of who you are that's making me into a jerk. The unknown freaked me out, numbed out my libido for a while. It's still a bit numb, but it's coming back. Nothing in you turned me off.

*Where'd you get the name "Razorfun"? What's that all about?**

I like knives, razor blades, and scalpels. I like to watch the blood run out of my skin, and sometimes out of other people's skin, if they want it. Blood is life force, powerful water of the body. Blades liberate it. Once again, in that room, we connected, that time through blood.

**Those are my questions for now. I'm getting on with my life, darlin', surfing and ::peering over my shoulder:: avoiding the law. Oh! Speaking of which, that Lt. Budge thinks you're a guy.

I'm real sorry it hasn't worked out with us, and I hope to see you from time to time when these wounds are healed. ::laughing:: No, I'm not being Ingrid Bergman, just realistic.
—W.**

Well, Budge is convinced you're a helpless sweet thang, so we must be doing something right. Motherfucker. Did he try to play you off me? Tell you I told him everything? You *know* I'd never, right?
—S.<<

End Toobe Entry

Narrative Entry, Jabbathehut

A weary, wary, Wally Budge clicks disconsolately at a small button on his screen. She said to read it, so he's gonna read it. A document opens up immediately, but is blocked by a window.

MOST TOP SECRET
ENTER PASSWORD NOW

Tip-tap-tip-tap-tip-tap-tip-tap.

Last night's garlic-soaked steak and pasta begins to rumble even more loudly in his gut as he reads the crisp, sharp document on the screen, complete with animated logo. Man, this T. A. of B. doesn't mess around. The only odd thing about it is it isn't addressed to him.

>>To: Undersec'y Labouchere, Bureau of Census and Statistics
From: Mr. Blaine, Triumvirate Assocation of Businesses
Subj: No Registration/No Money

I'll dispense with the amenities, Margaret, and cut to the chase. We are in deep brown sauce. Permit me to summarize:

Registration, only 74% complete, has ground to a complete stop. Rubes everywhere are Registering as "Scratch" or "Winc," and *that* has begun to foul up our database.

E-ads are being ridiculed to the point of ineffectiveness. Don't get me wrong, UnderSecretary, we *like* it when ads get ridiculed. People tend to remember them. We cheer every time Leno rakes an ad over the coals. But this is different: Ads are being *ignored*. Take a trip to the Web and find the Scratch and Winc page. You will see that a grassroots campaign has been mounted: "If Scratch and Winc Don't Need It, Neither Do I." And I thought this was America.

Direct email campaigns are failing. Rubes are sending back ads, they're not signing up for the giveaways. People are realizing they do not have complete access to the Net, but only to areas our demosurveys indicate they would *enjoy*. They are demanding COMPLETE ACCESS. Have you any idea what a mess that would be? And why do you suppose they want complete access, when most of them can't even access their microwave to cook their morning poptarts? Because Scratch and Winc have full access; *those* two are using illegal bypasses which your department cannot seem to stop!<<

Budge closes his eyes for a moment. What had he said to Shelly? Something about shit-canning the ads that had come to him. She'd said she'd done the same with most of the ones that came to her. But it had nothing to do with Scratch and Winc. What're they trying to hang on these two jokers? He lifts his eyes to the window and stares out at an amber-tinted sky. Then it hits him. They're trying to stick Scratch and Winc with their own fuck-ups. All that money sunk into the Net as the ultimate advertising medium, and it flopped beyond belief. To cover their asses, Scratch and Winc are taking the rap. Damn. He keeps reading.

>>Lastly: Scratch and Winc are trouble. They must be apprehended. If they are not behind bars in five days, I have been instructed to inform you that funding for the nation's infobahn will swiftly disappear.
Yours truly,
—Robert Blaine, esq.<<

Source1: persLOG/budge/harddrive
Source2: bckupfiles@FBCS.gov
Source3: TAB.confid/pers.com

End Jabba Entry

Toobe Entry

No word back yet from my pals. Guess it's a little early. Time for a bit of Net-surfing. Lookie what I got!

>>Subj: Announcing WinMark's E-MALE Bonus Club!
From: winmark@gw.tenpercent.com
To: malecitiz@gw.tenpercent.com
Introducing the WinMark E-MALE Bonus Club (R)
Men: community-oriented economic power can now be yours—discreet, at home and at your service. We're the clearinghouse dedicated to products, services, and specially chosen merchandise—all tailored to the interests of sophisticated men only. Our package—called DIRECT MALE—can be yours for the asking.
Magazines, Travel, Merchandise, it's all for you!
To begin receiving these free quality offers (nonsexual), just email us!
Copyright WinMark Concepts, Inc.<<

So I used the form letter that's been going around. Started out as a guerrilla document they said Scratch wrote, but ze swears ze didn't. Now it's standard operating procedure to keep sending these things back, with this attached:

>>Subj: Re: Announcing WinMark's E-MA . . .
From: I. Citizen
I'm really curious. How did you target me for this mass

mailing? Did it go to everyone, did you track certain patterns of my use of the Net, or did you just send this out to everyone and hope you'd get a few responses? I'm seriously interested, as I'm studying Internet advertising patterns.

Please let me know. I'm not a gay male, so I wanted to see why you'd take the risk . . .

—Citizen Individual<<

They just sent all that back with this added:

>>Please call us at 202-555-1300 and ask for David Canowicz.<<

Yeah, right. I'll just do that.

End Toobe Entry

Narrative Entry, Jabbathehut

There are times when it seems the entire Net is abuzz with activity. Anxiety and excitement, passion and pontification heat up the wires with a veritable hum all around the world. Other times, as impossible as it seems, a deep melancholy seems to infuse the scenery, not unlike a lone diner in the desert, one light on.

This night it feels as if there are two lights on. I conjure the image of a figure hovered over a rough table, feather pen and burning candle flickering over a piece of paper. Another figure, far away, stares out a window at a city long gone to sleep. I allow a message to be retrieved:

>>To: Jabbathehut
From: Johnny@BuschGard. antivir.parkdomain.bot:GwynCirce
Subj: Help
My friend:
Can you get this to Winc? I'd use Gwynyth's routes but I've already imposed too much. It's just email, but obviously I can't use my real name or the regular conduits anymore. It must get to hir, as a letter from Scratch. Thanks if you can.
—S.<<

The impartial stranger gives way, and I honor the request.

>>To: Winc
From: Scratch
Subj: Us

Midnight . . .

I'm a bear of little brain. I can't remember what our particular isms or differences are, and I don't care. I'm furious at this Budge character, miss you fierce, even miss Toobe, I mean, the old way we used to write to him. Lately my letters to him have been whiney.

I feel such love for you, my friend, my lover, my fellow traveler. Your vulnerability is overwhelming sometimes, until I realize it is my own. You're right, there is no support for outlaws, even among ourselves. Your path is so lone, as is mine, and we cannot help each other, any more than we do in comforting words. But we still return to relating, to the realizations, albeit alone.

I am sad that today, when I broached the subject of relating to people without a gender identity, or even sexual preference, the possibility of simply loving whoever comes along, I got blank faces, tinged with fear and judgment.

It kills me how the choices we make can instantly obliterate others. I appear to perch on fences because I cannot bear to lose sight of the other possibilities. As a grown-up, when I must make choices, I watch those possibilities slip away. My inevitable reaction is to turn inward, to write, to confide sometimes.

It's all the same thing—the connectedness of spirit, a capacity we're born with, and either spend our lives denying or searching out to the farthest corners.

I want that connection, to see and be seen, with someone. The point is, Winc, you do see. That's worth everything to me. More than any of my ignorance or fear of change. I miss you. Can we meet? Please.

Thanks for listening, my love. Goodnight.

—S.<<

The message was received.

End Jabba Entry

Toobe Entry

>>To: Toobe@SixFlags.TX.com
From: Winc@Firebreather.FunPark.com.bot:GywnCirce
Subj: Chat logs

This is trippy, Toobe. You're right, it's not just us resisting, it's coming from everywhere. What do you do when you're leading the parade (not that we wanted to, but I guess we are), and you look back and there's a bunch of people you don't recognize and some of them are downright scary? Read on. I'm Honeydew.

>>***OnlineHost: You are in "Gun Room." ***

John2334: Anybody know where I can buy a glock?
Tom NRA: Nevada, I think.

Member Profile
Name: Tom NRA
Age: 22
Sex: M
Gun: LUGER7
Occupation: Government worker
Hobbies: ARMY SNIPER, COLLECTOR
Quote: Get the government, before it gets you!

PDQ237: I had to settle for a Ruger Mini-30 . . .
Tom NRA: I have a Glock 17. GREAT GUN.
John2334: Tom NRA, can I buy it?
Davesnor: Anyone know what kind of guns Winc and Scratch pack?
Tom NRA: Sell my Glock? Sorry, never.
Georgia3: ::blushing:: Well, I've had some experience with *Winc's* gun, fellas.
PDQ237: Yeeeeeeee-HA!<<

[Toobe, I swear I don't recognize Georgia! Maybe under another name, though. ::wide grin::]

>>**Honeydew**: ::raising hand:: Question please?
Tom NRA: Honey: Go ahead.
Honeydew: Thanks Tom . . . figured this would be the place to ask: What do you think about govt intervention in online chats?
Tom NRA: Govt intervention generally sucks.
YoMan: Government should mind its own fucking business.
Spiker: What intervention?
Honeydew: ::nodding:: Do you think they're messing with us on *this* service?

YoMan: Yes, they definitely are.
Scoperfl: Ditto, government sux.

Private Message to Honeydew

Shooter: There were articles in lots of magazines. Check a library.
Honeydew: ::nodding:: Will do. It really spooks me. I *hate* the idea of being watched.
Shooter: And they can *control* you! If they don't like what I say or who I talk to, they can go after me. They don't do it a lot—there are lots of people online—but they do it.

Georgia3: Winc told me that's why he's running from the govt, Honeydew. They're watching, he said.
Honeydew: Ah. Hope he makes it.
Spiker: Here on this service they snoop?
Honeydew: More like peeking into our files, Spiker.
YoMan: They have Net cops roaming these rooms. Other services too.
Tom NRA: That's how they got on to Scratch and Winc so damned fast.
Spiker: ::muttering:: You think that's how?
Gunboy: Yep, goddamned Eyes.
Gundoode: Good old USA has everything tapped.
YoMan: Anyone else going to the Scratch and Winc rally tonite?

Private Message to Honeydew

Honeydew: ::shaking my head:: Cyberlife had so much promise.
Shooter: Still does. But it should be Anything Goes.
Honeydew: Anything?
Shooter: Who cares what I *type*? Can't harm anybody with keystrokes.
Honeydew: Exactly! Well, not quite exactly. I've had my feelings hurt several times.
Shooter: So they were hurt. Words aren't actions.
Honeydew: Uh huh.
Shooter: Actions are another story. I kill you, I should die too. But I say, "fuck you man, I'll kill you" online, means nothing.

Honeydew: Rally?
YoMan: Yeah! Time to fight back.

Spiker: ?

Tom NRA: We've got some plans, Spiker.

YoMan: If we're not careful, they're gonna catch Scratch and Winc. One of those poor slobs might screw up, and the govt will be listening.

YoMan: The NYC Police dept is looking for guys who want to talk to little girls.

Georgia3: It's true, I've heard from them.

YoMan: "Nothing to hide" isn't invite to snoop.

Spiker: Gee, Georgia, why have you heard from them?!

Barrel34: I know of a young lady who got nailed for sending out porno photos.

Spiker: Over the Net?

Barrel34: Yep.

Shooter: Bring on the gestapo!

Honeydew: Can they even look into private rooms?

MeStud: Sure, but the volume of traffic is too high for them to effectively monitor squat.

Shooter: You're paranoid dude.

Private Message to Honeydew

Honeydew: What you were saying about online stuff not hurting? I don't know, it's made me cry a couple of times.

Shooter: That's why tissues were invented. Have a good cry and get on with your life.

Honeydew: Yeah. Well, thanks for talkin'. You seem like a good guy.

Shooter: Thanks! Have fun, don't kill too many guys!

Honeydew: ::chuckling:: OK, you either!

John2334: Anybody know where I can get a glock 17 cheap?

Honeydew: You think they're really monitoring Scratch and Winc?

Tom NRA: Of course.

YoMan: They can't monitor it all, but they can be selective and frighten people.

Honeydew: They actually hire folks to check us out?

YoMan: Yes! Random checks like IRS.

Georgia3: Most common "charge" is Abusive Language.

Luger7: Glock 17, $475 any pawn shop.

Spiker: How do you know where to draw the line?

YoMan: Aw, shut up, Spiker, there's no line to fucking draw!

Luger7: Rem 870 $198, Walmart.
Georgia3: Well, I for one would fight for Winc.
SweetiePie: Scratch is more *my* style!

Private Message to Honeydew

Shooter: Do you have to fend off guys because you're so sexy?
Honeydew: ::narrowing my eyes:: Yeah, I'm just waiting for the next guy to ask me what I'm wearing,
Shooter: As long as it's sheer and sexy!
Honeydew: ::reaching for my dagger . . . deciding to forgive you::
Shooter: ::kiss . . . intense kiss . . . french kiss:: A dagger? That's my style!
Honeydew: ::growling:: Just be happy you're not in range. ::laughing::

Spiker: Lots of ways to fight back.
Honeydew: Fight back? Like how?
YoMan: Blow 'em up.
Spiker: Just shut off all our computers maybe?
Tom NRA: Spiker, then they win!
Honeydew: Yeah, wouldn't that be like cutting off our noses to spite our faces?
Tom NRA: Yes, Honeydew.
Spiker: Explain, Tom NRA.

Private Message to Honeydew

Shooter: Hey, you're a real tough cookie! :) I like my cookies with lots of crunch in 'em!
Honeydew: ::laughing softly:: Hope you find one . . . I'm strictly a ladies' girl, darlin'.
Shooter: Oh, too bad! :(But isn't there something I can still do for you?
Honeydew: ::smiling:: Wash the towels afterward?

Tom NRA: If we make ourselves suffer, they win. We stay on and practice 1st Amend., we win.
Spiker: True, but money talks.
Honeydew: ::waving:: Bye you guys. Take care!
Jay: Has anyone been shot before?
JEAN25: Before what?
Spiker: Anybody shoot anybody before?

Jay: Don't ask that!

Honeydew: ::pausing at the door, staring hard at Spiker::

Tom NRA: Don't anybody answer that question, I MEAN IT!

Spiker: Heh heh heh.

Honeydew has left the room.
End Chat log 20:37EDT.

Scary, huh, Toobers? I don't think they meant "fight back" through the ol' voting process . . .
<<

Toobe Entry con't

This is way too weird. They're doing it again. A few minutes after I got that log from Winc,
Scratch sends me this:

>>**To:** Toobe@SixFlags.TX.com..bot:GwynCirce
From: Scratch@Firebreather.FunPark.com..bot:GwynCirce
Subj: Gunnutz

Toober, it's a scary world out there in Normalland! I just
went to a gun room and they're obsessed! I got a couple of
Private Messages, but I was way too spooked to talk! I asked
them if they'd ever shot anybody. You could have heard a pin
drop. But no one said No!
—S.

Not only were they in the same room, but the random amusement park bypasses Gwynyth
gave us just happened to assign them each the same "random" addresses.

End Toobe Entry

Narrative Entry, Jabbathehut

"Hah!"

A third cigarette is burning in the ashtray, but Wally Budge takes no notice. There's a document scrolling down his screen, something Typhoid Mary found for him. Is this a Bingo?

"Locate Scratch/Winc @ Six Flags" was the query. Shelly had shown him how to send
Mary on what she called an "Open-Ended Search."

He'd had a bug up where it didn't belong about this amusement park thing. He'd turned
to Typhoid Mary for a list of all of Scratch and Winc's addresses. Wham, the file is scrolling down
the screen now, too quick to even read. Good sign.

But when he gets to the end of the download, it's a mess. He's kneading his brow with a
scratchy knuckle while he tries to make sense of this:

```
TITLE rec.roller coaster FAQ, part 2/3: Coaster info,
orgs, and refs
rec.roller coaster FAQ, part 2/3: Coaster info, orgs,
and refs
Archive-name: roller coaster-faq/part2
12:05:50 MDT
```

Uhhhhh ... huhhhhhh.

```
This is part 2 of the rec.roller coaster FAQ . . .
  Common abbreviations
  _____

A lot of things discussed on rec.roller coaster are in
acronym form. This is because writing out "Six Flags
Over Texas" several times in a posting is tedious, at
best; ``SFoT'' is much easier to write. Here are some
abbreviations you're likely to see in discussions on
rec.roller coaster.
```

What the hell?

```
ACE—American Coaster Enthusiasts
BGT—Busch Gardens Tampa, Tampa, FL
BGW—Busch Gardens Williamsburg, Williamsburg, VA
BTW—By the way
CI—Coney Island, Brooklyn, NY
DL—Disneyland, Anaheim, CA
FYI—For your information
GASM—Great American Scream Machine (roller coaster at
SFGA, Jackson, NJ)
```

His eyes are starting to spin. He lifts his eyes to the screen one more time. He's nothing if not game.

```
GP - General Public
IAAPA - International Assoc. of Amusement Parks and
Attractions
```

It goes on for pages. He'd been on wild-goose chases before ...

```
Definitions of Roller-Coaster terms
_____

Discussions among coaster enthusiasts can soon become
awash in jargon. Below is a list of coaster terms used
```

> by enthusiasts when discussing their favorite subject.
> This should help you impress friends and relatives with
> your knowledge of roller coasters. Cross-references to
> other definitions in the list are . . .<<

Cursing darkly, he stabs at the **Discontinue** button, putting a stop to the document transfer.

Transfer interrupted!

He calls Shelly. She takes one look at the mess he's accumulated, sighs, and fights to keep a smile off her face.

"Oh, Walls, I'm sorry. It's a Web site, and it's um . . . it's a really *great* collection of information about roller coasters. But it's not what you wanted, is it?"

He snorts. "You could say that." His teeth are clenched, he's got to stop doing that. "I want an explanation for why every time we do a search on Scratch, Winc, or Toobe we find them at some damn roller coaster!"

"It's so frustrating, isn't it?" Patiently she explains.

"Whoever set them up with the email addresses also attached a kind of circular loop. Every time you try to find out what the address corresponds to, you get this nice helpful file all about roller coasters."

"Well, isn't that special," he snarls. "There's gotta be a connection! First they're at Coney Island, and now . . ."

"Does it help to know that it's automatic? That there's nobody behind the screen doing this just to you? It's an automatic thing that will happen every time you try. There's no one behind it, really, just the guy who set it all up in the first place."

"Oh yeah, that helps a lot."

"Wally?"

"Yeah?"

"Maybe whoever set it up really likes roller coasters."

"So? That's about seventy million people!"

"You could do a stakeout."

"Huh?"

She's excited now. "A stakeout! Stake out the roller coaster Website. Tag everyone who signs on! Follow them down!"

His massive head swivels around until he's facing her.

"Shel," he says, "you're a peach."

Source1: persLOG/budge/harddrive
Source2: bckupfiles@FBCS.gov
Source3: diary.sdunlap@FBCS.gov

End Jabba Entry

Begin narrative entry, Gwynyth
Gwynythmydiary.logenterpassword ✶✶✶✶✶:

With satisfaction——I must admit——I note that the FAQ:roller coasters file has been accessed about thirty times. She's holding . . .

It seems word has gotten out that the orphans of the cyberstorm have a safe haven here at Farm Reports. Not good. If the "good guys," as Toobe calls them, can find these two, then someone else will, and soon.

The mail below came for Scratch, I forwarded it on to hir. At least no one else can intercept it. Can't say the same for anything that goes to Winc at that SixFlags address. Must remember the white light.

Hackers are afoot, breaking down bridges as soon as I build them. Winc has been tagged, and needs extra links, which still don't hold very long.

Note to myself: Collect more sage.

MailLog.autoforward: Scratchsecureverif.:

>>Email #1:
To: Scratch@FarmReports.com
From: TheStLouis7
Subj: We are . . . are you?

We are M.P.D. Multiple Personality Disorder. Only one of us likes the "Disorder" word, but that one is Boo who is down on everything about himself anyway. We want to know: Are you a gang like us? Is Winc? Is that why ✶you✶ are so many people online?

We look hard for others like us. We have certain signs we look for. The actual individual actions of each personality is probably the surest way to tell. And of course, sometimes there's time loss when one of us is being so much stronger than the rest. We've found among ourselves and other multiples is a fear of mirrors on the part of the host. She avoids looking in mirrors because she never sees the same face. Is it like that for you? Is that why you "change"? She also doesn't like clocks, they scare her. None of us like them. Time is an enemy, because time always disappears.

Do you have some time to write to us?

—StLouis7<<

End Mailog
autoescape: Gwynythmydiary.logclose
End Gwynyth Entry

Toobe Entry

>>**To: Toobe**
From: Scratch
Subj: Don't laugh . . .

I'm intrigued with these Multiple folks. They don't sound like kooks, you know, they sound cool, if you try to forget the fact that "they" is one person. Or "one person" as *we* know "one person."

How different from them am I? Maybe it *is* weird to insist on multiple genders. Or maybe it's not so weird to insist on retaining multiple personalities? They don't sound eager to "integrate" them all, or whatever the shrinks say they're supposed to do. Seems a sane response to the world.

Should I answer it?

—S.<<

>>**To: Scratch**
From: Toobe
Subj: Multiples

I had a long talk once with somebody who was diagnosed as MPD. Only ze called it Dissociative, I guess the newer term. I found hir to be totally together. (I didn't mean a pun there.)

—T.<<

>>**To: TheStLouis7**
From: Scratch@ (emailaddressscrambled)
Subj: Am I?<<

[I always have to remind Scratch it's Encrypted, not scrambled. Encrypted!]

>>Thanks for your note. I'm not a Multiple personality, but I really liked getting your letter. I related to a lot of it.

You should know that Winc and I never wanted to make any kind of statement, or that we know any answers to anything. We just did our thing and somehow a mirror was held up so all kinds of people are seeing different things, in us. I guess that's good, I just wish the Law wasn't one of them.

I just found out there's a Website on us, which has everything anyone's ever said about us. A Website's like a page of a magazine, where people can add their own stuff and read other stuff, right? And it's all held together by a computer network? Obviously I don't understand this stuff. I've always had a question. Where is the Web page actually located? I mean, is it in the air, made up of tiny electrons, or is it a physical thing held somewhere in a computer lab?

By the way, that Farm Reports address is not a good place to reach me. How did you find it? I'm afraid you can't reach me anywhere. My email address changes automatically every time I send something out. Sorry, it's the only protection I got right now.

—S.<<

End Toobe Entry

Begin narrative entry, Gwynyth
Gwynythmydiary.logenterpassword ×××××:

Toobe has kept me apace of the mail he's received from the lovesick ones. I'm slightly alarmed that several folks, although well intentioned, were able to get mail to Scratch. Must reenforce Circe.antivir.bot.

Mailog:

>>To: Scratch
From: Winc
Subj: Was reading some Zen stuff, and my brain fried . . .

Chuang Tzu taught that the mousetrap exists for the sake of the mouse: Once the mouse has been caught, you can forget the trap. He further taught that words exist for the sake of their meaning: Once the meaning has been grasped, you can forget the words. From his lessons, I've learned that identities exist for the sake of relationships: Once the relationship has been established, you can forget the identities. I find myself looking for one who has forgotten identity, so that we might be together in a relationship.

—W.<<

>>To: Winc
From: Scratch
Subj: My brain with fries to go

Me! Me! Take me! I'm forgetting identity! Trying anyway!

—S.<<

autoescape:Gwynyth\mydiary.log\close

End Gwynyth Entry

Jabbathehut Narrative Entry

And in a green office, bloodshot eyes stare at piece of email sent to Winc, asking for an online meeting. Stubby fingers rapidly type "Coalition" and punch for a cross-reference.

Source: persLOG/budge/harddrive

End Jabba Entry

✴

‹HAPTER TEN

Toobe entry

E-Pitti op the day

We've pretty much come to the end of a time when you can
have a space that is 'yours only'—just for the people you want
to be there. Even when we have our 'women-only' festivals,
there is no such thing. The fault is not necessarily with the
organizers of the gathering. To a large extent it's because we
have just finished with that kind of isolating. There is no
hiding place. There is nowhere you can go and only be with
people who are like you. It's over. Give it up.

—Bernice Johnson Reagon

>**To: Scratch**
From: Winc
Subj: Make it or take it

I guess you can know now: I don't live in Paris. I don't
even live in New York any more. Trenton, N.J., if you wanna
know the truth. I moved here about a week ago, when it started to get too weird. See, I was quite the fixture on the Lower
East Side, but I'm also a private person. You and I just have
different ways of being private. So: I was born in a small
town near here . . . the prodigal whatever returns. The bright
side: I kept my job. ::lop-sided grin:: You can do phone sex
from *anywhere*. It's pretty bleak here after NYC. I gotta
move back when all this blows over. There's this bridge here
over the river to Pennsylvania, and a huge sign that says,
"What Trenton Makes, the World Takes."

Look, you didn't do anything wrong. Neither of us did.
This whole thing is making me think deep, and that's always
good. I have a tendency to stick a smiley face all over myself,
like the great circus clowns. But too tired to make one up
now, for you.

What I want to know is why it matters so much to me,
how you feel about me, what we are to each other. Isn't that

what we've been discovering all this time: that we can be anything we choose? But I'm hurt because it's finally clear to me that this stuff *is* a choice, and you're not choosing me. ::looking out the window at Trenton, Joisey::

Battered tenements, factories half standing, the I-beams of their foundations protruding from the ruins like bones from a gaping wound. Talk about your war zones . . .

Truth is, Scratch, you're not exactly Ms. or Mr. Normal yourself. Let's forget the fact that we're both Most Wanted for a moment. You're still *far* outside everything I grew up with.

Wanna know the truth? I want to be in love with you, I want to be singing in the rain, *but* I don't want that to make me *be* anything else. ::sadly:: And with you, it looks like I have to be one thing only.

"Woman" hasn't measured up for me. "Man" *never* did. I've tried so hard to rest in one identity, one persona, one gender for all time. It never worked, because what I discovered with you is that I'm *so many kinds* of person.

Why can't the world just be glad two people met and let it go at that?

You say you want to "hang in there." Well, I've spent so much time trying to be what I was second-guessing you'd want me to be that I never bothered to figure out what I want from you. I'll work on that one now.

Yours in High Treason,

—W.<<

>>To: Winc
From: Scratch
Subj: Stuff

I don't see where it says in the instructions what we gotta be. (Christmas Eve: doityourself contraptions all around me, dog-eared paper in my grimy hands . . . "How do you put this fucker together?")

I am overwhelmed by the endless defining of ourselves. I just read a folder online about transsexuals and butches and femmes and then I went into the Deaf Chat room and they were talking about themselves vs. "hearies" . . .

Of course it's important to figure out who we are, or who we are in relation to who other people are, but I mostly think it's about connection. When I used to hang only with women, I mean, refused to deal with men for anything, including getting my car fixed, it was really about connection. I want(ed) desperately to engage, but did not want to be hurt anymore. I still want that, and the choices I make instantly are about not wanting to get angry, to feel invaded, to be *falsely led* by another person. I want to be smitten, and I don't want to waste any time with the "wrong" person.

I can pick and choose online, but usually none of the cues I rely on are there; the only one left is whether someone goes on too long onscreen.

That limited space online—and the true desire to hear what people say in response—makes a village square where people can talk to one another. But we also have the freedom to contemplate, and not respond at all and not be considered rude! That's an amazing freedom.

About connection: I think about the angry person who hates everybody (me in a former life, shades of me now). This person is really anxious to connect, but has been hurt, is weary, or even bored. If ze truly wanted to be left alone, ze simply would go off where ze has no fear of meeting anyone. Instead, ze continues to live in the world, but each encounter is a chore, as hir need for connection grows fiercer. The worst of these kinds of people (perennial victims) want to be rescued. They view each encounter with a hope that this will be The One. So when they get hooked by the "wrong" person, all that yearning leads to all that anger.

Like the cynic who is truly full of hope.

This weariness and grief is making me miss who you really are, when what I really want is to fuse with you, to connect.

This separation between us hurts.

—S.

P.S. Re: Treason? What?<<

>>**To: Scratch**
From: Winc
Subj: Grief

You are brave. You embrace rather than shrink from what you perceive as your own shortcomings. You do this without self-flagellation (well, for the most part), rather, with balance.

In Jewish tradition, there is said to be a number of people in the world whose life work it is to experience the pain and growth (or not-growth) of the rest of the world. ::wry grin:: In keeping with the early Jewish fetish for nailing things down, it's written that there are 500 of these folks in the world at all times: that when one dies, another is born. All they do, it seems, is move through the world and experience life that goes on all around and through them; this is their growth. And by the fact of their experience, by the fact that they witness the world, the world gets better. Maybe they're around to let people know that no one is truly alone. The texts don't go into it, but the legends do—these 500 people (there's a word in Hebrew for them and I can't recall it just now)—can enter any walk of life. They can be butchers, mothers, scholars, beggars, or poets, no matter what they do, they still fulfil their life purpose.

You raise the most difficult issue: maintaining some integrity and wholeness while striving for connection, communication, and companionship. And what you've helped me see is the fact that there are people in the world who've already lost the battle for wholeness, who are so submerged in the need to belong that their heart switch is *stuck* in the "intake" position. They've forgotten how to give. I am such a sap for them. (The part of being "woman" that I took on after giving up "man"?) But less so since I've met you. Thanks. —W.

P.S. Re: Treason. It's official, hon. You and I are conspiring to overthrow the govt. Or didn't you know?<<

Toobe Entry, cont.

No way Scratch could have read that announcement, ze doesn't know how to access things very well.

End Toobe Entry

Jabbathehut Narrative Entry

He's reading the government announcement for about the thirteenth time. If you were listening at the door to his office, you'd hear soft sucking sounds punctuated by the occasional:

"Aw, shit."

Memos are piling up on his hard drive. He's not answering them.

To: Investigations
From: Enforcement
Subj: Where are they?

We can be mobile with thirty minutes' notice. So, where are they?
—Henderson

... and ...

To: Ms. Budge
From: U-Sec L
Subj: Green Light

Attached warrant for the arrest of Scratch and Winc. Do it.

 click here to read attached file: "SWwarrant.DOC"

... and probably the most disturbing one, the one that's got the small hairs on the back of his neck standing up ...

To: All Bureau Personnel
From: Undersecretary Labouchere
Subj: Protocol

As you know, there are quite a number of citizens on the Net who are using the screennames "Scratch" and "Winc" in varying combinations. e.g., Sccratch, Wink, Wincc, etc. We must assume these citizens are sympathetic to the antigovernment sentiments of the originals.

In accordance with the Gingrich-Helms Free NetSpeech Act, the following safety precautions are hereby operative:

- Any persons with the screen names "Scratch" or "Winc," or any name similar to these names, will be located, detained, questioned and held, if necessary, on charges of aiding and abetting the overthrow of the government of the United States of America.
- All Websites or newsgroups, all chat rooms private or public, with topics including or referring to Scratch or Winc are to be monitored, and subject to immediate closure.

Take down names. I cannot warn you strongly enough that any ×abuse× of these provisions will land us in a media soup that ×none× of us will savor.

Let's do what we get paid to do.

—L.

Source1: persLOG/budge/harddrive
Source2: bckupfiles@FBCS.gov

End Jabba Entry

Toobe Entry

Great news. Check this out!

>>×××Online Host: Frankie has entered the room
"Fantasy Island."×××

Private Message to Frankie:

Hotdog: What up?
Frankie: ::purring:: G'morning ... still sleepy eyes.

Hotdog: R u m or f?
Frankie: ::mischievous eyes:: Ah, darlin' . . . I've made an oath not to tell.

Private Message to Frankie:
Johnny: Hey, dollface.
Frankie: YOU!
Johnny: Yep! We're safe for the moment. Wanna join me?
Frankie: I'm, um . . .
a bit tangled just now.
What's up?

Private Message to Frankie:
Hotdog: R u wet?
Frankie: ::laughing lightly::
Takes more than the question to get me wet, love.
Hotdog: Heh heh.
Frankie: Um . . . hang in there for a minute.

Private Message to Frankie:
Johnny: ::looking at you evenly:: We're live. We happened into this sector at the same time. Come to me.
Frankie: ::biting my lip:: Where?
Johnny: Private room "heat."
Frankie: ::nodding:: Be right there.

Frankie has left the room.
Online Host: Frankie has entered Private Room "heat."

Error: No host in the room.
Frankie: ::peeking in the door::
Johnny: No idea who Error is!
Frankie: ::shivering:: Everything like that has me thinking it's cops.
Johnny: I know. Me, too. I'll check it out, brb.

Johnny has left the room.
Johnny has entered the room.

Johnny: bak. It's Gwynyth's Safety!
Frankie: ::weak smile::
Johnny: ::smilin' back::
Frankie: Scratch . . .
Johnny: Yes?
Frankie: You're up awfully early . . . or is it late where you are?
Johnny: I'm not sure myself. Weird how it's dark whether it's early or late.

Frankie: Uh huh.

Scratch: What did you want to say?

Frankie: ::firmly:: Nothing important. What brings you here?

Private Message to Frankie:

Hotdog: Wood u like me to lick your clit? WHAT DO U HAVE ON?

Johnny: Look. I got one word for you, OK?

Frankie: Yeah?

Johnny: Hypothermia.

Frankie: ::blinking:: Is that supposed to be romantic?

Johnny: ::slow grin:: Want to know what it means?

Frankie: ::leaning back:: Uh huh.

Johnny: When a person gets hypothermia, it's very difficult to revive them. You have to take them to the hospital and work on them all night long, because there's nothing to replace body heat easily. ::deep breath::

Frankie: ::watching you, listening::

Johnny: In the mountains, when a hiker gets too cold and the body suddenly drops its heat level, ze's got maybe half an hour until ze's frozen. So the only thing ze can do is hope to find another person. ::pushing on:: That person gets into the sleeping bag with the cold one, they have to both be naked, and they wait. Sure enough, the heat from the rescuer heats up the frozen person. Almost instantly. They have to stay together until the person's heat comes back to normal.

Frankie: You're making me cry.

Johnny: I was frozen, Winc. You warmed me up. I want to stay in the bag with you.

Frankie: ::loss for words::

Johnny: Um, ::talking rapidly:: it's my favorite story. I've loved it since I first heard it from a crusty old ice climber.

Frankie: ::reaching my arms up around your neck::

Johnny: ::holding you close to me:: ::breathing you in::

Frankie: ::moving softly into your arms, crying crying::

Johnny: ::stroking your hair::

Frankie: Missed you missed you missed you.

Johnny: Samesamesame.

Frankie: ::willing my heat around the two of us::

Johnny: ::relaxing into you:: I used to bore people with that story, never had anyone get it.

Error: Window closing.

Johnny: We got to go. But now we're . . . we're all . . . you know?

Frankie: ::fiercely:: I know. We are. And we're *gonna* be.

Johnny: <--- loves when you get fierce.

Frankie: ::growling, extending claws::

Error: Window almost down, dearies.

Johnny: Wow! Gwynyth's personalized touch! And she's not even here!

Frankie: ::laughing:: Guardian angel!

Johnny: Bye, love. Amuseparkmail, OK?

Frankie: ::nodding::

Frankie: Scratch?

Johnny: ILY.
Yes?

Frankie: ::softly:: Simulpost.

Johnny: I figured.

Error: Window closed. Communication stopped.

5:59:25 a.m. Closing Log file.<<

Toobe entry, cont.

Yessss! As usual, they were oblivious to the treason thing. Do I nag them? Will they deal? Gwynyth still says to wait, but she got a tiny smile when I told her about that chat. Tiny smile on her means a big one on other people.

End Toobe Entry

Jabbathehut Narrative Entry

Wally Budge is biding his time. Let the rest of the Bureau roust up the folks named Ssscratch or Wwwinc. He's reading some very interesting correspondence, intercepted and forwarded to him by one of his hackers. (Assignment: Search names Scratch and Winc.)

> **>>To: HoneyDew**
> **From: Vina**
> **Subj: Is that you?**
>
> Please forgive me if I've reached the wrong mailbox, but I'm looking for Winc. The real Winc. We heard that this is one of your screen names. I represent a group called the Coalition, and we need to locate Winc ASAP.
> —Vina<<

With a satisfied grunt, he adds "HoneyDew" to his database, and chalks up another entry for "The Coalition." Patterns, patterns. Now we're talking. Familiar territory at last. He feels like a cop again. The next message, however, isn't so satisfying.

To: Ms. Budge
From: DevilsOwn
Subj: Progress, BUT . . .

We've got some leads. There was a nibble on some obscure agriculture node, and we've narrowed it down to a few thousand sites. Shouldn't be long now. But something *really* weird is happening. Someone is pulling all the Scratch and Winc clones offline. Is that you? If it is, STOP IT! We've been using them to determine leads.

And do you know about the rally tonight at the Scratch and Winc Website? DON'T mess with it, okay? We'll have it wired, and we're counting on at least one live lead attending.

—Your everlovin' Devil

Now ain't *that* a kick in the pants? He forwards a copy of the hacker's email to Shel, picks up the phone and dials. She answers on the third ring.

"Make it quick, I'm busy."

"Shel? It's me."

"Well, hello *Ms.* Budge."

He sighs, but lets it go. "Did you get that message from my hacker?"

"DevilsOwn? Yeah. I'm lookin' at it right now."

"How do I tell Her Ladyship to lay off all the Scratches and Wincs? How do I tell her to leave all the Websites and newsgroups alone?"

A pause, then, "Leave it to me. Dinner tonite at Antonio's. You're buying."

"I'd buy you the world, Shel."

"Yeah, and on *your* budget, I'd have some mortgage officer on my tail the minute I tried to move in. Now go be a cop. I gotta cash in some chips."

End Jabba Entry

Toobe Entry

Something fizzing in my brain. I think I'm on to something: People start acting the way people expect them to act. You know? Like right after Celia Donovan got her glasses everyone started to call her a brain. Just a few months later she *was* a brain. Before the glasses, she was a C-minus as far as I knew, but everyone was going "There's Brain," and she was A+ after that.

So same for my "criminal" pals. Check it out:

>>**To: Winc**
From: Scratch
Subj: Invites

I don't know if you've been getting mail, but mine (under every bypass location) is full of offers. All of them usually make my skin crawl, but I kind of liked this one. What do you think?

—S.

>>**To: Scratch**
CC: Winc
From: Coalition of G/L/B/T Folks
Subj: Help us?

We wanted to write and tell you that we think what you're doing is very important. While the media and the government seem to have focused on how depraved you are by not Registering, we've noticed that you refuse to say exactly what sex you are. As a coalition of gay, lesbian, bisexual, and transgendered people, we know how it feels to be marginalized. We have all had to deal with gender issues in our lives, and we think it would be terrific if you could publicly announce that you are queer.

There are so few role models for us, and now that you have everybody's attention, we think it would be wonderful if you could come out and give the movement a shot in the arm.

(signed by all)

—CGLBTF<<

What say you? I'm kind of mixed. I could call myself queer, not being your average Straight Amerikan, but I'm seeing that nobody much is.

—S.

To: **Scratch**
From: **Winc**
Subj: **The Coalition**

I got one, too. It rang true. Wouldn't it be kind of exciting to be spokespeople for this organization?

Let's find out more!

—W.

To: **Winc**
From: **Scratch**
Subj: **Hermit crab**

I don't think I want to do that. I don't know what I was thinking.

The fact is, I don't do groups well. People's IQ levels drop when they're all together in a room. Something about processing one idea until every member gets it or something. Then they'll start writing stuff they want us to sign, and I won't agree with one little sentence of it, and then they'll have to discuss *that* until the sentence is removed or changed, and then send it back to us . . . signed off by six people. ::throwing up hands:: Then we'll walk in and one of us will be wearing a fragrance somebody's allergic to, or someone will say they can't abide flash cameras because one person has epilepsy, and they'll have to vote about whether we can attend or not, etc.

Let's just write them a long letter saying thanks but no thanks.

—S.

To: **Scratch**
From: **Winc**
Subj: **Yes indeed you are**

Oh, I hadn't noticed that about groups, but you're probably right. But I think we might be having an impact. Maybe we *are* in a position to do something.

—W.

To: Winc
From: Scratch
Subj: (Nice to talk again)

    Do something about what?
—S.

To: Scratch
From: Winc
Subj: (Yes, indeed it is)

    People are getting pissed off, have you noticed? This week I got letters from Star Trek clubs, a disability rights organization, the right to bear arms people, and a million others.
    If we seem to speak to all those people, maybe we *should*!
—W.

To: Winc
From: Scratch
Subj: (Oh, good)

    You, too? I got letters from the Rainbow Coalition, the Latina Hermanas group, Mothers against Funk Music, blah blah.
    Let's go to a chat room. Your mail's coming back to me almost as fast; I know you're online right now!
—S.

To: Scratch
From: Winc
Subj: Armed rooms

    Meet me in room Arms.
—W.<<

I kind of trailed along, so my PMs are in here, too.

Online Host: You are now in the room "Arms."

Winc: See what I mean? Maybe we didn't intend it, but we stand for something.
Scratch: ::waving hand impatiently:: People are bored. We're just the latest thing to hit the charts.
Winc: I don't think so. And while I respect your cynicism, *I* think you secretly hope something will come out of this.

Scratch: Come out of this? What do you know about what I secretly think?
Winc: ::hiding a smile:: You're sputtering. It's a sure sign I've hit a nerve.
Scratch: ^&*(()#@!
Winc: Uh huh.

Private Message to Toobe

Orlio: Hey, doode!
Toobe: My man! Remember about not using this bypass unless it was an *emergency*?
Orlio: I'm at my dad's computer. His company has their own node and I made some, um, modifications. We're cool.
Toobe: Whoa! You've got direct access to a *node*?

Scratch: OK, so I hope they all fucking turn off their computers, stop buying stuff, and refuse to Register. What's so bad about that?
Winc: ::laughing:: Nothing. What do you mean turn off their computers?
Scratch: Ghandi's idea: Home Rule. If we stop using the damn things, they'll have to stop with the invasions. What's driving them anyway? Moneylust. Never mind how much they're getting already, they always want more.
Winc: They?
Scratch: Same old They.
Winc: I think it's a different They this time, dear.
Scratch: Government, advertisers, online providers--all They to me.

Private Message to Toobe

Orlio: Man, where've you been? The rally starts in ten minutes!
Toobe: Oh, that.
Orlio: "OH THAT?"
Toobe: ::muttering:: I can't go. This is the only screen name I've got left, and it's barely hidden from the Eyes. The person who coded it for me would have a fit if I pushed it.
Orlio: Cops? Wow, didn't know they were that close!

Scratch: Do you think They make any distinction about this kind of user or that kind of user? Like that this group is white males or that one is black disableds or whatever?

Winc: I suppose not.

Scratch: They look at money. Not whether we have it, but whether we'll spend it. Poor folks probably get more marketing shit leveled at them than anyone else.

Winc: But the govt says they're getting involved because they don't want porn trafficking or innocent children hurt.

Scratch: I think it's $.

Winc: ::thinking:: When we refused to Register, and then other people didn't either, T.A.B. swarmed all over people.

Scratch: Right!

Winc: Tell me, why *didn't* you Register?

Scratch: Oh, well. ::heavy sigh:: I don't do connectivity well.

Private Message to Orlio

Toobe: Wanna know a secret?

Orlio: Yeah!

Toobe: Scratch and Winc are online right *now*, talking to each other!

Orlio: Man! Can I say hi?

Toobe: No way. They're on these mondo bypasses, deep inside some killer encryption codes. No one can touch them.

Orlio: Shoot. I never got to meet them.

Toobe: Want another secret?

Winc: Connectivity?

Scratch: Driver's licenses, traffic tickets, library cards, memberships, taxes. I might build a whole philosophy out of resistance, but the truth is . . .

Winc: ::still listening::

Scratch: That's it. No big philosophy. No noble reasons.

Winc: ::covering my mouth::

Scratch: I knew you'd laugh. And you? Why didn't *you* Register?

Winc: Kind of similar. Nothing noble.

Scratch: Yeah?

Winc: Third question in the Reg form. Sex:_____.

Scratch: ::blinking:: Why not just put female? Or whatever you wanted?

Winc: It's not that easy. I'm still male on my driver's license, birth certificate, etc.

Scratch: Oh. I tried to put both and neither, no and yes. Come to think of it, that's about where I gave up, too.

Private Message to Toobe

Toobe: You know, you *have* met them. in the Anne Rice Room, the old hag cutting on her arm, that was Scratch. The boy who was really a girl, that was Winc.

Orlio: That was *them*? They're *ladies*?

Toobe: ::cracking up:: Not telling.

Winc: I take it you don't want to be the Coalition spokesperson.

Scratch: I'd fuck it up.

Winc: But I think your other idea is good.

Scratch: Which one?

Winc: The strike.

Scratch: Oh, that was just an example.

Private Message to Toobe

Orlio: ::glancing at watch:: Gotta go.

Toobe: ::snort:: You get all the fun.

Orlio: ::sputtering:: *You*'re talking with Scratch&Winc, and *I* get all the fun?

Toobe: Doode! Do me a favor?

Orlio: ::chillingly soft voice:: What's in it for me?

Toobe: Send me stuff from the rally, OK?

Winc: No, I mean it, we should strike.

Scratch: Yeah, right. How would we get everybody to do it?

Winc: ::looking at my mailbox, looking at yours:: I think we could get the word out.

Scratch: Email them all?

Winc: Email a few, the word will spread.

Scratch: You have a lot of confidence in our popularity.

Winc: Scratch, I think I understand you a little better now. You don't stay in touch with the world a whole lot, right?

Scratch: Well, sometimes. Some people. Some groups.

Winc: Right, well, at present they're staying way in touch with you. And me.

Scratch: ::thinking::

Winc: So we write everyone on the Net, and tell them we don't think the Reg process is fair, etc., and then see if everybody wants to join in.

Scratch: What if it doesn't work?

Winc: Then it doesn't work. Can't hurt! Just ask everybody to stop using their computers for a day?

Scratch: ::excitedly:: They should say something before they sign off. Something about themselves, about who they really are. Some true thing, not about what they buy or what kind of B.O. they have.

Winc: Yes.

Scratch: Let's tell this Coalition first. They'd get it.

Winc: Perfect! You want to write the letter?

Scratch: OK. Who *you* gonna tell?

Winc: Well, I think I get this software/hardware thing better than you, no offense.

Scratch: Oh, no, it's true. You know everything!

Winc: ::laughing:: Non non, darling.

Scratch: You do!

Winc: I'll write an announcement, from both of us, and send it from one node to the next, all around the world.

Scratch: To the nodes?

Winc: One node = thousands of computers. ::examining fingernails:: Might as well start at the top. But we *do* need a node to start with.

Scratch: Won't Gwyn's do fine?

Winc: It's safe, but it's *way* teeny. It won't handle traffic to and from everyone in the world. We need a corporate honker.

Scratch: Wow. ::shyly:: Do you really think anyone would give a damn?

Winc: Scratch, I have six letters from CBS News alone in my mailbox.

Scratch: Hmm, so do I. I thought it was advertisement offers.

Winc: From a news program?

Scratch: Oh, right. You know what Toobe has?

Winc: What?

Private Message to Toobe:	Private Message to Orlio:
Winc: Hey hon, are your ears burning? We're talking about you.	**Toobe:** Where are you now?
Toobe: Oh yeah? Well, I'm talkin' about *you*! Hey, do you think you could say hi to a friend of mine?	**Orlio:** At the rally! You should *see* this place! Hundreds of people here!
Winc: Email?	
Toobe: No, live chat.	
Winc: I'll check with Scratch.	

Winc: Toobe wants us to meet a friend of his, live chat.

Scratch: ::wincing:: Big risk.

Winc: Yeah, you're right. Skip it. You were saying Toobe *has* something?

Scratch: Right! An automatic responder from Jabba that says no to everything. Check it out! ::uploading::

Winc: ::chuckling:: Pretty great! But I'm sorry he's being besieged.
Scratch: Yeah, but the toy helped. It goes out automatically in response to email from anyone on a list Jabba made up.
Winc: ::shaking my head in amazement:: I like to see them all.
Scratch: But I don't.
Winc: Toobe may know where to get access to a mondo node!
Scratch: Uh, sure. That's a good thing, right?
Winc: ::purring:: I'll take care of it, hon. So why don't you have Jabba give you a responder, too?
Scratch: You're going to laugh again.
Winc: No, I promise I won't. Tell me.

Scratch: I use a Tandy, an old one from Radio Shack. It's a laptop, but they weren't even called that then.
Winc: When?
Scratch: Oh, 1988–89, when they were invented.
Winc: Don't tell me it's the kind that uses disks for all the programs. No hard drive? *That* one?
Scratch: That's the one.
Winc: :X
Scratch: You said you wouldn't laugh.
Winc: Not laughing! It's sweet! How did Gwynyth set you up with all the bypasses then?
Scratch: Why do you think we were at her console for so long? She treated me like some fossil in a museum!

Winc: Oh, I thought you and she . . . um . . .

Private Message to Toobe:
Winc: I ask you about major nodes and you go heh heh heh?
Toobe: More heh hehs. Hang on a minute.

Private Message to Toobe:
Orlio: I'm at the Rally! Ton of queers here.
Toobe: Hey, pal, just how big is your dad's company's node?

Scratch: Me and Gwyn? No! Anyway, this Tandy goes any-where, which was good re: the Reg stuff because it's not even listed in the registry of computers anymore.
Winc: You are such a dear.
Scratch: Its name is Sam. Or Sammie. She's a tomboy, and was never, ever called Samantha. My first female possession since I was ruled by a femme feline at the age of nine. I love her.

Private Message to Winc:
Toobe: I think we can feed two birds with one bag of seed.
Winc: Huh?

Private Message to Orlio:
Toobe: I think we can feed two birds with one bag of seed.
Orlio: Huh?

Winc: Scratch?
Scratch: Yes?
Winc: I love you.
Scratch: ::ducking head:: I . . . love you too. I've missed you.
Winc: Me, too, you. Let's just move on. OK?
Scratch: ::setting jaw:: OK.
Winc: Besides, ::tossing hair:: we have a cause!
Scratch: We do?
Winc: ::tapping my foot::
Scratch: Oh, right, we do! OK, off to write letters!
Winc: Goodbye, sweetie.
Scratch: Bye!

End Toobe Entry

Narrative Entry, Jabbathehut

Wally Budge has gone all out. He'd even brought daisies, her favorite flowers. Now they're sitting across from each other, and he's speaking around a mouthful of four-cheese manicotti.

"How'd you do it?" The muffling factor of the four cheeses cannot conceal the wonder in his voice. He'd gotten this memo just before leaving the office:

Shel is toying with her gnocchi al pesto.

"Well, it seems that *some* civic-minded citizen of these United States found out what we were doing and blew the whistle to the ACLU."

A grin spreads across his face, threatening to reveal a mouthful of food. He catches himself just in time, as Shel continues.

"The ACLU mounted an email campaign, and it seems that the undersec's mailbox was flooded with . . ."

She pauses, trying to think of the exact number.

". . . well, at last count, it was over 25,000 pieces of mail from outraged citizens."

"Last count?"

She smiles. "Wally, 25,000 pieces of email in less than an hour."

He whistles. A mistake. Hastily, he wipes his mouth and responds.

"Twenty-five *thousand*. What have we got on our hands here?"

She grins the grin that always gets him.

"The natives are restless."

As though on cue, both their beepers go off at once. Three beeps, repeated over and over. They look up at each other. Yellow alert. Get back to the office, pronto. They never even got to order the zabaglione.

Source: diary.sdunlap@FBCS.gov

End Jabba Entry

Begin narrative entry, Gwynyth
Gwynyth\mydiary.log\enterpassword *****:

Diary Entry: 48 Hours until Mercury Goes Retrograde.

Farm Reports is totally deserted. All systems are up. Nothing too startling, but where is everybody? Could our young lovers have hit on the goof of the century? To wit:

AutoMailLog:

>>To: Jabbathehut
From: Gwynyth
Subj: Was this "your" idea?

My friend,

I received this not fifteen minutes ago. Actually, I received about twelve copies of it. Apparently, it's being distributed daisy-chain style all over the Net. Once you receive it, you're supposed to send it to ten people you know. I've read it to nine o' my cats, so you make ten. Is this "you"? Or have they stumbled onto something smart?

—G.

>>To: All Our Friends
From: Winc@PalisadesPk.NJ.com
Subj: How does this strike you?

I'm writing for both Scratch and myself. Can't make this too long because some people would rather we took up residence somewhere with no windows. Scratch and I have been blown away by all the letters we've been getting. We can't answer them because of tracers. But we want to say thanks so much.

It's been a really weird time for both of us, especially now with this charge of High Treason. After they get us, who are they going to target "next"? So, we came up with an idea:

We want to call a general strike on the Net, shutdown for 24 hours, to let the govt know they can't get away with prowling online, and businesses can't tell us what to buy. Obviously there's a whole lot of support for this way of thinking, more than anyone realized, and we should let our helpful govt know.

The deal would be for everyone to sign off and shut down at once. Not forever, just a day. Everyone goes to the Website "Jumping Off," and posts a sort of farewell, an anthem. Everyone writes their own.

Every single user: corporate, online services. The only ones left on the Net will be the govt, and let's see how much fun they have talking to themselves, without us to spy on.

We hear there's a rally online tonight. Maybe you could talk about it there? Obviously Scratch and I won't be able to be there, but maybe this is something to do?

{{{Netfriends}}}

—S&W

P.S. We were thinking about 24 hours starting 8 a.m. Eastern Time, the day after tomorrow.<<

>>To: Gwynyth
From: Jabbathehut
Subj: I assure you . . .

. . . this had nothing to do with me. It hasn't the hope of a snowball in Hades. I, too, have received multiple copies, and I neither participate in nor condone the proliferation of spam on the Net.

Fighting God,

—J.<<

Gwyn.mydiary.cont.

Spam? According to the boy wonder, spam is any meaningless drivel posted to the Net or spoken in chat rooms.

Isn't it *all* spam?

Romeo and Juliet are planning their strike for the precise moment Mercury goes retrograde.

autoescape: Gwynythmydiary.logclose

End Gwynyth Entry

Narrative Entry, Jabbathehut

The pressing need to organize the sequence of events of late is crumbling under the persistent anarchy advocated by our protagonists. I have long stopped trying to fathom their motives, resigned to trying to keep them out of trouble. The following letter, for example, was sent from a Tandy laptop, for wailing out loud, and had it gone out as sent would have brought all the little peacekeepers on their shiny little cybercycles.

I have decided to forgive Gwynyth's insinuation that I would be behind such an idea as a strike. She has been under a great deal of stress and worse, has an adolescent stranger sharing her cat-infested home. At this point, I shall simply gather information to show her and anyone else who actually cares about history, how such a debacle came to pass.

>>To: Vina@USOL.com
From: Scratch@(encryption added)
Subj: The Coalition of Gay & Lesbian & Transgender & can't remember the rest

I checked your references, as it were, by asking everybody I know and having all my friends look you up. Sorry to be so paranoid but fact is, I've never worked and played well with others. As soon as I know what the party line is, I run screaming in the other direction, even if I *agree*. So we have to say no to your proposal. Assuming we *are* queer, and come *out* as queer, the straight mothers for legalization of marijuana would pout that we're not representing them. Fact is, we don't want to represent anyone. We want everybody to say their piece. So, what I do want to propose is this:

◎ Click here to read document: AllStrike.DOC

What do you think? You could reach lots of people. You could say an anthem that will tell everyone what you told me. Your Coalition sounds great, this is the perfect time. Go to that Jumping Off site and write everything you want. That way you'll get it right, and not leave it up to us to mess up.

Thanks a lot for your letters. You're very persistent. You must be good at civil rights stuff and everything.
—S.<<

Of course it never occurred to the Scratch-person that mail to organizations is never read by the addressee. Gwynyth would say it was protective of me to follow its trail, and its impact, but as stated before, I simply gather.

Source: mailerdaemon@coalition.com

End Jabba Entry

Toobe Entry

I hate when adults are right. Gwynyth isn't your average adult but when she's on a tear it amounts to the same thing. I would've snuck into the rally if she hadn't threatened me with permanent kitty litter duty. If I'd gone, it would have ended in tears, just like she warned. Note the next report I got from Orlio.

>>To: Toobe@Farm Reports.org.Monsterride.santacruz
From: Orlio@eor.com
Subj: Comin' Down!

I'm not making it up when I say everyone in the *world* is here! We're all in rooms called "The Rally," and each room holds around 500 people. So, you know how when there's an overflow in one room, another one gets created automatically and it's called, "The Rally 2?" Right now, I'm hanging out in "The Rally 1029." Heehee.

There are newspaper reporters here, and e-zine types; a whole group of deaf people; people from role-playing game rooms, people with split personalities. It's like a street fair. People selling Scratch and Winc T-shirts, buttons, commemorative dinner plates, and I'm not kidding: Scratch and Winc holsters!

I'm cuttingpasting, cuttingpasting, hopping from room to room, saving tidbits for you. A bunch of us are doing that, we've agreed to share what we find. Guess I'll have a pretty good picture for you by the time it's all over. Here's a giggle for you:

>>**BarBun**: Scratch is the best online lover I've ever been with!
HotHead: Too right there, grrl!
BarBun: Uh huh! Knows how to take time, build things up.
HotHead: She knows what fingers are for!
BarBun: She?
HotHead: Huh?
BarBun: He.
HotHead: She.
BarBun: He.
HotHead: Scratch is all grrl, you spritzhead!
BarBun: ::tossing hair:: I know a real man when I see one, you tramp!<<

And this:

297

>>**Tale2Tell**: Winc and I switch a *lot*! I love that
about hir.
Barnabus: Aw, that's sick!
Tale2Tell: No. You get to be everything, not just one
thing.
Barnabus: ::cautiously:: What's that mean?
<<

Just switched rooms and I'm in "The Rally 1622." Head spinning. Funny thing is, no one really knows why we're here.
People are starting to talk about that. I'm going to log it.
::smooches til later::
—Orlio<<

Well, at least people are talking.

End Toobe Entry

Narrative Entry, Jabbathehut

Wally Budge and Shelly Dunlap knew it was bad the minute they'd pulled into the parking lot. Every light in the place was burning. Except Budge's office. Like a Christmas tree with
one bad bulb.

When he'd reached his office, every alarm and whistle his computer was capable of gen-
erating had been flashing or beeping, demanding "read me, read me!" With a weary sigh, he
reads . . .

To: Ms. Budge
From: U-Sec L
Subj: Excuse me, but . . .
    I'm so sorry to disturb your dinner, lieutenant, but I just
received this little item, and I'd *really* like to answer it soon.
—L.

>>To: U-Sec L@FBCS.gov
From: press@whitehouse.gov
Subj: Request for Verification
Madame Undersecretary,
I'm sure you've got things under control on your end, but it's
getting *out* of control here. The Chief's in-basket is jammed
with mail about Scratch and Winc. I'm attaching some of the

Wally Budge reads down the list of events, crimes, threats, and heroics attributed to our stal-
wart cyberfreaks, his eyes growing wider as he proceeds from plot to theft, prank to lurid sexual exploit, and finally to a list of a dozen suspect organizations, each claiming responsibility for
the activities of Scratch and Winc.

To: U-Sec L
From: Ms Budge
Subj: Allegations
Ma'am: The president and his men can't be seriously thinking these two goofballs are *doing*
all this, can they?
—B.

Of course they can be thinking that. Why not? Everyone *else* is thinking it. He stabs at the well-
worn delete button, and starts again . . .

To: U-Sec L
From: Ms. Budge
Subj: I'm on it.
Ma'am: I have reason to believe the suspects have not in fact perpetrated the alleged crimes set
forth in the Press Sec's memo. I'm also reasonably sure they're not connected with any group,
terrorist or otherwise. I'll have confirmation before dawn.
—B.

He presses SEND, shaking his massive head. Time to be a cop. He leans forward to look into his
swollen database. Patterns. But Wally Budge is looking for something *outside* the pattern this
time. That's where they'll be. Where something doesn't fit.

The hackers have narrowed it down to agriculture. He calls up the list of several hundred
possible sites. Cows, chickens, corn, and government subsidies. Now, what *doesn't* fit with agriculture? Smiling suddenly, he enters a search pattern:

```
FIND: Agriculture + roller coaster
Parameter: One node containing both
Search: Agriculture sites from DevilsOwn
GO
```

Typhoid Mary sashays off the screen in search of the impossible.

And returns in less than ten seconds. Bingo! Stubby fingers fly over the keyboard.

To: Scratch@Farm Reports.org
From: Ms. Budge
cc: Winc@Farm Reports.org
Subj: Let's talk turkey . . . and chickens and corn

    I'm going online. Meet me in Farm Reports, room: City Slicker. I'll wait there until you show up. We need to talk.

—Budge

He presses SEND, and leans back, more content than he's been in days. He's whistling a mangled version of "London Bridge Is Falling Down."

Source1: persLOG/budge/harddrive
Source2: bckupfiles@FBCS.gov
Source3: shred@whitehouse.gov

Jabba Entry, cont.

Within every organization there is another organization. Some will acknowledge this, and bow to a natural order of leadership, while others delude themselves into believing they are all acting as a "tribe."

Before the S&W dyad (I prefer to see S&W as a reference to canned restaurant food) became such a predictable trend, several of my cracker cohorts were in the habit of monitoring the Coalition for various reasons. An automatic log set in motion in those days has now come forth. I would have missed it if it hadn't been so badly forwarded to me.

Online Host: You have entered room "Coalition Meeting."

Dave: You blew it, Vina!

Anne: You should have told us you were doing this!

Vina: ::startled:: I was charged with the task! Go to S & W and ask for their sponsorship!

Phil: Vina did great. Scratch trusts her, ze wrote back, didn't ze?

Carrie: Phil's right! Scratch doesn't write back to *anyone*.

Jahari: The strike is happening. There's a rally about it right now. Half the membership is there!

Dave: Move to go to Executive Meeting.

Phil: You can't do that!

Dave: ::patiently:: in the absence of a majority the Executive Meeting must occur.

Online Host: You have entered Private room "Exec.mtg."

Dave: Half the membership isn't here, but they voted by proxy. We can engineer our own vote.

Anne: Exactly.

Carrie: They voted to strike!

Dave: I have had it with this endless bickering. We're as effective as our dumbest member.

Anne: ::vigorous nodding:: Here here!

Dave: All that emphasis on coming out, educating in the heartland, when the real power is in *economics*.

Carrie: OK, don't start all that again, what's your plan?

Dave: We write the nice letter back, saying we agree to the strike. We have one of the largest nodes in North America, and that will promise them a huge number of participants.

Anne: Not that any huge business in its right mind would go along with this.

Manluv: Exactly. No point in even following this discussion.

Carrie: But what if for some reason unknown to us, this thing works?

Dave: Then we don't.

Carrie: I don't follow.

Dave: We don't shut ours off.
We'll be the last node alive, and the strike won't work.

Anne: Jesus, Dave.

Dave: Hey, it's hardball time. You really think all of us turning off our little computers for awhile is gonna do anything?

Anne: True.

Dave: But all of the nodes shutting down *except* ours will do something. The media would be all over us, dying for interviews. All of our issues will get out. They'll see we have real power.

Manluv: Why don't we tell Scratch and Winc that idea?

Dave: Because they won't do it. They're off on their little Ghandi pilgrimage and there's nothing so unstoppable as a dewy-eyed rebel with a half-baked cause.

Anne: Ain't that the truth.

Dave: We're agreed? All of us?

[all five members assent]

301

Dave: Let's do it.<<

>>**To: Jabbathehut**
From: Carrie
Subj: Urgent info

Just wanted you to know about the above. I voted yes because I knew they'd kick me out if I didn't, but thought you should know.

—C.<<

The above transcript was sent fully unencrypted, wide open for all the world to see. But its destination is shrouded, thanks to me.

Source1: mailerdaemon@coalition.com
Source2: shred@coalition.com

Jabba entry, con't.

Wally Budge is a very, very happy man. His years as a beat cop in the East Village are paying off. All that time with freaks, he can smell 'em a mile away. He files the minutes of the Coalition's Executive Committee under "Priority One," cross-references it to "Strike," and adds a new tab to the entry: "Betrayal."

End Jabba Entry

Source: persLOG/budge/harddrive

＊

CHAPTER ELEVEN

Toobe Entry

Winc uses "splatter" to describe playing different identities all at once. It happens when you're in Private Messages with lots of people, in more of your personas than you can count. Like when ze's boffing a guy as a guy and then turns around and does the same as a girl, both at the same time. But splatter works for me right now cuz all my worlds are in collision. My dad just got the concept of the Net, he's pissed at the advertising and the invasion of privacy. He went off on some story about the '60s when they blocked a railroad track and a bunch of his friends went to jail. I didn't get the particulars cuz he talked about him and mom a little and I kind of went off somewhere else.

Then there's Orlio, who's all excited about the rally (still going on), and Gwynyth, who's making incantations over her altar.

The megatons of mail I'm getting wears me out, even with Jabba's autoresponder. Seeing my emailbox full every fucking time I sign on is driving me nuts. What is the obsession with me? With Scratch and Winc?

I don't know what they're up to. Before, there was a whole cult around them, but they weren't really anywhere near it. Now that they've sent their letter, people are talking about them, the strike, about me, or what they think is me.

Coney Island must be making its biggest sales with the shirts, and the coaster still rattles the walls of my room every day. Funny, I've gotten used to it. Better than the jackhammers in my old nabe. I miss my dad: He seems kind of lost in all this. I want to explain the whole Net thing to him but he keeps saying he understands: "It's an old struggle in new surroundings." This may not sound very cool but I'd really like to go down to the beach with him and have an ice-cream cone.

Anyway, the update: The rally's been going on for almost twelve hours; Scratch and Winc are in some room together having a talk; Jabba was sending mail to Gwynyth, but now ze's not anymore, for some reason; Gwyn's hyper, bustling all over this place like one of her twitching cats, muttering a lot. "Sense of purpose." "Guides be with me." "Mercury's well timed . . ." Stuff like that. More later.

End Toobe Entry

Narrative Entry, Jabbathehut

Wally Budge is online in Farm Reports.

No word back from Scratch or Winc. Not yet, anyway. Time to set up the meeting room, he figures, and pulls down a Menu from the top of his screen:

> **CREATE**
> • **New Message Board**
> • **Meeting Room**
> • **New Society**
> • **Pomegranate Seed**

Shaking his head at the foibles of farmers, he looks down at his manual. He moves his cursor to "New Meeting Room," but a window opens up on his screen before he can click his Mouse.

To: Ms. Budge
From: DevilsOwn
Subj: Hats off to killer lady cop

Excellent hunch, supercop. Farm Reports *is* Target Zero. We've got a Scratch and a Winc logged on *in* Farm Reports, and we're ready to start the trace. Of course at present count there are 833 *other* Wincs, 656 *other* Scratches elsewhere on the Net. But it's a start.

We're seeing you online in Farm Reports. Be careful. Unbelievable traps. Skull got caught in a loop he still can't escape. Stay to the route marked "Pomegranate Seeds."

—Yr Devil

Pomegranate Seeds? Budge looks up at the Menu, where he'd nearly selected "Create New Room." Cautiously, he moves the cursor to "Pomegranate Seed" and selects the newly highlighted line. A musical note sounds, and . . . another menu takes its place.

> **CREATE**
> • **New Message Board**
> • **New Meeting Room**
> • **New Wardrobe**
> • **Pomegranate Seed**

Damned hackers. Again, he selects the highlighted line. Again, the musical note and yet another menu appears. He glances up at Devil's message. Why does he feel like the Cowardly Lion, itching to leave the yellow brick road and snooze in the poppies? Once more he selects "Pomegranate Seed," for which he's rewarded with yet another Menu.

> ### YOU MADE IT!
> **CREATE**
> - **New Message Board**
> - **New Meeting Room**

With a satisfied grunt, he selects "New Meeting Room," and types in his own room name: "City Slickers." And waits. Wally Budge knows how to wait. A lot of guys hate that part, but it's the part he likes. Budge is waiting for Scratch and Winc.

Source1: persLOG/budge/harddrive

Source2: AutoLog/courtesy.gwyn@farmreports

End Jabba Entry

Toobe Entry

You could divide the world up into people who think the strike will work, and people who don't. People who believe, and people who don't. Guess which category my old friend Jabba falls into?

>>**To**: **Toobe**
From: **Jabbathehut**
Subj: **Don Quixote rides eternally**

My little friend,

So glad you are still enjoying the autoresponder. Although why you would bother to respond at all is a mystery to me.

I am loathe to ask you your thoughts on this so-called strike currently clogging the airwaves. One cannot so much as tread a simple cyberpath without being harangued by some wild-eyed convert to the latest populist trend. No matter, I am whirring over the top of such gridlocks with ease, as hackers and coders have gone after much more visible fish than my elegant bypasses.

Still, you should know, my clients have been infected with the notion and are foolishly signing off for a 24-hour period. That window of time is the only shred of intelligence in this whole ridiculous charade. At least things will be back to a semblance of normalcy soon. For your amusement, and a curious sense of closure on my part, I excerpt the following:

>>To: Jabbathehut
From: JanStanM
Subj: The Strike

My wife and I are in agreement with the principle of the strike. We will be shutting down our computer and spending more time with our children this weekend. Since we have had nothing but excellent service from you (lockout for youngsters still holding, thanks) we assume you are among those who will close down their service in solidarity with the other strikers.

Thanks for your help, and see you in 24 hours.

—Jan and Stan Margolis<<

There are dozens more like this. Should you wish any electronic activity despite the prohibitions (apparently several small, commercial services will be closing down, in a pique of corporate conformity), I will be available as always.

Fighting God,

—J.<<

Something about Jabba always stays the same, and right now that's comforting. Of course I'm going to shut down. Gwynyth would have a fit if we didn't "join the tribe," as she puts it.

End Toobe Entry

Begin narrative entry, Gwynyth
Gwynythmydiary.logenterpassword ×××××:

Scratch and Winc are happily chatting in a safe area. Now that their auras are entwined again I have no need to pry into the nature of such conversations. But there's always my curiosity (which never killed a single cat, as far as I know).

The strike reminds me of ancient gatherings, where all responded to some unseen signal and met in the woods by the moon. Venus is so lovely this time of year. Uh-oh . . . alarms going off in Farm Reports. Hackers and Cops!

Tech note to myself: Strengthen Farm Reports.

The strike is set to begin in under twenty hours. What will I do for a twenty-four-hour absence of electronic activity in the house?

Resolution to myself: Clean house.

autoescape: Gwynythmydiary.logclose

End Gwynyth Entry

Toobe Entry

>>To: Toobe

From: Orlio

Subj: Man, you're not gonna believe it!

Hey, doode!

This is your roving reporter on the scene at the most amazing rally in the history of the universe! Thousands just spilling over onto more nodes. One minute it's impossible to get in there ("Room full, care to try another?"), and then another whole node opens up and you're there. I've been logging as much as I can, but I swear man, it's enormous.

You can see it's not all cozy. It's like *The Lion King*, when all the jackals got loose, and the animals went crazy. They all wanna do something, but no agreement so far.

::softly:: Thanks again for getting me together with Winc. I plugged him/her into my dad's node, and she/he was happy as a clam. So am I.

{{{{{{{{{{{(Toobe)}}}}}}}}}}}

—Orlio<<

End Toobe Entry

Begin narrative entry, Gwynyth
Gwynythmydiary.logenterpassword ×××××:

Diary Entry: 12 hours until Mercury goes Retrograde.

Tech note to myself: Breakthrough ... "Cupid and Psyche" have asked for bypasses allowing passage without being traced. Ha! My Guides have led me to code that would baffle even my large (strangely silent of late) friend.

I think the silence is a direct response to the care Jabba has been feeling for our three charges. That would send the large one scrambling for the fish tanks.

I poked my head onto the Net. Rally, indeed! It's a mess! When will they ever learn?

AutoLog Entry:

>>To: Winc"encrypted"
From: Scratch"encrypted"
Subj: Update

I wrote the Coalition and they were excited. They're gonna put together a statement. What do coalitions do best?! I am so glad I'm not gonna be in that room.

Have you seen the Gender Board? Abuzz. Not just about us, but themselves! ::tearing up:: It's happening:

>>Post: Gender Board

> I read that 90% of intersexed infants are altered at birth. I was furious when I heard that, but one thing relieved me, that we're all meeting here, online, and at least we've found each other instead of having to wonder if there are any others like us out there.

<<

"Intersexed" means hermaphrodites in this context. I didn't even think of that possibility!
—S.<<

The tribes are gathering. Haven't had this much fun since we all got naked in Central Park and passed out flowers to the cops! Speaking of cops, where are they?

autoescape: Gwynythmydiary.logclose

End Gwynyth Entry

Toobe Entry

I thought it'd be a good idea to send a note to Scratch. Every time I think I'm insulting hir intelligence by reminding hir of stuff, ze says ze had no idea what was going on. And *thanks* me.

>>To: Scratch@Batman.sixflags.com
From: Toobe@Buschgard.coaster.com
Subj: Rally

I have a feeling you don't know what's happening online. There's a huge rally about the strike, it's been going on for over 24 hours. But it's deteriorating into name-calling. There's thousands of people online, and they're talking about your and Winc's idea.

To: **Toobe**
From: **Scratch**
Subj: **Wow, thanks!**

I had no idea. I'll tell Winc. But no way I'm going there.
Makes me want to crawl into a hole.
—S.<<

End Toobe Entry

Narrative Entry, Jabbathehut

Wally Budge is online, biding his time. He's wondering who put "Farm Reports" together. Pomegranate seeds, cats, mythology, and roller-coasters. Almost as weird a combination as Scratch and Winc themselves. Speaking of whom, still no word. They're online in Farm Reports now—somewhere. He's patient.

A window opens up. He reads:

To: **Ms. Budge**
From: **DevilsOwn**
Subj: **Hats off to killer lady cop**

Glad to see you made it through the maze. This place isn't what it seems to be. We see you in "City Slickers." Can you get Scratch and Winc in there with you? That would make life very good. Do what you can from your end to keep them online.
—Yr Devil

P.S. There's one other person online with the three of you, but no way to tag him. We're guessing it's the sysop, so be wary . . .

Sysop? He glances down at the well-worn online dictionary. **Sys**tem **Op**erator, the one who set this place up and runs it. He continues reading Devil's memo.

P.S. again. Can you do anything about this strike? Make it against the law or something? Every node that closes down means another bypass we'd need to rig in order to find them. They won't ever do it, not fully, but it'll be a mess. According to my timer, 12 hours until Wipeout. Right? That's all the time we need.

To: **U-Sec L**
From: **Ms. Budge**
Subj: **Strike**

Ma'am: Urgently recommend issuing Netwide bulletin from our office for all citizens to ignore plans for this Strike. Am presently 12 hours away from locating Scratch and Winc, and shutdown would impede capture.
—B.

SEND!

He hasn't eaten since last night. Hasn't slept, either. Like the good old days. He's thinking about that Sysop, apparently online with them now. Toobe? Who? Where? He wonders idly what Shel is doing.

Within minutes, a window opens up on his screen.

To: Ms. Budge
From: U-Sec L
Subj: Good Idea, Good News

That's more like the Wally Budge I know. Notices will be up Net-wide in under 60 minutes. Go get them.
—L.

Wally Budge blinks in confusion at the memo. Must be some new secretary answering her mail.

He's pulling down menus at random, here inside this innocuous bulletin board "Farm Reports." He's very careful not to select any of the choices.

GO TO:
- **Grain Index**
- **Poultry Futures**
- **Hell in a Handbasket**
- **obe**

"Go To" obe. obe? Where the hell is that? Go To obe? Go . . .

Government employees of the Federal Bureau of Census and Statistics walking by the small green cubicle assigned to Lt. Wally Budge might have stopped and wondered at the laughter from behind the closed door, and two words repeated over and over:

Go To obe! Go Toobe!

Source1: persLOG/budge/harddrive
Source2: AutoLog/courtesy.gwyn @ farmreports

End Jabba Entry

Begin narrative entry, Gwynyth

Gwynythmydiary.logenterpassword ***:**

Shortly after getting a letter from Toobe, my little romantics slipped into another frenzy of email and chat rooms. The good lieutenant stumbled onto a safety passage I made for Toobe.

Tech note to myself: Time to break out the tar baby.

AutoLog Mail/Chat:

>>To: Winc
From: Scratch
Subj: UOK?

I'm ready to talk again, can we?

Meet me in room The Shore.

—S.

OnlineHost: *** You are in "The Shore." ***

Winc: ::sitting on the beach, knees up to my chin, watching the waves, turning to you and smiling::
Scratch: Hi.
Winc: ::opening my arms:: ?
Scratch: It's happening.
Winc: ::Carefully:: It? ::folding arms around knees, watching the water::
Scratch: ::waving at news bulletins:: The rally. The buzz. The happening.
Winc: ::nodding:: Momentum's building!
Scratch: I wanna hide. Have I mentioned I don't do crowds well?

Private Message to Scratch	Private Message to Winc
Toobe: Thousands and thousands of people at the rally, you guys (I'm double PMing you).	**Toobe**: Thousands and thousands of people at the rally, you guys (I'm double PMing you).

Scratch: I have a burning question. Hope it won't offend. Can't censor anything right now.
Winc: It's fine. What?

PrivateMessage to Winc	Private Message to Scratch
Toobe: They're all talking about you!	**Toobe**: They're all talking about about you!

Scratch: Acccccckkkkkk!
Winc: Don't worry, hon.

Private Message to Toobe

Winc: Great news, honey! But a little overwhelming just now. Can you hold off a bit?
Toobe: Sure thing! I'm sorry.
Winc: No, I really want to know, but Scratch is a little publicity-shy.
Toobe: ::smacking forehead:: I forgot about that.

Winc: ::continuing to stroke your hair, listening::
Scratch: How can you be so womanly, when you lived so long as man?
Winc: ::blinking::
Scratch: Offended? ::please hoping not::
Winc: ::smiling:: Offended? No, flattered. Let's see . . . I think it has to do with my phone sex, believe it or not, and . . . ::shyly:: reading Zen.
Scratch: ::snuggling in::
Winc: A lot of people in their gender change *layer* a new gender over what they had. . . . I think the deal is to destroy yourself utterly . . . to get to a point of zero, nothing . . . and then create.
Scratch: Like art.
Winc: Right. There's an art to gender.
Scratch: But the kernel of it was there, or you wouldn't have made the journey to your change. Is *that* what felt like not-boy?
Winc: ::laughing:: No, I was running away from boy, but had no clue what girl might be. We've got a bud for everything in us, don't we?
Scratch: ::muttering:: Oh yes.
Winc: So I created myself as a (culturally-correct) girl, and had to go through the same insights about that as anyone else.
Scratch: I'm not even talking about girl yet. But maybe how you felt, that was the not-boy part.
Winc: Maybe. People keep asking how did I know I wasn't a boy. I knew, that's all. I knew it wasn't me. Looking back, I think I knew that *both* the approved genders were too restricting for me.
Scratch: ::emphatically:: Me, too.
Winc: ::laughing again::

Scratch: Why you laugh?

Winc: If I don't laugh, I'll die.

Excerpt: Online Rally

Luger7: No special rights for homosexuals.

Vina: This isn't about homosexuals!

Scratch: ::stroking beard:: Were you creating from zero before or after surgery?

Winc: Definitely after. Before, I was just like everyone else, racing for (what I thought was) the finish line.

Scratch: Thinking your journey would end as you came out of anesthesia . . .

Winc: Yes, exactly.

Scratch: So did you say, fine, now I'm a girl, now what do I do? And then said, uh oh, what's a girl?

Winc: Sort of . . . I talked with some women and they asked me how could I be a woman like them? Other women said I was simply a castrated male.

Scratch: ::flatly:: I don't believe your womanliness is created . . .
It *is* you.

Winc: What's womanliness?

Scratch: Touché.

Winc: ::grinning::

Excerpt: Online Rally

MikeM666: Newbies die!

RainBeau: Hackers suck!

Success: Oh, for chrissakes.

Scratch: ::Putting my head on your lap:: Overwhelmed at the juggernaut we started. All I could think of was you, your cyberlap.

Winc: ::shaking my head:: You always make me smile, always know how.

Scratch: I feel messed up: I can fuck you, I can even be Leilia and carve on you, but to lie in your lap? Biggest risk of all.

Winc: Thank you for trusting me like this.

Scratch: ::sigh:: Is this where the lights go down?

Winc: Yeah, and the sun sets over our heroes.

Excerpt: Online Rally

StLouis7: I don't wanna align with NRA freaks!

StLouis7: Militia monsters!

Shooter: Fuck you!

> **Scratch:** Quite exhausted kitten now. But feel more calm.
> **Winc:** Glad to hear it. ::happy sigh:: You'd better go, then, huh?
> **Scratch:** ::nodding:: Thanks for putting me back together.
> **Winc:** I just sat here . . . you did the hard part.
> **Scratch:** Why just me? grumbling . . .
> **Winc:** Because you leave first, and I stay here waiting and that's how it works.
> **Scratch:** ::sighing, burying my head in you::
> **Winc:** ::holding you tight::
> **Scratch:** O . . . K. Good night.

End autolog

autoescape: Gwynythmydiary.logclose

End Gwynyth Entry

Narrative Entry, Jabbathehut

Wally Budge is a patient man. He's rereading the two messages that just popped onto his screen.

To: Ms. Budge@FarmReports.com
From: Scratch "encrypted"
Subj: Hold yer horsies

> We know where you are. Maybe we'll be there.

—S.

To: Ms. Budge@FarmReports.com
From: Winc "encrypted"
Subj: Hold whatever you please, dear

> ::brightly:: . . . and maybe we won't!

—W.

So they're back in touch with each other. This ought to be interesting. Then some good news/bad news.

Budge throws himself back into his chair, deep in thought. Why is this particular Sysop—who seems to know Toobe—so interested in protecting Abbott and Costello? Leaning back, Wally Budge is putting one and three together. Find the Sysop, find Toobe. Find Toobe, nab Scratch and Winc. Find the Sysop, paydirt. Ten hours until the strike.

Source1: persLOG/budge/harddrive
Source2: AutoLog/courtesy.gwyn@farmreports

End Jabba Entry

Begin narrative entry, Gwynyth
Gwynythmydiary.logenterpassword *****:

Evil, am I? He, am I?

autoescape: Gwynythmydiary.logclose
End Gwynyth Entry

Toobe Entry
Orlio just sent me this, but he didn't have to. You can't sneeze without their making sure you see it.

Ten seconds after I saw this, Orlio PM'd me that 500 people signed off. I risked going into the rally myself, and they were still straggling out the door. Steadily.

Godmofodammit.

End Toobe Entry

Narrative Entry, Jabbathehut

The halls of the office building that houses the Federal Bureau of Census and Statistics are ringing with laughter. Flasks are making the rounds; there's victory in the air. The first reports on the effects of the "practical joke" announcement show the rally dispersing. But in one small, green office, it's quiet. Sure, a flask is being passed back and forth between two people, but you'd have to press your ear to the door to hear the subdued conversation.

"So now the hackers have a better chance of locating them?"

"That's what they tell me. Right down to the room they keep their computers in."

She takes a pull at Wally's flask of Wild Turkey. "Sounds pretty sleazy to me."

His beefy hand reaches for the flask. "Yeah. The shrinks are real proud of the little bombs in the message. Half the people signing off are Mac owners who thought their computers were crashing."

A message flashes onto his screen, and the two of them read together:

To: Ms. Budge
From: DevilsOwn
Subj: Hellfire and Damnation!

Lost two *more* guys, and I don't even know how! One minute they were online, the next minute they're off, phoning me to say their screens filled up with graphics--cat graphics, man--and they were locked out. If they try to turn their systems on now, all they get is yowling. This Sysop dude is gonna pay.

Good news, though: we've narrowed it down further. Mid-Atlantic states. Hang in there. Next part is the trickiest: getting down to city and street address . . .

—Devil

"Does he treat you any different?"

"Huh?"

"If he thinks you're a woman, does he treat you differently than if he thought you were a guy?"

"I *am* a guy!"

"But he *thinks* you're a woman. Notice any differences?"

Budge leans forward in his chair, suddenly very busy retrieving the flask from her. "Shel," he says gruffly, not meeting her eyes, "I'm wondering who this Sysop is. I'm wondering why he's taking out my hackers one by one."

She leans back, looking at him. Waits. Shrugs. "Why don't you find out?"

"How am I gonna do that? Send him a letter and say, please let me know everything about you so I can arrest you on suspicion of harboring a minor and a pack of fugitives?"

Shelly's not saying anything. She's pointing at the screen, where Typhoid Mary is swaying back and forth. Typhoid Mary, the search engine. Of course!

"What's up, Boss?" asks the hippie chick icon. Wally gets a zing that he'd like to meet the woman who recorded that voice. But he's reading from his manual, typing in his instructions.

"Shel," he's saying, "What would I do without you?"

```
FIND: Agriculture + roller coaster
+cats + mythology + technology
Parameter: One user profile containing all
Search: Farm Reports
MODE . . .
```

He clicks on "Mode," and a menu drops:

```
MODE . . .
• Search
• Search and Tag
• Search and Disable
• Search and Destroy
```

"What?" he asks.

"It means you have a choice of what you want her to do. She's a friendly graphic interface for a complex search engine. She can search for you, or she can tag whoever she searches so you've got an electronic fix on them, or she can . . ."

"Yeah, yeah," he says animatedly, "I used the tag thing to locate Toobe in the first place way back when. But what's this 'disable' and 'destroy'?"

She takes a deep breath, and an equally deep pull on the flask.

"Okay. If you choose 'Search and Destroy,' she'll wipe out the hard drive of whoever she's after."

He gives a low whistle.

"Or," she continues in professional mode, "if you choose 'Search and Disable,' she'll freeze whatever program's running on their computer."

He's getting it. "So," he says, "if I tell her to disable this Sysop, it leaves all systems running, but he can't *do* anything with them?"

"Bingo. But it's not perfect. Whoever interrupts Typhoid Mary once she's in that mode, their computer will freeze up as well."

He makes his choice: SEARCH AND DISABLE. Typhoid Mary is off on a Sysop hunt for the one who's been knocking off the hackers; the one who's been harboring Toobe. He'll bet his badge on it. He lifts the flask to his lips, but freezes as another message opens up on his screen.

To: Ms. Budge
From: Sysop (oooh, what an archaic word!)
Subj: Peek-a-boo, I see you!

> Ten little hackers,
> Working on a fix.
> Four met a kitty-kat.
> Now there are six.

>> Mind your step, dearie.

"Shel?"

"Want me to stick around here for awhile?"

"Yeah. That'd be great."

Source1: persLOG/budge/harddrive
Source2: AutoLog/courtesy.gwyn@farmreports
Source3: diary.sdunlap@FBCS.gov

End Jabba Entry

Begin narrative entry, Gwynyth
Gwynythmydiary.logenterpassword ×××××:

The wolves are at bay for the moment.

Perhaps it was foolish, but I couldn't resist flicking the nose of the chief wolf himself. We're actually having a lively interchange.

AutoLog/Mail:

>>To: Sysop
From: Ms. Budge
Subj: Re: Peek-a-boo, I see you!

Dear Sir or Madame,

I'm guessing it would be entirely redundant to tell you who I am and who I work for. I'm also guessing you know where Toobe is. And where his two buddies are. I want you to know I'm on their side. I want them to give themselves up and come in on their own. It'll be a lot easier for them if they do. Do you have any idea how much this investigation has already cost U.S. taxpayers? But I want you to believe me: There's no way anyone can make these charges *stick*. I'm also guessing you could cybersquash me like a bug with the flick of your little finger.

Please don't do that. I'm looking for them, but I'm not their enemy. They need me on their side. At least let me meet with them.

Thanks.

—Wallace T. Budge, Lieutenant

Federal Bureau of Census and Statistics<<

Oh call me an old softie, but I answered him:

>>To: Ms. Budge

From: Sysop

Subj: Yer ass is MINE, copper

Ha! I've always wanted to say that. Please forgive me.

Since it seems you learned some manners from your mother, I'll not now "cybersquash" you as you so quaintly put it. But I warn you: I'm watching.

**And this sweare I by Code and by Craft:

If you so much as touch one hair on their precious little heads, I shall become the Fury whose name only your night-mares dare whisper. So Be It.**

Sincerely yours,

"encrypted" <<

autoescape: Gwynythmydiary.logclose

End Gwynyth Entry

Narrative Entry, Jabbathehut

The two of them are staring into the screen. Shelly speaks first.

"Your Sysop is a woman."

"Huh?"

"That's a mama lion you're dealing with; she's protecting her cubs."

"But Typhoid Mary can disable her, right?"

"Right. Typhoid Mary is gonna disable anything that gets in her way."

Source: diary.sdunlap@FBCS.dov

End Jabba Entry

Toobe Entry

It's coming apart at the seams. Collapsing. I hate stupid grown-ups who believe anything that's printed. I hate it when people flap their mouths instead of their ears. Too much like school. And Orlio—I can just see his face, like a kid who just learned there is no Santa Claus.

```
>>To: Toobe "encrypted"
From: Orlio@eor.com
Subj: Uh oh
```

It was all going so well. I mean, sure people were yelling at each other, but they believed in Scratch and Winc, y'know?

```
>>Shooter: It's a damned lie! The govt *always* lies!
Brknstck: Maybe not always, Shooter. Personally, I
think it does sound like some drug-dealer's prank.
AWESOME: No way, Brk . . . I *met* Scratch. Good sense
of humor, but not mean. I believe it.
FredMan: Fine, Awesome . . . *you* sign off at 8 a.m.
I'm not!
Brknstck: Me neither, Fred. My online time is too self-
affirming. I'm not going to throw it away on some joke.
HotHead: *You're* the joke, don't you see that?
::fuming::<<
```

People are dropping out of the rally left and right. Have to ask you . . . *was* it all a practical joke?

—Orlio<<

I wish I could hug him. I feel like it's all my fault, and it isn't. But I did write back that it wasn't a joke.

End Toobe Entry

Narrative Entry, Jabbathehut

Their flask is empty. In the halls of the government building, good cheer abounds. Within the walls of his office, Budge is losing it.

"Shel?"

"Yeah?"

"I think I've had it."

"Tell me more."

Shaking his shaggy head in confusion, he does.

"It's been twenty-four hours since I sent that message to Scratch and Winc to meet me here, and they haven't shown up. I've been sitting in this damned bulletin board fun-house twiddling my thumbs, reading up on turkey gizzards and grain prices in seven countries I can't pronounce, and I've had it."

She's listening.

"So," he continues, "I'm thinking, fuck it. No word from Scratch and Winc. No word from Typhoid Mary. I'm old-fashioned. I don't belong here. I thought I could catch them with the tried and true ways I learned on the streets."

She's still quiet, looking at him with one eyebrow raised kindly.

"Fuck it," he continues. "The rally's breaking up. The system is working without me. Let Devil find the two of them. Let Henderson go catch them. Let the Supreme Court of the United States of America find them guilty of high treason. Let them hang those two poor bastards for conspiracy to overthrow *their* fucked-up conspiracy. I've had it."

"Wally," she says gently.

"What?"

She's pointing to his screen.

"You've got company."

Scratch has entered the room.

> **Scratch**: Hello, Cop.

Wally Budge glances upward and thanks some deity or other. Stubby fingers type as fast as they can.

> **Ms. Budge**: Hello, Scratch. Where's your pal?
> **Scratch**: On hir way.
> **Ms. Budge**: Do you taste all her food before she eats it, too?
> **Scratch**: Don't try "Divide and Conquer." It didn't work last time, it won't work now.
> **Ms. Budge**: You're quite right.
> **Scratch**: So what the hell do you want, Ms. Budge?
> **Ms Budge**: I need to know if you and your partner in crime are in any way connected with any terrorist groups trying to overthrow the govt?

Scratch: Ah, same ole . . . I thought you had something new today.

Winc has entered the room.

Scratch: Careful, Winc, he's already started on the wrong foot.
Winc: ::sweeping grandly into the room à la Donna Reed:: *Has* she now?

Private Message to Winc
Gwynyth: He's got hackers tracingyour phone lines. What would you like me to do?

Private Message to Scratch
Gwynyth: He's got hackers tracing your phone lines. What would you like me to do?

Ms. Budge: ::raising my hands:: Sorry. Can we talk, please?
Winc: ::purring:: Oh look, Scratch, she's being nice!
Scratch: ::evenly:: OK, lieutenant. Talk away. (Winc, scroll up for the brilliant question re: terrorist groups.)

Private Message to Gwynyth
Winc: Should we be scared?
Gwynyth: Not this very minute, no.
Winc: Phew! Thanks *so* much!
Gwynyth: You want to stay on, then?
Winc: Uh huh, please?
Gwynyth: Then so you shall.

Private Message to Gwynyth
Scratch: How can they trace our phone lines?
Gwynyth: All too easily, I'm afraid.
Scratch: What should we do?
Gwynyth: Winc wants to stay on and talk.
Scratch: Cool. Me, too!

Ms. Budge: And I'll keep asking the same questions until I get some answers.
Winc: ::rolling my eyes:: Do you really think we're *that* connected?
Scratch: ::checking address book:: Nope, no terrorist groups here!
Winc: ::peering over Scratch's shoulder:: Ze's right, officer . . . no terrorist groups there at *all*!

Shelly starts a bit, peers closely at the screen. "Ze?" she asks.

Budge jerks his head almost impatiently, still typing. "It's what they call each other, to avoid pronouns."

"Ah."

> **Ms. Budge**: Haven't you heard the charges against you?
> **Scratch**: Oh yeah, corrupting minors, getting our modems in a twist, etc.
> **Winc**: ::softly:: I don't think that's what he's talking about, Scratch.
> **Scratch**: ::Yawn:: What're the charges?
> **Ms. Budge**: You are currently being charged with High Treason.
> **Scratch**: Whoa! ::looking over at Winc:: Did you know this?
> **Winc**: ::hands on hips:: Scratch, I *told* you that. It's the whole conspiring to overthrow the govt thing.
> **Scratch**: ::turning to Budge:: Do you honestly think that's what we're doing?
> **Winc**: ::sweet innocent smile at Budge:: Li'l ol' us, officer?
> **Ms. Budge**: High Treason is punishable by death in this country.
> **Scratch**: I hate when that happens.
> **Winc**: ::folding arms across my chest:: Well, we didn't do it.
> **Scratch**: Yeah, right, we didn't do it.
> **Ms. Budge**: Will you two stop clowning for one minute? This is very serious. We have evidence.
> **Winc**: What evidence?
> **Scratch**: What evidence?

Shelly laughs and punches his arm. "That got 'em!"

> **Winc**: ::looking over at Scratch fondly:: simul . . .
> **Scratch**: . . . post.
> **Ms. Budge**: You both have called for a riot. You're instructing your cohorts to sign off.
> **Scratch**: Ah, what a load of crap. We made a suggestion.
> **Ms. Budge**: That's considered . . .

His hands freeze on the keyboard. Wally Budge suddenly realizes he doesn't know what to say. Shelly is holding her breath. Before either can speak, another window opens on his screen.

To: **Ms. Budge**
From: **DevilsOwn**
Subj: **Yahoooooo!**

    We see you got them in there with you. Good going, supercop!
Winc is in South Jersey, Scratch is in Northeast Pennsylvania. Now
keep them online for another 30 minutes, and I'll tell you what they're
having for dinner.

—Yr Devil (who wants to meet you when this is all over with)

Their eyes dart back and forth from the new memo to the chat room onscreen.

> **Scratch**: Cat got your tongue?
> **Winc**: ::leaning across the table toward the handsome
> officer, allowing cleavage to show:: Something distract-
> ing you, officer?
> **Ms. Budge**: Why do you pull that shit with me?
> **Scratch**: Maybe she'll go for this: ::straightening my
> tie:: Can I buy you a drink, hon?
> **Winc**: ::leaning back, stroking my mustache, watching
> Scratch pick up the pretty girl cop::

Wally slams a beefy fist down on his desk. Hard.

"See what I mean, Shel? Why do they *do* that?" She shakes her head grimly; he goes back to
his keyboard, oddly buoyed.

> **Ms. Budge**: Why do you have to play at being something
> else?
> **Winc**: ::blinking:: Why not?
> **Ms. Budge**: Why not just be yourselves?
> **Winc**: ::gently:: Maybe this *is* ourselves. All of our
> selves. Maybe it's fun. Maybe that's all there is to
> it, Occifer.
> **Ms. Budge**: Why are you being so stubborn? Just come on
> in, and we can straighten this whole thing out.
> **Winc**: ::cracking up:: You're chasing *us* and *we're*
> stubborn?
> **Ms. Budge**: You said you're innocent. So come in and let
> us help you.
> **Scratch**: Will they give us room service? A parade?
> **Winc**: ::warily:: Who's "us"? You and your little squir-
> rels trying to trace us?

Wally's hands fly back off the keyboard as though he'd received 200 volts.
Shelly's massaging his shoulders.

"All you gotta do is keep them online until Devil and his gang get them. You're the one who's gonna have the last laugh. Just hang in there."

> **Ms. Budge**: If you two could try to be serious for a
> moment--
> **Scratch**: We're dead serious, Ms. Budge.
> **Winc**: Damned serious here, Mister. What about those
> squirrels?
> **Ms. Budge**: What squirrels?
> **Scratch**: Oh, don't play dumb.

Wally Budge makes the unfortunate decision to do just that.

> **Ms. Budge**: ?

Private Message to Scratch

Toobe: Get the hell outta there!
Scratch: Why?

> **Winc**: We know you've got hackers all over us. You lost
> four and have six left.
> **Scratch**: Besides, if we were to come in, *you* wouldn't
> be in charge anyway.

Shelly's cell phone goes off. She answers and listens while Wally stonewalls valiantly. If Wally had been able to turn to see her face, he would've seen big trouble.

> **Ms. Budge**: None of this would be necessary if you would
> just cooperate.
> **Scratch**: You don't sound very convincing.

Private Message to Scratch

Toobe: They're arresting people at the rally!
Scratch: What? Bouncing them offline?
Toobe: No! Arresting them at their houses!
Scratch: Jesus.

> **Ms. Budge**: I mean it.
> **Winc**: ::turning to Scratch:: He means it.

"Wally," Shelly's saying, "It's Henderson on the phone. There's been a new development." But Lieutenant Budge is deep in conversation, self-righteous indignation making him type fast for once.

Ms. Budge: I know what is right and what is wrong. And I know my job.
Winc: ::gently:: You know all that? Do you know what *we* are?
Ms. Budge: No. I mean, yes. You're wanted criminals.
Winc: No. Who are we, what are we?

Private Message to Winc

Scratch: Winc! Did you get the message from Toobe?
Winc: No. I'm flooded with other messages. What'd he say?
Scratch: People are being arrested at the rally. I mean, in their homes. They're tracing them to their private accounts.

Ms. Budge: My job is to locate and apprehend you.
Winc: Really, that's all we are to you? That's all you think of us as?

Toobe has entered the room.

Toobe: You guys! I didn't get any answer from you, and I mean it, they're arresting everyo . . .
Ms. Budge: You!

Toobe has left the room.

Private Message to Scratch

Winc: Tell me you're kidding.
Scratch: It's true!

Scratch: Listen you fucker, what's this about arrests?
Winc: Scratch? Arrests? You mean it?
Ms. Budge: What?

Private Message to Toobe

Winc: Are you OK?
Toobe: I'm OK, but I'm outta here fast.
Winc: Go with care. We'll talk later.
AutoHost: Toobe is no longer online and did not receive your last message.

Scratch: I mean it. I'm gone. You're a fuckhead, Budge. I was actually starting to like you.
Ms. Budge: Wait. It's got to be a rumor!

Even as he types he catches Shelly's grim face out of the corner of his eye.

Private Message to Scratch

Winc: That fucking . . . I'm speechless.
Scratch: Sign off now!

> **Winc**: Mister, I don't know how you're gonna sleep
> tonight. That is *so* low.
> **Scratch**: No more waiting.
> **Ms. Budge**: Even if it's true, the two of you could stop
> this thing.
> ## Scratch has left the room.
> ## Winc has left the room.

Private Message to Scratch

Winc: ::grimly:: I can't believe this.
Scratch: ::furious::

"Damn!" He lights a cigarette with shaking hands.

"It's true, Wally. They've made over sixty arrests nationwide in the last thirty minutes.

His jaw drops.

"Did Lieutenant Henderson happen to mention *who* he might be arresting?"

"He said they're accomplices," she answers. "You already have two cigarettes going, babe. I don't think you need a third one."

Source1: persLOG/budge/harddrive
Source2: AutoLog/courtesy.gwyn @ farmreports
Source3: diary.sdunlap @ FBCS.gov
Source4: bckupfiles @ FBCS.gov

End Jabba Entry

Begin narrative entry, Gwynyth
Gwynyth\mydiary.log\enterpassword *****:

The witch hunts have begun. My now-offline ward (who foolishly jumped into the crossfire to alert his friends) received the following, which I retrieved for him out of the kindness of my racing heart.

Auto/Mail Log:

>>To: Toobe∂″encrypted″
From: Orlio∂″encrypted″
Subj: Every rap nightmare you've ever heard

Hey, kiddo, this is *scary*. I was in this rally room, and people starting dropping off the line, right? And we all thought it was a node overload, but look at this:

>>**BarBun**: Hey, where'd Thesman go?
FredMan: I'll call him live. brb.
Hansoo: So, you guys gonna strike?
HotHead: Well, I was, but now I don't know.
FredMan: bak! I . . . this is TERRIBLE! They've arrested Thesman! They think he's conspiring with S&W. They came to his fucking HOUSE!<<

General noise and confusion. Then at least there was this:

>>**BarBun**: ::firmly:: That does it. I'm pissed.
Hansoo: What can we do? Lodge a complaint?
BarBun: Let's go ahead with it.
Fredman: The strike?
BarBun: Yep.
FredMan: Yes.
Hansoo: Me too.
Azazello: What about online shopping, BB?
BarBun: I'll deal.
HotHead: Go, grrl!
BarBun: ::grinning at HotHead::
HotHead: ::grinning right back::<<

My hands are shaking. It's like a war, man. My dad says he's closing down the whole company node, but he's gonna wait until the last minute to do it.

Miss you.

—Orlio<<

While the witch hunts themselves did not succeed in the long run, there were over fifteen million killed in the short run. This could be a long siege.

Jabba would find me dramatic, but accurate.

autoescape:Gwynyth\mydiary.log\close

End Gwynyth Entry

Jabbathehut Narrative Entry

He's no longer in Farm Reports. He's in his office, he's pissed, and he's typing.

No sooner does he push SEND, then another window takes its place.

He's too close to give up. It goes like this every time, he reminds himself. Halfway through the
pursuit, it always looks too dark to see. He types:

SEND! And yet another window opens.

To: **Ms. Budge**
From: **U-Sec Sec**
Subj: **Your recent memo**
Dear Ms. Budge: The undersecretary thanks you for your concern in this matter and assures you that she has every bit of confidence in you to do your job in such a manner that would make your government proud.

Sincerely yours,
—Ronald McVey
U-Sec Sec

He's wondering how to attach a paper bag full of dogshit to his next memo, when one more window opens up.

To: **Ms Budge**
From: **DevilsOwn**
Subj: **Double our treasure, double your fun**
Yes ma'am!
—Devil

Source1: persLOG/budge/harddrive
Source2: bckupfiles@FBCS.gov

End Jabba Entry

Toobe Entry

That bastard! Budge started arresting people! He says it's not him, but I'm starting to believe like my dad that all cops are pigs.

People started dropping out of the rally like a scene from *Jaws*. Little heads pulled under the water. Scratch and Winc were talking to Budge, for gawdsakes, at the time. Do they have any idea how close they were?!

End Toobe Entry

Narrative Entry, Jabbathehut

Shelly Dunlap is reading some email.

>>To: **Shel**
From: **Ms. Budge**
Subj: **Speechless in the saddle**

Encryption: SDunlapOnly
Dear Shel,

I'm writing this because I don't trust my voice not to shout. I don't trust my hands not to make fists and do some serious harm. I don't know who to trust. Here:

>>To: **Henderson, Enforcement**
From: **Budge, Investigations**
Subj: **Confirmed Locations**

Scratch positively confirmed in Dingmans Ferry, Penn. Winc in Trenton, N.J. Street addresses to follow ASAP.
—B.<<

>>To: **Ms. Budge**
From: **Henderson Sec**
Subj: **Re: Confirmed locations**

Ma'am, Lt. Henderson has asked me to convey his thanks and his regrets that he cannot act on this information as his task force is now operating independently, ref FBCS Charter&Code Ch. 6, Sec 114, Para 12, SubPar c.15.
—Sgt. Anna Pepper
Sec'y to Lt. Henderson<<

and this . . .

>>To: **U-Sec L**
From: **Ms. Budge**
Subj: **I need 24 hours!**

Ma'am, I have them located down to the city. Give me 24 hours!
—B.<<

>>To: **Ms. Budge**
From: **U-Sec Sec**
Subj: **Your recent memo**
Dear Ms. Budge,

The undersecretary thanks you for your concern in this matter and assures you that she has every bit of confidence in you to do your job in such a manner that would make your government proud.

Sincerely yours,
—Ronald McVey   U-Sec Sec<<

Shel? I've been "reassigned," like to a dumpster, right?
—Wally<<

Shelly Dunlap blinks twice, then calls up an electronic edition of the Bureau Charter and Code on her screen. She's tapping the tip of a pencil against her teeth as the rules and regulations scroll by.

Source: diary.sdunlap@FBCS.gov

End Jabba Entry

Toobe Entry

Winc just sent me this stuff. Ze said, "Isn't this weird?" I don't think that's the word for it.

Private Message to Scratch

Winc: Scratch?
Scratch: Yeah?
Winc: Did you see what I just saw?
Scratch: What?
Winc: It was a cartoon: a little hippie chick parading across the screen.
Scratch: Oh, that. Sure. Doesn't show up that well on Sammie, but I saw it.
Winc: OK.

Then a little while later, same thing:

Private Message to Scratch

Winc: Scratch?
Scratch: Mm?
Winc: The hippie chick just went back across the screen, and . . .
Scratch: Yeah?
Winc: She waved at me!
Scratch: Cool!

When I was getting these, an alarm went off in my head, but not in theirs. I know they're the grown-ups, but . . .

Private Message to Scratch

Winc: Scratch, the little hippie chick is making me nervous.
Scratch: Huh?
Winc: She keeps walking back and forth.

Scratch: Wait a minute. Are you saying she doesn't belong to you?
Winc: ::hands on hips:: I should say not! Look at those *shoes*!
Scratch: ::looking:: Right.

Figured something out about adults. They never trust their first hunches.

Private Message to Scratch
Winc: The hippie chick is ba-ack.
Scratch: I figured it out! Must be one of Gwyn's guardian angels.
Winc: Of course!

Then Gwyn peered over my shoulder, and my whole body just relaxed. She typed this in so fast all I saw was a blur.

Private Message to Winc
Gwynyth: The little hippie is not mine, my dear hearts, but I'm watching.
Winc: Anything we should do?
Gwynyth: Nope.

Private Message to Scratch
Gwynyth: The little hippie is not mine, my dear hearts, but I'm watching.
Scratch: It's a spy!
Gwynyth: Yup.

Private Message to Winc
Scratch: Um, the hippie's got company.
Winc: I see! What *is* that?
Scratch: Beats me. Looks like an Uncle Remus Stories character.

Oh, man! Gwynyth wouldn't tell me any more about it!

Private Message to Winc
Gwynyth: Don't be alarmed if you see my tar baby. Whatever you do, don't touch her!
Winc: Tar baby?
Gwynyth: Br'er Rabbit and the Tar Baby. Uncle Remus, *Tales of the South*.
Winc: Scratch knew! Isn't ze cool?
Gwynyth: Yes, dear, very cool.

Private Message to Scratch
Gwynyth: Don't be alarmed if you see my tar baby. Whatever you do, don't touch her!
Scratch: ::blinking:: I don't think I get it.
Gwynyth: ::wryly:: Hopefully, they won't either.
Scratch: Ah.

I had already told them to sign off, but they never pay attention when I say that. Guess who has a little pull?

> **Private Message to Winc**
> **Gwynyth:** You two should seriously consider signing off.
> **Winc:** Right!

> **Private Message to Scratch**
> **Gwynyth:** You two should seriously consider signing off.
> **Scratch:** Right!

Then there's really, way pull.

> **Private Message to Winc**
> **Jabbathehut:** You must get offline. Email for you both in the usual manner.
> **Winc:** Right!

> **Private Message to Scratch**
> **Jabbathehut:** You must get offline. Email for you both in the usual manner.
> **Scratch:** Right!

>>To: Winc@"encrypted"
From: Jabbathehut "encrypted"
CC: Scratch
    Toobe
Subj: Offline

    There are hackers, working for (at the moment) Lt. Wally Budge. They are able to close in on you because there are fewer nodes online at this hour of the morning, but more importantly because of this: They are my colleagues, and therefore very, very good. You mentioned in some previous mail that you had access to the EcoTech node. I suggest you both get yourselves--physically--there, posthaste. Repeat, you are within hours of being physically located. GO!
    Fighting God,
—J.<<

Think I'll just do that (get offline). Wish I was going with them, but it's back to wandering on the boardwalk again, with my spy tape recorder.

End Toobe Entry

Toobe Entry

Three minutes later. They're back online, talking with each other! Can 15 year olds get gray hair?

End Toobe Entry

Narrative Entry, Jabbathehut

Lieutenant Budge has just received what should have been the best news of his already distinguished if somewhat erratic career.

To: Ms Budge
From: DevilsOwn
Subj: Streetwise!

State Street in Trenton, Elm Road in Dingmans Ferry. I can't *believe* those two actually went back online. Are you using a psychic? Street numbers in one more hour, tops! Can I take you to dinner when this is all over?
—Devil

Wallace Budge is chuckling. His laughter disintegrates into a wracking cough, and still ... he can't stop.

Source: diary.sdunlap@FBCS.gov
Source: persLOG/budge/harddrive

End Jabba Entry

Begin narrative entry, Gwynyth
Gwynyth\mydiary.log\enterpassword ***:**

Spam it all. I don't like playing it this close to the vest, but they still need to send their little notes apparently.

AutoLog:
>>To: Scratch
From: Winc
Subj: The Fugitive(s)

Wow! Did you get J.'s email? Exciting, huh? Let's go one more time to a room "Confession." We've got to go to that node, but there's a *little* time left.
—W.

To: Winc
From: Scratch
Subj: One-armed man

I'm way depressed about the rally. They didn't get anywhere. But anyway, yeah, we've got time for a little chat. Why "Confession"? What's a node again? You mean physically?
—S.

To: Scratch
From: Winc
Subj: They'll never take us, pal

Yes, physically. It's the node belonging to Orlio's dad,
Orlio being Toobe's little friend who was in the A.R. room
with us so long ago?
::patiently:: A node is the central location for a whole network of computers, it covers thousands of accounts. We're
going to hole up there, until we're the last ones online. Then
we'll shut it down, and the strike will be complete! The node
is EcoTech. It's in Manhattan. How far are you from there? We
need to go to it now, well, after I tell you what I need to tell
you.
—W.

To: Winc
From: Scratch
Subj: Not far

I can be there in about an hour and a half. Tell me what?
—S.

To: Scratch
From: Winc
Subj: It's a date

One and 1/2 hrs is cool. ::sigh:: But meet me in
"Confession." I'll tell you there.
—W.

×××Online Host: You are in Room "Confession."×××
Scratch: So why "Confession"?
Winc: I have one to make.
Scratch: Yes?
Winc: Oh, I did a little media interview.
Scratch: You're kidding!
Winc: ::small voice:: Just one! I don't even know if
they're gonna air it.
Scratch: But I thought we agreed not to do them!
Winc: I couldn't resist. ::mischievous grin:: It was
that one with David Berkowitz, Real Sex, Real Personal,
something like that.
Scratch: But we gotta get outta here!
Winc: I know!
Scratch: So, how'd it go?
Winc: Extremely well!

336

Private Message to Scratch

Winc: Hippie chick's back.

Scratch: I see her, and Gwyn's tar baby.

Winc: It's a showdown! What *is* a tar baby?

Scratch: Uncle Remus's story: If you hit a tar baby, you get stuck, which of course makes you angrier, so you hit it again, you get more stuck, until you can't move.

Winc: You're so smart!

Scratch: Gwynyth is.

Scratch: Give me some of the funner questions he asked you.

Winc: "How does a person like you get dates?" "If you can't adjust to being male or female in this world, there's something wrong with you." "Describe your first sexual experience as a woman."

Scratch: ::snort:: What else?

Winc: "What were your sexual fantasies as a teenage boy?"

Scratch: <---likes that one.

Winc: ::nodding:: Me, too. I actually felt good talking about sex.

Scratch: Your answer to that last one?

Winc: Fantasy as a teenage boy was to be a teenage girl . . . having sex with another teenage girl!

Scratch: ::smiling:: You sick thang you . . . and brave.

Private Message to Scratch

Winc: Whoa! Did you see that?

Scratch: What?

Winc: Hippie chick took a swing at the tar baby and now she's *stuck*!

Scratch: Just looks like a bunch of Xs and Os on my screen. Keep me posted.

Winc: ::purring:: I'll keep you anything you wanna be kept.

Private Message to Winc

Scratch: I can read what they're saying to each other!

Winc: Cool! I only have visuals.

Scratch: Hippie keeps asking tar baby, "Where's the Sysop?"

Winc: And the tar baby keeps holding out its hand to give her something.

Scratch: Saying, "Sysop's right here!"

Winc: Every time Hippie touches the hand she gets stuck.
::cracking up::
Scratch: ROTFL!

Scratch: What else did you say?
Winc: ::softly:: First time I had sex as a woman was
with a wonderfully gentle butch lesbian who took her
time with me and taught me how to love my new body.
Scratch: Vicariously proud of that girl.
Winc: But then the host asked: "What's the difference
between orgasm as male and orgasm as female?"
Scratch: Gulp.
Winc: Told him since I wasn't exactly female or woman I
didn't know if mine would *be* like a woman's ::grin::
but that I could describe what I do feel now. So I
described a boy orgasm, and he got all hyper and said
yes that's the way it is! ::giggle:: Then I went kind of
dreamy describing orgasm now ::blushing:: and halfway
through, the jerk interrupted me!
Scratch: You're kidding!
Winc: Nope! I called him on it: "Just like a man to
interrupt before I get finished!" He got all embarrassed, then ::tossing hair:: I finished!
Scratch: You dawg. On national TV! Hee-e-e-e-e-e-ee!

Private Message to Scratch

Winc: Hippie's down for the count!
Scratch: Her words are comin' out all garbled!
Winc: Don't you just love Gwyn?
Scratch: Glad she's on our side.

Scratch: Anything you wished you'd said?
Winc: No, that's the funny thing. It felt complete. And
don't worry, they said they won't show the police the
tape. Said they'd release it after their lawyers got
through with it.
Scratch: Lawyers?
Winc: Well, harboring a fugitive and all that.

Private Message to Scratch

Winc: Let's both thank Gwyn in PMs.
Scratch: Right!

    Winc: I have a feeling we are way past time.
    Scratch: Oh, no doubt. So, I'll see you in Manhattan? ::dancing to imaginary swing band::
    Winc: ::looking into your eyes:: Manhattan.

Scratch has left the room.
Winc has left the room.

autoescape:Gwynyth\mydiary.log\close

End Gwynyth Entry

Toobe Entry

    Okay, gonna sign off, this time for real. How will I reach anybody? Gwynyth told me S and W are coming to New York. Cool. Wonder if I'll get to see them real-time. She says they're gonna hole up at Orlio's dad's node. I know they're about the same distance away from the city, but that's over an hour for each of them: Winc by train, Scratch in hir li'l beater. ::fretting:: All I can do is wait.

    This just came in.

    >>To: Toobe"encrypted"
    From: Jabbathehut
    CC: Scratch"encrypted"
        Winc"encrypted"
        Gwynth"encrypted"
    Subj: Perhaps if I'm more direct
        Get the hell off the line. Everyone is in danger. Physical locations are being discovered!
        ::sitting back down in my chair::
    —J.<<

Oh Jesus Christ on a silicon crutch, Scratch is still on, maybe Winc, too. I'm outta here.

End Toobe Entry

Jabbathehut Narrative Entry

Wally Budge is staring at his screen, whereupon a woebegone and bedraggled Typhoid Mary is struggling beneath a mess of clinging . . . something. Black, sticky. Tar? He picks up his phone and dials.

"Yeah?"

"Shel, it's me. Whatcha doin'?"

"I'm still researching the Bureau Code to find out how Henderson snagged this case out from under you."

"Hey, do me a favor? Pull up my screen on your monitor and tell me what you see."

"Will do. Hang on."

Typhoid Mary's movements are getting slower and slower, the mess of goo larger and larger on his screen. Shel comes back on the line.

"Uh, Wally . . . I see what you're seein'."

"Is it bad?"

"It's worse. Listen. Whatever you do, *don't* touch that mess with your cursor, OK? It's the mother of all viruses, and if you touch it, your entire database is gonna make the LaBrea tarpits look crystal clear."

"Ah." He can feel himself sweating.

"Stay calm. Click your mouse *outside* the mess, and hold it there."

He does. "Yeah?"

"Good. Now, hold the mouse button down, and drag it across the top of the mess. It should make a little box *around* the mess without touching it, right?"

"Uh huh." Damn, he feels like he's being talked through defusing a fucking bomb!

"All right, now let go of the mouse button. The box is gonna stay around the mess. When it does, hit DELETE."

"You mean delete Typhoid Mary?"

"Yes, Wally. Do it. Fast."

"Is this gonna be permanent?"

"Move it!"

He clicks. His screen goes clear.

"Thanks, Shel."

"Don't mention it."

"She was a good soldier, Shel."

Her laughter makes him smile for the first time in hours.

Source: diary.sdunlap@FBCS.gov
Source: persLOG/budge/harddrive

End Jabba Entry

Begin narrative entry, Gwynyth
Gwynyth\mydiary.log\enterpassword *****:

Guides be baffled, they have ignored the warning and gone into yet another chat room. I will send them a warning myself if they don't disappear soon.

AutoLog:

>>**Scratch:** Winc, we gotta go but I wanna talk about sex. I'm horny as hell.

Winc: You are?

Scratch: I'm gonna see you soon and we're doing something dangerous: That combination is sexy as shit!

Winc: True, and contagious. ::dropping to my knees::

Scratch: It's why I like gayboyz: the complete intrusion of sex into everything; they can't keep their dicks out of it.

Winc: Nope, they can't. ::leaning my head on your thigh::

Scratch: The rude insistence of it . . .

Private message to Scratch

Gwynyth: ::averting eyes:: I'm not prying, but you must get off the line. The whole node must be shut down.

Scratch: Have to go darlin'.

Winc: ::kissing your thigh gently::

Scratch: ::desire welling up:: I love you.

Scratch: ::softly::

I love you, Winc

I love you, Digqueer

I love you, whatever your boy-name was.

I love you, Frankie, and Tasha Yar.

Winc: ::tears filling eyes::

Scratch: Bye, dollface.

Winc: ::softly:: Bye handsome.

I shooed them out the door; it felt odd to watch their screen names disappear.

autoescape:Gwynyth\mydiary.log\close
End Gwynyth Entry

Narrative Entry, Jabbathehut

Midnight. The building is quieter now. Word is out that a few hundred crackpots will have shut down their computers seven hours from now, but so what? Alone in his office, Wally Budge has another kind of so-what going on in his mind. What did Winc say again? That maybe they were just being themselves? Christ knows he'd seen his share of whackos in his day, and most of them had been harmless.

But he'll never get to know about Scratch and Winc. He knows where they were before they signed off, but his hands are tied now. Poor slobs. Henderson doesn't use kid gloves. If only there were some way to get back into the driver's seat.

The phone rings.

"Budge here."

"It's Shel."

"Too tired for dinner." God, he *sounds* tired.

"That's not why I called."

"Yeah?"

"It's about your being taken off this case."

"Yeah?"

"I found a loophole."

Source: diary.sdunlap@FBCS.dov

End Jabba Entry

Toobe Entry

I am way glad that all I know *isn't* what I read in the papers:

>>Scattered Attempts at Strike Holding Steady

by Thomas Fulton

The first signs of an online Net "strike" appear to be occurring, despite predictions that the idea is a hoax, or the ill-conceived plan of cult followers of Scratch and Winc. Nonetheless, some fairly large online services such as E-world and Emerald OnRamp have shut down completely, citing agreement with the essential ideas of a net strike. Experts at MIT and other computer labs across the country assure citizens that a strike on this level is impossible, and point to the government warning regarding such a strike, namely that this strike is alleged to have its roots in a practical joke.

<<

End Toobe Entry

Narrative Entry, Jabbathehut

I rather liked my young friend's habit of posting a thought for the day, though many of his sources were somewhat pedestrian. I shall continue the tradition, but from a somewhat loftier plane:

Epitti of the day

Anyone who can be proved to be a seditious person is an outlaw before God and the emperor; and whoever is the first to put him to death does right and well. . . . Therefore let everyone who can, smite, slay and stab, secretly or openly, remembering that nothing can be more poisonous, hurtful, or devilish than a rebel.

—Martin Luther (1483–1546)

I am one of the few rational people scanning the InfoBahn. No great revelation, that; but it is with great difficulty that I note that some members of the Internet and World Wide Web systems are actually closing down entire nodes, not to mention millions of people personally signing off altogether. They have also taken, as suggested by two persons I haven't the stomach to name, to scrawling anthems across the cybersky seconds before discorporating.

***

A train is speeding northward along the Northeast Corridor. Wally Budge is surprised to note that even though it's close to one in the morning, nearly every seat is taken. Talk is animated. Several boom-boxes are tuned to public radio affiliates and AM talk shows, making conversation difficult.

"Isn't radio use illegal on board a train?"

Shelly Dunlap turns to him and smiles. "Not during a national emergency."

"Oh, yeah," he grins. "That."

He goes back to his laptop. How did he used to occupy himself in dull moments before he got one? Chuckling to himself, he calls up the series of memos that brought about this train ride.

To: Ms. Budge@Investigations
From: Henderson@Enforcement
Subj: Assignment

Check the duty roster, Lieutenant. You have a squad assigned and stakeout point X-Ray is yours. Don't fuck it up. I don't know how you wormed your way back onto this case, but don't get your hopes up. I'm keeping you as far away from them as I know how.

—Henderson

The second memo had made more sense.

To: Ms. Budge
From: SDunlap
Subject: It worked!
Classification: Ms. Budge Only

Henderson used a loophole to get you off the S&W case. I found another one to get you back on. Stick with me, we'll go places.

—Shel

He'd sent a memo back to Shel, calling her the angel she is, and asking her what "stake-out point X-Ray" was. He drops his eyes to the answer she'd sent.

Ah, well. He'd always liked trains. Gives a man some time to sit still and think.

Narrative Entry, Jabbathehut (con't)

Memo: University of Washington
As the Regents are responsive to the students, staff, and faculty of the college, and since we are approaching a weekend, we have decided to comply with the unanimous request to shut our Webserver node down. All normal Internet activity will resume Tuesday morning, 8 a.m. EST.

Signoff Sunday 8 p.m., EST
***

A National Emergency: Shelly's loophole.

Even now, Wally Budge is chuckling. Shelly turns in her seat.

"What's so funny?"

"Tell me again how you trumped Henderson's big trick."

Smiling, "I must've told you three times already."

"Tell me again"

So she tells him, how Henderson had manipulated both government higher-ups and media to label the threat of the Net strike a national emergency. How Henderson pulled the *first* loophole: In a national emergency, jurisdiction of all ongoing cases rests solely with Enforcement: Henderson's sandbox.

 "Which is how he locked me out!"

"Uh huh," says Shel, feeling like a baby-sitter reading a bedtime story to a particularly cute child. She tells him again how she found an obscure paragraph in Henderson's loophole: in cases of National Emergency, *no one* is assigned desk duty except communications personnel. Every able-bodied Bureau worker was supposed to be out there.

He's smiling contentedly. "Puts me slam-bang back on the case!"

"*Station stop Phila-DEL-phia, Thirty-Fourth Street Station. This will be the only stop in Philadelphia. All doors are open.*"

Narrative Entry, Jabbathehut (con't)

It's well past midnight when Lieutenant Budge looks out the window at the crowds of people waiting to get on board the train. What the hell is going on? Why is everyone out and about at this hour? Why is everyone so damned cheerful? In the background, an endless series of announcers from the National Public Radio Network are going on about how many nodes have shut down; how many people are estimated to have signed off already.

"Lieutenant Budge?" The quavering voice pulls Wally out of his reverie. He swivels his head to find himself inches from the face of some kid in his early twenties.

"Who wants to know?" he asks gruffly. Ever since his "television debut" at the Coney Island debacle, people have come up to him on the street to say hello.

The young man goes beet-red. "It's me, Sir. Frank Norton."

Wally's puzzled. Shelly leans in close and whispers, "Your communications chief, Lieutenant." Wally nods, but continues to stare at the nervous young man.

"What was your job before this assignment?"

"Hard copy routing and expediting, Sir."

Wally blinks. "You work in the mail room?"

The young man's wince is painful to watch. "Yessir. But we don't call it that any more, sir."

Source: diary.sdunlap@FBCS.gov

Narrative Entry, Jabbathehut (con't)

University of Colorado

As the Regents are responsive to the students, staff, and faculty of the college, and since we are mid-weekend, we have decided to comply with the unanimous request to shut down our Webserver node. All normal Internet activity will resume Tuesday morning, 8 a.m. EST.

Shutdown 11:45 a.m. Sunday EST

***

"What is it you want, Agent Norton?" says Lieutenant Wally Budge. The young man's face flushes with shy pride at the lieutenant's use of the title, as Budge had known it would.

"Well, sir," says the neoagent, in a near parody of earnestness, "You asked me to tell you when we were halfway there. We are, sir. Halfway there."

"Thank you, Agent Norton. Carry on."

Wally and Shel share a crooked smile as a more self-confident Frank Norton returns to his seat. Wally looks back out the window. How had he ended up with this crew? National emergency or not, it was a motley one indeed.

Thanks to that little subparagraph, the entire staff of the bureau had been sent out around the country to stake out nodes that hadn't shut down yet. Nodes—those electronic transfer stations that service hundreds, sometimes thousands of computers, representing a hefty number of citizens. One of those nodes would lead them to Scratch and Winc, went the reasoning.

"All aboard! This train is making stops at Trenton, Princeton, Newark, New York City, Hartford, Providence, and Boston."

Source: diary.sdunlap@FBCS.gov

Narrative Entry, Jabbathehut (con't')

The weak-kneed McOnline services fall in, one by one.

Memo from John Metzger, CEO, Prodigy
To: all service users

As Prodigy is responsive to its vendors, users, and the general population, we have decided to honor the unanimous request of our customers to shut our Webserver node down for 24 hours. All normal Internet activity will resume Tuesday morning, 8 a.m. EST.

Shutdown 12:01 a.m., Monday EST

***

Back on a train speeding northward along the Northeast Corridor, Budge turns back to survey the people aboard. They continue to appear exuberant.

"What the fuck is everyone so happy about?" he murmurs out loud.

"Next station stop TrrrrrreENton, New Jersey," calls the conductor.

End Jabba Entry

Source: persLOG/budge/harddrive

Begin narrative entry, Gwynyth
Gwynyth\mydiary.log\enterpassword *****:

I am delighted to include a bit of chat that was risked just before Romiette and Julio finally got offline and sped towards the Big City:

Begin AutoChatLog:

Private Message to Jabbathehut

Gwynyth: Care to go to a private room, O great one?

To my surprise, Jabba joined me, grumbling about it being too dangerous to continue in Private Messages.

Online Host: You have entered private room "Cythera."

Gwynyth: I had a feeling you might be lurking until the bitter end.

Jabbathehut: ::eyebrows raised::

Gwynyth: I thought you might like some company.

Jabbathehut: Madame, I do not lurk.

Gwynyth. Of course you don't, dear. You are very busy, I know.

Jabbathehut: Purpose of this intrusion?

Gwynyth: Oh, slide down off that horse, you old fart. I'm just making contact.

Jabbathehut: Forgive me. I'd forgotten the social convention.

Gwynyth: Well, you can learn again, it's very easy.

Jabbathehut: I have had no reason.

Gwynyth: I know, dear, I know. And someday maybe you'll tell me why. I miss you. I don't *just* think of you as a genius, you know.

Jabbathehut: Nor I, you. It is rather strange to be here in this the ever-diminishing cyberspace, just the two of us.

Gwynyth: Three of us, dear.

Jabbathehut: Three?

Toobe has entered the room.

Jabbathehut: ::gruffly:: Very well, then, three of us.

Toobe: Better make that five.

Jabbathehut: ::lifting an eyebrow:: Five?

Winc has entered the room.
Scratch has entered the room.

Jabbathehut: ::sighing heavily:: Five.

Winc: Oh, it's a family!

Gwynyth: ::suppressing a smile:: *Jabba Knows Best*?

Toobe: *The Jabba Bunch*!

Scratch: ::eyeing Jabba's scowl:: *All In the Family* ::ducking::

Jabbathehut: ::utterly speechless::

Jabba signed off immediately, of course, but if you can tell such a thing onscreen, I think the old dear might have been secretly pleased.

autoescape:Gwynyth\mydiary.log\close

End Gwynyth Entry

Narrative Entry, Jabbathehut

"Next station stop Pennsylvania Station, New York. New York will be the next station stop."

Finally, he thinks to himself. Wally checks his watch: 4:30 a.m. This train has been like a goddamn party for the past four hours.

"Wanna round up the troops, Shel?"

"Yes, Lieutenant," she grins, and moves up the aisle searching for sleeping agents, whose somnolence sets them apart from the revelers on board. Wally Budge leans over to the woman seated across the aisle, vaguely wondering if she's one of his "men," since she doesn't seem to be chatting like all the other lamebrains around him.

"Pardon me, ma'am, I couldn't help notice you weren't joining in the festivities here."

She turns to him slowly, strawberry blond waves falling down across her right eye. She's smiling. "Is that a crime, Officer Budge?" Husky voice, kind of Lauren Bacall. He'd always liked Lauren Bacall.

"Heh heh," he laughs nervously. "Saw me on television, huh?"

"And who in the entire country hasn't, officer?"

He shakes his shaggy head. "Yeah, I suppose. Do you have any idea why everyone's so happy? It's a national emergency, after all." Damn, her legs go on for*ever.*

She laughs lightly. "Well, Lieutenant Budge, I suppose it's the adult equivalent of getting a day off from school. The Net is shutting down, people are actually talking with each other—without keyboards and monitors. They're not stuck in their houses." She shrugs. "It's a holiday."

"And you?"

The train is pulling to a stop.

"Me? I'm visiting an old friend in New York." She shakes her hair out of her eyes, revealing a waterfall tattoo dropping from her right eye down to her cheekbone. Wally can't stop himself from asking. He points awkwardly at the tattoo.

"So, you're a Winc fan, huh?"

"This is Pennsylvania Station, New York."

She raises her hand, drawing a long, slender finger down the length of the design. Smiles into his eyes. "Who in their right mind *wouldn't* be a Winc fan, officer."

She's up in the aisle now, pulling a bag down from the rack above her seat. Wally Budge is up in a flash, standing by her side. She turns to him, startled.

"Yes?" She's got a good four or five inches on him.

"Let me get that bag for you, ma'am."

A slow smile, her head inclined just slightly, and that long hair falling over her eye again. He feels like a teenager. The smile doesn't leave her lips.

"Why, thank you, officer." With a small laugh and a wave, she's through the door and out on the platform.

A tapping at his shoulder. It's Shel, amused.

"Agent Budge? The troops are ready to disembark."

Source1: persLOG/budge/harddrive

Source2: diary.sdunlap@FBCS.gov

End Jabba Entry

Begin narrative entry, Gwynyth
Gwynyth\mydiary.log\enterpassword *****:

True Romance, take two. The young lovers are back online. Toobe and I were skimming through the farewell ditties when Winc's first email arrived. I don't know who was more excited, Toobe or me.

AutoMailLog:

>>To: Gwynyth@"encrytped"
From: ScratchnWinc@ecotech.com
Subj: We're ba-a-a-a-a-a-a-ack!

We made it! We're on *Wall Street*! Can you believe it? I waited outside the address Orlio gave us, and it's about 5 a.m., right? Streets are empty, hardly any lights on. This kid comes right up to me, eyes popping out of his head, and he says, "Winc?" I say, "Orlio?" He's laughing, saying over and over "Wow, you really *are* a lady!" And I say "Sometimes, dear." And he keeps laughing.

Oh! I sat across the aisle from a certain lieutenant the whole train ride up here! Long story, I'll tell you in person.

Then Scratch *roars* up to the curb, screeches to a halt, and leans out the window with a crinkly grin and says, "Hey, Dollface, kept you waitin' long?" Swoon. Ze must've broken every speed limit getting here on time.

Orlio couldn't get over Scratch. "Oh man, that is so cool: You're a dyke!" Scratch kept smiling, glancing at him all gruff-but-not-really, and finally said, "Sometimes, dear." I swear!

Anyway, Orlio's dad let us in, they both went home, and

now we're just cozy as can be. It was easy enough to set up this account, so . . .

—Scratch here. Hey, Gwyn. We're safe and sound, watching for the last node signoff. Any words to the wise would be appreciated. See you and Toobe soon, I'm thinking.
—ScratchnWinc

To: ScratchnWinc⌐"encrypted"
From: Gwynyth⌐"encrypted"
Subj: Watch Your Tootsies

::wagging a finger at you:: Careless, careless! You sent me your last note without encrypting your address. I've taken steps to vanish it from the cyberether, but no telling who's watching. Budge's minions continue to prowl, nasty creatures every last one of them.

That said, I'm so glad you're here! Fortunately, you left those hackers a cold trail from your homes and now they have to start--forgive me--from scratch. We're working out new bypasses now, so I can't stay too long.
—Gwyn<<

autoescape: Gwynythmydiary.logclose
End Gwynyth Entry

Toobe Entry

Audio file:
NPR broadcast, Special Edition
This is Bob Edwards in Washington. Despite the exultation in the streets, there are still a few nodes left functioning, effectively gutting the strike. But try to tell that to the revelers in the street, who seem to be comprised of serious freedom-of-speechers as well as those who go wherever they sense a party.
End NPR Transcript
End Toobe Entry

Narrative Entry, Jabbathehut

On the still silent streets of lower Manhattan, beneath the unlit neon sign of Papaya King, two doors down from the drab entrance to EcoTech Technologies, Budge glances down at his watch. It's almost 5:30 in the morning. He looks up just in time to catch nine out of his ten squad members look up from their own watches. He closes his eyes, wearily.

"Nothing to do but kill time, Shel," he says sotto voce. "Henderson is sure to station himself at the most likely node."

Shelly turns to face him. She's been peering intently into the window of a local piercing parlor. She bites back a smile, and pats the laptop at her side.

"That's not what your hackers have been saying, sir."

Source: diary.sdunlap@FBCS.gov

Narrative Entry, Jabbathehut (con't)

The Node Room

[I must excerpt here from Toobe's adolescent journal, as he is still, thankfully, offline:]

>>Toobe Entry

I actually just talked to my pals by phone. That was bizarre. I guess they made it from Dingmans Ferry (Scratch) and Trenton (Winc). They're at Orlio's dad's. He handed the keys to them and left the building. He says he's going to plant himself in front of the TV with his radio on, because he's never been this "disconnected" from the Net before. This is so weird to be offline, and know that they're on. But I do have their phone number. I can't believe he's going to let them play around over there. What a cool guy.

End Toobe Entry<<

Narrative Entry, Jabbathehut (con't)

We are down to approximately 30 nodes at present, the lowest number I ever would have imagined. brb.

bak.

Make that 29.

Fighting God,

—J.

End Jabba Entry

Begin narrative entry, Gwynyth
Gwynythmydiary.logenterpassword xxxxx:

Toobe has asked me to record one of the radio updates. Such a dear.

>>NPR Broadcast, Monday morning:

This is Bob Edwards in Washington. And now for our update in what is becoming the top story of the day: The so-called Internet strike. A number of factors have contributed to what looks to be a greater participation than expected for the strike, which is set to be in full effect four hours from now, Monday, at 8 a.m. Even this morning the notion had seemed impossible to all but the most zealous of online users and civil liberties groups . . . but the stunning fact is, there are only about 30 more nodes left and functioning at present. The total number of nodes is in the hundreds, a figure which contributed to the skepticism of Net watchers and longtime communications experts. With each passing hour, more of the nodes simply close down, often preceded by thousands of individuals signing off their accounts.

[End NPR broadcast excerpt]<<

AutoMailLog:

>>To: Gwynyth
From: Jabbathehut
Subj: Your gracious offer

My dear witchful wonder, I wish to avail myself again of your kind offer to protect our two friends. They are online, together, in the same physical room apparently, speaking with one another via keyboard. Words fail me.

—J.<<

J.'s right; they are indeed sitting together in the node room, typing to one another side by side (Winc's idea of an ice-breaker, I imagine). The two of them seem quite oblivious to the machinations of Budge's hackers, who by now have pegged them to New York State.

AutoChatLog:

>>*Online host: You are in Private Room "Hee Hee."*****

Winc: ::sleepy smile:: Good morning.
Scratch: Check this out! Dueling computers!
Winc: ::blinking:: You seem very awake.
Scratch: Way! Do you know one of my passwords is "Winc"? Are you reading the "Scratch and Winc" board? Have you missed me? Do you have enough stuff to read? Read this: ::uploading::

Post: Scratch and Winc Website

It's working, it's working! Very few nodes left!
Signing off now!
—Alternative to Loud Boats Node, San Diego

Winc: Do you know you make me happy beyond words?
::shaking my head:: Delighted to see this side of you.
Scratch: So many sides. So happy to see you!
Winc: Me too you! ::softly:: Why are we typing then?

Scratch: We're shy. And we have to keep activity on this line.
Winc: To show that we're still here?
Scratch: Yeah. Our assignment!
Winc: ::dimly:: Still haven't had any coffee yet, dear.
Scratch: Then when all the nodes shut off we're the only ones left!
Winc: You seem pretty happy.
Scratch: Hysterically happy! ::measuring:: 85% you, 30% rebels with a cause.
Winc: While I believe your math needs some work, I'm happy too. Do you know what?
Scratch: ::stopping short:: What?
Winc: When you're happy, you tell stories.
Scratch: Hmmm, guess you're right . . .
Winc: Lovely to see, darlin'. You're full of joy.
Scratch: Joy's got me picked up by the holes like a bowling ball. You wanna hear something else?
Winc: Always.
Scratch: ::demonstrating:: I put my fingers inside your cunt, then I put two more in your ass, then I rock you back and forth and up and down and then I kiss you and then I pick you up and you come and then we are happy-happyhappywackos!
Winc: ::gasp:: Yeah, that's sort of what I had in mind . . . like that . . .
Scratch: Then Razorfun comes in all dark and scary and cuts you and then we bleed all over naked bodies and roll around in the daisies . . .
::circuits crossing and jamming::
::Technicolor explosions::
Winc: ::laughing at your sweetness::
Scratch: . . . and then Scratchgrrl jumps into Winc's riotboy arms and we slamdance around while I pull his cock and then Digqueers trips us up and we fall down on the green grass with all kinds of wet stuff and lots o' flowers . . .
Winc: Scratch. I am so glad you're back.
Scratch: Back ain't the half of it. You may fear you've created a monster . . .
Winc: ::purring:: You have always been my favorite monster.
Scratch: Do you think we should be logging this? Hard to recreate hysterical joy . . .

Winc: ::rolling my eyes:: Do you for one moment believe I wouldn't save this masterpiece? But I'm a little scared of going offline. To be with you face to face again. ::carefully keeping my eyes glued to the screen::

Scratch: Yeah, me, too. But there's no other way but forward. We gotta be together for this last thing. ::using all my willpower to keep fingers on the keyboard:: I'm sorry I was gone so long, must have been very difficult for you . . .

Winc: ::nodding, smiling gently:: Made sense, though. Look how long we took to get to know each other, not just in surfing, but . . . I go away too.

Scratch: I know. Feel like I'm a floating hotel, too many functions to keep up. So I just shut down.

Winc: Understand.

Scratch: Trying not to think about you on the floor . . . red marks on your back . . .

Winc: ::moaning::

Scratch: You've got to protect yourself from my going away. I have NO idea when it's coming . . .

Winc: ::Pressing legs tightly together:: Listen, you . . . it's all part of love.

Scratch: ::slight grin, continuing to type:: Wanna get you all wet, always want to get you all wet and messy . . . weirdest thing . . .

Winc: Wanna be on my knees in front of you.

Scratch: }->

Winc: Is that a picture of Razorfun?

Scratch: Uh huh.

Winc: Wanna press my face against your boot.

Scratch: Wanna slap that face and kiss that face and slap it some more . . .

Winc: Yeah, wanna feel you slap me.

Scratch: Wanna mark you with me.

Winc: Wanna be yours.

Scratch: Guess what?

Winc: NO! ::small voice:: g'bye?

Scratch: Yeah, we should do our signoff soon.

Winc: ::gulp:: Right you are. ::waving::<<

My bet is their next words to each other were "hello" and "hi there."

autoescape:Gwynyth\mydiary.log\close

End Gwynyth Entry

Narrative Entry, Jabbathehut

Six a.m. Sun's coming up on a Manhattan Monday, still no traffic. No early-to-work types rushing to their offices. A gaggle of government types stand on the sidewalk, holding cups of sticky-sweet concoctions from the now-open Papaya King. They're all listening to Budge hold forth about his days as a beat cop. Only Shelly Dunlap notices that he keeps shifting his eyes to the EcoTech building, up to the third floor, where one light is burning.

"What're we waiting for, Wally?" she asks.

"We're waiting for Henderson to wake up and give us the damned go-ahead," says Wally. "Until then," he grins, "we wait." He looks over at his shabby crew of "men." "Have I told you the one about busting the pickets at the abortion center in Chelsea?"

Source: diary.sdunlap@FBCS.gov

Narrative Entry, Jabbathehut (con't)

>>To: ScratchnWinc
From: Jabbathehut
Subj: Errant nodes

Although I wouldn't bother concluding anything from this, there appear to be only four nodes left online. I doubt this situation will continue, as most of them will probably come back once they've seen their folly. However, since you continue to fritter away your time, I shall inform you that one of the nodes is Gwynyth's, one is yours of course, one belongs to "The Coalition" (of an endlessly long name regarding sexual minorities), and the other is mine. I assure you I will continue to operate as usual, as it is not my nature to be a joiner of any kind. Please excuse that inconvenience.

Fighting God,

—J.

To: Jabbathehut
From: ScratchnWinc
Subj: Naughty nodes

The Coalition? Are you sure? We're puzzled. Can you please check again? Also, if for some reason they go offline, and then we go offline, you'll be the only one left. Could you please consider taking a holiday for 24 hours? We wouldn't really count you among the strikers, but it would make everything perfect.

—S&W.<<

But three minutes went by, which of course is far too long for cybergnats to remain still. Again risking capture, including of this correspondent, the W-person used the *telephone* to inform me that in their mindless tinkering at the node, they had discovered the Triumvirate Association of Businesses database file. Successfully fighting my panic, I calmly informed them that they must not attempt any sort of interaction with such an enormous database. It is coded and protected, but I have come to believe that any electrically powered machinery is at risk when in the vicinity of the canned food twins.

This, of course, did nothing to dissuade them:

>>To: Jabbathehut
From: ScratchnWinc
Subj: Code in the node

Please excuse me, our dear friend, but Winc has found a few entry level codes that look familiar even to hir. Ze says Toobe taught hir some when he was setting up one of your bypasses for hir. Is it possible you know these codes? Just checking.
—S.

◎ click here to read attached file: CoolCode.DOC<<

Looking back now I realize I was completely ambushed by my own vanity. The codes were frighteningly familiar, the most basic elements of encryption. My shock at seeing how vulnerable was such a powerful database perhaps fogged my reason. Before I could come to my senses, I had fired off a memo with the corresponding code breakers. I can only say in self-defense that I had no idea the W-person would have any idea how to input them.

End Jabba Entry

Begin narrative entry, Gwynyth
Gwynythmydiary.logenterpassword *****:

Collecting all these sources is challenging. My admiration for the child grows, for he has been doing this sort of thing for many weeks now.

As promised, I am retrieving missives from all who wish to reach us, and placing them in their proper order. My laugh lines are deepening.

>>**Scratch Entry:**

It was stunning to discover the database, because it was like the black box in an airplane, totally secret and indestructible, and carrying all this information I guess is crucial to Big Brother. I got off on just looking at it, but Winc went right in. It was like ze knew in an instant how to hack it. Ze said that was a shocking idea since ze's "a real bonehead," but it wasn't to me. After ze got Jabba's codes ze sat down at this console and started typing. I was telling hir to be careful because I was sure the thing would start shooting acid out its portals or something if it felt someone messing with it. Ze said machines weren't like that.

Of course the first thing ze tried was to delete the whole thing, but it wouldn't even respond. In fact it kicked hir out a few times, but ze kept going right back in. Then we got to the database spreadsheet itself, which showed all those stupid Reg questions in the order they're asked and all that. You could go down to each field and highlight it. They were in alphabetical order, but I remembered the questions themselves weren't, so I asked Winc if you could just rearrange the order. Winc looked at me like I was Einstein or something.

Then we got another note from Jabba. We were surprised, because ze was always going on about how we shouldn't email.

>>To: ScratchnWinc
From: Jabbathehut
Subj: Confirmation

I have completed my tests and can assure you the last node besides Gwynyth's, mine, and yours is in fact the Coalition's. More importantly, perhaps it needs to be pointed out to you, this makes you extremely vulnerable to actual capture. Any fool would know that you appear to be in either San Francisco or New York. Neither my node nor Gwynyth's reveal themselves to the average eye— average eye being, I assure you, an accurate description of the law.

F.G.,

—J.<<

We went right down to the third question, our favorite one to hate:

Sex: M/F

We were silly by then, bored out of our skulls, but wired from all the waiting, adrenaline, and sex we weren't having. We put our fingers together and hit the "delete" key as one, fully expecting a big old nothing.

Apparently when you delete a field the whole database has to be put back together all over again, minus the field. We didn't really know what we'd done, but if it'd been written online, we would've looked like this:

> **Winc**: Wow, it's an hourglass.
> **Scratch**: What does that mean?
> **Winc**: It's thinking.
>   (Pause.)
> **Scratch**: Wow, it's still thinking.

Only we were side by side (much better). Every time we looked back at the screen the hourglass was still there. And the little lights blinking on the console. S L O W L Y.

Meanwhile, in came another memo from Jabba:

>>**To: ScratchnWinc**
From: Jabbathehut
Subj: Coalition
    Lest you get hurt, it might help to know that the reason for the noncompliance on the part of the Coalition is not the general membership, with whom you apparently had much correspondence, and in whom you (oddly) placed much trust. There is, as is often the case, another stewardship within the organization; this handful of people have commandeered the node. Perhaps this makes a difference to you, perhaps not. In any case, there appears to be no means of having your little action work, so long as this node is open.
—J.<<

I started looking for candy in the desk drawers and Winc sat quietly and scarfed Cheezits. We were, needless to say, seriously bummed.

End Scratch Entry<<
autoescape:Gwynyth\mydiary.log\close
End Gwynyth Entry

Narrative Entry, Jabbathehut
Dire circumstances lead to dire memos:

Private Message to ScratchnWinc

Jabbathehut: I choose this primitive and extremely dangerous method to inform you that you must get offline immediately. The police, despite their obvious limitations, will divine your location in Manhattan within minutes.

Even *I* was not prepared to see what followed that missive:

Private Message to ScratchnWinc

Gwynyth: Yeah, what J. said.

I'd forgotten that she can read even my most private memoranda.

End Jabba Entry

Begin narrative entry, Gwynyth
Gwynythmydiary.logenterpassword ✕✕✕✕✕:

>>**Scratch Entry:**

It always fucking goes this way. One stupid little scared clutch of people fuck it up for the rest of us. I know it wasn't the real Coalition members, but it doesn't matter. All people have to do is temporarily throw in with each other over one or two issues, it's not like they have to sign their lives away. But no, they gotta fight about every little thing, hold out when they feel the groundswell, as if taking a stand on something, anything, would fucking kill them.

What else could we do? We had to sign off. I certainly wasn't gonna meet up with that ugly Budge over the scared shenanigans of some A-list queers.

End Scratch Entry<<

autoescape: Gwynythmydiary.logclose
End Gwynyth Entry

Narrative Entry, Jabbathehut

How I became entangled in a series of telephone conversations with S & W is beyond my imagination. I simply offered to let them know of the progress of the hackers, and they have chosen to contact me frequently and without purpose, as far as I can tell. They typed an inane series of chats while sitting in the same room, have probed the offices of EcoTech, and other bizarre activities, and I finally concluded that they were very bored. True, they had nothing to do but wait for their silly little strike to materialize, despite the fact that anyone can see they would have been waiting forever. At the same time, as the nodes have closed down, they have frustrated the pursuing hackers. Accept this childish image, if you will: It is as if they are in a cave, with many tunnels leading to them; as each node closes down the tunnels collapse, and the hackers are forced to find another conduit to them.

By my calculations the hackers should be at their door by 8 a.m. I have called Tweedles Dee & Dum twice to update my predictions, but see no need for further chat as that prophecy is holding.

End Jabba Entry

Begin narrative entry, Gwynyth
Gwynythmydiary.logenterpassword ×××××:

>>Narrative Entry, Scratch

One by one, morning lights are going on in this city that never sleeps. I am imagining that with each light that goes on, a computer shuts off. I bet people are dancing, or painting, or writing letters in longhand, maybe reading magazines, turning past the ads to the letters to the editor, making hot chocolate. I feel a tingling inside, which I can't tell is from lack of sleep, desire for Winc, or the excitement of this strike (I still have hope—something might make the Coalition shut down). Nothing like a little authority closing in to galvanize the previously unpolitical. After that bullshit with arrests, people scrambled to get the fuck off their computers.

We're supposed to be composing our own anthem but after all this, there seems nothing more to say. We're having a great time reading the other people's, though, except they're slowing down to a trickle. Makes sense: only four nodes supporting what's left of the system. Winc says to be patient.

End Scratch Entry<<

The last of the hackers has fallen prey to my cybercats. Time to prepare my adieu. Toobe has begged to be allowed a private email to Jabba. How can I refuse?

>>To: Jabba
From: Toobe
Subj.: Just please

::looking at you straight in the eyes:: Please help us. Isn't there something you can do about that Coalition? I guess I'm asking you again for help, which I know I've done too much lately. But it's really important.
—T.<<

autoescape:Gwynyth\mydiary.log\close
End Gwynyth Entry

Narrative Entry, Jabbathehut

Had I not had my disbelief suspended days ago I would be sputtering at the evidence on my screen, but there are, at present, only two nodes left. I am operating on a temporary conduit from the EcoTech node myself, as that is the only one available to me. I shut my own down hours ago as there was no activity on the line, and it is far too costly to keep up appearances. The fish tanks are sparkling. I have made my temporary conduit safe from the bored antics of its two occupants.

>>**To: Toobe, Scratch**
From: Winc
Subj: Giddy

I feel free! Figured out this chart to break through the two-party gender system. It's what I was, what I was *trying* to be, what I am now. Three genders, that's not all of 'em, but it's a start. There's this whole big space that can include *lots* of genders. ::fade in *Star Trek* theme:: I feel like Captain Kirk or Janeway . . . going where no man has gone before. What do you think? Engage!

—W.

	As boy	**As girl**	**As outlaw**
Favorite ice cream	vanilla	chocolate (no nuts)	tutti-frutti
Star Trek role model	Mr. Spock	Lt. Tasha Yar	Lt. Dax
Movie I'd see again and again	*King of Hearts*	*Desert Hearts*	*Wild at Heart*
Favorite comic	*Superman*	*Dykes to Watch Out For*	*Shade, the Changing Man*
Often greeted by	"What charisma!"	"Quelle mystique!"	"What the hell was that?"
Object of affection	girls	women	Scratch
Mission in life	Change the world	Change the system	Change my mind
Theme song	"I Wanna Be Your Man"	"I Am Woman (Hear Me Roar)"	"Fool on the Hill"
Major use for telephone	telemarketing	professional phone sex	modem connection
Book read most avidly . . .	*Siddhartha*	*Encyclopedia of Women's Myths and Secrets*	*The Story of O*
Burning question	"What's a woman?"	"What's a man?"	"Who cares?"

Narrative Entry, Jabbathehut (con't)

The cyberwitch has joined the ranks by taking her node offline. The two nodes functioning at present belong to my bored correspondents and the Coalition. Although that node is protected with encryption, I ran a series of tests that revealed a standard protection device, adequate if unimaginative.

Their strike will not happen, as I predicted.

>>Narrative Entry, Scratch

Just read Gwynyth's anthem, she's shut down! Called Toobe and we laughed and cried over the phone lines until Gwyn warned us to get off. Here's her signoff anthem:

>>And this I state

I started getting cranky around the time they called in the mortgage on the Coney Island Freak Show, and put up a McDonald's in its stead. Let me tell you—there weren't many places left for a bearded lady to work.

Memories: "Can I help you, sir?"

"Look at the man in the dress, Mommy!"

"Sorry, this land is for women only."

I have always found refuge in my computer. Next to my cats, that ornery pile of chips and circuits was the most forgiving creature in my life. I plied quite the thriving trade in online credit card tarot readings. But one day some hacker pranked my routings, and I had men signing on for, of all things, credit card cybersex. Gave the damn fools a tarot reading anyway, and realized they never knew the difference.

I found my life's work at the nexus of spirituality, technology, and desire.

I felt fulfilled. In the years that followed, I built vast cyberdomains to allow all who could find them to enter, explore, experience, and emerge enlightened. I flourished.

I had but one friend in the world who could match me in my speed and desire for things techno.

My large friend and I built cyberworlds in which we romped. Cyberplaymates. Detectives, too, hot on the trail of the world's great criminal masterminds. This went on for seven years, and never did we meet face to bearded face. We once believed in the fathomless soul of our humanity. Until, one day twelve long years ago, my friend was simply no longer there. I've no idea the reason for this. I'm sure ze believes I have simply accepted the absence with my usual aplomb. But I was suddenly alone in an empire of zeroes and ones. Slowly I dismantled that empire, myself retiring from the worlds I'd created. I built and fortified my cyberfortress, my secret domain. I practiced my Code and my Craft, waiting to discover my *raison d'être*. I missed my large friend.

I've kept tabs on my friend, and to this day I hold no key to the sudden disappearance. Now, after twelve years of virtual and quite real solitude, I have three *new* friends who've gazed upon my furry face and never blinked an eye. It's been worth the wait. And lo, my first friend and I have spoken again of late. You can call it chance. You can call it a twist of the fates or a turn of the dial. I call it the power of an open heart. Now I know the reason for my cyberpowers. I know the reason for my understanding of the Craft. And the reason for my beard.

From this day forward, I pledge my life to opening my strong arms to all my family members everywhere. By Code and by Craft, I do. So Be It.

—GWYNYTH

Signoff Monday 5:20 a.m. EST<<
End Scratch entry<<

Narrative Entry, Jabbathehut (con't)

>>To: Jabbathehut
From: ScratchnWinc
Subj: What gives?

We're taking your advice and getting out of here. But we've got a question: We thought you said we'd be the last node online! This way anyone using the Coalition node—and you know that could be *thousands* of people—is in danger of being arrested, and they'll go after them before us, to try to flush us out! Can you please email those guys (we can't seem to get through) and ask them why they haven't shut down yet?

—S/W.<<

I responded that I *can* do such a thing, but the dynamic duo fails to understand avarice and its relation to power. Nonetheless, they did finally leave the premises, so to speak, so I am resting slightly more easily.

My cherished public radio has perhaps a better summary of events that happened next:

Despite earlier predictions that the so-called Internet Strike would have no effect, it appears at present that there are only two nodes left functioning. One is located in San Francisco, the other in New York.

As we speak, apparently a last "ScratchnWinc" anthem is being transmitted, though from which node is not yet clear. An automatic shutdown of their node should, however, follow. We will have the full text of that anthem in a few moments.

>>Scratch entry, Winc entry

We can't wait any more to see if the Coalition will change its mind. We have to do this.

Question Authority ain't the half of it. Question everything. We don't have any advice, just big hearts and no common sense, and we hope nobody gets hurt in all this.

Until we can meet again,

Digqueers/Luvboyz
Frankie/Johnny
Leilia/Karn
Spoiler/Lt.Yar
Razorfun/Gyrl
Spiker/Honeydew
Scratch/Winc<<

ScratchnWinc signoff 7:58 a.m. Monday, EST

End NPR transcript<<

Narrative Entry, Jabbathehut (con't)

Eight a.m. Wally Budge is still out of breath from climbing the three flights of stairs up to the node room of EcoTech Technologies. He's grinning ear to ear, though. Henderson's tone of bitter resignation over the phone had made it all worthwhile.

"They're not here, Budge. They must be at your site," Henderson had growled.

"Is that an order to search the premises?"

Henderson had simply hung up the phone. Budge started issuing directives.

His dirty dozen, whom he has come to regard fondly, swarms through EcoTech like ants at a picnic. Budge himself is reading posters on the walls. He knows he's just missed them. Shelly Dunlap looks up from one of the monitors.

"Got something interesting here, Wally."

He ambles over, peering over her shoulder at the hourglass endlessly humming on the screen.

"What is it?"

"It's the master database for the Registration. They tapped into the T.A.B. masterfile!"

"What'd they do to it?"

Shelly pauses before answering.

"Well," she says slowly, "They've given it a command it can't comply with."

He lifts a craggy eyebrow. "What does that mean?"

"It means," she says, "there's gonna be no more database, no more Registration, no more online marketing, and . . ." She pauses.

"And?"

"And you won't have to be Ms. Budge any more."

"Well, ain't that a pleasant surprise."

The two of them stare into the screen for a few moments. Behind them, the James Bond wannabes are searching through paperwork.

"They won't find anything, will they, Wally?"

"I doubt it. But we've got them. On my home turf. I'll have them in custody in less than three hours."

On the screen before them, the hourglass sits squarely in the middle of the screen.

"I know a great deli up on Houston Street," he says. "Let's grab a bite there until our fish surface again."

Source: persLOG/budge/harddrive
Source: diary.sdunlap@FBCS.gov

Narrative Entry, Jabbathehut (con't)

Perhaps an update of the "fish" is in order: Predictably, they had no idea how to turn the EcoTech node off. They did lock the building, though.

::flicking my wrist::

The EcoTech node is disabled. There is only the Coalition's node. No strike.

Pity. But I do so enjoy being right.

End Jabba Entry

‹HAPTER THIRTEEN

Transcript: *NPR Morning Edition* with Bob Edwards
Day: Monday
Time: 8:30 a.m. EST

Cutaway from NPR, Bob Edwards
To: WXPN, Philadelphia

This is Bill Luxor with a special report. Early this morning the last node of the worldwide Internet system closed down without a whimper. No comment was available from spokespersons of the sexual minorities organization known simply as "The Coalition," which owns and manages the last node to shut down.

The Internet strike, less than one week ago an idle fantasy of a few, is now the bewildering reality of many. No one could have predicted the impact of such a strike, the first of its kind, but its effects reach almost every corner of the civilized world. Instigated by the so-called cyberfugitives known as Scratch and Winc, the movement spread in a matter of seconds, reaching São Paulo and Capetown as quickly as San Francisco and New York. We'll be keeping listeners posted as the day progresses, Bob.

Home Anchor, Bob Edwards: Tell me, Bill, how does this Internet really work?

Bill Luxor: Good question, Bob. The Net is made up of hundreds of clearinghouses, as it were, which are called nodes. Those nodes in turn serve smaller sites, much like electricity comes to each house through larger transformers. Only the communication here is through telephone lines. Each node affects thousands and even millions of individual users. Once a node shuts down, an Internet pathway is effectively closed. The apparent goal of the strike was to shut down the entire Internet, just by closing off all of the nodes.

Anchor Edwards: Is such a thing really possible?

Bill Luxor: No, in fact the experts said it was impossible. The public sector nodes of the government and military are still technically "online," but without the private sector nodes they've come to depend on, the vital links are missing. That effectively means no Internet, just a few isolated government nodes running, but connected sporadically. In fact the only people they have to chat with is each other. But the timing was very swift. Even as recently as a few days ago pundits were pointing out other crucial flaws in the shutdown.

Anchor Edwards: And what were those flaws?

Bill Luxor: Well, cooperation for one. If even one node had held out the whole thing would have failed, just as with any strike. That's what it looked like early this morning, when there were two nodes left, then just the one, belonging to the Coalition. We've still no idea why that particular group waited as long as it did. If that node had stayed functioning the strike, as it were, would have failed. But unlike a group of workers, these nodes represent so many different kinds of people and organizations, it is quite unbelievable there was any cooperation at all. There were as many *reasons* for shutting down nodes as there are nodes. Two hours ago three-quarters of the world's connections, impossible as it may seem, went completely offline, taking millions of personal computer users with them.

Anchor Edwards: Indeed, the entire news-gathering process of National Public Radio has been effected. I understand that this has forced us to use a little shoe leather to do our usual reporting!

[Edwards, Luxor laugh]

Bill Luxor: Exactly, Bob. Last night, with the Coalition's node still in operation, it looked like the shutdown would be crippled. Mysteriously, at 8:00 this morning, that node simply shut off, accompanied by the anthems that had become standard procedure for node shutdown.

Anchor Edwards: For further details on this story, we go to Janine Brownwill, our Internet expert, for the details:

Insert actuality: Janine Brownwill.

Actuality, Janine Brownwill: Bob, I'm standing at the heart and soul of MIT's computer labs, normally a bustling center of activity any time day or night. But today it is completely empty, save for a curious technician or two, as they try to piece together the phenomenal events of the past few days. As each node dropped offline, automatic "bots"—programs designed to catch such events—were sent to the sites. But those bots had *also* been turned off before node shutdown, rendering them completely ineffective.

MIT technicians and others around the world have doubted that this strike was remotely possible, but as they watched the connections fall offline one by one a kind of reckless abandon seemed to permeate these and other Internet headquarters. The closest analogy I can think of is the Wall Street Exchange floor on a Friday afternoon. Paper was everywhere, engineers were flying around with printouts of thousands of logs.

When it looked early this morning like the last node was still in place, there was almost a disappointment here, as if they had watched a giant experiment about to fail, even though technically, such a strike could spell disaster for MIT itself.

But at last, when it simply shut off, a great cheer went up here, an enthusiastic response for engineers. With nothing more to do, all the technicians left, going outside as so many people are doing now. It's an event, a time when you remember exactly where you were when it happened.

Anchor Edwards: Exactly how did that final node go off, and what do we know about the people who managed it?

Brownwill: As near as we can tell, Bob, that last node center was managed and maintained by a political action organization comprised of, according to their press release, "gay, lesbian, bisexual and transgendered people and their friends." No one had been sure just why this group, of all of the participants, had held out from the strike. Apparently the general membership didn't know of the situation, or that their node was the last. When the members did learn of it, they held an emergency meeting at 4 a.m. Eastern time, to determine what had happened.

Anchor Edwards: Janine, why was the membership in the dark about the fact that they were the last holdout?

Brownwill: It's a matter of a group within a group, Bob, although the details are still sketchy. Apparently the Coalition had been one of the first to join supporters of the strike late last week. Word is that they have had direct contact with Scratch and Winc, and had helped them orchestrate the strike in the first place. But some core members of the group went against the vote, and refused to cooperate.

Anchor Edwards: So those few people with the keys to the castle, so to speak, simply refused to "throw the switch"?

Brownwill: Exactly.

Anchor Edwards: I'm curious, Janine, how were you able to put these pieces together, especially without your usual electronic assistance?

Brownwill: Well, that was a bit tricky. I'm often on the Net at night, monitoring the activities of the last few days. I was amazed to watch all the pathways disintegrate last night and into the morning, and frankly wouldn't have believed it if I hadn't seen it with my own eyes. Since that node was the only one still alive last night, I routed my account to that node, and was able to stay online and watch the conversations. It was obvious the general membership was furious, and confused as to what was happening.

Anchor Edwards: So how did the decision come down?

Brownwill: That's the funny thing, we're not entirely sure. All we know is that at about 8:00 this morning, there was no more Internet.

Anchor Edwards: And was there one of those "anthems," like there have been with the other shutdowns?

Brownwill: Yes, but it's fairly mysterious. No one's quite sure what its purpose is, and certainly not who the author is. The Coalition informs us that the writer was not one of its members. A full transcript will appear in the local papers, on TV, and over this station at the top of the hour.

Anchor Edwards: Thanks, Janine, and Bill, from member stations WXPN and WHPR.

Chicago:

It's a Party— Sort Of

This is the most social this reporter has seen Chicago in a long time. It's oddly reminiscent of the Fire, or the day JFK was assassinated. The streets are full of people, people who've never met each other, all talking about one thing: the Internet shutdown.

Not only are many people's jobs affected by the strike, but the very nature of their workday has instantly changed. Without access to the information they normally get with such ease electronically, people are forced to ask each other what is going on. But the surprise aspect of this phenomenon is that people are discovering each other's online screen names, sometimes meeting up with people they've only known electronically.

There are even a few reports of romances, between people who have known each other only via computer screen. More commonly, there are real-time "salons" springing up everywhere, usually centering in a coffeehouse or bookstore.

Pissed off,
Not gonna take it anymore

Scratch and Winc may have been the spark, but there's a whole lot more behind the Net strike than originally met the eye.

Citizens are angry. Once favorable to government Registration, a strong suspicion and even distrust has replaced the growing hope that Registration would bring more options, not less. But anyone who has had obnoxious ads hurled at their screen names can tell you it's annoying to fend off campaigns for hair replacement implants when you're trying to find a law library, or worse, when you're taking the occasional cyberstroll through the world of the Net as a member of the opposite sex. The joy of the Net is its freedom.

Update: NPR

Radio On Scene Report, KRUW Wichita.

You can go from one block to another hearing news of the Internet shutdown. As with any major event, people's radios are turned on everywhere, and one can walk for blocks listening to the same broadcast without interruption. It's a sunny day in Wichita, people are strolling, some are scratching, some are winking, the apparent signals of those who follow the cyberfugitives Scratch and Winc.

There's a different feel to the crowd today. I've never seen such diverse groups of people in all in the parks. In one corner of the park is a group using their hands to communicate, in another, young people with pierced noses and big combat boots are talking animatedly. There is just about every color of the rainbow represented here, it's phenomenal. It was like a demonstration, but there is no agenda, no speeches, and no discernible cause. It's something like the love-ins of the '60s, I suppose, but involving virtually everybody.

Anchor Edwards: For some more details on the mechanics of the strike itself, let's go back to Janine Brownwill, our Internet expert. Janine, there is one nagging question behind all this. Granted there are a lot of angry people out there, and maybe many of them are following the tenets of Scratch and Winc regarding gender and cybersurfing, identity changes and so on. But this strike involved virtually every private sector node in the world. Surely all these people are not united in some common, humanitarian struggle.

Brownwill: Bob, that is a very good point, and you're right, there is certainly not the warm fuzzy unity that followers of Scratch and Winc would have wanted. For an effect this large, all the corporate nodes had to be involved, and corporations are not known for their strong emotional or political stands. But apparently the key to the success of this action, for lack of a better word, is its 24-hour time period. There were enough "squeaky wheels" on most of the nodes that the corporations simply declared it good business practice to comply. To have refused to shut down would have lost them customers; these businesses did not want to take an unpopular stand. So they simply closed for the day. Not a long enough period to seriously damage them, but I think the prevailing sentiment was, "Why risk it?" when they knew everyone would come back online again.

Anchor Edwards: And now for a fresh perspective on our top story of the day, here's Rap Shoopman, NPR Youth Reporter.

Shoopman: Amid all the celebration of former Net users, there is a very serious raid going down. Scratch and Winc have been spotted on a side street in Manhattan, or at least their car has. Police are probably no less than a mile away, as last reports had pegged raids by various officers in various cities. Of course there are many false Scratch and Winc sightings; no one has known the kind of car they drive. In Manhattan, many people do know Winc, a Lower East Side resident, and some have known Scratch. At any rate, the car is a small Honda Civic, bright blue, with bumper stickers all over the back. The car is currently parked outside the Midtown TravelLodge Hotel on Eighth Avenue, its occupants probably inside. The police have been preparing for action in this area, having focused on Times Square and Madison Square Garden, while other SWAT teams were camped out at City University and SUNY. This is Rap Shoopman, reporting for NPR.

Anchor Edwards: Hold on, Rap. You say you know Winc. So maybe you can tell us what Winc's real name is?

Shoopman: [laughs] No one seems to know, Bob. Winc has always been Winc to us.

Anchor Edwards: Thank you Rap. We'll keep listeners posted as to events in that area as they happen.

Excerpts, Corporate online services

Memo from Steve Case, president, America Online

Our company has always prided itself on being responsive to its customers, and when we noticed that there was almost no one online last night, we decided to give this strike idea a new listen. We resolved that we would indeed shut down the node, which accounts for over 4 million users in the United States and worldwide. The customers are making a statement, and we listened. We look forward to seeing you again on Tuesday at 8 a.m. Eastern Time.

CompuServe statement:

We have shut down our CompuServe node until there is more activity. At present the distracting news of a net strike has forced us to go offline. It would not be feasible to continue operating this costly business without the support of our users.

Excerpt: LINEMADNESS

Gonzo reporter on the street: Despite the official statements of various online companies, it was the individual users who facilitated the shutdown. There were no people online, therefore no service. The nodes shut down but I wish we could say it was born of ethics. Of course not: purely economic reasons, save for a few alternative colleges whose presidents issued statements of support for the strike. At any rate, maybe it was a trickle-up theory that can be used again. It's gotta start somewhere.

Narrative Entry, Scratch
Route: Hard disk to be uploaded in the event of my capture
<encrypted>Confirmed, Toobe upload

We were depressed. We'd been up all night and it certainly looked like the whole fucking thing had failed. I was embarrassed—it was my stupid idea—but Winc wouldn't hear of that. Ze kept saying things like, "We made a splash. At least we did that." So we're driving around and my radio's doing its static thing as usual. Winc finds a station at last before I smash the little contraption to smithereens.

That's when we hear what's happening. The Net is shutting down. Ours was the second-to-last to go—we thought that was the end of it, that's why we were so glum. But somewhere in the time we'd been driving around, that last one did go off. We had felt betrayed by the

Coalition, because Jabba told us that theirs was the one still online. Then we'd gotten excited because Jabba was going to shut down (ze said it was because it cost too much money to keep hir own node going). And the Coalition node stayed online.

Anyway, there were all these noises out in the street, everybody was talking about the strike. But it was like they didn't know the whole thing had failed. So we started listening, and it turned out the strike did work! It was all over the news. The Coalition node shut down. We looked at each other and then I pulled over. I ran into a coffee shop to get us some brew and when I came out I saw Winc looking at me through the car window like ze'd always ridden in there with me. It was like some movie. The sun was still in its early morning place, making everything feel new. Winc was smiling at me, the light right behind hir hair. I jumped in the car and handed hir the coffee, and we were off, for gawd knows where, but we were going.

So we got a few blocks and all that relief and tension flooded through me and it went to my crotch. All of a sudden I had to get my hands on hir, my Winc. I looked over at hir all shy but later ze said it was more like sly. There was this cheap hotel right in front of us, so I screeched into the parking lot.

We were in the room and I was swimming in desire, but also I was totally aware that ze was real, not online, big as life, hir body warm and real and right up close. Every time I touched hir, just a little, it was like electricity zapping me. Ze said it was the same for hir, like we needed to take an hour for every inch of skin, but we had no time and the electricity was fierce. We had to go almost too fast, the hunger was deep; we hugged and I felt like I was swooning, a word I've never understood, but I couldn't breathe and I was dizzy and all I could do—all I wanted to do—was hang on. I knew, right then, that despite all my great philosophizing, it was her gyrl stuff that turned me on right then, hir breasts and hir smell and hir hair and hir eyes looking at me so womanly and open and ready for me. Ze was female. I wanted hir.

I'm not even sure I got all our clothes off but it was a fast, furious, glorious fuck—I felt I could eat hir bones with my teeth and smash our skin together so it would never come apart. We tore up that room, with the radio blaring about the strike, about "Scratch and Winc" who sounded like the totally made-up cardboard heroes they were. We fucked when the stupid commercials came on and then we took a shower and practically broke the door fucking in there.

I splattered: Even though I had to conquer the hell out of hir and tell hir all those dirty things I think in my head and vulgarize hir and make hir want me and need me and crave me, at some point we became this one passionate body that didn't have a name or a sex or a place that was anchored down anywhere, we were us, juice and blood and kisses.

Until we heard on the radio about the police swarming, at which point . . . we got the hell out of there.

Later: The only thing that would make me any happier now is if we could be with you, Toobe. While I was checking out the street to make our sloppy getaway, Winc—in one of hir typical bursts of calm efficiency—called you at Gwynyth's and told you guys we were on our way. You said everything was fine there, but you were excited beyond belief like the little boy I wish you could be more.

End Scratch Entry

Transcript: NPR Report update

Bob Edwards: We now have the full excerpt of the final "anthem" issued by one Sysop, which means systems operator, screen name Jabbathehut. This was keyed in just before the final node was shut down.

> ## To: All who care to listen
> ## From: Jabbathehut
> ## Subj: My statement
>
> It is not in my nature to be public in any way, nor to join the activities of others, for organized efforts are at best mediocre and lack creativity. However, I have been surreptitiously aided by the desperate idealism of some people I have come to regard as friends.
>
> I have retired to my lair for a good twelve years, driven there by forces of evil in part, but mostly of cruelty and chance. Such is the nature of God, who is a malevolent fellow, and appears to suffer the same boredom many of us do in these uncertain times. I doubt I shall appear again, at least in this guise, as my conduits have become far too known to too many. So I shall attempt to explain myself.
>
> Many years ago I loved fiercely. She was intelligent and beautiful to me but not to herself, and blessed with a ferocious determination I had not seen before nor since.
>
> I wish there had been a reason for the events of February 25, twelve years ago, but as usual, it was random and arbitrary. She was walking with her best friend, the wife of *my* best friend, through streets not known to be unsafe, when a gang of marauders overcame them. But they were interrupted by well-intentioned youth, and the evildoers panicked. Blows were thrown, until guns were drawn. My beloved and her friend were gunned down within seconds.
>
> It happens every day, I know. But there are some events from which one can never recover.

Oddly enough, the smallest of circumstances saved me from joining her on her bier. My beloved's friend, her partner in death, had left behind a son, three years old, and a husband, my best friend. Quite simply, they needed me. John, the little one's father, is a sensitive sort; it was all I could do to keep him feeding the dogs and shaving himself each morning. You might say that little Toobe, although he was not called that then, saved us both, with his wondering eyes and quick heart; he toddled between both of us with questions, endless and irritating hugs, and an insatiable curiosity that perhaps appealed to this battered ego.

Once I was assured that his father was skating on all wheels, I retired to this peaceful room with my fish and electronic spiderwebs. It is not my wish to sustain physical contact with anyone again, and the little child has grown too fast to remember any visual image of me. But we have kept in touch, to say the least, although he doubtless does not know why.

At any rate, that Toobe should be a part of a movement so large and so successful, by some standards, is no surprise to me, but it was some time at three this morning that I realized it was he who had saved me, not I him. And so, when I discovered the stench of evil leaking from the last node belonging to one "Coalition," I decided to end my own strike against the world, and at least facilitate the wishes of my beloved charge.

It was quite simple to arrange an electronic soldier to attack the recalcitrant node with a "nerve gas." Perhaps if the organization's higher echelon of decision makers had spent more time on their software and less on their ambitions, they would have had the simplest of measures to prevent such a preemptive incision from rendering their operation useless. In a matter of minutes the last, and thus all nodes, were shut down.

Fighting, but perhaps not God any longer,

—J.

Anchor Edwards: You're listening to a special edition of NPR news . . . this is Bob Edwards. And now for a special on-scene report from our youth reporter Rap Shoopman, who has discovered a possible arrest situation regarding Scratch and Winc. Rap, how did you come to be in the heart of it all when sting operations have been going on in virtually all parts of the city?

Shoopman: Well, some of us recognize Winc from the Lower East Side, and we've been pretty sure this was Scratch's car for some time. We could tell by the weird bumper stickers. Oddly enough that car's been there for quite awhile, but the police were apparently not aware of it. Then I'm assuming the police were tuned to the radio and heard our descriptions . . . they got over here pretty fast.

There's a kind of irony in the fact that this particular squadron is led by Lieutenant Wally Budge, the policeman from the Bureau of Census and Statistics who's been trailing Scratch and Winc—via computer—for weeks. From what I've been able to gather, he had no idea his assignment would lead to this sting. All units have been instructed to watch and wait, but this situation sort of fell into his lap.

Anchor Edwards: So what's happening now?

Shoopman: Scratch and Winc came out of the hotel, and I must say they didn't look like fugitives. One's short, the other tall, they had their arms around each other, looking kind of spacey. They seemed to be in no hurry to get to their car, which they drove perhaps a block before they were stopped. Quite suddenly they were surrounded by police, and they looked absolutely stunned, like they had no idea how big a moment this is.

Anchor Edwards: Were they stopped by Lieutenant Budge?

Shoopman: That's the odd part; they were stopped for a traffic violation. It seems that old parking tickets had gone to warrant on Scratch's car; it was a routine stop. The license plate number was already in the computer. Of course when the plate came up the officer on duty saw the connection, and called for more backup, and a rather comical situation developed. The government agents pushed through the crowd to reach the scene. The NYPD Blues were yelling and waving their arms at the government cops to lay off their collar. In the confusion, no one was watching Scratch or Winc, who were sitting there in the car, spaced out.

As I'm talking, the local cops and the feds are at some kind of bureaucratic standoff, so the officer has not approached the occupants again. Apparently he's waiting for the backup to arrive, or the question to be resolved about who has jurisdiction in this case.

Narrative Entry, Scratch
Route: Hard disk to be uploaded in the event of my capture
<encrypted>Confirmed, Toobe upload

I've always said the only time I'm totally present is while fucking, but I guess you could say that extends to afterward, too. We were so dreamy we could hardly stand. If I had had my antenna up I never would have let us walk out of that hotel. We'd heard the news on the radio that they'd found my car so duh . . . we went out to the car.

At any rate we took off, but didn't get far before we were pulled over. Goddamn parking tickets. Do they have nothing better than to go after people with parking tickets? Did you know when a cop sees the warrant come up on the database the arresting officer has no idea if it's for parking in a loading zone or murder?

Anyway, they were taking way too long to check my record with my driver's license. All of a sudden I knew this was it, they'd connected me with cyber "Scratch" and it was all over. I got this flash of jail, then my stomach went totally cold when I realized Winc would go to jail, too. I remembered how hir license still says male, so she wouldn't be sent to a women's prison. It would have been totally fucked. I told hir to get out of the car, all I could think of was to run. Winc got it right away and we took off down the alley like our shoes were on fire. All the cops were standing there, yelling at each other, so we got a headstart before someone noticed. I really thought we were going to make it.

Then shots behind us, Toobe! I thought it was my car backfiring, then Winc fell down. They fucking shot Winc!

End Scratch Entry

Transcript: NPR Special Edition

Anchor Edwards: This is Bob Edwards reporting from Washington: In an incredible development, Scratch and Winc are very close to being captured, but it is not without a certain amount of confusion. Apparently shots were fired at them just moments ago, when they tried to run after being stopped for a traffic violation. The New York City police were able to connect the violation with the warrants for high treason.

Because of that charge, the officers were instructed to proceed with extreme caution. The warrants list Scratch and Winc as high-priority criminals, at the top of the FBI's most-wanted list. When Scratch and Winc fled the scene, an officer who had not been briefed on the situation drew his weapon and fired. It is not known at this point if anyone was hit, but for all intents and purposes, Scratch and Winc are still at large, and it looks like the government agents on the case have just been granted jurisdiction over the local officers. This places the balance of the hunt-and-chase in the hands of Lt. Wally Budge of the Federal Bureau of Census and Statistics . . . the man responsible for the Coney Island fiasco only weeks ago. His was the first in a series of fruitless government raids on the nation's amusement parks.

We will keep you posted as we await further developments.

Narrative Entry, Scratch
Route: Hard disk to be uploaded in the event of my capture
<encrypted>Confirmed, Toobe upload

I didn't give a fuck what happened next, I just wanted Winc to be right where ze was, lying in my arms. The cops were nowhere to be seen. I don't think they knew they'd hit hir because ze just kept running. I didn't even know until ze fell down, and I thought ze'd just tripped.

Suddenly there was absolutely no hurry. I remember a watery beam of sunlight somehow peeking its head over the tops of the skyscrapers. We found a little hollow for us to lie in, me leaning against a brick wall with hir collapsed into me. I could feel hir blood, sticky and hot against me, like I'd always imagined. Ze was murmuring how much ze loved me and looking into my eyes and then I realized something, and got all panicky, and I said Winc, No! No! I knew ze was blissed out beyond all comprehension, hir little self happy to be lying in my arms, frozen for all time, just like that, with me.

"How I always wanted it to be," ze said, and hir eyes were so near, so deep, and changing colors every five seconds to a shade more beautiful than the last. I knew it was a perfect moment too but I also got really pissed, like I always do when I feel everything's just going the path of least resistance and not trying to change itself into something better. I got pissed at hir and the police and the radio and the Net and people and subways and cars and skyscrapers, and I practically hauled hir to hir feet and made hir walk, willing some hospital or medicine man or some*thing* to be around the corner. My survival instincts kicked in: Get out of there before the enemy comes back.

Then this big belly laugh welled up in me: up to this point the biggest issue for Winc and me had been what would we be for each other in the world, how would we make this work, and now all of a sudden this big cartoon had been painted for me that said: live, Winc, just live.

End Scratch Entry

Anchor Edwards: We've learned more about the arrest situation regarding the so-called cyberfugitives Scratch and Winc. We now go to youth reporter Rap Shoopman, who has been at the site since morning.

Rap Shoopman: Well, it's a mass of confusion around here, Bob. Impossibly, the fugitives appear to have slipped away. Or perhaps they were never as close as we thought. Here's what's confirmed: Two people were stopped driving Scratch's blue Honda, but there was no actual contact, except for one of them handing over a driver's license, which the police still have. They're going to dust the license for fingerprints to make sure the driver was indeed Scratch. I could've sworn it was Winc that I saw in the passenger's seat, but now that I'm looking back on it, I was pretty far away, and who knows, maybe Winc's been through some changes in the last year or two.

At any rate, what I do know is this: At one point an officer took some shots at the pair as they fled down the alley and the taller of the two fell to the ground. We have to assume it was a result of having been hit, but I'm not sure of that either, because when the smoke of the general confusion and hollering cleared, the two had vanished. Hospitals in the area have been alerted. Lt. Wallace Budge, of the Federal Bureau of Census and Statistics, apparently did spot the two and is detailing his unit for pursuit. A squadron of officers has moved out in a singular direction, so they seem to have a fairly sure idea where the pursuit will lead.

This is Rap Shoopman, reporting for NPR.

Anchor Edwards: That's our update for this hour, we'll keep you posted. Meanwhile, the strike is still holding. Not one node has been turned back on, nor are people inclined to go back online. All eyes and ears are tuned to the media for the developments with Scratch and Winc.

Narrative Entry, Scratch
Route: Hard disk to be uploaded in the event of my capture
<encrypted>Confirmed, Toobe upload

Winc was having a lot of trouble walking, so we took a break, sitting up against a pile of boxes in an alley, hir back against my chest, my hands doing their best to stop hir bleeding. Ze looked so pale.

Then I looked up and saw him. Standing just a few yards away at the mouth of the alley. Nicotine-stained fingertips, shabby suit, good shoes but worn to hell.

If he'd spoken I would have recognized the voice, but I already knew who he was. We locked eyes for one of those long moments. My mind started formulating some acknowledgment, a warning, a thank-you, a quip. But there was only that silence, Winc and I looking at him, him looking at us. Then, he turned away. Yes, he did.

He walked very fast, very deliberately to the other end of the alley. He went to the crowd of cops, but I didn't panic. I took my time, getting Winc to hir feet, adjusting hir against me, and kept walking. Down the alleyway, I heard him, a voice that matched the one I'd created for him in my head, telling the others he'd seen us going away *directly opposite* from where we were. It was the classic line: I saw his shadow etched against the gritty brick buildings, his thumb stabbing the air. "They went thataway," he said, and he kept his gaze steady on them. There was a shuffle of feet, like pigeons taking off in a rustle of feathers away from us. I heard his footsteps following the others, and then it was very, very quiet.

We were alone again, Winc and I, and I knew there was no place else, no*body* else that I wanted to be. It wouldn't matter what happened, we were together, alone, as we'd always been, and that would have been enough. Hip to hip, we walked slowly, me half holding hir up, my Winc, bleeding hir life into mine.

***

Narrative Entry, Toobe

This is my last entry at Gwynyth's; I'm going back to my dad's in a few minutes. I've been saving this part to tell cuz nobody would believe it:

They managed to hitch a ride with somebody who didn't say a damn word. Scratch said later it was as if a magic cloud swirled around them, bringing them to Gwynyth's like the Good Witch's bubble. Somehow they remembered how to get to the secret door under the roller coaster, which no police had thought to stake out. Not that they'd find anything cuz they never did realize there's a whole house under here. Anyway, Winc was bleeding way bad but they knew if they'd gone to a hospital they would've been nabbed sooner than you can say Circe.bot.

Winc was out of it for a few days but Gwynyth's an amazing doctor (she says healer).

But she had help:

Turns out Winc was wearing hir favorite belt, the one that embarrasses me and always makes my dad smile, it's such a relic. Ze bought it in Haight Ashbury somewhere. It says LOVE in these huge letters across the buckle, the O slightly tilted. Guess where the bullet went through? Uh huh. Now the O is completely rounded out, when the bullet went through it hit the edges, which slowed it down. Gwyn got that out, but it was the O that was cool; Winc put it on a chain and gave it to me to wear. There may be about a hundred different cliques at school but everybody agrees the necklace is cool.

Anyway, I get to do a special youth film school internship, and I think my first project will be: *The Legend of Scratch and Winc.* I have this image of Wally Budge walking out of that alley like he's just lost the prize, pointing to that squadron of cops and saying thataway. And then I'll drop in this song by Leonard Cohen (as a kind of present to my dad), but it's my film so it'll be one of his new ones: Democracy is Coming, to the USA . . .

It's an idea. Meanwhile, people are online again, but they laugh at the ads and I think they're gonna disappear soon. The ads, not the people.

Love,

Toobe

The End

GLOSSARY OF TERMS I USE IN MY JOURNAL

...... : Emphasizes a word, since you can't use italics.

::action statement:: Describes how something is said, or how somebody does something. Like we're having sex maybe, and I'm saying what I'm doing by going ::kissing you roughly::

<- - - : When this is pointing back at your screen name in a chat, it means your name starts the sentence, like:
Toobe: <--- is the one writing this glossary

>>   <<: Used as excerpt marks. People use them when they're trying to keep track of all the different "bulletin board" postings, and who said what.

bak: Back at keyboard

brb: Be right back

btw: By the way

Chat: To "talk" electronically, meaning to type back and forth on a computer via a communication service.

Chat Room: A "place" to chat. Anyone can open one and give it any kind of name, then other people can join if they want to.

Cybersex: Having virtual sex online, via computer. The dialogue is typed instead of spoken or acted out.

Cybersurf: To move around the network sporadically, kind of like channel surfing with a remote.

Email: Electronic mail. You can send it anyone who has an email setup. Can be used for short notes several times a day, or you can attach a whole file. The communication service "holds" the mail until you sign on and get your mail.

Emoticons: Those too-cute little faces you can make on your screen to let the other person know how you're feeling. You have to look at them sideways to know what they mean. :) is a smile. ;) is a wink and a smile. :X is Winc's favorite around Scratch... means clamping your hands over your mouth to keep from laughing.

Eyes: Online police, supposedly without any real power (right). I put them in my journal with this symbol: ///
///Can I be of any assistance here?///

FBCS, or FBC&S: Federal Bureau of Census and Statistics. The part of the govt that makes sure the Net doesn't get obscene.

Hir: A non-gender-specific possessive pronoun (I didn't make this up!).
E.g. The cop sat at hir computer and typed.

Log: To save a conversation or file. You can chat or read for as long as you want, and while you're doing that, your computer can make a copy of what you're saying or reading, for you to look at later. I log everything.

LOL: Laughing Out Loud (see ROTFL)

Member Profile: A "résumé" you make up for yourself (you can write anything) that other people can look up to see who you are, or say you are.

Modem: Device that connects your computer to the phone line.

Net or Internet: Aka the Information Superhighway, aka the Infobahn. It means the network of computer connections, all hooked together via modem. A commercial or educational site holds all the phone lines together, individual computers are then connected to those.

Offline: To be not connected to the computer. The real world. Real life.

Online: To be using the computer, usually connected with a communication service, in contact with other members. Sometimes feels more like real life, though.

Private Messages, or PMs: A way to privately communicate with another member within a service. Nobody else can see the message.

Private Rooms: An electronic "space" where two or more members can gather and talk, without being monitored. What's cool is you can be anywhere on the Net, even in a room or two, and "call" someone and chat with them privately at the same time.

Reg.: Registration.

ROTFL: Rolling On The Floor, Laughing

Sysop: System Operator, the person who does the day to day running and managing of a bulletin board service.

Vader: Short for evader, somebody who's is avoiding Registering online.

Web: Part of the Net where there are "sites" with key words and pictures, and you can use them to link from one place to another. Everything's connected; you can get pretty dizzy jumping from spot to spot.

Website: A place which has an address you punch in where whole "pages" are displayed, full of all kinds of information. Record companies have them, and regular people have them. Sometimes they're way boring, sometimes full of really cool information. Like NASA has one, and so does my stupid English teacher.

Ze: A non-gender-specific pronoun (I didn't make this up either!). Example:
Ze sat at the computer and typed.

***